SNOW WASTE

Snow Waste

Michael E. Bemis

Writer's Showcase
New York Lincoln Shanghai

Snow Waste

Writer's Showcase
an imprint of iUniverse, Inc.

For information address:
iUniverse, Inc.
2021 Pine Lake Road, Suite 100
Lincoln, NE 68512
www.iuniverse.com

ISBN: 0-595-26460-3

Printed in the United States of America

This book is dedicated to my mother, whose unrivaled inspiration and support provided the impetus for its existence.

CONTENTS

▼

Acknowledgements

Over the past several decades, the art and science of snowmaking has become increasingly complex. While the author's interest and passion in this technology has always been significant, years of intensive research, including many site visits, were required for the writing of this book. However, all the author's efforts would have fallen far short had it not been for the expertise of Greg Warner, a veteran snowmaking supervisor at Sunday River Ski Resort, Newry, Maine. His willingness to engage in countless personal and telephone consultations over a period of many months provided superb technical content, and planted the seeds for many real life scenarios. The author is deeply grateful for his time and effort.

The author also wishes to acknowledge the time and effort put forth by many employees at Sunday River Ski Resort, Newry, Maine, whose cooperation in the writing of this book has been most helpful.

The cover of this book was designed using images provided courtesy Sunday River Ski Resort, Newry, Maine.

The author also gratefully acknowledges the cooperation of the State of Maine—Department of Environmental Protection; Mead, Publishing Paper Division, Rumford Mill, Rumford, Maine; Natural Resources Council of Maine; Northeast Laboratory Services, Waterville, Maine; Kennebunk, Kennebunkport, and Wells Water District, Kennebunk, Maine; and New England Chemical and Explosive Disposal Co., Inc., Winthrop, Maine; all of whom contributed significantly in the writing of this book.

Finally, the author would be remiss if he didn't thank the scores of people, too numerous to mention, who responded to newspaper requests for information with valuable facts and remembrances, those who steered me in the right direction when my research lost its way, and a multitude of tolerant librarians scattered across Maine.

CHAPTER I

▼

ANOTHER SEASON

The autumn leaves Joe didn't have time to rake were blowing in the wind as he left the house that mid-October morning. As he backed his pickup truck out of the driveway, the cloudless blue sky and bright sunshine lifted his sprits. Turning off the gravel surface of The Johnson Road onto the smoothness of the state highway he punched a few buttons on the radio console, tuning in the latest weather forecast. Weather was, after all, Joe's life. It literally dictated his next move.

The monotone voice of the weather service droned out the usual facts and figures. As he had a thousand times before, Joe made note of what he needed, and the rest, well, he didn't really hear it. The road was desolate at this hour, at least during the off-season. A month ago it would have been clogged with leaf peepers, as the natives called them, moving at a snail's pace as they gawked at the colorful foliage unfolding before them across still fields and rolling hills. In a month, seven or eight of every ten cars, with fancy pairs of skis attached to the roof, would be moving like jack rabbits on their way to a single destination. But this was between seasons and Joe was alone, in the cab and on the road.

The dull-voiced announcer cycled through the state zone forecasts amidst a background of intermittent static, finally stating that the weather for northern Webster County, including the Western Mountains, would bring the first threat of frost to the area, with temperatures possibly dropping into the upper twenties with light northeast winds. It was music to Joe's ears. The National Weather Service always talked of frost this time of year, but as Joe knew, they were talking to farmers. Not snowmakers. To farmers the first frost meant harvesting or protecting crops still in the field and bringing home live stock left in warm weather shelter. For Joe, the first dipping of the mercury below 32 degrees was opportunity. The chance to make snow.

"Good morning, Ethel," Joe said breezing past the counter on his way to the back of the small country store to get a coffee. "How you doing this morning?"

"Coffee is fresh, Joe."

When was it not, he thought, as he poured a large cup, leaving plenty of room for the extra cream his taste buds demanded.

Ethel had owned and operated the Cannon General Store at the intersection of Route 2 and White Woods Road for 32 years. While things outside and those who came inside had changed dramatically over the years, Ethel and the store itself had defied that change. "I'm no Cumberland Farms," she would howl when a familiar customer would expect more, but actually that was somewhat rare, because Ethel had most everything you would expect her to have and what she didn't stock her caring motherly service made up for. Joe took two big swallows of coffee, something the extra cream allowed him to do, and went back to the front of the store where Ethel was still hunched over a small section of counter hidden by display racks that she called her desk.

"They say upper twenties tonight, Ethel, looks like we'll be working," Joe said.

"Just one minute, Joe," Ethel replied. But almost immediately she put down her purple ballpoint pen and turned to him, smiling. "So there's truth to the talk of a frost then?"

Joe shrugged. "I don't know about all over, but it sounds good for up above."

"Well, I'll be praying you get it up there. But I got to hope the rest of us get spared. Some of the boys have still got a fair amount of work to do."

Joe slowly shook his head. "Gee, another season, where does the time go?"

"Yeah, the older ya get the faster it goes," Ethel said.

Joe leaned over the worn but smooth wooden counter, depositing a neat stack of coins totaling fifty-five cents on the wide metal edge of the cash register and walked away.

"See you later," he said, already halfway to the door.

Ethel raised her voice. "I expect I'll see a ribbon or two of white on the mountain come morning," she said.

Joe turned around, holding the rickety screen door open with the small of his back. "I hope," he said.

Joe settled himself behind the wheel of the running truck, eased it into gear, crept across the uneven gravel of the parking lot to the White Woods Road exit and headed for the mountain, two miles away. Balancing his coffee in the same hand that gripped the steering wheel, he used his other hand to turn up the weather radio. He loved to listen to it. Maybe it was his job or perhaps it was something else, but he was always content listening to the official sounding voice of the National Weather Service, particularly when stormy weather was in the forecast. He had just turned onto the access road when he met Johnny, the night security guard, coming in the opposite direction. Like a planned rendezvous, they pulled their vehicles onto the ample gravel shoulders of the road, the mainstay of the ski resort's meager network of streets, and stopped.

"Hey, Johnny, how's it going?" Joe asked across the blacktop.

"Same old," Johnny replied sleepily. "I'll be glad when things pick up, it sure is boring around here. Except for some people at River Locks and a few at White River that beat feet at six this morning, the place was deserted last night. Course, being a Sunday night I suppose you got to expect it, but the sooner you make some snow the happier I'll be."

Joe cracked a big smile, most of which he put on for Johnny's sake. "Just so happens we might be starting tonight," he said, taking a generous mouthful of coffee to get it down before it cooled.

Johnny's enthusiasm bubbled. "No shit. Wow. This is early, huh?"

"Yeah, they're talking upper twenties tonight."

"Really. That's cool. Hey," Johnny said, his smile fading, "on your way up check out the overflow lots, particularly the one near the hotel. Them little bastards were cutting donuts again last night big time. If I catch them doing it I'm going to call the sheriff for sure."

"Do you know who it is?" Joe asked, trying to appear interested.

"Not by name," Johnny answered seriously, "but I've run them out of here before, it's local kids."

"Yeah, well, they're probably just screwing with you, leaving their mark to piss you off."

Johnny nodded. "It's working. So you really think you'll be making snow tonight?" he asked.

"Yeah, looks like it. Don't you be a stranger now."

"I'll be over for sure. See ya later, Chief."

"Take care," Joe said, taking his foot off the brake and letting the truck creep from the gravel that crunched loudly beneath the truck's big tires. When he reached the pavement he accelerated lightly, holding his coffee cup in mid air to prevent it from slopping.

Outwardly, Joe was nonchalant about starting operations; he wasn't one to show his emotions to anybody except his mother. Nevertheless, the thrill of another season was quietly building. He didn't know why it excited him, but it did. If he had to put his finger on something, he'd guess it was his quest to do better than the season before, the challenge of trying to deliver a tenth straight year of growth. In the beginning it had been easy to open earlier and stay open later because the season was already short, but with each passing year of doing better the pressure became greater to squeeze out a little more.

The huge growth spurts of the eighties that most everybody took notice of and applauded had slowly transformed into an expectation. The glory days were gone. White Woods Ski Resort was at the top now and keeping it there was no easy feat. Any retraction would surely gain attention and leave people from the boss to ski magazine writers wondering what was happening. It was a weight on Joe's shoulders that he willingly carried. If they started on this night, if they made enough snow to ski on, it would be the earliest ever, a week and a day ahead of the previous record.

Turning the corner onto the access road straightaway, he instinctively looked up at the broad section of mountain that was suddenly before him. Characterized by a dozen ski trials, it was an inspiring sight that caught your attention, particularly in winter when the winding trails were long blankets of brilliant white beckoning to be skied. While the locals usually glanced, Joe was more like the people from away. He stared.

As the road ascended on its final stretch before the overflow lots he sped up, forgetting to look at the escapades of last night that had seemed to be of undue importance to the youthful Johnny. Turning into the maintenance area parking lot, he switched off the weather radio and backed into his usual spot beside the pump house, a fairly large structure that sat beside the maintenance building on the side of a hill, low to the ground, near the Abbott base lodge, but far enough away to keep the public out.

Like most of the buildings at White Woods, the pump house was dark green with brown trim, colors that blended into their natural surroundings, and like the lodges, it had a rather odd shape, the result of having been added on to more times than an architect could hide. Except for a couple bright yellow signs on the front door warning people not to enter without head and ear protection, the building was unmarked.

Joe stuffed his coffee cup under the seat, slid out of the truck's cab, and arched his body back, allowing the sun full access to his face. Straightening up sooner than he wanted to, he walked slowly across the dusty hard packed gravel to the pump house, spun his key in the dead bolt lock, and opened the dented metal door to a melody of squeaking hinges. As the door slammed shut behind him the musty smell of the building was everywhere. Like the shack that sheltered a pump by pond's edge at the farm where he had worked as a boy, the pump house was largely a seasonal place. Once snowmaking ceased in the spring, the small crew of full-time snowmakers switched their base of operations to the maintenance building, largely because of its full kitchen and spacious dining area.

Walking briskly down the corridor, he thought about how the stale odors of summer would soon give way to the smells of winter—the reek of tobacco smoke, overpowered only by the frequent aroma of brewing coffee and popping corn. Stopping at the control desk he fixed himself a cup of instant coffee. Taking a sip, he grimaced and shook his head. It was too hot. Carrying the coffee to his office, he sat down at his desk and punched in the three-digit extension number for the corporate offices. Doris answered in her usual early morning voice, professional but somehow dry sounding.

"Looks like it's a go for tonight, Doris, weather service says mid-twenties."

"That's nice, Joe," Doris replied. But Joe knew it was just one of her canned responses.

There had been a time when Joe had liked Doris, most everybody had. But that was before her affair with Warren, before she had become the company princess, which she had taken advantage of in the extreme.

"Has the weather report from Northern been faxed in yet?" he asked, not really expecting she would have checked the machine.

Northern, a weather reporting and forecasting service in neighboring New Hampshire, supplied detailed reports specific to mountain weather, information that came in handy, particularly when conditions were marginal as they would be tonight.

"Haven't seen it," she answered, which probably meant she hadn't checked.

"Hey, Doris, it sure sounds good for Carter don't it. If we go all the way this summer it will make us one of the biggest in the East."

"Yeah, that's what I hear," she said, making no effort to conceal her lack of interest. Like everything that didn't feather her own nest, Doris despised White Woods' planned expansion onto Carter Peak, a project that was sure to mean more work for her.

"If you're looking for Warren," she added, "he's not in yet. I think he said something Friday about seeing the lawyers in town this morning."

Warren was always with lawyers Joe thought, either getting himself out of some mess or trying to get somebody else into one.

"Okay, have him call me about tonight when he gets in."

Joe sighed out loud as he seated the handset, thinking about how he'd like to send the regulars home to get some sleep as soon as possible and make a few calls to the seasonal workers, which he figured he might need. Despite the fact that making snow when conditions permitted was as certain as the sun rising the next morning, Warren had to approve them starting, and God forbid if Joe tracked him down in town, he'd never hear the end of it. Besides, he really didn't dare do that anyway. Taking one last swallow of coffee, he flung the cup into the wastebasket and headed to the pump and compressor rooms to check on things. Mostly he strolled around, killing time as much as doing anything productive. He had just made a mental note to pick up a box of light bulbs to replace the half dozen that were blown out when the pump house door slammed. It was Marty.

"Hey, Marty," Joe said, "How are ya?" Joe had only seen Marty, his pump operator, a few times in passing during the summer and hadn't seen him at all since mid-August.

"Oh, not bad. You?"

"Good. I was going to call you."

"Yeah, I thought, maybe. I was delivering wood at the condos and saw your truck. Are we on for tonight?" Marty asked, ejecting a stream of tobacco juice through the gap in his front teeth onto the soiled concrete floor.

"Looks like it. I've just got to talk to Warren."

"Christ, if you get us skiing this week you'll be some kind of hero around here won't ya?"

"Yeah, right," Joe said.

"So did ya keep busy over the summer? There wasn't shit to do was there?"

Joe knew Marty was making reference to the full-time crew, a mix of snowmakers and maintenance workers. For the first time in ten years, there had been no expansion work on the mountain, which was the source of Marty's cynicism.

"Oh yeah, we kept plenty busy, mostly with the condos, trail maintenance, we did some cosmetic work all around, you know, taking the rough edges of things, stuff you won't notice but you would if it wasn't done."

Joe hesitated, trying to think what else they had done. He knew Marty was jealous of the full-time crew, even though he always declined the offer to take one of the positions.

"Yeah, I bet, like housework I suppose," Marty said, a tone of skepticism in his voice that few bosses would tolerate for very long. But Joe knew Marty well enough to understand his ways, which meant ignoring the comment.

"Well, as long as ya got our hardware in place," Marty said.

"Oh yeah, every hose and gun. It's a good thing we started mid-September instead of waiting. We just finished up Thursday. It takes longer every year. Remember when we had only a couple hundred guns. With those new ones we got the season before last we got close to a thousand now."

Marty sneered. "Yeah, but them old ones ain't worth shit, Joe, and you know it, least not compared to that new design you came up with. What about the intakes at the pond? Did you check them good?" Marty asked, not waiting for a reply. "Remember that time a few years back, them fish that we sucked up, we didn't know we'd done it and we damn near pumped those poor bastards halfway up the fucking mountain. Now they would have jammed the shit out of everything, don't you think?"

"Oh yeah," Joe said, disgusted with the swearing and knowing full well that the new screening system that had been installed and their pre-season checks would keep if from happening again.

Marty took off his soiled green cap and put it right back on for no apparent reason. "So things are squared away then?" he asked, releasing another stream of spit onto the floor.

Joe nodded. "We charged everything up, air and water, and went over it with a fine tooth comb. There shouldn't be any leaks to deal with tonight. That reminds me, there was a water hydrant on Exception that was darn near off at the weld, a groomer must have caught it late last spring after we'd quit. It never ceases to amaze me they don't report that stuff but they never seem to."

"You sure it wasn't one of them fucking hikers, Joe? We're getting more and more of them every year."

"No, the cut hose was still on it, it was a tiller job for sure."

Marty shrugged. "Well, you think tonight then?"

"Yes. I'll talk with Warren and call you. You gonna be at home?"

"I guess," Marty said turning around and waving his right hand in the air as he walked away, his voice trailing off as he muttered something Joe couldn't understand, probably something about his home life, which for Marty was not the best. While Marty was a hard worker, he was tough to be married to. He was known to cut firewood for ten hours straight, drink a six-pack of beer, and fall asleep in his old soiled recliner in the living room that he wouldn't part with, getting up early the next morning and doing it all over again, paying no attention whatsoever to his wife of 27 years.

Joe went back to his office, tidied up a bit, and called Doris again. Warren still wasn't in so he decided to head over and wait for him. There wasn't much else he could do. A dozen trucks—contractors, delivery people, vendors—filled the loading zone that surrounded the main lodge, a sprawling three level building that, like the pump house, had an appearance uniquely its own. As Joe rolled to a stop in front of the Reception Center that was adjacent to the lodge, he noticed Warren's car tucked into its usual shady spot. "Good," he said out loud, pressing hard on the parking brake. The warmth of the morning sun heated his face as he skirted an unmarked panel truck and crossed the wide concrete pedestrian plaza.

"Good morning," he said, holding the door for a young man in a flashy uniform shirt and blue jeans dragging a hand truck piled high with big cardboard boxes plastered with faded labels that barely declared their contents of frozen crinkle cut french fries.

"Thanks," the worker said, moving with determination across the spacious entryway toward the resort's huge walk in freezer in the far reaches of the basement, which on the mountain side of the building was below ground. Joe climbed the wide flight of metal edged stairs to the lodge's main floor to the sound of hammers and saws coming from the ski shop where a horde of workers scurried about in an effort to finish the renovation job they had started too late. Skirting another semi-uniformed man with a hand truck in tow, he climbed the narrow unmarked stairway that led to the corporate offices. Walking briskly down the long hallway—past the offices of accounting, marketing, and sales—Joe didn't look right or left, hoping to avoid meaningless greetings with workers who were always peering out at those who came and went.

He ducked into the cluttered alcove adjacent to Doris' office and plucked the one page plain paper fax from Northern out of the machine's otherwise empty bin, his eyes scanning the data that filled the page from margin to margin in a matter of seconds, confirming what he had suspected. A solid window of opportunity above 3,000 feet starting as early as dark.

"Yes," he said softly, clenching his right hand into a fist and making a gesture that resembled a single hammer blow. He folded up the weather report, shoved it in his back pocket, and passed by Doris, who was doing her nails, without a word being spoken, which was not uncommon.

As he entered Warren's spacious office he immediately noticed Warren was on the telephone so he turned to leave, but Warren nodded and waved him in, motioning toward the three upholstered captain's chairs that formed a semi-circle in front of his desk. The call continued for several minutes with Warren saying little.

"Yeah," he kept repeating, nodding his head and occasionally rolling his eyes for Joe's benefit. Five minutes had passed when Warren held up a single finger to signify to Joe that he'd be another minute, which turned out to be about right. The handset had barely hit the cradle before Joe was getting the usual greeting from Warren.

"Joseph, how are you?" he said as a big smile spread across his flawless childlike face.

"Fine, thanks."

"Well, you're looking good. How's your mom?"

"Good, slowing down a little, you know how it is."

Warren tossed his head upward. "You bet I do and I'm only pushing fifty."

Darn, Joe thought to himself, that wasn't what he meant, not that Warren was slowing down. He didn't get the chance to correct himself.

"So Doris said you're looking for my blessing to start tonight?"

"Yes, if it's all right with you."

"Damn right it is," Warren said, raising his voice. "We need to make some money and keep the season pass holders happy."

Warren's familiar words made Joe smile.

"And see if you can lay down some white asphalt," Warren added, referring to the type of heavy wet snow that was best early in the season to build a base.

"Definitely," Joe said, "it sounds like things will be perfect for that."

Warren nodded. "You're going to use that new additive too, right?"

"Yeah, we got…"

Looking at his watch, Warren interrupted. "Oh shit, I was supposed to meet Art up by Lift 7 at ten. He's convinced it won't make it through another season without problems."

He paused for a minute, thinking, before he raised his voice and spoke.

"Doris."

There was no answer.

Joe turned around in his seat and could see she wasn't at her desk. "She's not there," he said.

"For Christ Sakes, what's his pager number, I can never remember those blasted things," Warren said fumbling through the big Rolodex he had retrieved from the far corner of his cluttered desk. He still hadn't found the number when Joe saw Doris out of the corner of his eye walking back to her desk from down the hallway.

"She just walked in," Joe said.

Warren pushed the Rolodex away with disdain and stood up. "Doris."

"Yeah," she said, appearing in the doorway a few seconds later.

"Would you page Art. I was supposed to meet him up at Lift 7 at ten. Tell him to do whatever he needs to, short of ordering a new quad, that is."

"Will do," she said, "but it's close to ten now, he may already be up there."

"Whatever," Warren said sitting back down, shaking his head. "I just hope to hell we're not talking much money up there. He should have gotten that taken care of in the spring. Our cash flow is shit this time of year and he knows it. I'll be dammed if I'm going to borrow at twelve and a half percent even if it is only a 30-day note."

Discreetly, Joe turned his head to see if Warren was talking to him or Doris. She wasn't in the doorway.

"Yeah," he said, not knowing what to say, particularly since Warren was criticizing Art, the resort's Mountain Operations Manager, which made him feel uncomfortable. Warren was always doing that, chastising people when they weren't around to defend themselves. Joe figured Warren said things to the others about him when he wasn't there.

"Of course, I might be able to manipulate those blood sucking contractors that overhauled it a couple years ago into believing they screwed it up, which they probably did in the first place. I'll get a deferred payment at least," he said, looking directly at Joe with a sneer on his face.

Talk like that, particularly when it came from Warren, made Joe uneasy, mostly because he never knew what to say. What was he supposed to say? It didn't matter. Warren spoke again.

"Doris," he yelled sharply, apparently not realizing until he'd said it that she was on the telephone paging Art.

Warren smiled and turned his attention back to Joe.

"So you ready to start working nights again, Joe?" Warren asked softly with a tone of voice that implied he was genuinely interested in the answer.

"I guess, it comes with the territory," he said, trying to sound upbeat, which, except for quick encounters, was difficult for him in the morning. Joe didn't advertise it, but he was a hard-core night owl. He figured it was best not to publicize the fact he was at his best from late afternoon on, because if a day position he wanted opened up they might consider him unfit.

"Did Doris tell you, I was with the lawyers this morning about Carter, that land use issue isn't behind us."

"Oh," Joe said, knowing he had squandered his chance to leave now that Warren had broached a new and broad subject area.

"No, the stuffed shirts in Augusta are fiddling with those god damn green zones and the line out toward Carter is getting too fucking close for, oh shit, that reminds me, Doris," Warren said, raising his voice and rising from his chair.

Joe turned around and could see Doris hanging up the telephone. Again she appeared in the doorway.

Warren said, "I just remembered, I promised the attorneys we would get them that old conceptual stuff. Could you dig it out? Don't send the originals though, you'll have to make copies."

"Why?" Doris asked, walking further into the room, stopping a few feet from Warren's desk, in full view of Joe.

"Because that stuff goes back to when we had the law firm in Portland, remember? The lawyers in town haven't got that stuff."

Doris grunted and shook her head. "Well, can't they get it from them…from Portland I mean?"

Warren sat down shaking his head. "Not from those bozos they can't."

"Well, I have no idea where it is," she said, waving her hand across the long bank of file cabinets that served as storage for most of the resort's records. What hadn't been filed, which was a lot, was heaped on top of the cabinets or stuffed into the collection of cardboard boxes that were stacked in both corners flanking the cabinets. The bottom boxes, crushed and bulging were spilling their contents of brochures and trail maps from years past. Despite the fact they were outdated and useless, they remained there. Joe couldn't help but think that if she couldn't find the file it was her own fault. Her filing system was hopeless to non-existent, so much so that he had resorted to maintaining his own meager set of records.

As usual Warren took pity on her, his tone of voice bordering on apologetic. "Don't worry about it, I'll have Dwight help you find them."

"No, I'll take care of it, but that's a big file, did they say what they wanted?"

"You better give them everything," Warren said with a smile. "That Intent to Develop, even if it was only in concept, might change where they draw the line. That's what the attorneys think anyway."

Obviously dejected, Doris turned and walked away without a word. Joe knew all too well that she was bothered by the thought of doing the work that Warren's request would entail.

Warren turned his attention back to Joe.

"I'm telling you, this crap is a pain in the ass. There's a good chance we're going to catch shit with Carter, which is why we've got to fast track it. It seems the environmentalists are doubling their efforts every time you turn around. It's like this," he said, picking up a section of shabbily folded newspaper and almost immediately throwing it back down, snapping his ring finger on it a couple of times for effect, "it's yesterdays Globe, Clarkson is getting hammered on because they're trying to expand. It isn't their fucking fault their ridgeline is covered with some rare high altitude vegetation. It doesn't matter that their future, the terrain they got to have to survive, let alone prosper, is on the other side of it. Christ, I think we've got it bad, dealing with the state, those poor bastards are going head to head with the Forest Service."

Warren paused, cleared his throat, and continued. "I don't know why, but they seem to think they got to side with the environmentalists, so much so that they're considering taking the expansion acreage by eminent domain despite the fact they know damn well that if Clarkson doesn't survive, the town won't either. They do something in Augusta or Washington to appease those green devils that I suppose looks like nothing to them on paper, but out here in the real world it does nothing but hurt the little guy."

Joe didn't have anything to say so he remained silent.

Warren was plainly pumped up, probably from his meeting with the lawyers. Again he picked up the newspaper and dropped it, shaking his head from side to side.

"We're the god damn life blood of Northern New England in the winter. What the hell else is here between foliage and mud season but snowmobilers? Not a goddamn thing, that's what, nothing. We pump hundreds of millions into the economy with an industry that's as clean as a whistle, but all we get is shit, like we're just another fucking Exxon or something."

Warren appeared poised to continue his tirade when Doris walked into the room again with a couple of messages she had taken earlier and laid them on his desk.

"Did you get a hold of Art?" Warren asked her.

"Yeah, he's all set, he said he'll talk to you later about it."

The telephone rang. Doris leaned over Warren's desk and answered it. A few seconds later she jabbed the hold button with her finger and hung up the handset.

"It's Peter Richardson, something to do with the meeting this morning."

Warren turned to Joe. "This will only take a minute," he said picking up the handset.

As Warren talked on the telephone Joe's mind shot ahead to what he had to do. This early in the season they often ran a single overnight shift rather than the usual two eight to ten hour shifts. Considering they might be able to turn on guns around eight, he'd have the crew start at six, which meant they wouldn't have much time to get any sleep, always a concern, especially since they'd probably be working until morning. He was trying to decide how many seasonal workers he should call in when Warren disconnected the call with the console button and slammed the telephone handset back into the cradle. Surprised, Joe looked up. Warren was staring directly at him.

"Those god damn bastards," he said, shaking his head.

Joe raised his eyebrows, feeling uncomfortable, but didn't say anything.

"You see, Joe, this is what I mean, bullshit, plain fucking bullshit. Peter just talked with Augusta, they're talking about another study, the first one was nothing but horse hockey and they want to do another, but I suppose it's better than them doing something definite, at least it buys us time."

Warren was about to continue when Dwight, White Woods' vice president, walked into the office, greeted them both softly and sat down, pulling up the fabric of his pant legs mid-thigh and crossing his legs, letting the papers he was holding come to rest in his lap below his folded hands. As usual, his dress was formal. A crisp white oxford button-down shirt with his initials embroidered on the pocket in dark blue, gray twill slacks with a knife like crease, matching socks, and pointed brown leather shoes with little tassels that bounced to the movement of his feet.

"Looks like we'll be able to blow some snow tonight," Warren said for Dwight's benefit.

Dwight turned to Joe, adjusting his body position slightly to look directly at him. "Oh wow, that's great, and so early, goodness, another season is upon us, can you believe it. So does this mean I'll see you early tomorrow morning, Joe?"

"I guess," Joe replied, forcing a smile, still trying to plan his escape from the office.

"Did you tell Joe about the reporter from the Bangor paper?" Dwight asked, looking back at Warren.

"No, not yet," Warren said, realizing that he had forgotten all about it but not willing to admit it. He turned to Joe. "There's a reporter from the *Bangor Herald* that wants to do a story on the first snow we make. I told her you'd call her."

Joe was not happy about the thought of having a guest with him, especially on their first night when there was so much else to do. His mind raced ahead and he found himself thinking about all the introductions and small talk that it meant and the endless entertaining he would have to do to make him feel welcome. Besides, the chance to get back in the saddle and make snow was the high point of Joe's year and he sure didn't want it messed with by a reporter. Even though he knew better, he resisted.

"This isn't the best night for that," he said. "With the usual equipment problems and…I mean, you know how important it is to get a trail or two open. I just won't have the time to spend with him that I'd like."

"It's a she, Joe, and that's the point, she wants to see what might be the first snow in the country being made, that's the crux of the story."

Having been involved in the initial arrangements, Dwight was quick to convince him.

"She's a real nice gal, Joe, easygoing, you'll like her."

Joe knew he didn't have a choice. Continuing to complain about something he knew he'd being doing anyway didn't make any sense.

"So I'm supposed to call her?" he asked, looking first at Dwight and then at Warren.

"Yes," Warren said, "I told her you'd call as soon as it was a go for sure."

"Do you have her number?"

"Ah, somewhere," he said, his eyes sweeping across his cluttered desk, "it's in the book, it's the Bangor paper, her name is Brenda," he paused, shaking his head and frowning, "Brenda something, I don't remember."

"I got it in my office, Joe, if you want to drop in on your way out," Dwight said.

"Okay, thanks."

"As a matter of fact, I've got to run anyway, I'll have it ready for you," Dwight said getting up. Then, turning to Warren, he said, "I'll talk with you later if you're going to be around, I've got a ton of things to get done this morning and I've got to pop into the house around noon. The little one is with a sitter, we were up half the night with her, she's got the bug."

Warren nodded as Dwight walked briskly toward the door.

"Did the reporter say how long she was going to stay?" Joe asked, immediately realizing that he probably shouldn't be questioning it. "Just so I know," he quickly added, "so I can plan."

Warren was indifferent to it. "Just tell her what sounds good, show her around, she'll be satisfied. That reminds me, get a media kit from Doris to give her, I think we sent her one, but give her another anyway."

"Okay," Joe said, his face blank.

"Look, Joe, I know you don't like PR stuff interfering, but media coverage is free advertising. Even if it isn't the Boston market, every little bit helps. Who knows, they might even put it on the wire. Regardless, what they write, especially if it's strong, is worth ten times what we get from that fucking rag of ours, which everybody knows is nothing more than our very own mouthpiece."

Joe was surprised. He thought Warren liked the resort's weekly newspaper, which they had started five years before. Growing from a few pages to more than thirty last season, every story in it was about White Woods, or in some way promoted the resort.

"Besides," Warren continued, "you've got quite a knack for talking to reporters. If you didn't insist on being a half-assed vampire all the time, I'd have you do more of it."

Joe was taken aback. He didn't know what to say. That was exactly what he would like to be doing more of. He would jump at the chance to be a spokesperson for the resort, which would lead to recognition, and that, inevitably, would lead to better jobs. More importantly, Joe knew it would give him some badly needed exposure within the corporate hierarchy, which seemed impossible to achieve working nights. He also knew, all to well, that while Warren was generally a fair boss, the employees who fared best were the ones that were close. Joe was aware of many occasions when some plum had been given out to somebody simply because they happened to be there when Warren turned around.

"I understand," Joe said, "and don't worry, I'll..."

Without waiting until Joe finished or even excusing herself, Doris waltzed into the office, announcing a long distance call for Warren from a person who was not familiar to Joe. He waited in the office for a few minutes, hoping that he'd have the chance to talk more about his future, something he rarely got the chance to do since he hardly ever had the nerve to broach the subject. But when Warren swiveled sideways in his oversized chair and leaned back, his right hand draped causally over the uneven row of books held firmly in place by a set of large pewter book ends in the shape of skis, Joe figured it was his cue to leave. He glanced at his watch, got up, and walked out, waving to Warren as he went.

Dwight's office was adjacent to Warren's, but the door was fifteen steps down the hallway, diagonally across from the alcove. Doris, who was rocking gently in her chair, didn't look up from the advertising flyer she was reading as Joe passed quickly by and entered Dwight's office. It was empty. But Joe wasn't concerned. He knew Dwight wasn't the type to keep him waiting long. For a moment he considered sitting in one of the red leather chairs that were centered before the desk, but decided against it. Instead he stood just inside the door, allowing the doorknob to nudge the small of his back, his eyes wandering around the immaculate surroundings.

Half the size of Warrens office, it was a beautiful room with pure white walls and dark green carpet that looked as good as the day it was laid. The matching mahogany furnishings, decked out in that sparse but tasteful touch of interior design, looked as if they were still on the showroom floor of the Portland furniture store they had been purchased from five years earlier.

With only the heel of his right boot touching the floor, Joe pivoted slowly toward the eight-foot high hutch on his right, silently reading the titles of the books that were evenly placed along the eye level shelf. He was almost finished when he heard footsteps.

"Oh I'm so sorry, Joe," Dwight said as he entered the office and scurried behind his desk. "I just popped into marketing, goodness, I do hope I haven't kept you."

"No, no problem, I just got here, I knew you'd be right back."

Dwight put a stack of papers, the same ones he had with him in Warren's office, on the desk, squaring them off neatly like you might do with a deck of cards. Then, taking his appointment book from the middle desk drawer, he opened it to a place marked with a red plastic paper clip, and flipped back several pages.

"Here it is," he said, placing his finger below a neatly penciled entry and looking up at Joe. "975-NEWS, which is 6397."

"975-6397," Joe said, jotting down the number on the back of the folded weather report.

"If you need anything, don't hesitate to call, I'll be home all evening."

Joe nodded. "What do you plan to do with that when Carter is finished?" he said, pointing at the large framed artist's rendition of the resort that hung on the wall behind Dwight's desk. Dwight did a quarter turn in his chair and looked up at it, resting his fingertips on his chin. "Goodness, you're right. They've been able to keep it current these last few years by just adding the new trails in the wooded areas, but we sure can't do that with Carter."

"Yeah," Joe said, motioning toward the right side of it, "Carter just isn't there."

They stared at it in silence for a minute.

Finally Dwight spoke. "I guess I'll just have to commission another one."

Joe nodded. "Well, anyway, I guess we'll see you in the morning."

"Yes. And again, Joe, I'm sorry to have held you up."

"No problem," Joe said, waving his hand as he walked out, thinking about how Dwight was such a pleasant person. Joe didn't know too much about his past, but he figured Dwight had nurtured his business and social skills working in sales. Fresh from college, Dwight landed a job as a sales representative for a sporting goods company that specialized in putting together packages of equipment for rental. When the company was driven out of business by manufactures intent on capturing a bigger piece of the pie, he became a sales representative for Head, hawking retail and rental equipment to ski resorts in the northeast. Being privy to a wealth of ski industry growth data and demographics, and being partial to the culture of resort life and all it would mean for his young family, he took the job of vice president at White Woods, despite the fact he had the inside track to become director of sales for Head's northeast region.

Back at the pump house Joe rounded up Al, Andrew, John, and Pete, and sent them home. "Be back by six," he told them, "and get some sleep. The window sounds decent so we may be working straight through till morning."

Since they would be blowing snow on just two trails, Joe needed only a few seasonal workers to round out the crew. He made the necessary calls, telephoned the reporter, and headed home to take a nap, sleep he'd need for the long night that lay ahead.

CHAPTER 2

▼

FIRST NIGHT

When Joe got back to the pump house at four-thirty, Marty was already there, readying the control desk for another season, something Joe felt he should have attended to before this. Located beside the locker room, the control desk was an enclosed area designed to shelter it from the deafening noise that filled the building during operations. The most apparent evidence that Marty spent most his time there was the ring of tobacco stains on the concrete floor that circled his rickety rolling chair. While Marty always had a spittoon handy to use at Joe's insistence, he would inevitably get worked up about something personal—which was the only thing that ever bothered him—and start spitting on the floor. If Joe was there, he's chastise him loudly, and Marty would revert to using the can, but the cycle would always repeat itself.

"Thanks for calling me," Marty boomed sarcastically as Joe walked into the building, "you must think I have fucking ESP or something. It's lucky I saw John at the store."

"Sorry, Marty, I saw you earlier and forgot about you."

"I guess…damn, somebody has been screwing around here again," he said, peering behind the counter that served as their kitchen, his cap falling from his head when the bill pushed up against the cinder block wall. "Nobody has got any business messing with my things."

Joe knew what he meant. Over the years the control desk had become cluttered with dozens of things Marty had brought from home, the fruits of his wife's obsession with garage sales. In addition to a coffee maker, hot shot, toaster oven, two coffee-cup warmers, two radios, and a nice color television set that sat on a shelf above everything else, there were a couple of portable space heaters under the desk. All of it was supposed to stay to the right of an invisible line on the counter, away from the resort's two computers and the bank of dials and switches, but like spitting on the floor, Marty wasn't known to care a whole lot about those kinds of things.

Joe stood near by, watching him trying to sort out the electrical cords that were tangled, mumbling to himself about how if they were going to borrow something they at least ought to put it back the way they found it. Twice Joe offered to help, but Marty was oblivious to his presence and his words.

Convinced he didn't want any help, Joe left for his office. It was just after five when he heard the voice of a woman. She's here already, he thought to himself, knowing it had to be the reporter. Rather than waiting for her to come to his office, which might never happen, he went to the control desk. The well-dressed woman, with shiny brown hair that flowed halfway down her back, tried to acknowledge Joe's entrance, but Marty was determined not to allow a distraction, at least not just yet.

Joe waited patiently on the sidelines while Marty finished his story, eyeing the woman who looked to be in her early thirties. She was big, almost stocky, but not overweight, at least from what Joe could tell, although the big L. L. Bean jacket that covered three quarters of her body was not revealing as much as he would have liked to see. When Marty finally finished talking, Brenda turned to Joe, and they introduced themselves. When he shook her soft hand, Joe wondered if he had squeezed to tight.

"So I guess you two have met," he said, watching Marty's eyes roam her backside.

"Yes, Marty was telling me some interesting things."

Joe nodded, silently wondering what Marty had told her.

"I was telling her about the First Night we had two years ago," Marty said, not knowing when to yield the floor to the boss. Joe kicked himself for having left him an opening.

"You remember, Joe, them squirrels that hoarded up a bunch of acorns or nuts of some sort in the line on Exception. It clogged damn near every gun all the way up. There wasn't one that we didn't have to blow out. Them squirrels probably starved to death that winter considering the cache of feed they lost. Course I've always hated them anyway, nothing more than gray rats in my book."

"So you found us okay?" Joe asked Brenda, intent on quieting Marty.

"Well, not really, I had to ask, but it wasn't your directions, it was finding the right building."

"Yeah, a lot of people miss it or just ignore it because it's not marked. I suspect the thousands of skiers that pass it from a distance every day during the season probably never realize what it is and how important a role it plays in their sport."

Joe hadn't finished speaking when Brenda reached into her oversized brown leather pocketbook and took out a small notebook. Pulling a white cap less stick pen from its spiral top, she flipped the cardboard cover, folding it underneath. Joe watched silently as she scribbled, pleased that what he had said was appealing enough for her to write it down. Encouraged, he continued.

"It's true though, we've had a lot of mild winters over the past ten, twenty years. Snowmaking is no longer a luxury. Without it there wouldn't be any early or late season skiing and at times there wouldn't have been any skiing at all. When I started we used to think of snowmaking as the frosting on the cake, but nowadays it is the cake, if you know what I mean. It isn't just for success, you got to have it today for survival."

Brenda continued to write at a furious pace, flipping pages over the top of the notebook that she allowed to dangle. Joe paused, allowing her time to get caught up. He figured she didn't know shorthand and if she was going to quote him he wanted her to get it right. It wasn't that he wanted to be quoted, but if he was, it was important to him that it be what he said.

The last time he was in an article for the Cannon Gazette about expanded snowmaking the reporter had almost completely botched his words and even when she got it right it was out of context. For him it was made worse because being a weekly, the papers that were chock full of the words he'd never spoken stayed on the newsstands for a week and every time he saw a stack of them sitting somewhere he cringed. If he could have afforded to, he would have bought every last one of them and taken them to the recycling center.

"Well, we're kind of getting ahead of ourselves," Joe said.

Brenda stopped writing, lowered her notebook, and looked up with a smile on her face. "No, this is great, really, thank you."

Regardless, Joe was the systematic type. He had already decided on a course of events for her visit and to do different now would bother him, even if it was a self prescribed plan that probably served his needs more than hers. Besides, it was only a matter of time before Marty piped up again.

"Well," Joe said, "I thought we'd take a tour of the pump house and then talk in my office."

"Sounds great."

"Later we'll go out on the mountain and after that you can spend some time with Marty at the control desk or go out on the mountain again, or both, whatever you want."

At the mention of his name, Marty spun around in his chair, obviously having been listening the whole time.

"Well, no offense or nothing," he said, "but now that you're writing things down I ain't got nothing to say."

Brenda ignored the comment.

"Please don't change a thing for me, Joe, I'll just shadow you or whoever, just do what you normally would, that's what will work best for me."

"Okay then, lets take the tour, and don't let me forget, when we get to my office, I've got a media kit for you."

She appeared puzzled.

"It's a packet full of information about the resort," Joe added. "It will give you a lot of background information, it's really good."

"Yes, that would be great."

"Why don't we start outside and then move inside."

Joe's tour of the pump house didn't last long, a combination of his brevity, which was a straight forward to the point kind of approach, and the building's limited contents. He ended the journey at his office, which was tucked away in the far corner of the building. As they entered he couldn't help but wonder what she would think of it. He felt compelled to say something. Positioning himself behind his desk, he smiled at her. "I suppose I'm stretching it calling this an office."

"No, this is nice," she said, looking around, but he knew she was only being polite.

Prior to making chief, Joe had longed for the day he would have his own office. To him it was the pinnacle of success. But he knew it looked more like the storage room it had been than an office. People he knew who visited for the first time often commented about its windowless, unpainted cinder block walls, its stained concrete floor, and the absence of a ceiling which allowed you to see the roof through a maze of dull red iron trusses. He had considered painting it but never had; afraid that the crew would think he was more interested in being an administrator than a snowmaker.

Besides, years earlier, when the resort's supplies were centralized at North Slope Lodge and he'd converted it into an office, he immediately coined the phrase "my real office is on the mountain" to dispel any notion to the contrary. The saying stuck and the fact he had an office turned out to be a nonevent, so he felt uneasy about taking a chance on making improvements. He knew it didn't matter to the crew that his job had changed considerably as White Woods had grown or that he really wanted to be out on the mountain in the thick of things anyway. So he followed his self-imposed rule that his office remain the same, keeping it neat and clean but nothing more.

"Well, sit down," Joe said, motioning toward the single chair that sat in front of the desk.

Joe handed Brenda the media kit, briefly describing its contents. As soon as he finished he realized he hadn't looked at this season's version, but he wasn't too worried because it never changed much anyway. Brenda opened the glossy presentation folder and leafed through the collection of brochures, guides, and recent news releases that were stuffed into its two pockets. Deciding it was a good chance for him to take a break while she looked over the material, Joe excused himself and headed for the control desk, realizing halfway there he hadn't offered Brenda anything to drink, not that there was anything except water and instant coffee. Finding Marty and Al talking at the control desk, Joe briefed them on what needed to happen.

"We've got to do the safety review in the locker room right off, then lets get Exception and Starburst pulled up. I don't expect that we'll be able to get going until eight or nine, but let's be ready."

"I don't know about that," Marty said, drawing out his words for emphasis, "the summit is already bouncing between 29 and 30."

"Good," Joe said. "Oh, Al, I don't know if Marty told you but we've got a reporter with us, she's in my office. I don't know how long she'll be staying."

With a cigarette dangling from his lips, Al cupped his hands over his breasts. "Yeah, Marty was telling me," he said.

Joe immediately turned around to make sure they were still alone. They were. He turned back to find Marty and Al smirking. He struggled not to show the concern that had engulfed him as it always did when somebody said or did something offensive, particularly when it could be construed as sexual harassment. What if Brenda had followed him? He knew that half the reason they did it was to get a reaction from him and as usual he had given them one.

"Lot of cushion for pushing there," Marty chimed in, hoping to keep it going.

Joe knew he shouldn't have paused long enough to give Marty the chance to speak. Regardless, he could avoid the issue if he focused on work.

"Make sure the guys are all set with gear," he said to Al, "we got some new stuff if anybody needs it. I'd like you to demonstrate the equipment, you know the drill."

Al shook his head, his playful mood gone. "Yeah, but it's bullshit," he said.

Joe knew what he meant. The safety review for experienced snow-makers did seem unnecessary, but even if they only absorbed or took seriously one thing, Joe reasoned, they'd be that much better off. Besides, the insurance company required it annually, even for return-ing workers, as part of a statewide program aimed at decreasing job-related injuries through pro-active approaches like better awareness and equipment.

Joe returned to his office and found Brenda reading the second page of a press release. He sat down at his desk as she gathered the papers together and put them back into the folder, not bothering to insert them into the pockets.

"So did you have a chance to go over some of that?" he asked, rais-ing his eyebrows.

"Yes, it's great stuff. I didn't realize how much there was to it."

"If you have any questions now, or whenever, just ask," he said, real-izing he should have told her that right from the start.

"So what time does the crew get here?"

Joe leaned back in his chair. "Well, it depends, we run two shifts, evenings and mid-nights, sometimes we do a day shift, but usually only if we have to recover from something, like an ice or rain storm. So about half the guys work evenings and the other half work midnights. Depending on what time the evening shift comes in, how much overlap there is at shift change, and what time the midnight shift goes home in the morning, they might work up to ten hours. We have to keep things fairly fluid so we can bob and weave around the weather."

Brenda was writing again so Joe figured what he was saying must be of interest.

"The guys are expected to be here for every scheduled shift, which can mean they work every day for weeks at a time. Their days off come when conditions don't allow us to make snow, and of course they can have days off if they need them, within reason. But basically they're expected to be here if we're operating. Marty, I don't know if I told you, he's the pump operator, he works both shifts..."

Brenda interrupted. "Every night?"

Instantly, Joe regretted his words, afraid that he had sent up a red flag. He knew it amounted to a lot of hours, and while he was pretty sure the ski industry had some exemption to labor standards that allowed it, he wasn't sure exactly how it worked. All he could do was a little damage control and change the subject.

"He's allowed to because it's inside duty, sitting down. It's an important job but he doesn't do much more than take care of the computer, the base station radio, and answer the telephone if it happens to ring. And we have other operators who can spell him if necessary and who can work for him if he wants time off."

"What about you?" Brenda asked.

"Excuse me?"

"What's your schedule?"

"Oh, well, I pretty much work a variable schedule. I get here before we start in the afternoon and I stay until things are running smoothly, or at least until after the midnight shift comes on. Al is the midnight shift foreman so he takes over when I leave."

The issue of Marty's work hours was still lingering on Joe's mind when Brenda asked, "Now, this is your first night, right?"

"Well not for me and a few of the others, we're full-time, but it's the first night we'll make snow, as a matter of fact, that's what we call it, 'First Night.' It was a phrase we were using long before those New Years Eve celebrations came along."

"First Night," Brenda said, jotting it down, "I like that. So how do you decide where you're going to work first?"

"Oh, that's easy," Joe said, "making snow this early doesn't leave much of a choice where to start because it's only cold enough at the higher elevations, up in what we call the blue and black zones. We'll start tonight on two of the major trails from the summit of Abbott Peak called Exception and Starburst and make snow down to mid-station. I don't know how well you know the mountain, but Exception is a top to bottom intermediate and Starburst is an expert trail than runs into Planet, which is an intermediate."

"So if you make snow on those two trails tonight, then what?"

"Well, if we lay down enough, we'll open tomorrow."

"I guess I don't understand," she said. "How can you open if there is only snow on top of the mountain?"

"Oh, I see what you mean. We'll open using mid-station, that's usually how the season starts, and ends for that matter. Skiers ride the lift to the top, ski the top half of the mountain, and ride the lift back down to the lodge."

Brenda nodded.

"Once we get from mid-station up open, assuming we don't get any natural snow, we'll spend a week or two, depending on the weather, building base depth down the mountain on the same trails. The intent is to reach the base area and the quad that services those three trails. From there we'll just branch out and keep adding terrain." Joe looked at his watch. "Well, we better get going," he said standing up, "we can talk more later."

"Oh sure," Brenda said, gathering her things from the floor and rising to her feet.

They walked silently down the hallway with Joe trying to think of something to say, but as usual, nothing came to mind. Everybody was either in the locker room or at the control desk, drinking coffee or soda, smoking cigarettes, and talking. Joe quickly took stock of who had arrived, losing Brenda to the crowd at the control desk who were more than content paying attention to her. Five minutes later Joe herded everybody toward the locker room and waited while they got settled. With his standard introduction out of the way, he delved into the safety issues and Al's demonstration of the equipment. It was six-twenty when they finished. It would have gone on longer if anybody had asked questions, but as usual, nobody had.

Joe walked to the back of the room to talk with Brenda.

"So what do you think?" he asked.

"Well, I'm getting enough to write a book," she replied. "I never realized there was so much to it."

Joe nodded. "Any questions?"

"Yes, lots. I guess I didn't mention it before, but the article, at least the way my editor envisions it, is supposed to focus on the fact you might make the first snow in the country. So that's what you'll be doing tonight, right?"

"We hope so," Joe said smiling, choosing not to mention that Shapleigh Ski Resort had beat them every year but one and that year it was a draw.

"Could you tell me a little more about that?" Brenda asked.

"I'm sorry, about what?"

"Your snowmaking ability. Which is tops, right?"

"Sure, well, that's been the success of White Woods, our ability to make good snow, and lots of it. We're one of the biggest snowmakers in terms of production output and we're the industry leader for snow quality in New England."

"I see," she said.

"We've got one of the most powerful snowmaking systems in the East so we routinely have some of the first skiing in the region and most often we're still skiing when most of the other resorts have shut down. We make snow whenever the weather allows it, we even make snow when it's snowing."

"If you don't mind I'm going to sit down so I can write," she said.

"Oh sure, do you want to go back to my office?" Joe asked, turning around to find the room empty.

"No, this is fine," she said, preparing to take notes again.

"Well, we better go anyway. The guys will be in and out of here."

They walked back to Joe's office where Brenda picked up right where she had left off.

"So what is it that sets you apart from the rest, I mean, what gives White Woods the edge."

Joe felt her questions were becoming more pointed. Maybe she was smarter than he thought.

"Me," he said smirking.

Bewildered, Brenda said, "Excuse me?"

"I was only kidding, it's a lot of different things, like our computer system, which constantly monitors weather conditions at various elevations on the mountain. It allows us to make ten different grades of snow, from what we call a Type One, which is real dry, to a Type Ten, which is base snow, or what we call white asphalt. Anyway, the crew…"

Brenda interrupted. "What will you be making tonight?"

Whatever the hell we can, Joe thought to himself. "We'll shoot for Type Ten, for a base," he answered.

She nodded, looking at her notes. "How does all that work, the computer and the weather?"

"Well, the crews on the mountain call in to Marty their location and he puts it into the computer which does some number crunching based on the ambient air temperature, the relative humidity, the wind direction and speed, the air and water pressure we have available and the type of snow we want to make. The computer gives the ideal setting for that particular gun."

Brenda shook her head. "I'm sorry, I didn't get that."

Joe repeated it slowly, not satisfied that he had said it a little differently than the first time. He prided himself in being able to recite things like that the same every time.

"Thanks," she said, "I got it that time. Now the setting, what do you mean by that?"

"How much water and how much air."

"I see, so it's nothing but air and water then?"

"That's right. Lots of air and water," Joe said, avoiding the question. It was common practice not to mention the additives that enhanced production, but he still didn't like the idea of lying.

"So you use a lot of both then?"

"Oh yes," Joe said smiling, "but we've got it. We have a high pressure air system which can deliver 140 pounds of pressure per square inch, which is a lot, and we can pump 12,500 gallons of water a minute up the mountain."

"12,500 gallons a minute," she said slowly, like she was trying to figure how much that was.

"Enough to fill an average sized swimming pool in about a minute and a half," Joe said with a smile, knowing what she was thinking.

"So any given night you're using a lot of water…like…"

Again, Joe was ahead of her, having been through the routine before.

"Millions of gallons a night, but we recycle it. We pump it up the mountain, make snow with it, which essentially just stores it there, and then it naturally returns to the watershed on its own. It's really like one massive recycling system. Think of it that way."

"I see what you mean. So where does the water come from?" she asked.

"Our own pond, called Jordan Pond. It's a manmade pond down in the valley that has a capacity of roughly a hundred million gallons. It's almost always full because it takes runoff from a thirty-five square mile watershed, which is basically the whole range of mountains from here right across," he said, sweeping his hand through the air to symbolize the area, "and it's also spring fed, sometimes we pump from it all night without the level changing a whole lot."

"So there are pumps down there?"

"Yeah, that's right," he said, nodding, "there's a pump house down there with five pumps that each do 2,500 gallons a minute. That's what gives us a total of 12,500 gallons a minute. We'll take a look later."

"So these pumps are boosters then," she said, motioning toward the pump room.

"No."

"I'm confused then."

"I think I know what you mean. The pumps at the pond feed these pumps, not unlike the ones down there getting fed by the pond. We do have one booster pump here for the far end of the mountain. Does that help?"

"Yes, thank you, now…" she hesitated, looking at her notes, "oh, I know what it was, how many pipes are there from the pond to here?"

"Just one," Joe said, holding up his right index finger. "All the pumps at the pond feed into a 20 inch main which runs up here five feet underground to protect it from frost."

"So when it gets here, it divides again?"

"Right, it just feeds the pumps here, then each pump here supplies a different section of the mountain with water. I'd be glad to draw it out for you if you want or I might be able to get you a map of it."

"No, thanks anyway. But I think I've got it now," she said with a smile.

"Good, now I'll confuse you again. About a mile beyond Jordan Pond is the Salem River, which we can also pump from if we need to. We've got an identical set-up of pumps there and a 20 inch main that runs to the one at the pond."

"Really, wow. So the river is like a backup then?"

"Yes, just in case we need it. The river intakes are located just up river from a hydroelectric dam that the paper mill in Waterford owns and operates. We have an agreement with them to regulate the dam flow if necessary, which means we really have an unlimited water supply. We have a permit to pump 30,000 gallons a minute from the river. But except for biannual testing in the spring and fall we've never pumped from the river to make snow, we just don't need it. You'll find some of this information in the material I gave you."

They talked for an hour and a half, rehashing most of what they had already discussed and touching on some things they hadn't talked about. Brenda's interest in snowmaking, which seemed to extend beyond journalism, baffled Joe, but he didn't say anything. It was close to nine o'clock when Joe declared it was time to get Brenda out on the mountain.

"But first, we need to get you outfitted properly. Nobody is allowed on the mountain without the standard issue, and to do that we've got to go back to the locker room."

"I dressed warmly like Dwight said, I've got four layers on," Brenda said, gathering her things from the floor.

They walked to the locker room in silence where Joe went to the corner and started sorting through two piles of paperboard boxes that were stacked almost to the ceiling. "What size foot do you have?" he asked, scanning the labels on the boxes.

"Excuse me?"

Joe stopped, turned around, and smiled at her. "What size shoe do you wear? I need to find you a pair of boots."

"Oh, ah, a women's eight and a half would be fine."

"There's no half sizes here," Joe said, turning back to the piles, "and I think you're going to have to settle for something a little bigger, but we got plenty of socks."

After several minutes of rummaging, Joe finally found a new pair of size nines and laid the box on the picnic table bench, instructing her to try them on while he repositioned the stacked boxes.

Five minutes later, the boots, with literature still dangling, were laced and tied. Brenda stood up. "These seem fine," she announced, sounding unsure of herself.

"They take a little getting used to, but they'll take care of you up there."

"I really thought these would be okay," she said, patting the toes of her smooth soled boots, which she had neatly placed on the bench, laces tucked inside.

Joe grinned. "Those wouldn't give you the kind of traction and support you need out there. Like I said, nobody goes on the mountain without the right boots or the right head and ear protection, and of course the right clothing. It's not just a liability thing, something we do to satisfy the insurance company, I mean. After you've been up there, even on an easy night like tonight, you'll appreciate the need."

Joe repositioned the size adjuster inside a white hard hat he'd gotten from a long cluttered shelf that ran the length of the locker room and handed it to her.

"What are these?" she asked, grasping the hat by the black plastic ear protectors that hugged its sides.

"Ear protection," he said. "They pull down. Try it on."

Slowly she placed the hat on her head. "Seems fine."

"Okay then," Joe said, "we're getting there. Now a light and you'll be all set. Are you wearing a belt?"

Brenda groped at her waist. "Yes," she said blushing. "I sometimes don't so I..." her voice trailed off when Joe thrust the light in front of her.

"This," he said, shaking a metal box the size of a paperback book and ten times as heavy, "is your battery, it attaches to your belt on the back." He didn't bother to explain the rest of the setup, which he figured was obvious. Instead, he turned his back on her, pretending to be checking the two-way radios in the wall rack, knowing if he watched her she might get embarrassed, especially since she was probably already feeling awkward standing there in unforgiving boots and a hard hat. A minute later she was still grappling with her belt and the battery, trying to get the metal loop in the proper position under her clothes. Thinking he should probably offer to help but knowing he had no intention of doing so, Joe excused himself, went to his office, and returned wearing his equipment. He was relieved to find Brenda ready to go.

They left the pump house and headed for the triple chair that would take them to the summit of Abbott Peak. They didn't speak as they walked along in the chilly night air, feeling the early season cold despite their layers of clothing. A four wheeled ATV raced by them and stopped at the base of the lift. It was Al. Fishing a cigarette out of his pocket, he lit up, and disappeared into the shack just as Joe and Brenda got there.

"What's he doing?" Brenda asked.

Joe motioned her onto the loading platform. "We can't ride the lift unless there is somebody at the base to run it, or at the top, whichever."

"Oh, I just figured they were running," Brenda said.

Joe shook his head. "Oh no, that wouldn't make any sense, these things use a lot of electricity, it would cost too much, anyway you need somebody to run it. Used to be that we did it ourselves, but not anymore."

A second later the lift started, and the chair that would be theirs circled behind them, slowly gaining speed as it approached.

Al remained in the brightly lit lift shack, peering at them through the window. Neither of them spoke as the chair whisked them away into the darkness. Despite the fact it was a triple chair that had plenty of room for two people, they ended up sitting closer than Joe felt comfortable with. He considered moving away but was afraid she might be offended. Instead he lowered the safety bar.

"You were saying you used to ride without a lift operator."

"Oh yeah, all the time in the old days. But since Balloon Boy, that was what we called this guy that used to work here, got his beater stuck in the chair and darn near got killed we have to have an operator. Somebody at the top or bottom, so if there's a problem, they'll know it. The way it used to be, somebody could have gotten into trouble, even hurt, and nobody necessarily would have known, at least for a while anyway."

"What happened to…to that guy you mentioned?"

Joe was cognizant that he was talking to a reporter, most of who were always in search of a story, but he figured since this had happened years earlier there was no harm in sharing it with her. "Balloon Boy, well, he was riding up alone and when it came time to get off, his beater got stuck somehow on the chair, nobody ever knew how exactly, but…"

"Excuse me, but what is a beater?"

"A beater? It's a tool. It's nothing more than a hunk of metal we carry to knock ice off the guns, everybody has one, they're all different but serve the same purpose. Anyway, Balloon Boy had a tire iron he had cut down to size but it was still curved on one end. When it got caught, he was hanging off the chair, held only by the beater. If it hadn't been for the stop arm at the top that he grabbed with his hand he'd have kept going, and who knows what would have happened."

"You mean he would have gone back to the bottom?"

"Well, yeah, but if his beater let go he'd have fallen, forty, maybe fifty feet in some places, or coming into the base hanging like he was he could have got hurt. It happened a long time ago, couldn't happen today, not with the precautions we take."

"I see. If you don't mind me asking, where did he get that name?"

Joe grinned. "Probably not what you think. He wasn't fat, you know, shaped like a balloon. It was that whenever he got winded, which he did all the time, he'd start exhaling real loud and fast, like he was blowing up a balloon."

"Oh. So he's not here anymore?"

"No, nothing to do with what happened, he just left. Actually he died a couple of years ago in a sled accident up north."

"Oh, I'm sorry."

"That's okay."

"Is that hissing noise snowmaking?" Brenda asked, pointing into the darkness.

"Yep, that's the guns."

They didn't talk much more on the way up. Joe couldn't think of anything to say, which was often par for him in social situations, particularly when it was a twosome and he didn't know the other person well. Instead he pretended to be adjusting his clothing, which served to diminish the awkwardness created by the silence. Knowing that Al had the chair running as fast as it would go so he wouldn't have to wait as long to shut it down, Joe asked her if she would be okay getting off as they approached the top. "You've got to move fast, it's not like with skis on."

"I'll be okay," she said.

After they got off Joe radioed to Al that they were clear. Almost immediately the lift stopped, jolting the seemingly endless line of empty chairs into a slow back and forth swing. Joe clicked on his helmet light, prompting Brenda to do the same. She fiddled with the hat-mounted beacon, finally finding the little switch. They walked silently a hundred feet or so toward the backside of the mountain, where the sound of the hissing guns faded. The trail narrowed and became rough, but was nonetheless well illuminated by the combined candlepower of their bobbing helmet lights.

"Is this a trail?" Brenda asked, scurrying over a large outcropping of ledge that skirted the path, which Joe traversed with remarkable ease.

"Oh, no, sorry about that, I forgot. This is just a footpath we use to get over to the summit; hikers use it in summer. It'll give a nice view of town from the backside in a minute. We can't use the high-speed detachable lift, so we use the triple for summit access. There, look over there."

The trees and thick vegetation that had lined the path had suddenly given way to a mostly rock surface, dotted with scrub brush that seemed to be growing from the rocks themselves. Joe waved his arm in a small arc at the cluster of twinkling lights that seemed closer than they were.

"That's Cannon in the distance," he said. "Pretty isn't it?"

"Yes, it's beautiful, and bigger than I thought."

Without a word Joe set off with Brenda in tow. The path narrowed again and got rough, causing Brenda to slow down.

Joe turned around just as she spoke.

"Sorry."

"No problem," he said, "we've got all night."

"I feel like an astronaut walking on the moon, if you know what I mean."

Joe figured she meant the rock surface, the altitude, the gear she was wearing, maybe all three. In any event, he didn't pursue her remark, knowing they were about to break out onto the summit of Abbott Peak. But Brenda was talkative.

"That hissing sound is the guns again, right?"

"That's them."

"They're louder, how far away are they now?"

"About a hundred yards. They'll get a whole lot louder when we get closer."

As they passed a small weather-beaten shack with a bright red cross on its door, Joe turned to her and was about to speak when she pointed at the rusted iron cables that dropped diagonally from the corners of the building into eye hooks the size of donuts that were embedded into the rock surface.

"Are those what I think?" she asked with childlike awe.

Joe smiled. "Oh yeah. Up here it's got to be either tied down or planted in concrete."

"Wow. So it would just blow away otherwise?"

"It could, lets put it that way. Now, you need to lower your ear protectors." He watched her, making sure she did it correctly, before continuing along. They passed behind three guns placed in the shape of a V that circled the summit lift house, their output blanketing the ground in virgin white, and stopped.

"All right," Joe said, raising his voice and positioning himself beside the two pipes that lay across the frozen ground, obscured in places by a tangle of thick vegetation. "These are the mains, one for air and one for water," he said, patting each of them in turn. "Now every place there is a gun, there are hydrants, which control the flow. We have two hoses for each gun, one for air and one for water, they connect in the back like this." He grabbed the gun by the tripod and leaned the football shaped head toward the snow, exposing the connections. "Can you see it okay?" he asked.

"Yeah, I guess."

"Let me shut one down so you can take a closer look," he said. Joe went to the hydrants, eased off the air and water, and returned to the dormant gun, motioning Brenda closer. "See," he said, grabbing the air hose just below where the coupling was fastened to the gun, "it connects in the back with what we call ears, which are really clutches."

"I'm sorry, what are the ears?"

"These," Joe said, resting his thumb and forefinger on the two pieces of metal that jutted out at three and nine o'clock. "They hold the hose in. Without them the pressure would just back the hose right out of the gun."

Joe pulled on the rings attached to the ears and yanked the hose free from the gun, repeating the procedure with the water hose. "That's all there is to it," he said, rolling the gun over so Brenda could see the seven little holes that dotted its flat front.

"It seems so simple," she remarked.

Joe stuck the gun's legs back into the snow. "That's because it is," he said, looking back at her with a wide smile. "The complexity isn't the equipment, it's the ingredients—air, water, temperature, humidity— all in the right combination." He paused. "Here, let me show you what I mean when I say how dangerous these things can be. Go down the trail a little way and stay put."

Brenda passed by Joe and carefully picked her way down the steep slope. When she was close to eighty feet down, twice the length of the hose Joe had disconnected, she turned around for the third time and he signaled for her to stop. Joe went to the air hydrant, positioning himself behind it so he had an unobstructed view of Brenda below, and eased it slowly open. Almost immediately the motionless yellow hose wiggled to life. At first its movement was sluggish and low to the ground, but within seconds, powered by 115 pounds of air per square inch, it was dancing wildly across the mountainside, spewing snow into the air. Like a python striking its prey, it rose into the dark night one second and slapped the ground with a loud thud the next.

As soon as Joe had cranked the valve fully open, he started closing it until the hose once again lay limp on the snow. Joe started toward the gun, gesturing for Brenda to join him. By the time she arrived, winded by the climb, the gun was back in place, the hoses connected.

"That was neat," she said, gasping for air.

"I thought you might like that, everybody does."

"Yeah. It's so powerful."

Joe nodded. "And deadly."

Joe returned to the hydrants, put the gun back in operation, checked its output, and waved Brenda along, stopping short of the next gun.

"We try to work entirely along the mains, behind the guns," he said, waving his hand across the carpet of virgin snow that was dotted with protruding rocks and weeds. "Skiers like it that way."

As they continued down the steep grade of the mountain, Joe's eyes never left the trail as he carefully inspected the work of the guns. Occasionally he would reposition a gun slightly, adjust the flows at a hydrant, or pick up a handful of snow and squeeze it, but mostly he just looked. They had passed more than a dozen guns when the trail merged with a wider one and started to level out just a little. Joe stopped and turned to Brenda.

"You see, we got darn near perfect conditions tonight, there isn't much we need to do to this trail, coverage is good, quality is good."

Brenda nodded but didn't say anything.

They kept walking, down another steep section, then across a wide bumpy area that was almost level, where a small wooden building sat trailside. Except for its pitched asphalt roof, it always reminded Joe of the tree forts he had built as a kid. Walking to the back of the building, Joe pulled a fat ten inch spike out of the rusted hasp, laid it on the roof, wrestled open the rickety door, and crawled inside. Brenda poked her head through the opening.

"This is a valve house," Joe said. "There's six of them up here. We use them to isolate sections of the mountain. It's also where we can blow off the main from."

"What's that do?"

"Blow off the main means to flush it. You see this," he said, running his hand across a rusted pipe that exited through the wall of the shack and extended twenty feet into the woods where it was difficult to see against the brown forest floor. "We can open the valve in here and dump all the water we want without affecting the condition of the trail."

"Why would you want to do that?" Brenda asked.

"To flush it out."

Brenda smiled. "You mean to clear it of acorns."

Joe laughed, backed out of the shack, slammed shut the door, and put the big spike back in place.

"So these guns get put out when you start?" Brenda asked.

"Yeah, that's right. They get stored behind the mains, hose and all. When we're going to make snow we do what we call a pull-up, which means the guns get extended up hill as far as the hoses will reach. As the night passes we lower them, which gives us the coverage."

"How many guns are there?"

"I assume you mean on a trail. That depends on two things, whether it's what we call an opener, and of course, the length of it. This trail, Starburst, is what we call an opener, it's one of the first trials we make snow on every year, so we got hydrants every twenty feet, because you need that kind of placement early in the season. We got forty-five hydrants here, which is a lot for its length. The most hydrants we got on any trail is…I think it's sixty-eight, on Infinity. Needless to say, the guys don't like pulling up that one."

A hundred yards further down they turned a ninety-degree corner and mid-station was suddenly before them. Joe went into the lift shack and made a call, commenting to Marty out of earshot of Brenda about how well the new additive was working. When he finished they stood on the platform and talked.

"Part of the reason I called Marty was to see what we had for air. This time of year, with conditions marginal like they are, you need a lot of air. We got a little to spare right now, so we'll start a few more guns around here to beef up coverage in this basin area which gets the most skier traffic. If the temperature drops later we'll free up some air and be able to do more. Usually just before dawn you get quite a drop."

Joe started the guns that circled the basin area, finishing just as Andrew and Pete, with cigarettes dangling from their mouths, rounded the corner on Starburst. They talked briefly on the mid-station deck, then, at Joe's direction, Andrew started the lift, and he and Brenda rode back to the summit and came down Exception, which didn't require the summit hike, arriving back at mid-station forty-five minutes later. Joe radioed the pump house and several minutes later the lift started. They boarded it and rode down in silence, Brenda obviously awed by the lights below, which slowly revealed the buildings and poles to which they belonged.

"Well, that's pretty much the fifty cent tour," Joe said as they walked to the pump house. "Do you have any questions?"

"Yeah, I'm confused about which trail, I mean, it's probably just me, but the first time up we hiked along the summit to the quad where you were making snow, but I don't see how they can ski that if only the triple is open, early in the season I mean."

Halfway through her question, Joe knew why she was confused, but interrupting was out of the question. When she finished he smiled. "When we started from the quad we were on Link, which joins Starburst a couple hundred yards down. Link exists to connect Starburst, and Abbott Peak in general, to the quad."

"So why were you making snow on Link then?"

"Because we're using the lines on Abbot. You got to realize the system was built piecemeal. It was easier to service Link from Abbot than from White Peak. So it only makes sense to go all the way at once. Otherwise, when we open the quad we'd have to come back and fire up Abbot for just a ten gun deal."

"I see."

"Did I lose you with that?" Joe asked.

Brenda smiled. "Maybe a tad," she said, holding up her hand, "but never mind, really, I'm all set."

"Do you have any other questions?"

"Nothing I can think of," Brenda replied, "but this has been great, really."

If she was faking it, Joe couldn't tell.

"Well, I know you wanted to be here for First Night, and that makes sense, but you would be surprised at how different things are when we're going full tilt. Our output would amaze you."

"Maybe I could come back sometime."

But it'll never be arranged, Joe thought to himself, which was always the way it was.

"Well, I'll take you down to the pond and the river, after that you can sit with Marty for a while, or if you want, you can take another run, maybe with Al."

Joe felt he should stay with her for the duration, but he could only take so much socializing. They walked to the control desk in silence, where Marty was stretched out in his chair, holding the remote control to the television, which wasn't on.

"Everything okay?" Joe asked as they approached.

"Haven't heard that it isn't," Marty said.

"I'm going to take Brenda down to Jordan and Salem," he announced, not expecting an answer from the docile Marty who had apparently slipped into one of his quiet moods that he had a habit of doing without notice.

The keys to the truck weren't on the control desk board so Joe figured he'd find them in the truck. But they weren't there. As he radioed Marty, Brenda struggled to climb into the cab, stymied by the trucks high clearance, the slight downward grade where it was parked, the stiffness of her boots, and the bulk of her clothing. Joe felt he should assist her, but he was afraid if he did she might be offended, so he called Marty on the radio again, using the transmission as an excuse not to help.

"They're here on the counter," Marty replied after several seconds.

All the way to the control desk and back Joe chided himself for not helping Brenda. But if she'd expected it, you never would have known. Settled comfortably in the passenger's seat, her safety belt fastened, she smiled broadly at him as he climbed into the cab, started the engine, and slid the truck into gear.

Puttering along deserted roads, asking and answering questions that inevitably led to others, Joe and Brenda talked easily. Joe was beginning to like her, no, he already did like her, but it was a feeling that he kept to himself. Maybe if he hadn't been working it would be different, but he was the chief, she was a visiting reporter on assignment, and a mountainside of subordinates were hard at work trying to deliver the earliest start on record. So he did the only thing he could do. He suppressed his feelings, and went about the business of giving her what she had come for.

When they got back to the pump house a half hour later, Joe reiterated her options. She choose the control desk, which didn't surprise Joe, given the harshness of the mountain. As Joe walked away he was still thinking about how she was probably wondering why he had dumped her. Maybe I'll get with her later if she's still around, he thought, reminding himself that he had a job to do. Regardless, he could only engage in conversation for so long before he was talked out, and, on top of that, he wanted a cigar, and he didn't feel it would be right to smoke in front of her, even if everybody else was.

When he returned to the control desk an hour later, Brenda, who seemed relieved to see him, was still sitting rigidly in the chair where he had left her, feet planted firmly on the floor, pocketbook resting in her lap. Marty, who not surprisingly, had abandoned his speechless stretch, was talking up a storm. True to her obvious Christian upbringing, she let him finish his story, giving him her full attention, before she turned to Joe with a pleading look.

"I was wondering if we could talk some more, I've got a few questions, if you don't mind that is."

"Oh sure," Joe said sincerely, having recovered nicely during the break, "why don't we go to my office."

"That would be great," she said with a smile, jumping to her feet. Then turning to Marty, she said, "Thank you for your help, I appreciate it."

Marty grunted an unintelligible farewell.

"How'd it go?" Joe asked, turning around slightly as he led the way to his office.

"Great," she said with a laugh.

"So now you know it all."

"Excuse me?" she said, walking a little faster to catch up with him.

"You know everything now."

"Oh, yes."

They walked the last few steps to the office in silence, taking their chairs. Joe leaned back in his, expecting her to ask a question. When she didn't he spoke.

"So you had some questions?"

"Oh yes," she said, grabbing the notebook from her pocketbook on the floor and wildly flipping the pages like she was trying to beat the clock. As he waited, Joe wondered when she'd had the time to write them down. After turning pages for almost a minute, first in one direction and then in the other, she spoke without looking up.

"I've got so much here."

"That's okay, take your time," Joe said, trying to sound patient.

Ten minutes later, with the snowmaking questions asked and answered, Brenda closed her notebook and stowed it away. For the next half hour they talked easily about a variety of things. As the subjects of their conversation changed, Brenda kept trying to bring up Joe personally, but each time he managed to deflect her prying that he was pretty sure was based on personal desire. With no wedding band on either of their fingers, he figured he knew what she was up to and he didn't feel he could afford to be interested even if he really was. With the season just starting, he wouldn't have time for her, particularly because she no doubt lived in Bangor. From here on in, he'd be working seven nights a week, or as close to it as the weather would allow, which meant sleeping close to noon, which just happened to suit him fine because it allowed him to be in the thick of work during the evening and early night when he was at his best. So what was the point in leading her on? It was close to midnight when she said she better be going.

"It's a long ride to Bangor, and I'd like to start writing this tonight while it's fresh in my mind."

"So it will be in tomorrow's edition then."

"No, probably not, it's the kind of thing they usually keep for a weekend feature. All I know is I'll have to submit it by tomorrow."

"I'm curious about one thing, why no pictures?"

"Oh," she said, almost like she was relieved he had asked, "that depends on the story. They might not do much with it and run it without, or they might run it with a file photo or two, or if they feel it's worth it and they have the space, they'll send one of our photographers over. When they want good pictures that's what they do, send over a staff photographer."

"I see, so it's kind of wide open then, I mean, as to what they'll do with it."

"Always is, it depends on, well, I suppose I shouldn't say this, but it really depends on advertising, the amount of copy in any edition depends on the advertising. Every page, regardless of the worthiness of even news stories, has to be paid for. It's no different than any business, somebody has to pay the freight, if you know what I mean."

Joe nodded, absorbed by what this woman of common appearance was saying. He was right. She was smart. Suddenly she was on her feet, thanking him and promising to send a copy of the story. He walked her to the edge of the parking lot.

"Drive carefully," he said as she stood in front of her little foreign car, frantically digging in her pocketbook for keys.

Joe walked back to the pump house and paused at the door, just out of sight, waiting for her to leave, just to be sure she got off all right. He didn't want her to feel she was being watched, something he despised, but he did want her to know, just in case she was paying attention, that he cared enough to see her off safely. Knowing he wouldn't be able to hear the car's four cylinder engine start above the screech of the pumps, he waited and watched. A minute later her car crept slowly across the parking lot and down the access road. Joe waved, waited until the oval taillights of the late model compact disappeared, and went to the control desk, where he helped himself to a cup of coffee.

"Everything going okay?" he asked Marty, whose eyes were glued to a soundless football game.

"Haven't heard that it isn't," he said. "Did the gal leave?"

"Yeah."

"She wasn't bad, aye," Marty said. "And available to boot, there you go, Joe."

Joe didn't say anything as he watched the ball go out of bounds on the silent screen, hoping Marty would drop the subject. He didn't.

"If I was you, being single like you are, I'd be all over that. She's probably got her own place and everything."

Joe grunted an acknowledgment which could just as easily have been taken as disapproval.

"Hey, since you're just standing there, suppose you could spell me for a bit, I've got to use the little boy's room," Marty said.

"Yeah, go ahead."

Joe sat down and leaned back, wondering as he often did when he sat there what it was like to spend the entire shift, really two of them back to back, in that chair.

The remainder of the night was uneventful. By daybreak 15 tons of fresh snow had been laid down over 30 acres of terrain high on the mountain. Just as Ethel had predicted 24 hours earlier, two white ribbons of snow adorned the summit of Abbot Peak.

Joe was dragging and would have liked to head home, but he couldn't. First Night was always the longest one for him, and this year would be no different. At daybreak, Dwight would compete for first tracks. Not because he wanted to do it, but because Warren insisted on it for the bragging rights it brought. That was Warren, always vying to be the first resort in the East for everything, and that meant being able to claim you had skied first. It was nothing more than a gimmick, but it did grab the attention of the media, which supplied a ton of free publicity.

Joe made the call to Dwight just before six, knowing he couldn't put it off any longer, like by doing so Dwight would call in and spare him the drudgery of waking him.

Dwight's sleepy voice answered halfway through the third ring.

"Dwight, this is Joe," he said, realizing that such an introduction was hardly necessary. "It looks like it's a go. We put down six or eight inches on Exception and Starburst. It looks good."

"Okay," Dwight said, not needing any reminder of what Joe was talking about. "I'll get ready. I should be there by seven. See you then."

Joe broke the connection using his finger and dialed again. While they had been successful laying down a decent snow cover, it was Joe's opinion that it was wholly inadequate to open with. Regardless, procedure required him to call ski patrol, the first step in a progression of events that could lead to opening that morning.

Joe easily convinced Tom, the ski patrol coordinator who was serving his first year in the top spot, that things weren't good enough to open.

"It's thinner than my forehead hair on the head walls and there's more turtles up there than you can shake a stick at," he said, referring to the ice and snow covered grass and branches that protruded above the otherwise virgin snow surface.

Despite the hour, Tom was jovial, a sure sign Joe was conversing with a morning person who had probably already been up for at least an hour.

"Thin I accept, protrusions I don't," Tom said playfully. "If you got turtles on the mountain we'd best act fast, patch me through to trail maintenance, will you."

They both laughed.

"I'll look forward to waking you up again tomorrow morning," Joe said, trying to sound snide.

"No such pleasure with me," Tom said. "I'll look forward to something I can ski on. Talk to you later, bye."

As he hung up the telephone, satisfied with the conversation he had had with Tom, Marty walked into the office. "You call Dwight?" he asked.

Joe didn't answer right away, but that didn't matter to Marty.

"The stupid bastard will probably hit a rock and kill himself," Marty said. "If you ask me he ain't too swift, I mean, why the hell do it at all? It don't make sense."

"I don't know," Joe said, determined to stay loyal to White Woods, "being first, tradition, whatever, it does get us some attention, you've got to admit that."

Unconvinced, Marty shook his head and walked away. "See ya in church," he said.

Joe didn't really expect someone like Marty to understand what he was talking about. The rest of the crew had left now and without the whining sound of the pumps and compressors it was quiet for the first time in twelve hours. Joe sat down at his desk, intending to work until Dwight arrived, but almost immediately he decided against it, he just wasn't thinking clearly—sapped by his first graveyard shift since they shut snowmaking operations down last March.

Instead, he pulled a cigar out of the package on his desk, unwrapped it, and reached into his jacket pocket, taking out his shiny metal cigar cutter, an expensive tool imported from Germany that had been a gift from his mother the Christmas before last. Opening the cutter, he placed the end of the cigar into the cup and pressed down, forcing the sharp V shaped blade across the moist tobacco until it snapped its finish. Tapping the cutter on the edge of the desk to remove the dissected tobacco that he let fall to the floor, he inspected his work. It was a good clean cut, the kind he liked. Next, he fished his brass Zippo out of the same pocket and primed the cigar by rolling the end to be lit over the flicking flame of the lighter. Finally, he stuck the cigar into his mouth and fired it up. Leaning back in his chair, he drew heavily, exhaling equal amounts of white smoke from his mouth and nose.

For the next ten minutes Joe sat there puffing his cigar, watching the thick grayish haze that filled the small room glide slowly toward the office door, where it disappeared into the hallway. Like the smoke, his mind drifted through future events—Dwight's first tracks, opening day, the prospects for Thanksgiving and Christmas—but nothing stuck, probably because he was too tired to dwell on anything in partic-ular.

He was halfway through the cigar when he remembered that Dwight would probably want coffee. He didn't want any, it would just keep him from getting to sleep, but he figured he'd best make a pot. Dwight was the number two man at White Woods and it didn't do a guy any harm to please him. Besides, he ought to quit smoking so the air would clear before Dwight got there.

Dropping his cigar into the ashtray, he went to the control desk, made the coffee, and puttered around the locker room till quarter of seven, when he went to the pump house door to watch for Dwight. He hadn't been there more than a few minutes when Dwight's late model Volvo station wagon pulled in. Joe went out to greet him.

"Looks good up there, Joe," Dwight said. "I'll change in the locker room."

"I made coffee, would you like some?"

"Yes, that would be nice," Dwight said, "cream, no sugar, please."

Joe got the coffee, preparing himself a watered down version because it was the polite thing to do, and went back to the locker room, where Dwight, now dressed in a brightly colored Descente jumpsuit, had just finished folding his street clothes.

"I take it everything went well last night," Dwight said, accepting the coffee from Joe.

"Yeah, it was really smooth."

Dwight sipped his coffee. "How did it go with the reporter?" he asked.

"Good, real good. She was satisfied," Joe said, setting his almost full cup down on the cluttered wall shelf with no intention of picking it up. He just couldn't stomach another cup of coffee.

"I'm glad to hear it. Well, I suppose we ought to get going. Who knows what the boys at Shapleigh, or heaven help us, Sugartree and Parkland, are doing," he said, referring to their archrivals in the battle of firsts. If White Woods had made snow last night, then they probably had also, and no doubt would be in the race for First Tracks.

As usual, Joe would drive his pickup truck up the service road to mid-station. From there, Dwight would hike to the summit. He could have run the triple for Dwight, but he didn't even offer, knowing that Dwight preferred the old tradition of driving and walking. In the early years of getting first tracks there was no mid-station, so while you could have ridden up from the base area, you'd have to walk down. Joe also remembered that Dwight liked the strenuous climb that gave him a good workout during a time when his bicycle was put away and cross country skiing wasn't an option.

Dwight transferred his skis and poles from his car to the truck and got in. "You know, Joe, considering it's just you and I, who'd know if we just said we did it. I could go over to the office right now and fax the press release."

Joe knew Dwight was only kidding. It was something he just wouldn't do. "I'd tell," he said smiling as he started the engine and put the truck in reverse, "besides, you…"

"Oh fudge," Dwight said, as hot coffee slopped on his hands and pants.

"Sorry," Joe said, looking between and under the seats for a napkin or cloth to give to him. Finding nothing, Dwight shook his hand off and rubbed his pant leg, obviously unhappy with having to do that. Neither spoke as they started up the overgrown service road, the bumper pushing over bushes while tree branches scraped and slapped at the side of the truck, occasionally hitting the windshield. Every minute or so a loud crack filled the cab as the tires snapped dry sticks lying in their path.

The service road, a single lane trail that had been made during mountain construction, was used to haul timber from newly cut trails and move vehicles, equipment, and supplies. Unlike the trails and slopes, where bushes and trees had to be cut often to keep them from protruding through early season snow that lacked adequate base depth,

the service roads received only enough maintenance to keep them pass-
able.

"Looks like we'll need to do a little work on this road come summer," Joe said, not taking his eyes off the road.

"It sure needs it, but you know very well if we do Carter there won't
be time."

"It looks good, don't it," Joe said, trying not to seem like he was
prying for information from White Woods' second in command.

"Yes, but it's a big project, we'll see."

Despite the fact he had brought it up, it was obvious Dwight didn't
want to discuss the expansion in detail, or at least he didn't want to talk
about the chances of them carving the future of White Woods from
the ruggedness of Carter Peak.

They emerged from the woods, into the openness of Exception, not
far from mid-station. Joe turned around, positioning the truck so they
were ready to drive out.

Dwight opened his door, rested his right foot on the ground, and
looked back at Joe as he pulled on his green knit hat that matched the
shoulders pads of his silk-like jumpsuit.

"Wish me luck," he said smiling as he stepped out of the truck.

"Take it easy now," Joe said, setting the parking brake harder than
usual. Joe got out, resting his arms on the side of the truck bed just
behind the cab.

Dwight reached into the back of the truck, pulled out his skis and
poles, and marched off up the mountain without another word. With
the leaves off the trees, the neon pink stripes that blazed the back of
Dwight's suit stayed in sight for a long time, finally disappearing a couple hundred yards up.

For the second time that morning, Joe took pleasure from the total
silence that enveloped him. Turning around, he admired the cloudless
pre-dawn sky, marked only by the fading night stars, which promised
another nice fall day. Scanning the distant landscape, he searched for
movement, but there was nothing. It was these views on clear cold

nights, he remembered, that used to keep him going during his early days doing gun runs. Nights when he was colder than any man should have to bear, or tired beyond caring, or just plain bored, he would look out and up into the dark endless distance and somehow find meaning in it, an ability to go on. Mostly he would scan the distant horizon, knowing that even a fleeting glance of the Northern Lights dancing in the far off heavens would lift his sagging spirits.

Standing as still as a statue, Joe watched the sun appear over the distant mountains, bathing the summit, and probably Dwight, in its warm brilliant rays. By seven-thirty it had reached Joe. Suddenly, he was wide-awake, absorbed by his surroundings. Beside him, a mix of birches, maples, and pines, seemingly arranged by the careful planning of a landscape artist, rose up like towering giants, framing the valley below and the distant mountains beyond. The further his eyes traveled the less detail there was, until only the purple silhouettes of far-off mountain tops could be seen, the farthest probably 50 miles away. He thought about how he could see so much, but really so little. What was happening below the trees tops in the hundreds of square miles that lay before him on this cold October morning? An icy mountain stream running briskly over a bed of rocks—a herd of deer feeding, their heads occasionally jolted to attention by some unknown noise—a sleeping hiker who would soon rekindle the fire that had cooked his meager supper.

"Hello," Dwight yelled as he approached the truck.

Joe spun around, realizing he had been caught daydreaming. "How'd it go?" he asked, raising his voice.

"Great, just like a mid-winter run," Dwight said. "As long as you know where the ground starts."

They climbed into the truck and drove down the mountain the way they had come.

Dwight was suddenly talkative. "You know, I probably say this every year, but one of these times I'm going to get a television station to come do this with us. Wouldn't that be great? Most any weekday morning, like this year, would work. You know, they have those live features, maybe even the Today Show. We'd get a ton of publicity out of it, don't you think?"

"Yeah," Joe said, knowing he was subdued by the grip of his mind, brought on, as usual, by being alone. Realizing he needed to return to the real world, he struggled for something to say. "You should invite them, I bet they'd come," he added, knowing that agreement was the safest thing to say in the midst of one of his encounters with whatever it was that made him distant.

"I think I will," Dwight said, "as long as you make sure that First Night is a weekday. And if they wouldn't come, we could tape it with one of our camcorders and release it to them, I bet they'd use it."

"Another good idea," Joe said.

The rest of the trip down was silent, something that Joe blamed on himself. When he got into one of his thinking moods it wasn't easy to shake.

Back at the pump house, Dwight returned to the locker room where he quickly changed. Joe was standing by the door waiting for him when he finished. They left the building in silence and Joe locked the door.

"There," Dwight said, still bubbling with enthusiasm, "another season has officially begun."

"Yeah," Joe said, forcing a smile, still unable to muster any enthusiasm.

"Well, thanks, Joe, we'll see you later. I don't want to waste a minute getting the press release faxed."

Dwight hurried off, churning up a small patch of dust as he shot across the parking lot and down the connector road toward North Slope Lodge. Weary, Joe climbed into the cab of his truck and rumbled down the access road with Dwight's empty coffee cup rocking on the passenger's side floor, wondering if they would beat the others.

Chapter 3

▼

Opening Day

The first few nights on the job they always lost a worker or two. This year was no different. They were usually guys who had taken the job without realizing how difficult it was or how vicious the weather could be. When Joe and Art interviewed them they would try their best to screen out those who for whatever reason didn't seem to be the type, unless, of course, they were one of Warren's nephews or cousins, who they had to hire.

But regardless who they were, it was inevitable that one or two each season would end up quitting after a few hours or days. The record time for bolting was just a half hour set two years earlier. It had stopped the crew's long-standing practice of taking bets on whether the previous years record would be beat because nobody figured you could leave any quicker.

It was just past 1 a.m. the second night of operations when John radioed the pump house asking if anyone had seen Eric, a first-year worker.

"He left to take a piss and I haven't seem his since."

"How long has he been gone?" Marty asked.

"I don't know, a while I guess."

Joe was on Starburst, just above mid-station, checking snow quality and thinking about heading home. He didn't like what he was hearing. They were supposed to stay together, or at least keep an eye on each other, particularly the new workers.

"Pump house, 508," Marty said, "how long has it been since you last saw him, since you saw Eric last, I need a time."

"It's been…maybe a half hour," John answered hesitatingly, his finger keeping the mike keyed longer than his words lasted.

"Christ," Joe said out loud as he headed for Exception where John and Eric were assigned, "why did he wait so long." Based on past experience Joe figured Eric was probably already home, but he couldn't assume anything, especially because John's half hour might mean one, which was long enough for a new guy to get himself in trouble.

"501, pump house," Joe said.

"Go ahead," Marty bellowed back.

"I'm a hundred yards down Starburst. I'll check Exception from the top. Have Al check the base lift shacks and you check the pump house."

With the lodges and maintenance building locked up tight, Joe knew those were the only two places that would draw Eric if he were still on the mountain. Joe had just reached the summit of Abbott Peak and was preparing to start down Exception when Marty called.

"Pump house, 501," he said not waiting for a reply, "his stuff, I guess it's his, is in the locker room, he must have come in and changed and left."

"Okay, I'm on the way in. Do you know what he drives?" Joe asked.

"Nope."

"502, 501, Joe, I believe he drives that Volkswagen Rabbit, the one with all the bumper stickers on the back, it's dark green." Al said.

When Joe arrived back at the pump house fifteen minutes later he checked the parking area. No Volkswagen Rabbit. In the locker room, sitting on one of the benches in front of the lockers was a helmet, light, jacket, and boots, all neatly arranged in a pile. Joe had never had a guy just leave without checking in with him or somebody. While he didn't doubt Eric had left, he didn't want to assume it, so he went to his office and called the telephone number listed for him on the crew roster, but there was no answer. Still concerned, Joe confirmed with Al that he had seem him get out of the Volkswagen Rabbit that night, so short of the car having been stolen, Joe would just have to assume he had quit. He didn't like it, but there was nothing more he could do.

"I guess he left," Joe said as he approached the control desk. "I called the number listed for him, it's an 824 number, so it's around here, but there's no answer."

"Well, if his car ain't here he left," Marty snapped.

Joe hadn't expected Marty to understand the need to follow through on something like this.

"It would be nice to know for sure," he said, "but we've done all we can."

Marty, who was feverishly flipping through channels on the television, changed the subject. "Jesus Christ," he said as he quickly skimmed through another ten channels, "we got forty-five stations on this cable system but not a damn thing that's even halfway decent to watch. You get this cable at home?"

"No, it doesn't get out my way."

"Me neither, course at home I don't much give a damn anyway, but my wife would like to have it for the soaps and maybe some of those talk shows."

"Yeah, my mother would love it. Sooner of later it'll probably reach us."

"If it's like anything else, count on it being later."

"Well," Joe said, "you got to realize that if it weren't for White Woods there wouldn't be any cable in Cannon, period. At least we got a chance to get it."

"Yeah, I suppose."

Unable to find a ball game on, Marty settled on the resort's bulletin board channel, muting the background music.

After a couple of minutes of watching public service announcements flip across the screen, Joe said, "Well, I guess I'll leave a note for Doris to call the next guy on the interview list to replace Eric. I'd like to wait, you know, to make sure he isn't going to show up tonight, but that will leave us short?"

"Yeah, particularly if somebody else bangs out. With these kids today you never can tell. But you don't have to worry none about him, he's gone all right."

"Strange, isn't it, how they just disappear."

"It isn't for everybody, but you'd think they would quit normal-like."

"I suppose they're embarrassed."

"I guess."

Joe sensed that Marty was sliding into one of his quiet moods, so he leaped to his feet and marched off to his office. He'd have considered going home except for the fact they were probably going to be able to open that morning, and if they did, he needed to be there. At three-thirty he traipsed down Starburst and the top section of Exception. With the predawn temperature dipping, he ordered the crews to switch to drier snow. While it wasn't as efficient to produce, it made for better skiing.

Following established protocol, he made the call to Tom at seven o'clock sharp. By seven-thirty, the lanky six-foot-six patroller was at the pump house, dressed like he'd just come from the slopes instead of home.

"So it looks pretty good, huh, Joe?"

"I think so, I checked it top to bottom, it looks smooth."

"Okay then, if you'll drive me up there, I'll put her to the test."

With the crew gone, Joe drove him up to mid-station and started the lift. When Tom disappeared from sight, Joe turned around and walked to the end of the deck, where he placed his folded arms on the weathered wooden rail and looked out over the valley to the mountains in the distance. The patchwork of clouds that had allowed peeks of sun early had now given way to a solid overcast. Following a car through the trees as it came up the access road, Joe wondered who it might be, but he turned away when it disappeared behind North Slope Lodge.

Instead of shutting down the lift like he might have done, on the chance Tom would decide to take a second run, he walked to the opposite edge of the deck, where he waited to greet him. Just as he expected it wasn't a long wait. Tom whizzed around the corner, stopping on a dime just feet from where Joe stood, spraying his ankles with a shower of powdery snow. With his poles dangling from his hands, Tom raised his goggles.

"Nice," he said, "very nice."

Joe smiled, more pleased with Tom's assessment than he'd ever allow himself to show.

"So it's a go then?" he asked.

"Seems fine to me, but I'm going to take another run. Any excuse, don't you know," he said as he prepared to load the chair.

Joe nodded, walked to the lift shack, and started the propane heater, something the lift attendant that would soon be there was sure to appreciate. When Tom got back he gave his official blessing and they drove back to the pump house.

Tom headed for North Slope, without a minute to spare, where he would put the opening day preparations in motion. Joe's job was done. He locked up the pump house and returned to his truck that he had left running and headed for home, happy they had such an early opening, but hoping it wouldn't be a false start. This early in the season, with little terrain open and a limited snow cover, it was possible that warm temperatures, or worse, rain, could damage conditions to the point where they would have to suspend operations. It was something that had happened to him only once, which was how he wanted to keep it.

*   *   *   *

Jim joined the snowmaking crew the night after Eric disappeared. He was sitting on the doorstep of the pump house with a good-sized bottle of spring water between his legs when Joe arrived at about three-thirty, rising to his feet when he parked in front of the building. Joe was bothered by the fact that a stranger blocked his path to the building. Who was it? What did he want?

Joe eyed him good from behind his dark sunglasses while he pretended to be adjusting the weather radio mounted under the dash. Judging from his preppy looks, Joe would have sworn he was a skier. But why was he hanging out in front of the pump house?

The kid continued to mill around the front of the door with his hands in his pockets, occasionally glancing at the truck. Suddenly it occurred to Joe who he was. It must be the new worker, he thought to himself. It had completely slipped his mind that he had left a message for Doris to notify the next one on the list.

Realizing he probably wasn't going to go away, Joe shut off the truck and headed for the pump house door as casually as he could, despite the fact he was still irritated. He preferred to get settled before dealing with people, even the crew. That was why he always showed up at least half an hour early, so he could have the place to himself.

"Hi, can I help you?" Joe asked, trying to sound upbeat even though it was still the equivalent of morning to him. Up close the kid looked familiar. He had a boyish face and thick neatly trimmed jet-black hair that almost touched his shoulders, although it didn't look long tucked behind his ears, both of which sported small rings that hugged his ear lobes. I must remember him from the interview, Joe thought.

"Yes, my name is Jim Cabot, I was told to be here to start work at four," he said as a wide smile broke across his face, exposing a set of teeth that looked like a freshly painted white picket fence. Braces, Joe thought to himself, the kid has undoubtedly worn braces, so he must come from money.

Joe introduced himself and they shook hands. Then, unlocking the door, Joe said, "You're early."

"I didn't mean to be. I wasn't sure where things were and I didn't want to be late."

Joe opened the door and held it for him. "Well that's a good thing."

"Excuse me?"

"Not being late," Joe said, "come on in."

"Thanks."

They started down the hall in silence. Halfway to the control desk Joe held out a brown paper bag so that Jim could see it from behind. "I've got to put my lunch in the refrigerator, did you bring anything."

"No, but I had a late lunch," Jim replied, "I'll have some dinner when I get home."

Joe was tempted to mention Jim's misuse of meal terms, at least for this part of the world, but figured it wouldn't make for a good first impression, at least coming from the boss. Besides, he'd find out quick enough from the crew, and that in itself would be a learning experience. Joe put his lunch in the almost empty refrigerator and started a pot of coffee.

"Listen," he said, "I've got a few things I need to do, so why don't you just hang around here for a while, feel free to look, but please, don't touch anything."

"Yes sir," Jim said.

Walking to his office Joe wondered if Jim's military like reply was sincere or the product of the way he had come across. It was quarter of four when he heard talking and laughing coming from the control desk, so he knew some of the crew had arrived. There was no question Marty was there. He'd know his voice anywhere, mostly because it was always an octave above everybody else's, eclipsed only by the penetrating sound of his laugh that permeated the entire building if the pumps and compressors weren't running.

Some of the guys speculated that Marty couldn't hear himself because he had long ago gone half deaf from being exposed to the screeching of the pumps and the hum of the compressors for so many years, but Marty said it was bullshit. It's "inheritance" he'd growl whenever it got brought up, meaning to say "hereditary." But Joe knew Marty was just protecting his turf by trying to make sure that Joe didn't make any changes in the pump house to reduce the noise he was exposed to, or worse, make him keep the control desk door closed. Joe knew OSHA would probably cite them for it if they were inspected during operations, but their remote location made a night inspection unlikely.

When he got to the control desk he found Jim exactly where he had left him, leaning against the far wall, holding the bottle of spring water that was near empty. Joe introduced him as Eric's replacement, which they no doubt already knew. Nobody said anything. Joe looked at Al and spoke.

"We'll be in my office going over things, it'll probably take a half hour or so."

Al raised his right hand in a kind of comical salute, oblivious to the ash that fell to the floor from the cigarette that hung from his lips.

Joe tried to make quick work of Jim's orientation, but didn't succeed. His lecture quickly turned into a conversation that Joe found interesting. Although he would never admit it, he knew it was because he enjoyed talking to savvy people from away whose experiences were different. It was something he rarely got to do. There was no question Jim was brilliant. Having just graduated from the Massachusetts Institute of Technology near the top of his class with a Bachelors degree in structural engineering, he was already admitted to a top notch Masters degree program that he was slated to begin the following fall.

"So why not this fall?" Joe asked.

Jim's reply was straightforward. "Boredom."

"Oh," Joe said, nodding his head.

"Counting kindergarten," Jim explained, "I've been in school for 20 straight years. I feel that I've done okay for a person my age, so I decided to take a year off."

"That makes sense I guess. So what brought you here?"

"It's simple really, I spent this past summer as I had in previous years, hiking and camping, often for weeks at a time. When I wasn't on the trail I lived in campgrounds or sometimes in my car. Probably sounds a bit boorish, but I don't mind living that way for the summer, and after a year of unrelenting academic pressure it's a welcome change. Besides, I love it up here. I'd have my mail delivered to my parents house in Winchester and occasionally pop in there. Mom said I only came to get my laundry done, which was mostly true."

"Winchester, Massachusetts?" Joe asked.

"Yeah, down near Lexington, just northwest of Boston. So anyway, unless I wanted to go home and live, which I didn't, I really had to work somewhere. I love to ski, so I figured my best bet would be to find a job at a ski resort where I could work and ski all I wanted. Plus, I knew the job would end about the time I'd be ready for the trail again. It all made sense. At the job fair I went to in Portland they told me that snowmaking jobs started first and since I needed work I checked it off as my first choice, but I would have taken anything. As a matter of fact, had you not called when you did, I would have been starting as a lift attendant in a couple weeks."

"You may wish you had," Joe said, using the opportunity to change the subject back to the job. "You do realize that this job is tough and it's dangerous."

"That doesn't concern me, I'm used to hiking ten, twelve hours a day."

Joe smiled. "This is a bit different."

Jim didn't seem to grasp the difficulty of the job, despite the fact that he and Art would have painted a fairly bleak picture of it when they interviewed him like they did for all the applicants. While Joe didn't doubt Jim's physical condition, he had an obligation to make sure that anybody who worked for him understood what it took. Doing so improved the odds considerably that the Eric types of the world never got the chance to fail themselves and White Woods.

"Listen, Jim, it's been a while since we interviewed you and now is a good time for me to reiterate what this job is all about. This isn't the kind of job where you can fake it till you make it. In a nutshell, snowmakers push the limits of human endurance to the maximum. We work seven days a week if the weather is kind enough to allow it. Even if you're in top physical condition, which I don't doubt you are, and even if you're not tired, hungry, or fighting the latest strain of flu, which sooner or later you will be, you're still at a disadvantage. Have you ever worked a midnight shift?"

The smile was gone from Jim's face. "No," he said tersely.

"Well then, you've never had the feeling of wondering if you were going to make it through. Add in isolation, cold, wind, and work that defines the term back breaking. I'm telling you, there aren't a lot of people that can do it."

Jim nodded and Joe was satisfied his message had hit its mark.

"But that isn't to say that you can't do it, and do it well, and stay healthy. Mother Nature and that mountain out there," he said, waving his arm toward the slopes, "can and will be vicious, as vicious as anything a man can face in life."

Joe paused for effect, but he needn't have. Jim was motionless, ready to absorb what ever else spewed from Joe's lips.

"But," Joe said, sticking his index finger straight up for emphasis, "it ain't like war either, where your enemy can be a sneaky devious sort, that will out flank you. There isn't a hidden agenda out there, and that's the good news. With a few rare exceptions, if *you* get caught, it's because *you* went out there without preparing your body and your mind, that's the bottom line you need to take from here, be prepared."

"I think I understand," Jim said, obviously humbled by what he had just heard.

Content he had told Jim what he needed to know, Joe moved on to the other things to be covered. By the time he was finished they had been in Joe's office for over an hour.

"Well, it's high time we got you out on the mountain. I've arranged for you to work with Andrew, he's a good man and knows his stuff, just follow his lead and you're be all set, and welcome aboard," Joe said, rising to his feet, forgoing the opportunity to shake hands again.

When they got to the control desk Andrew was there waiting.

"He's all yours," Joe said to Andrew, who was already on his feet.

Andrew nodded and took over, sizing Jim up from top to bottom. "Okay, let's get you outfitted," he said, "this way."

"Everything going okay?" Joe said, turning his attention to Marty.

"Haven't heard that it isn't."

"Well, things are looking pretty good for so early, wouldn't you say?"

"I'd say," Marty answered, "that if we go top to bottom Saturday you'll be some kind of fucking hero around here."

"We all will be."

The rest of the week went smoothly. True to the prediction Marty had made, Dwight dubbed Joe as the best there was when they were able to start top to bottom operations on Saturday. It was the earliest on record and Warren was pleased. As he usually did, Joe made sure that strong doses of humility preceded his every word when it came to such things, but quietly he knew the credit was his. Just as he'd have been blamed for a weak start, he collected the honors for a strong one. Things were good.

CHAPTER 4

▼

THE EXPANSION

As October drew to a close, the polar jet stream dipped low across the Northern Hemisphere, allowing chilly Canadian air to dive south, setting up a string of unseasonably cold nights across the Western Mountains, which allowed for continuous nighttime snowmaking operations. Base depths on Starburst, Exception, and Planet had deepened quickly, and now averaged 17 to 27 inches. The crew had started to branch out onto Leader of the Pack and Supply Side, two trails that made up the remainder of the terrain from the summit of Abbott Peak.

When Joe got to work Monday evening there were two messages from Doris, both scribbled on the same piece of paper that was taped to one of the computer screens where it was impossible to miss. Doris must have brought it over, Joe thought as he pulled the paper from the screen. I bet it had been her ticket to leave for home early, a ploy she used often.

The first message was labeled simply "FYI" and said that Eric had called her and asked that his paycheck be sent to his home in Milford, a small town in Southern New Hampshire. At least she got back to me about it he thought, never expecting to hear the outcome.

The other message was from Warren, asking that he attend a meeting at his office the next day about the Carter Peak expansion project. Joe knew that Warren and Dwight needed to pick his brain about the cost of snowmaking for Carter, which was sure to get 100 percent coverage like the rest of the mountain.

Joe relished the opportunity to be involved at that level, but he wished they would meet in the afternoon or at the very least give him better notice. But that was the way it was with people who worked days. They could schedule a meeting for the next day without any disruption to themselves, but it shot Joe's plans to hell. Even if he left work early, which he'd have to do, he wouldn't get enough sleep, which he didn't like. He also knew that the meeting probably wouldn't end until mid-afternoon, preventing him from taking a nap before work. At least Warren would buy them lunch; he was always good about that.

With everything running smoothly, Joe left for home at twelve-thirty. The roads were deserted. He plucked a cigar out of the package between the seats, opened it, and pinched the end off with his long fingernails, foregoing the use of his cutter. With the cigarette lighter glowing brightly, the result of him holding it in its socket for a few seconds after it popped, he lit the cigar and drew heavily, slowing exhaling the smoke through his nose till it burned his membranes. As the cab filled with smoke he cracked the passenger's side window, drowning out the barely audible weather radio that he hadn't been listening to anyway.

He was deep in thought about the expansion, which sounded every day to be more of a sure thing. What would it mean to him? He'd been doing the same job for a long time, and while he loved it, he wanted to move up. Snowmaking chief didn't qualify you for much, but with his knowledge of grooming and lift operations, things he had taken the time to learn about, he could try for Mountain Operations Manager if the position opened, which was the rumor.

The problem was that Mountain Operations Manager was mostly a white-collar job, and Joe felt that Warren saw him as a blue-collar type, which was something Joe didn't blame him for, considering that the only work he'd ever done at White Woods was to make snow. Joe also knew it was common-place to hire from away for such positions, and surely Warren knew a slew of qualified people in the industry that he could tap for the job, like he had done when he hired Art.

His train of thought was interrupted when his headlights picked up three deer standing in the road, staring at him. Joe stopped, hoping they wouldn't run off, but he had gotten too close. Together they dashed into the woods, their white tails bobbing up and down as they picked the course of least resistance through the recently logged forest littered with slash. Barely visible fifty feet from the roadside tree line they stopped, looking back over their shoulders, no longer dazed by his headlights. But the lack of cover afforded by the bare branches of the hardwood tree forest must have made them uneasy. They moved on and Joe went home.

*   *   *   *

Joe wasn't late for the expansion meeting, so he was surprised to find everybody there drinking french vanilla coffee and eating sticky honey buns from three brown cardboard bakery boxes that filled the center of the conference table somebody had cleared for the occasion. From the looks of what was dumped on the floor under the windows, it appeared that Doris had done it, probably at the last minute. Joe went over to the kitchenette and was making a cup of coffee when Dwight came up behind him.

"Did you hear we beat Shapleigh?" Dwight asked, his voice unmistakable.

Joe didn't know what he was talking about. Beat who? At what? Then he realized that he hadn't seen Dwight since they did first tracks. But it was too late. Dwight was already refreshing his memory.

"They didn't make snow until the night after, I guess they were a bit warmer down there, or somebody was asleep at the switch, or whatever, but we beat them by 24 hours, a first."

"Hey, that's great," Joe said. "Remember, we're going to have a TV station there next year."

"You bet ya," Dwight said, taking his seat.

Almost immediately, Warren brought the meeting to order.

Just as Joe expected, it was boring. They spent the morning discussing what would be developed on Carter and how it would relate to what they already had. While Joe was surprised at the difficulty they faced in meshing the existing terrain and facilities with Carter, he felt they droned on too long about it, seemingly beating the subject to death. They only briefly discussed snowmaking, which was the only time Joe got to talk, so he was glad when Warren asked Doris to take the lunch orders at around eleven-thirty. None of the restaurants at White Woods were open yet, which meant the only place for lunch on the mountain was the Abbott Lodge cafeteria, and Warren made no bones about the fact that he wasn't going to eat tasteless burgers churned out by minimum wage workers that were probably getting their training on the job.

"We'll get lunch from the deli," Warren said. "They make a decent sandwich and they'll charge the order."

Doris circulated a yellow legal pad, waiting impatiently while everybody wrote down what they wanted, and left for town.

Warren was about to continue the meeting when he heard Art and the marketing people talking about Parkland and Sugartree, two side-by-side ski resorts that were merging and expanding.

"Did I hear somebody mention the competition?" he said, raising his voice and looking directly at Art.

The room fell silent.

"I was just saying that the latest I heard is they're going to try and connect Parkland's north face area to Sugartree with lift service."

"Gee whiz," Dwight said, surprised by the information. "I figured they'd tie them together with bus or trolley service or something, but with lifts, you're talking a lot of money, that's a mile or more."

"Money they probably got in a merger," Art said. "Like us, they're doing what they have to. They're land locked over there to the right, I guess it would be the southern end, so it's either this or the backside which has got an exposure they wouldn't want."

"True enough," Dwight replied, "but that kind of project raises a lot of obstacles."

Art shrugged. "What are they going to do though, people today expect more—more lifts, more terrain—it started happening years ago in the west when I was there. People are more likely to ski at a resort with a hundred something trails. It doesn't make an ounce of sense because you can't ski them all in a day or even a week, but it's that bigger is better phenomena, the perception and the reality that you have more choices. That's why I think we've only seen the tip of the iceberg in terms of consolidation. The big places are either swallowing the smaller ones or putting them out of business. I read the other day that the number of ski areas has declined by 200 in this country since '83."

"Including that backwoods place you came from, but you're right," Warren said, intending to steal the soapbox from him, "and it's not just trail count and lifts, it's everything, and that's where we're ahead of them—with quads, snowmaking capacity, hell, they got a serious water problem over there."

"That's right," Art said, "I heard their water problem just went from bad to worse. They didn't get approval to draw down the river any further. They're going to be held to the level they're at. They've got an alternative plan to build a fifteen acre storage pond that they would fill when the river is high in the spring, but that is a couple years away if the environmentalists don't derail that too."

Warren nodded. "And that's exactly why we need to press on, not just for the obvious competitive reasons. Let's face it, the tree huggers could strike anytime, anyplace, and not necessarily with any rhyme or reason. They might just decide they don't want further development here. If they're successful next week restricting the paper companies, who the hell knows what they'll do next. In fact, if they get that damn thing through, they may make a case that the per acre clear-cut restrictions are applicable to us."

Dwight was surprised. "I haven't heard about that."

"Me either." Art said.

"That's because you're hearing it here for the first time. But why the hell wouldn't they make the case, think about it. We sure as hell clear-cut, we sell the trees, for pulp to boot. And sure as hell these wide-open trails we're cutting are over fifty acres. Leader of the Pack is a hundred acres top to bottom."

Dwight shifted in his chair. "I haven't delved to deeply into that law because I don't think it's going to pass, but it must exempt recreational uses, otherwise it would set a dangerous precedent. What about golf courses and the like?"

"I'm not saying it can be applied, will be applied, or even that anybody has thought of it, but nothing succeeds like success. We've got to get our heads out of the sand and realize that the greens have long-range plans. Those bastards are like the Japs, they got a hundred year plan. They recently introduced legislation that would bar development of all new homes and businesses in five million acres of northern forest. It won't pass, at least not as it's written. It covers too much area, amounts to nothing more than the taking of private property. But it's indicative of what the greens want, and they know that by pushing crap like that they're bound to get something sooner or later. They got a lot at stake here, or so they think. People don't realize it but we're the most heavily forested state in the nation, that's something they don't want to change. That's how they're getting national support."

Nobody said anything so Warren continued.

"Don't under-estimate what they can accomplish. At the very least they'll drown a project in court appeals for years, which effectively kills it. The sad part is they don't know it but they're not fighting a real threat, they're trying to balance things. They have this half-baked idea that big business is so extreme in its abuse of the environment that they have to be equally as extreme caring for it. They're battling a perception that is of their own making, which naturally gets reacted to, it gets answered, so we're always at opposite ends. It's crazy."

Art spoke up. "They think we're a bunch of blue blooded elitists who sit in smoke-filled rooms and conspire about how we can rape the landscape. They've convinced themselves that we're bad people, that we do a lousy job."

"Exactly," Warren said.

"But you know," Art said, "there are plenty of owners who don't care, whether they conspire or not, I don't know, but they sure as hell put profit first."

"And what may I ask is wrong with that?" Warren said, shaking his head. "Profit is not a bad word, it's not a bad thing."

When Doris walked in with lunch fifteen minutes later, Joe hoped the discussion, which he felt was getting emotionally charged, would end, but it didn't. Doris was taking the sandwiches out of the bag one at a time and reading what was written on the white deli paper in black marker, passing them to whomever she thought was correct. Warren continued to talk despite the whispering and swapping of sandwiches.

Finally, Dwight raised his hand like a frustrated traffic cop trying to stop a lane of uncooperative traffic.

Warren fell silent.

"Did anybody order turkey on rye, no mayo?" Dwight asked.

Nobody answered.

"Fine, I'll eat it," he said.

For the next hour they ate lunch, went to the bathroom, used the telephone, and talked amongst themselves. It was after one when Warren brought the meeting back to order. With an hour break and full stomachs, they got quickly back into the particulars of Carter. But by three-thirty, with most everybody squirming in their seats, Warren decided it was either time for a coffee break or to wrap things up. He chose the latter.

"One word of caution before we go," he told them as he stood up to make his point, "I don't want what we discuss in these meetings to leave this room. Not the fact we're doing Carter, hell, that's already out. But I don't want the details, the what and where of it to get out. I'm not aware of anything that has, but we need to be mindful of what we say, particularly when it comes to Carter." The room was silent as Warren's piercing eyes swept the table. "Okay then, we'll meet again next Tuesday, same time."

Joe slipped out of the office before anyone else and headed for his truck, anxious to open the big manila envelope Doris had given him despite the fact he knew what was in it. Even if the return address hadn't been the *Bangor Herald*, the scrawled mailing address matched what had filled Brenda's notebook pages on First Night. He pulled out the contents—three copies of the article clipped to a card. The card started where he figured it was supposed to, on the inside lower flap, but Brenda's large handwriting and all that she had to say combined to fill the back and finally the top flap.

Joe wasn't particularly surprised that most of what she said seemed to gush with desire, at least if you read between the lines, which he was inclined to do. There were compliments galore, professional ones, but no less glowing; an invitation to call, with both work and home numbers, if he found any problem with the article or just wanted to comment on it; and finally, a thank you for seeing her off so nicely.

So she had noticed him watching until she left, he thought to himself. Putting the card aside, he read the article which was shorter than he expected, but surprisingly accurate. At least he'd be able to say he liked it. The story included a single picture of guns blowing snow that could have been anywhere, but looked surprisingly like the design White Woods had when Joe started. Its caption was simple. *Local snow guns at work high on a mountain.* Its *File Photo* label, on the far right in tiny black type, didn't surprise Joe."

Joe re-read the card again, noted it was a two-dollar Hallmark, and stuffed it back into the envelope with two copies of the article. The other he would tape up over the control desk. Even though he was tired, he decided to check in with Marty before heading home. He found him in the compressor room.

"This one is all fucked up, Joe," Marty cussed as he walked in. "The frigin thing couldn't blow up a kid's balloon. If we don't replace her soon she going to quit on us altogether."

Joe wished he hadn't stopped. He just likes to bitch, Joe thought to himself, if it wasn't the compressor it would be something else. Besides, it was their oldest compressor, which they pressed into service only early in the year when they were strapped for air. They hardly needed it most of the season.

"How did the meeting go?" Marty asked, leaning against the compressor.

"Good, I guess, we made some progress."

Joe didn't really like discussing administrative things with the crew, including foremen. He never knew what was okay to say and what wasn't. He turned to leave but Marty spoke again.

"So are we going to do Carter for sure or what?"

Joe turned around and answered. "I think we will," he said, trying to sound optimistic.

"Well, if we don't, it'll be because of money. Rumor has it he's fixing on doing the whole of it at once from scratch, which will cost big time, and I bet we'll hit ledge up there, which could up the price tag."

"Yeah."

"No, I mean it, we've been lucky up to now, but it don't take a fucking rocket scientist to see that Carter is a frigin rock pile and a half." Marty rolled his dirty baseball cap around his head, expecting Joe to say something. He didn't. "I'm not saying that it ain't worth it, Joe, hell, if there ever was a diamond in the rough Carter is it, but she's different than what we've been doing, you know what I mean, cutting a few trails here and there. Carter is a whole new area, a whole new ball-game."

Joe understood what Marty meant, but it was just talk, talk that Joe had little patience for, particularly coming from somebody like Marty. The best thing to do was to change the subject. "I'll talk to Warren about a replacement compressor. If you're all set I'm going home."

"All set," Marty said as he shuffled back toward the control desk.

Joe made a quick check of his office for anything that might have been left for him. Finding nothing, he went home.

*   *   *   *

The unseasonably cold weather that had settled across the Western Mountains almost two weeks earlier showed no signs of loosening its icy grip, which was just fine as far as Joe was concerned. They were blowing snow dusk to dawn now, which was a decent stretch of time considering the shorter days.

With nothing more for problems than occasional freeze-ups, they were averaging a new trail opening every two to three days. Word got back to the crew that business was up in double digits, the result of their hard work and the fact that it had been dry, which meant that competition for skiers was limited solely to what a resort could make for snow. With White Woods powerful snowmaking system operating at or near capacity, they had more terrain and better base depths than any other resort in New England. So Joe wasn't overly concerned with running short when two workers on the midnight shift called out sick the night before the second expansion meeting.

Briefly he considered staying all night to take up some of the slack, but decided against it. Instead he stayed till four-thirty. Warren must have been able to tell he had only gotten two hours sleep. During the morning break he suggested Joe go home.

"Jesus, Joe, you look like death warmed over."

"Yeah, I didn't get much sleep."

"And it shows, we're all set, go get some rest."

Normally Joe would have declined the offer outright, but he was dragging. Besides, he reasoned, he'd been at the first meeting and he'd be at the next. He got up and started for the door, wondering if the back-to-back cups of coffee he'd had were going to keep him awake. He was halfway to the door when Warren raised his voice.

"Oh, Joe, and everybody else for that matter." He paused while the room quieted. "Don't forget to vote. There's every indication it's going to be close and surer than shit they'll have their people out."

Joe nodded and left. As much as he hated going to bed for a short period of time, he knew he needed to. But he forgot to leave a note for his mother to wake him at three. He would have overslept had it not been for the telephone ringing on his mother's line.

As he drove to the mountain, he felt refreshed. He knew the nap wouldn't stand by him for long, but short periods of sleep had a way of making him feel good. His thoughts turned to the note from Brenda. He had considered calling her quite a few times since receiving it, but kept putting it off. He knew if more than a week or two passed, he'd never call her because he'd be afraid that something had changed in her life.

As he started up the access road he resolved to call her from work that night. He had a new calling card his mother had just given him from some promotion she had done through the mail.

With the crew settled and everything running smoothly, Joe went to his office, closed the door, accessed the calling card account, and dialed the number that was on the card he had tucked away in his wallet. Brenda answered, her tone of voice changing immediately when she found out it was Joe. They discussed the newspaper story.

"I had written a much longer article but they cut it on me. No matter how many times that happens you never get used to it. I was especially disappointed with your story because the X-Acto cut so deep but those are the breaks, at least in this business."

"Well, I liked it, it was great. I hung up one of the copies you sent at the control desk."

"Great. So how are things going over there?"

"Good, we've had guns going every night, we're way ahead of last year, at least so far anyway. It's shaping up to be a good season. I never like to say that, you know, like I'm tempting fate or something, but everything right now looks real good for us."

"Great. That reminds me, what can you tell me about the new area you're developing. It's called Carter Peak, right?"

"Yeah, but not much really, that would have to come from upstairs."

"Oh, I'm sorry, I didn't mean to put you on the spot, I just thought I'd ask. Marty mentioned it when I was over, and I read about it in the Gazette."

"Yeah, they really didn't say much of anything, I wondered why they bothered."

"For them that's not unusual given their coverage area. I bet there isn't anything else more important in Cannon than White Woods and its future."

"Yeah, I suppose. So you're thinking about doing a story?"

Brenda's answer was immediate. "If you'll give me one."

Joe laughed. "I don't have anything and even if I did I couldn't give it to you on the record."

"And I wouldn't expect you to. I discussed it with my editor. We'll wait for something definitive to happen."

"You mean like a ribbon cutting ceremony?"

"Well, it doesn't have to be quite that decisive, we'd settle for a formal announcement, maybe an approval of some sort from somewhere. It has to be newsworthy. It can't just be speculation, like what might happen, that kind of thing."

"I see."

Before the call started, Joe had set his watch to know how many minutes had passed to avoid getting cut off by the calling card company. With only three minutes remaining on the ten-minute card it was time to bring the conversation to the point of the call. With what he feared was apprehension in his voice, he asked her if she would like to get together sometime, an offer she readily accepted. They arranged to meet in Bangor the following Monday, which was her night off.

As Joe hung up the telephone, clicking his watch to a stop at slightly better than nine minutes, he felt good. He needed some time off and he looked forward to spending it in Bangor with Brenda.

The following day, after sleeping for ten hours and getting some chores done around the house that the expansion meetings had put off, Joe freed himself in time to tune in the noon news. He watched with interest as the numbers announcing the passage of the clear-cut ban were displayed on the screen—51,342 in favor, 49,789 opposed with 97 percent of the precincts reporting. Joe didn't know the significance of the ban's passage; only that Warren and Dwight had panned it as destructive.

He had his usual one o'clock meal with his mother and left for work, stopping at the store for coffee. Several day-shift paper mill workers, who often stopped at the store on their way home, had Ethel in an uproar, despite the fact they'd left ten minutes earlier.

"Those boys at National have given their lives to that plant and now it's all on the skids because of this clear cut thing, it's a darned shame if you ask me."

"Yeah, I guess it's going to happen. I don't know a whole lot about it, but it's going to have a spin-off effect that will probably be felt here in town, I mean besides the local guys that may lose their jobs."

Ethel was all ears. "What do you mean?" she asked.

Joe wished he had kept him mouth shut. "Just that the ban could be applied in ways people never intended."

"How so?" she asked without waiting for an answer. "You mean it's going to affect the mountain?"

Joe had put himself in a corner he didn't want to be in. "I just mean the spin off," he said, hoping to spell closure to the issue.

It probably wouldn't have except that a customer, his arms laden with breakfast food, approached the counter. Edging Joe out of the way, he dumped his purchases on the counter, oblivious to their conversation. "I still have a few items to get," he announced.

Joe smiled at Ethel and left, knowing that anyone who was as pompous as that customer would probably take his sweet time getting checked out.

*   *   *   *

Kay and Doug had moved to Cannon from Dracut, Massachusetts five years earlier. They had come for a simpler life, but mostly they had moved to escape what they considered to be Dracut's unrelenting growth and the unwillingness of city officials to control it. In the ten years they lived there, huge housing developments had transformed vast tracts of farm and forest land into suburban-like neighborhoods, its highways had became miles of strip development, and a sprawling industrial park had been allowed in the name of lower taxes.

From the beginning, Doug saw it coming. He spent many long evenings in stuffy meeting rooms at city hall, trying his best to make a difference, but never feeling he had. City officials would patiently listen to what he had to say, and then do whatever they pleased.

"It's my past," he would tell Kay, fresh from a meeting and brimming with frustration, "that's why they're not listening to me." Kay would usually succeed in convincing him that their reluctance to do as he proposed was seated in something greater than his personal history, which they likely didn't even know about, but occasionally they would still be sitting there long after their bed time debating the issue.

Finally, Doug realized that Dracut's land use policies were hopelessly mired in politics. The city's brand of conservation—the setting aside of one acre out of a hundred as green space, or laying down 12 inches of grass between a five-lane highway and the sidewalk—was not going to change no matter how much he tried.

Having vacationed in Maine, he and Kay were keenly aware of its unspoiled natural beauty, and, unlike Dracut, they were convinced it could be saved from the kind of development that seemed to be taking a greater hold in more and more places. Their decision to relocate had been made for them.

During one of their many weekend trips in search of a new home, they found a place just on the outskirts of Cannon's small business district. Like many of its kind, it sat too close to the road, the result of no zoning when it was built and the road being widened. It was run down and lacked modern amenities, but Kay loved the big kitchen and the large attached barn was perfect for their planned antique shop. Several subsequent visits to Cannon and discussions with those involved from their Realtor to the Postmaster convinced them it was a good place to settle.

The town was well known for its avowed opposition to development and its embrace of strict community planning, the product of people like themselves who had come years earlier. The only unknown they were aware of was Cannon's unguarded commitment to nearby White Woods Ski Resort. That was why the headline in the Cannon Gazette immediately caught their attention.

"White Woods makes ready for major expansion" would undoubtedly mean different things to different people. To Kay and Doug, with memories of Dracut still fresh in their minds, it could spell trouble. The newspaper's plastic sheaf was still in Doug's hand as he paced the kitchen floor reading the article. Despite the fact that it had been rumored and even reported on before, this made it official. Doug was quick to share it with Kay who was making dinner.

"Listen to this," he said, folding the paper so it was easier to handle. "White Woods Ski Resort, already one of New England's most skied mountains, is poised to get even bigger. At a sparsely-attended meeting Tuesday night, selectmen wasted no time in agreeing to a town meeting warrant article for $100,000 worth of improvements to White Woods Road to accommodate the planned development of Carter

Peak, estimated to cost 14 million dollars. The project, approved in concept by the town in 1986, requires little municipal action because the area is already zoned for it. White Woods presently has 73 trails, ten lifts, and two base lodges. Depending on which of several development plans is implemented, Carter Peak could increase the size of White Woods by almost one third. First selectman Abel Johnson, blah, blah. Now what bothers me is those seven little words, 'approved in concept and already zoned for,' how do you figure that?"

Slicing carrots into inch-long quarters on an oversized cutting board, Kay said, "Sounds like foresight to me."

Doug ignored her comment. "You know, Carter Peak is untouched. I'm pretty sure it's the mountain to the right of Abbott Mountain if you're facing the resort. It's like opening up a whole new area."

"Dinner will be a tad late, honey."

Doug growled an acknowledgment as he headed for the den, where he continued reading the article that concluded on an inside page. Like old times, he felt himself getting overly interested in White Woods. He knew where any degree of involvement in it would likely lead—his mere interest today would probably turn into a burning passion tomorrow—but for some reason he was powerless to stop his environmental fascinations once they were triggered. While he wasn't outright opposed to the expansion of White Woods, its size and scope bothered him. He'd have to find out more about it and monitor its progress.

The next day while picking up a copy of the town's zoning ordinance, he learned from a plain and prolific-talking town hall clerk that Cannon's conceptual approval of Carter Peak, which she couldn't find a copy of, would probably become final with little or no review. That evening, relaxing in the den in front of a cracking birch wood fire with Sam, their miniature collie, stretched before them, Doug poured over the quarter-inch-thick zoning ordinance for the better part of an hour while Kay quietly knitted. Despite having lived in Cannon for five years, Doug was not familiar with the document. Up until now there had been no reason to be.

At quarter of nine he closed the book, laid it on his knee, and spoke. "This thing is really strange," he said, his hand pressing down on it.

"What do you mean?" Kay asked, not looking up.

"I think it's been written around White Woods."

"What do you mean?" she asked again.

"It completely exempts ski resorts or the issues that pertain to them, and something that is exempted can't be regulated."

"Was it written before?"

"No, you don't understand, I don't mean it ignores the ski area, that wouldn't worry me so much, what it does is it uses language to exempt them, almost like those who wrote it knowingly crafted it so it wouldn't effect White Woods. I mean, we got strong zoning in this town, but this thing clearly exempts recreational land uses in a circle that White Woods just happens to be at the center of."

"Just like that?"

"No, no it doesn't say that, honey. I culled that from ten, fifteen places, but that's it in a nut shell."

Having reached the end of a row, Kay stopped and looked up for the first time. "Really, what's it dated?"

"It was drafted, I think…" he paused as he flipped to the inside front page, "1986."

"Well, you know how important White Woods is to Cannon. I suppose when it was written they wanted to make sure that they didn't do anything to hurt the resort."

"Well, that's fine, I guess, but this thing," Doug said, holding it in his hand and shaking it back and forth, "allows White Woods to do whatever they want, it's that simple."

"What about state, federal regulations?"

"To some extent they would be involved with an expansion, I guess. I really don't know what permits are involved in ski terrain development, but Cannon is a municipality, so they do their own zoning. I think the only state or federal issues would be waterways, wetlands, maybe if they're operating with a forest service permit which they're not."

"So what you're saying is that this expansion is a done deal."

"If I'm reading this right, White Woods is golden. This isn't easily undone," he said, slapping the book.

"Well I can't see why you're so concerned, it's only a ski resort and White Woods is already a big place. I don't see that it will change things a whole lot except to draw more skiers, which will be good for us."

Doug nodded. "True, but you know how it works. More skiers means the need for more lodging, more stores, more services."

Kay put her knitting aside and reached for the remote control.

"Sounds like there's a pretty good movie on at nine, do you want to watch it?"

"Let's give it a try," he said, tossing the zoning ordinance manual onto the nearby couch. "I think I'll meet with the owner of White Woods and get a copy of what they approved in concept."

Chapter 5

▼

Trouble for Carter Peak

A weak fast-moving low pressure system that dropped out of the Great Lakes and swept across New England after dark brought White Woods the first snowfall of the season. It was gone by dawn, leaving behind five inches of wet snow that clung to most everything it touched. Each time the sun peeked out from behind a patchwork of clouds on the eastern horizon, the snow sparkled like a million diamonds. With the temperature hovering around thirty and sure to rise, Joe took his time driving to the store that morning, relishing the fairy tale sight that was sure to be gone by mid-morning.

The store's parking lot was crowded with the trucks of road crews on break and deer hunters taking advantage of the snow's tracking potential. Passing a group of state highway workers, who were drinking coffee just inside the door, blocking the way more than they should have been, Joe made his way to the back of the store, where he fixed himself a large coffee. Unhurried, he drifted toward the front. When the line dwindled to two men, dressed in blaze orange, who were buying cigarettes, Joe stepped up to the counter.

"Good morning, Joe," Ethel said with a big smile as the hunters moved away. "I didn't see ya come in."

"Good morning," he said, dropping fifty-five cents into her waiting palm.

"What brings you out, didn't ya work last night?"

"No, I've got a meeting this morning."

"Looks like you're getting some good early-season skiing."

"Yeah, we've done well, our visits are way up."

Joe wanted to ask Ethel if she had noticed an increase in business, but another customer was behind him. He sidestepped out of the way, intending to continue their conversation, but Ethel hadn't finished with the first customer when a second one arrived. Backing away from the counter, he waved goodbye, and left.

The highway workers were outside now, still standing in a group talking, still blocking the way. Joe climbed into his truck and headed for the mountain, listening to the weather radio.

Unlike the first meeting, they spent the day discussing specific details of Carter Peak. As the day drew to a close Warren announced that he and Dwight would finish up.

"The rest of you are off the hook," he told them. "Dwight and I will firm up the package. I plan to fly to New York the first part of next week to arrange financing."

Now the frequency and length of the expansion meetings made sense to Joe. Warren was obviously trying to get prepared for the trip. Joe didn't know much about that stuff, but it figured that Warren would need hard numbers to convince investors.

He also knew that time was running short if Carter was going to be developed that summer. An expansion project the size of Carter was ambitious by any standards. Depending on the money available, it could add as many as 18 new trails serviced by three new quad lifts including a high speed detachable to Carter's 3,726-foot summit. If Warren had his way, there would be a new lodge nestled on a wide plateau between Abbott and Carter Peaks.

Construction couldn't start in earnest until the worst of mud season had passed, usually sometime in April, which left only about six months to get the job done figuring on an October completion date. Weather delays, like washouts caused by thunderstorms and high winds that grounded helicopters, could slow or stop work, and despite the best efforts of the engineers there were always unforeseen problems, such as ledge they didn't know about. With adequate funding, sufficient time, and a little luck, Carter could be ready next season, but it wouldn't be easy.

"Any questions?" Warren asked as he scanned the room. There was silence. "Okay then," he said, "I guess we're all set. As you know, the surveyors started last week and we'll have a design team hired at this time next month."

Warren's resolve to make Carter happen surprised no one in the room. They were well aware of what he had already accomplished and his desire to do more was a given. But each of them, to varying degrees, silently wondered if it would be different this time. Carter did not hinge on vision or innovative approaches to old problems. This time it was money. A lot of money. Not a single one of them was aware of anything that was going to stand in the way of raising that money, but each of them was aware of telltale signs that foretold of White Woods precarious financial situation.

Art spoke up. "If we can't fund the whole package, I'm curious about the phasing of it. We really haven't addressed that. I think…"

Warren interrupted. "Not an issue. Carter is going to happen just like the script," he said sharply, patting the three quarter inch stack of papers before him. "A year from now, we'll be a national destination."

Art smiled, and Joe couldn't help but wonder why Warren always found it necessary to preach to the choir. After all, the room was filled with his management team, his foot soldiers; he didn't have to fluff it up for them. They knew the potential of it. They wanted to know the probability. But that was Warren, too often talking as if someone was going to quote him, or put him on the six o'clock news.

"And one more thing," Warren said, "I'd like to get together Friday morning, say," he looked at Doris and Dwight before continuing, "I guess the same time, so we can review the package before we assemble the final proposal. It shouldn't take more than an hour. That way we can make any changes and have it ready by the end of the day." He paused, sweeping his eyes across the semi circle of blank faces before him. "Well then, if there aren't any questions, that's it," he said, rising to his feet.

Joe timed his departure so he could walk out with Art, which might give him the chance to find out about his plans. It was common knowledge on the mountain that Art was considering moving back to California. It had only been four years since Warren had lured him away from a small ski resort in the shadow of Squaw Valley, but his wife, a California native, longed to return. While she liked the better weather of the west, it was mostly the cultural and social opportunities in Sacramento, where they kept their home, and San Francisco, where they often spent weekends, that she missed, things that the Western Mountains of Maine sorely lacked. Art, understandably, was torn. While he, too, loved California and wanted to please his wife of fifteen years, he loved his job, where he was, for all practical purposes, his own boss for the first time in his adult life, and, having been born and raised in upstate New York, Art was no stranger to tough winters.

"So what do you think?" Joe asked Art as they walked down the stairs from the third floor and entered the lodge's main seating area, which was devoid of the hordes of skiers that had been there only an hour before. Joe looked across the expanse of scattered furniture and littered tables to the far corner, where two employees, tackling the first stage of cleanup, were stacking chairs in piles higher than they should have. If he'd been alone, Joe would have told them so, but he figured it was Art's place to say something, not his. If Art saw them, he ignored their carelessness.

"Oh, I don't know," he said. "The expansion would be good for everybody, but I just don't for the life of me see where the money is going to come from. It sure as hell isn't going to be financed with the money from the timber we cut, which from what I can tell is the only uncommitted capital we got these days. The rest is buried in those god-forsaken condos. My capital improvement plan is shot to hell. I put in for an upgrade to Lift 7 from a double to a quad, not even a detachable, two years ago, and there's no money. If that thing was any older it would be gasoline powered."

"Yeah," Joe said as they exited the building.

"I don't know when we'll be able to replace the older groomers, I don't know," Art said, repeating himself. "Maybe Warren is saving everything for Carter, but if you want my opinion those condos have bled him dry. The darn things aren't selling, you know."

Joe didn't know about that, he didn't want to know, but he wasn't about to tell Art.

Art continued. "The market for that top end stuff, all of it really, has just dried up along with everything else. Not too many people know it, but against the advice of his accountants he kept a lot of units in that last phase, more than he should have. I guess he likes the rental revenue from them or some darn thing, but he's paying their freight—mortgage, taxes, association fees. Course he's trying to unload them now, but that's what saturated the market."

Joe nodded. "Yeah."

"Course, you're half to blame you know."

Joe looked at Art, confused. "What do you mean?"

"What the condos haven't gotten, you did."

"What do you mean by that?"

Art laughed. "I'm only kidding, but you know you've been at the trough for years when it comes to snowmaking, getting whatever you wanted, whether or not you needed it."

Despite Art's preface, Joe could tell he had wanted to get in a dig about Warren's propensity for snowmaking, which bothered him. But there was nothing to be gained by dwelling on it so Joe clenched his teeth together behind closed lips and changed the subject.

"What about you?" he said. "Are you still thinking of heading West?"

"Mary won't let me stop thinking about it, she's got her heart set on it."

Joe paused a few feet from Art's car while he unlocked the door and opened it.

"You know, if I do leave," Art said tossing his briefcase onto the passenger's seat, "or should I say, when I leave, it will make a great opportunity for you. I'd even recommend you for all the good it would do."

"I'd appreciate that," Joe said. "Your support would mean a lot all around."

"You'd have it," Art said as he slid behind the wheel of his cream colored late model Volvo waving his hand.

Joe plodded across the near empty parking lot to his truck, watching Art's car disappear down the access road. Despite being encouraged by what Art had said, Joe was thinking about the differences between them, which could be summed up in the fact that he drove a Ford F-350 and Art a Volvo. "Ah, thinking again," he said out loud as he pulled himself into the cab of his truck and reached for a cigar, the first one he'd had all day. But he hadn't taken two drags on it when he decided that Art had probably trumpeted his support for Joe at that particular moment to make up for what he said about snowmaking getting all the money. Despite the fact he knew it was foolish, particularly since it was Art doing the talking and not some blowhard, it lingered on his mind.

*   *   *   *

It was nine twenty-five Thursday morning when Doris buzzed Warren to tell him that Doug Andrews had arrived for their nine-thirty meeting. Warren wasn't sure what Doug wanted specifically, if anything. Doris had arranged the meeting, telling Warren only that Doug wanted to discuss the status of the expansion and its potential effect on

Cannon. Warren had never met Doug, but he did know that he was one of a growing number of environmentalists in town, so he wasn't surprised when Doug turned out to be tall and thin, with a thick well trimmed beard and small wire rim glasses that framed meek eyes.

Warren met Doug halfway across the room, where they shook hands. Then, gesturing toward the semi-circle of chairs in front of his desk, Warren asked, "Can I get you something, coffee, tea, juice?"

"No thank you," Doug replied in a soft voice as he settled himself into the nearest chair.

Warren slipped behind his desk and sat down. "Do you ski?" he asked.

"Yes, well, cross country."

"Great sport."

"Yes, me and my wife do enjoy it."

"Well you're in the right place to enjoy it, we are certainly blessed to have such beauty here."

"Yes, I couldn't agree more."

"So what can I do for you," Warren said.

"Well, I'd like to learn more about your planned expansion. I read the piece in the paper. Just so you know, I'm mostly interested in the environmental aspects."

Warren nodded. "If you've read the paper you pretty much know it all, the expansion is just that, the need to make us a bit larger so we can better compete with our neighbors to the north and west."

Doug nodded. "Carter Peak is to the right looking at the mountain, correct?"

"Yes."

"According to the piece in the paper, you haven't settled on exactly what it will involve. But that's what interests me, what you're planning besides actual terrain?"

Warren was definite. "Very little. Maybe a small lodge, nothing else."

Doug nodded. "Well, let me be straightforward with you. I've read the town's zoning and it seems to give White Woods free reign within the recreational land use zone that is centered here."

"Don't worry, Mr. Andrews, you…"

Doug interrupted. "Call me Doug, please," he said with a thin smile.

Warren nodded. "You needn't be concerned about a water slide here or anything of that sort. White Woods and Cannon have enjoyed phenomenal success, the product of cooperation. Clearly it's been a win win relationship, which is exactly how I want it to stay."

"I don't doubt that, and I don't oppose White Woods per se, but Carter Peak is untouched. There are environmental issues that concern me."

"And me. With all due respect, Doug, I must point to our track record, which is unblemished."

"Again, I don't doubt that, but there are issues," Doug said, wishing he had come better prepared. While he knew there were a host of environmental matters concerning ski resort expansion, he couldn't think of a single one with Warren staring him down. So he said the only thing he could. "I'm a member of the Natural Environmental Council, and while I'm not here officially representing them today, it may come to that."

"I know who you are," Warren said smiling. "I read that piece in the paper, you were the fella that was arrested at Seabrook way back when, right?"

"Me and 1,413 others," Doug replied, silently damning the newspaper article that made it impossible for him to shed his past. Even if he didn't necessarily want it forgotten, it irked him that the choice wasn't his.

"Yes, of course," Warren said, content to back off and change the subject now that his jab had registered. "Listen, not to beat a dead horse, but I welcome your interest. I feel strongly about working together. Like I said, without the cooperation of the town, White Woods wouldn't be where it is."

What a bunch of bullshit, Doug thought to himself, he must think I'm new at this.

Doug and Warren talked for ten more minutes, but every question Doug asked, Warren answered in some general way, more times than not concluding his response with more fluff about cooperation.

As Doug drove home he thought about the difficulty that came with trying to come together. He wasn't sure, but his gut reaction, the result of listening between the lines, was that Warren considered him the mouthpiece of a cause he despised. If he was right, there was no sense trying to work with him. Doug purposely held off discussing the meeting with Kay until they were settled in the den after dinner.

"I met with the owner of White Woods this afternoon."

"Oh, that's right, how did it go?" Kay asked, putting the clothing catalog she had been reading aside.

Doug shrugged. "Terrible."

"What do you mean?"

"He's just one of those guys that says a lot but doesn't really say anything, if you know what I mean. How business is trying to learn from the environmental community and how they're going in the direction we want but we haven't embraced their efforts. Stuff like that. He's real shrewd, but I can see right through it."

"What about future development?"

"He says no, but it doesn't really matter unless the zoning is changed. Like I told you, they're exempt."

Kay thought for a moment, and then said, "It just doesn't seem to me that a ski resort is much of a environmental threat, I mean, I never really considered them like the rest."

Doug smiled. "Well they're certainly better than the smokestack industries if that's what you mean, and they're better than the extraction industries—timbering, mining. But you can't say because they have less effect they're okay. When you build an urban like infrastructure at the base of a mountain, which is what White Woods is well on its way to doing, it comes at a cost."

"It just seems to me that White Woods has a vested interest in keeping the area the way it is. I mean, what have they got if they don't."

"I know what you mean, and you're right, and I'm sure to a degree they're good stewards of the land, but let's face it, they're a business like any other and the bottom line is profit."

Kay smiled. "Sounds like somebody has got a project on their hands."

"No way," Doug said. "You know how people feel about that place. We'd be run out of town on a rail." He thought for a moment, then said, "Of course, if it was presented right, I mean, I think people would buy into oversight. Yeah, if you could present it that way, the need to have some level of control, it would probably work."

Kay nodded. "Yeah, and I bet dollars to donuts," she said, pausing to make her point, "that this isn't the same town that gave him carte blanche way back when. We know more than a few people who would agree with you."

"Yeah, I suppose you're right. The trick, though, would be in selling it because they'd be quick to get the wrong idea and get defensive."

"Well I'm going to unload the dishwasher," Kay announced.

Doug nodded as she left the room, already deep in thought about the best way of clipping Warren's wings.

*   *   *   *

On Thursday Joe slept late in preparation for the all night shift into Friday. The early part of the shift went smoothly, but it was just past twelve when that suddenly changed.

"506, 501."

Joe turned up the volume and answered from behind his desk, but 506 was in a dead spot, so they didn't receive Joe's reply.

"506, 501."

Marty intervened. "What do you need, 506?"

"506, pump house, we need to see him ASAP."

"10-4, hold on," Marty said as Joe hurried down the hallway toward the control desk, appearing just as Marty finished punching in Joe's office extension number.

"Oh, you are here," he said, hanging up the handset. "506 is chomping at the bit to see you."

"Where are they?"

Marty spun around in his chair, his right hand keying the microphone in one fluid motion.

"Pump house, 506."

"506."

"Where are you? 501 is right here."

"We just finished Universe, we're approaching The Junction."

Always mindful about letting his words be heard in the background, Joe waited until Marty's finger released the transmit button before he spoke.

"Tell them I'll meet them at The Junction in five minutes."

"Pump house, 506, stay put, Joe will meet you right there in five."

"10-4," came the distant reply.

Joe went to his office, gathered his equipment, and went out the door into the frigid cold, wondering what Andrew and Pete wanted. It was rare to call a foreman, and rarer still to call Joe when Al was working. Whatever they wanted probably didn't require his attention. Regardless, Joe didn't mind going.

He climbed onto his sled and started the engine. Letting the cold motor idle for a minute, he leaned back on the palms of his hands, and looked up into the cloud-free blackness, his eyes darting from star to star until he closed them. He'd have liked to lean back further, letting the soft vinyl of the seat's upright section massage his stiff back, but he'd look foolish doing that if somebody happened by, and besides, Andrew and Pete were waiting. So he eased the sled into gear and roared off, across Go Between and up the gentle incline of North Slope.

When he crested the final rise before The Junction, where the lay of the land leveled off in an area the size of a football field, he looked toward the two lift shacks that graced the edge of the hillside, knowing that considering the cold Andrew and Pete were in one of them. Sure enough, a helmet light flickered inside the booth that belonged to the quad, the newer of the two, and the one with electric heat. Joe aimed his sled for it and got there just as the door opened.

"What's up?" he yelled as Andrew emerged from the doorway, which was quickly filled by the bulk of Pete, who was dragging deeply on a stubby cigarette.

"We just come down Universe, we ain't looking to get nobody in trouble or nothing, but we counted three guns with ears open. Somebody on first shift is getting some sloppy."

"Really," Joe said.

"Yeah. Three in a row. Like I said, we ain't pointing the finger or nothing. But I value my hide more than that, if you know what I mean."

"Where were they?"

"Up at the top," Andrew said, turning toward Pete who tossed his cigarette onto the metal platform and twisted his heavy boot over it.

"Yeah, that's right," he agreed, "up toward the top."

"How open were they?" Joe asked, hoping to gauge the seriousness of the situation.

Andrew's experience came through loud and clear. "Enough for them to break free. This wasn't vibration that jiggled them out a little or ice or snow jammed in them. They were left that way, no two ways about it."

Joe nodded. "Okay, thanks for letting me know. I'll take care of it. Everything else going okay?"

"Oh yeah, it was just that," Andrew said.

Joe nodded, started his sled, and left. Leaving ears half open on a gun or two was reason to be concerned, but doing so on three was a serious matter. Back at the pump house Joe seized the operations log from the control desk and went to his office. Flipping the pages to the previous shift, he ran his index finger up and down the data that was squeezed into columns that weren't wide enough. He wasn't surprised when the information revealed that Alan and Jason had done the last gun run on Universe, just prior to shift change. It would be just like them, with thoughts of post-shift partying on their minds, to slack off the last hour of their shift.

Joe was tempted to address the situation right then and there by calling them at home, even though he knew he'd be doing nothing more than waking up family members or leaving messages on answering machines. Instead he wrote down verbatim what Andrew had told him, folded it in half, and tucked it underneath the triangle corner of his blotter. He left the logbook on his desk where it was still accessible should it be needed, but where idle minds would be unlikely to retrieve it for the very information he had just culled from it.

The remainder of the morning was uneventful and Joe emerged from the double shift with surprising ease. Instead of hanging around the pump house for the eight-thirty review meeting, he decided to wait at North Slope Lodge. He immediately regretted it. As he pulled into the parking lot a little past seven, he noticed Doris' little red car, parked in its usual spot. A tinge of uneasiness settled over him as he braked his truck to a stop, his eyes never leaving the car. Doris wouldn't have arrived early, so she must have stayed late. Which could only mean one thing. That she and Warren had spent the night at Ridge House.

Located beyond the ski trails, perched high on the edge of a rocky cliff, Ridge House was a small but immensely beautiful place that offered total seclusion. If he was right, and he knew he was, they would be coming down in Warren's car soon, and for him to be there presented an awkward situation.

As he sat there, the truck straddling three parking spaces and still in gear, his apprehension was quickly replaced by bitterness and he felt some misguided need to catch them. Why should he be inconvenienced just to further the mere perception that they hadn't spent the night up there in that den of iniquity?

But his rush of emotions finally settled in safe territory, and he slid his booted foot off the brake, letting the truck slowly creep away, his eyes fixed on the rear view mirror on the chance he'd catch a glimpse of Warren's car descending Ridge House Road. As he crested the incline and slipped down the opposite side he turned his attention back to the road and how he was going to pass the next hour. But his thoughts went right back to them. Who did they think they were fooling?

When Ridge House was under construction, there was speculation Warren was going to move there, but rumor later had it that his wife of twenty years had soundly rejected the idea of living in what she called "hell with a view." Warren maintained he built it for family and friends who wanted privacy beyond what the hotel afforded and for visiting VIP's he needed to impress, like executives from the National Ski Association or magazine writers. But most everybody who did more than flip burgers or park cars at White Woods knew what it had become—a place for Warren and Doris to slip away to for a few hours or a night. No doubt that was what they had done last night.

As he reached the state road, still puttering along, it occurred to Joe that Warren would claim they had stayed late last night to finish the presentation. That was always the way it was. Something to cover his tracks with. There always seemed to be an excuse. The bitterness, which had become all to familiar to Joe, welled up again. He just had to keep reminding himself that it was none of his damn business. And it wouldn't be except that he felt things didn't run the way they should because of her. Warren was the boss, he could do what he wanted, but she held an important position, and by doing little more than warming the seat, it meant more work for everybody and a resort that wasn't as good as it could be.

His pondering ended when he eased his truck into the store's parking lot. He helped himself to a large coffee with extra cream and had guzzled half of it before he reached the counter. Tossing a dollar bill onto the worn wooden surface, Joe said, "You look tired, Ethel."

"I am," she said with a faint smile, completing the transaction without moving from the stool where she was perched. "I guess I've got a touch of flu or something. Started yesterday afternoon."

"You ought to get yourself some help," Joe said, taking the opportunity to say something he had often thought.

"Maybe," Ethel replied, "but a person mustn't slow down you know, you got to keep going, and you can as long as you do."

Joe didn't say anything. It was a response he'd need to think on before answering.

"I know one day things will change," Ethel said. "I'm in no hurry for it, but it will just be there."

Again, Joe was silent, reflecting on her soft-spoken words.

"I've had those men in smart suits come here more than once, ya always know who they are even before they step up here and tell ya. They'd buy this place from me in a heartbeat, not because they want the store, lord," she said, sweeping her arm through the air across the mismatched aisles of merchandise, a third of which was collecting dust, "who would want it, no, they want the land, this corner to be exact. I know that. But I'm not fixing on selling it till I'm ready. But I'm no half-wit either, although they'd just as soon make you feel you were. I know that if I hold out too long, sooner or later they'll get a chunk of land that will do them okay, and they'll build a fancy store with lots of those colored neon lights, and prices no independent like me can match. At first the local folks will tell me they won't go there, but they will and I won't blame them, a person has to be mindful of their pocketbook. That's my lot in life, Joe, I know it, but I ain't hurrying it, not today anyway."

"Well I hope not," Joe said shaking his head, unsure of what more to say.

"When it happens it won't be a bad thing. I think the only reason it hasn't happened is because of everything they got up on the mountain. If Warren hadn't done all that he's done up there, they would have been here by now, but it's just a matter of time and they will be here. I suspect Carter will be the turning point. We'll see though."

"Yeah, I suppose we've been lucky really, when you think about it, there isn't a national chain here except for the two gas stations, the Mobil and the Exxon."

"The way I understand it, that won't change anytime soon, because they don't usually go for seasonal business regardless of how strong it may be."

"Oh really," Joe said, backing away from the counter to let a customer in. When he saw the woman pull a credit card from her wallet he figured it was time to go.

"See you later, Ethel," he said, waving as he left.

When he got back to the mountain Warren's car was tucked into its usual parking space. Still twenty minutes early, Joe sat in his truck until Art pulled in a short time later, timing his exit from the truck so he could walk in with him.

The review meeting was a meaningless two hours spent poring over a document that was in Joe's opinion already complete. When the meeting got over, most everybody ended up in a huddle with Warren, debating the finer points of appropriate percentages for novice, immediate, and expert terrain.

Joe waited on the sidelines for a while, but he was tired and they weren't. Despite the fact he hated to leave first, he slipped out quietly and went home. Because he didn't get to bed until noon and insisted on getting up early enough so he wouldn't have to rush, he only got a couple hours sleep.

Despite three cups of coffee, one more than usual, he knew he was grouchy when he got to work, but something as serious as leaving ears open couldn't be put off, so he summoned Alan and Jason to his office and chewed them out for five minutes. Then he waited in his office just long enough for them to clear the pump house and went to the control desk. Marty was expecting him, a big smile on his face.

"What's the matter with you?" Joe asked.

"What did you do, chew them new ass holes?"

"Why?"

Marty's grin broadened. "Because they're some pissed."

"It's their own fault. Somebody could have been hurt up there. You know that."

Marty shook his raised hands. "I ain't defending them party boys."

"Well then."

"What did they have to say for themselves?"

Joe shrugged. "I'm not interested in what they got to say because nothing they say matters. They were negligent, period, and that's the end of it. Anything from ski patrol today?"

"Haven't seen anything. Christ, with the coverage we got out there they better not be complaining."

"Yeah, but that's just it, our visits are up, way up I guess, because of the coverage, so it's getting skied off sooner than it normally would this time of year."

Marty shook his head in disgust. "But that ain't it and you know it. If marketing would get off your ass about opening more terrain, and let you put down a decent base in the first place, there wouldn't be anything to worry about, now would there? All they give a damn about is how many trails they can say we got for Thanksgiving."

Joe bit his lip to keep from laughing at the way Marty had emphasized the word Thanksgiving. When the urge had passed he spoke. "But that's what it's all about, Marty."

"'Course it is, but they lie half the time anyway about conditions, so why the hell don't they just say what sounds good to them and let us do our fucking job."

"It's not that bad, Marty."

"No, it ain't. It's worse. Their fibbing is only half of it. You know damn well we got trails that need maintenance and some of those we cut in the last few years didn't get cleared proper 'cause there wasn't time. They're littered with rocks and stumps and who knows what other shit. Some of them need a foot and a half, maybe two feet of snow to be right. It don't make an iota of sense to me. If one of the groomers fucks up his tins on some protrusion up there it won't be his fault, but they'll lay it on him just the same."

"Whatever," Joe said getting up, knowing that no matter what he said Marty would find a way to be negative.

Sensing Joe's displeasure, Marty changed the subject.

"What's the latest on Carter?" he asked.

"It's all set I guess, it's just a matter of financing now."

Marty groaned loudly. "That's gonna be tough sledding. Is he still planning on going all the way this summer?"

"Yes," Joe answered, offering no more.

"Well, time will tell," Marty said reaching for the television remote.

"That it will," Joe said, disappearing down the hallway.

$$* \qquad * \qquad * \qquad *$$

With no expansion meeting the following week Joe planned on having a normal seven days. He hadn't been able to work his usual schedule since the first week of operations. But Monday when he got up his mother broke the bad news. She needed him the next afternoon to drive her to a three-thirty appointment with a foot doctor in Bangor so she could be fitted for a pair of special shoes. While his mother was able to drive around town and occasionally to Waterford, the fifty-five mile trip to Bangor was more than she could handle.

He probably could have rushed through it and got to work by seven, but because his mother loved to eat out, and one of her favorite restaurants was in Benton, on the outskirts of Bangor, he took her there for dinner. They got home at nine-thirty and Joe called the pump house to check in.

"Everything quiet?" he asked Marty, who must have been checking pumps or sleeping because he didn't answer until the tenth ring.

"Haven't heard that it isn't," he said.

"Okay, good, I just thought I'd check, see ya."

Joe hung up the telephone, watched the ten o'clock news, and went to bed.

*   *   *   *

Warren returned from New York mid-week and word spread quickly he had come back with nothing. He tried to put the best face on it he could, saying there were clearly other options, but even he had his doubts.

The investors, with one notable exception, felt that White Woods was too heavily capitalized in real estate. Real estate, they said, that was mostly far from producing a decent return. They also told Warren that Sugartree and Parkland were goal to go with their planned merger and expansion, which cast doubt on the return possibilities of anything White Woods had to offer, particularly given the economic slump that the country was slowly slipping into, which was expected to affect the northeast more than any other region. They also feared efforts by the environmentalists that could stop the project cold or delay it for years in a sea of regulatory red tape.

Either Warren had misjudged somewhere or the investors had done their homework or maybe both. Regardless, the moneymen 500 miles away that Warren was depending on to bankroll Carter seemed to have a pretty good picture of what could happen, and they weren't biting.

Warren knew that any one of their concerns could be addressed, but not all of them, and because big money investors were a tight group, approaching others wasn't likely to change anything. The project was now labeled as risky, and even getting a meeting would be difficult.

"We're not dead," Warren said the next afternoon at a hastily called expansion meeting. "The real estate is the problem."

Dwight spoke up.

"We've got condo units worth well over five million retail that are near completion or under construction, and another three million that we can break ground for tomorrow if we want to. If we start moving units aggressively, maybe at lower prices, it's conceivable we can generate a down payment, if you will, in a month or two, we might be able to do…"

Warren put up his hand, stopping Dwight in his tracks.

"Too much time," he said. "I'm going to find a buyer for everything that's on the drawing boards. If Carter is for real, which it is by Jesus, that stuff is attractive, even in the short term."

Warren's plan to sell surprised everybody. They knew White Woods' success to date had to do with the fact it was wholly owned by Warren. They had heard him say on countless occasions he would never sell or lease any revenue source.

Art shook his head. "Those darn condos. I didn't like them when they were blueprints, and I don't like them now, they're nothing but…whatever."

Silence enveloped the room. Warren regrouped and continued.

"Look, our existing lodging is adequate, we all know that. And for the most part those condos are far enough along so that completion isn't an issue, so we'll have those beds whether we retail the units or somebody else does. Then of course, as much as I hate to admit it, there are those projects in town that will bolster what we have as well. The bottom line is, we can't have real estate development at the expense of capital improvements, particularly with the industry getting so darn competitive. We didn't come this far to lose our way. First and foremost, we're a skiing company. The name of the game is terrain, snowmaking, lifts, that's what put us on top and that's what's going to keep us there."

Dwight nodded his head feverishly. "I agree, it makes good sense all around, besides, all we're losing is the per-unit profit on sales which is a onetime thing. I bet we'll still be managing those units in the rental pool, or at least most of them, and we'll still enjoy the benefits of having increased lodging right on the mountain. It's really a no brainer, letting them go, I mean."

Art spoke up. "It might take time to unload them with the market as soft as it is, and you might want to give some thought to making the sale conditional on completion, maybe even have a bond. A lot of condo developers have gone belly up. We sure don't want them abandoned on us."

Warren was obviously annoyed by Art's opinion. "I'm not going to worry about that. Besides, who the hell cares if the bank has to unload them at auction, I'll buy them back and make a decent profit in the process."

"It might not be that simple."

Warren ignored Art's comment. "Carter is going to happen, come hell or high water, we're going to do it." Then without hesitation, probably to prevent further discussion, he turned his attention to Jamie, his marketing guru. "New York did seem to feel we had a problem with the fact that most of Carter was not visible from the access road or even the base lodges. They felt that was a problem, a what you see is what you get kind of problem, anyway, they may be right, it's something for you to be thinking about."

Jamie looked confused despite the fact she was nodding.

Warren continued. "So you'll address that then?"

Jamie continued to nod; obviously convinced that acceptance would take her out of the limelight, which turned out to be right. As quickly as he had targeted her, Warren turned away, closing the meeting on a positive note of general interest.

"Skier visits for October were seven percent ahead of last year," he told them. "We should all be pleased, especially you, Joe, you had some good terrain open and you kept it open."

"With the help of Mother Nature," Joe said.

Dwight looked at Joe. "Warren's right. Some of the smaller places still aren't operating and we're skiing almost half our best terrain. At this rate we'll be in fine shape for Thanksgiving. By the way, did any-one notice what Parkland and Sugartree had this morning?"

"Well if you can believe them," Art said laughing, "they're reporting something like 50 for Parkland and 55 for Sugartree. But you know how it works over there, they count the paths to the lodges as open trails."

Everybody laughed.

"Really though, that's how they just upped their trail count," Art said. "They added probably ten, fifteen trails, or I should say trail names at Parkland and maybe half that at Sugartree without adding a foot of new terrain. No kidding. They've split trails in half and named both of them and tacked names onto what were nothing more than nameless cutoffs."

"It's gotten to be such a number's game, but I fear we all play it," Dwight said.

"No question, but you've got to these days," Art said. "You've heard the latest one, haven't you?"

"No," Dwight said with an exaggerated sigh. "What now?"

Art loved the camaraderie that came from talking shop with col-leagues and the good feeling he got when he had novel tidbits of infor-mation to share. "Well," he said, clearing his throat, "the resorts aren't counting slope-side beds anymore like before. You ready for this, it's pillows now, they're counting pillows in terms of how many people they can sleep a night mountainside. That way they got big numbers to boast about. It doesn't matter of course that a solitary person might use a one bedroom condo that sleeps eight."

Most everybody shook their heads and smiled.

"Well, if there isn't anything else, I've got an important dinner meeting in town tonight," Warren said, rising from the table. Every-body followed suit.

As they gathered up stacks of papers and manuals and funneled toward the door, the talk was one on one. Warren caught the attention of Joe who was listening to a conversation between Art and one of the marketing people, and pointed his left index finger toward the floor, indicating he wanted him to stay. When the room was clear, Warren gestured again, this time for Joe to close the door, and then a third time, for him to sit.

"How are you doing, Joe?" Warren asked.

"Fine," Joe replied, feeling a little shaky about what Warren wanted.

Warren smiled. "Art and I talked this morning. He says he's leaving us this spring, on closing day, or as close to it as he can wind things down."

"So it's definite."

Warren leaned back in his chair and answered. "That's what he told me, I think his wife is determined. It's really too bad, Art is a good man. He may be headstrong at times, but we'll miss his ability, no question about that."

"Yes," Joe said. Awkwardness had now replaced uneasiness as he anticipated what was coming next. His future, at least what he considered to be his future, hinged on what Warren said in the next few minutes.

"I want you to take Art's place, Joe. I think you're the man for the job. If all goes well you can take over at the end of the season. You'll have the summer to get your feet on the ground, and god only knows, you'll need it. In the meantime, you need to spend time with Art, as much as you can without interfering with your schedule or his. I suspect you feel you're up to it, but Mountain Operations Manager is one hell of a lot different than blowing snow. You've got traffic, parking, lifts, ski patrol, grooming, and a ton of bullshit to make it all click."

"This is what I want, this is what…I can do the job," Joe said, stumbling over his words. "I really appreciate this."

"We'll talk more about it, there's plenty of time for that. Now If I don't high-tail my butt to town, mother is going to have my hide."

Knowing that Warren would soon be exiting the lodge on his way to town and not wanting to be seen sitting there, Joe decided to drive to where he could digest what he had just been told, forcing himself not to think about it until he was there. It was dusk, and he knew the carpenters, plumbers, and electricians would have left the almost completed town houses perched high on the rocky ledges at the base of Abbott Peak.

He drove to the end of the long line of units, dodging the building materials that dotted what would be the parking lot, turned around at the edge of Planet and parked. With a cigar going, he analyzed every word Warren had said, determined not to feel good about it, at least not just yet. Hadn't Warren seemed more committed to him in the beginning and seemed to back off near the end of the conversation? What if Art didn't leave? What if he made a grievous error before spring?

He knew, all too well, that those were mere thoughts, thoughts that were rooted in his wariness of anything that hinged on a variety of ingredients coming together, so halfway through his cigar, like he had done a hundred times before, he put them aside and moved on, hoping they had been dealt with. If all went well, he was about to be more than he ever thought he could be. Mountain Operations Manager. If Carter happened he'd be doing it for one of the largest ski resorts in the East.

It was close to six when he tossed the stub of his still-lit cigar into the ashtray and eased the truck into drive, deciding to go home and take a nap before going to work.

Creeping down the winding mountain road, Joe took a mental inventory. His reaction to things was like a roller coaster, and sooner or later it stopped. This time it appeared to have settled easily in contented territory. Yes, he was happy, so happy in fact, that he did what he rarely allowed himself to do, fire up another seventy five cent cigar, even though he knew he'd only have time to smoke half of it.

The truck bounced up and down on the rutted road, tossing him from side to side, but he didn't care. He wasn't even bothered by the pair of glaring headlights glued to his rear bumper that had appeared behind him seconds after turning onto the access road.

His mind wandered back to the beginning of the season, recounting how good things had been going. The earliest First Night on record, the coveted distinction of First Tracks, an opening so far ahead of schedule that the ski and rental shop wasn't even ready. Most important, a decent Thanksgiving lay ahead, and having the mountain at 100 percent by Christmas would be easy.

*   *   *   *

When he arrived at the pump house later that evening Joe found Al, Andrew, and a few others at the control desk talking with Marty. As Joe approached, Andrew, who was leaning up against the wall opposite the control desk, stood up straight, feeling uncomfortable he and his partner weren't out on the mountain working.

"Where did that come from?" Joe asked, pointing to a collection of plastic buckets with spoons stuck in them, a metal tray strewn with crumbs, and three or four bakery bags.

Marty answered. "It's leftovers from something they had over at the hotel, they dropped it by on their way home. The potato salad ain't bad, but I wish they'd sent over more of them little sandwiches."

They send us what's left over, Joe thought to himself as he gave it a closer inspection. To him it was disgusting, particularly the potato salad, which had already attracted several flies. Joe knew the food would sit there until morning, without refrigeration, and the guys would keep eating it. He shuddered at the thought. A few seconds later Joe dropped the bakery bag he had peered into and asked, "How are we doing tonight?"

"Smooth sailing so far, except for the wind," Marty said as Andrew and his partner gathered up their gear and left. "We may have to shut down Orbit."

As soon as they were gone Joe spoke. "Since you're both here, let me give you an update. The…"

Al interrupted him. "It'll have to be short, Joe, I've got to do the chair for them."

Joe started again, this time interrupted by the radio.

"510, pump house, we need a lift operator," Andrew said.

"No shit," Marty boomed before keying the mike and answering.

Deciding it was bad timing for a conversation, Joe told Al to go ahead.

"Yeah, okay, I'll take care of the lift and then I'll go up to Orbit and check on the wind, it's blowing like a bastard up there," Al said, pulling on his gloves and walking out.

Marty spoke up. "We got one hell of a dry gale, least up top. It was okay earlier, but instead of going down with the sun it seems to have come up with it," he said, making a sensible statement for the first time since Joe arrived.

Joe went to his office to tackle the pile of mail he had picked up at the administrative offices earlier in the day, making sure his radio was on. Most of the mail was junk or could be safely included in that category, which to Joe was testimony that everybody in the world who cared knew he was a snowmaking decision maker.

Twenty-five minutes later, while he was leaned over pushing down the contents of his small overflowing wastebasket, Al called the pump house.

"I've checked Orbit, it's blowing off, especially near the top, we're not getting much of any coverage here."

Joe headed for the control desk, knowing they'd probably have to curtail operations on Orbit, at least near the top of the trail, where it was almost naked, surrounded by nothing but oxygen-starved scrub brush, ledge and small boulders. Putting and keeping snow on its wind-swept forty-five degree surface was difficult at best and impossible when it was blustery, like tonight.

"Did you hear that?" Marty said as Joe approached.

"Ask him if repositioning the guns will do any good."

Al's answer was immediate. "The only snow we're making is in downtown Cannon," Al replied sarcastically.

Joe smiled, rolled his eyes, and sliced his neck with the narrow part of his right hand.

Marty keyed the mike. "Okay, shut her down," he said.

The radio traffic between Marty and Al prompted the crew working on Leader of the Pack to call in.

"510, pump house, the wind is blowing some wicked up here to."

Joe looked at Marty. Despite the fact that they were miles apart in most ways, they understood each other. For the second time Joe slid his hand across his neck.

The only other snowmaking that night was taking place on the sheltered slopes of North Slope, where the width and side-by-side configuration of the trails made blow-off less of a concern.

To a chorus of complaints, Joe sent the most junior half of the crew home. He hated cutting their hours, but couldn't justify having them on duty. He knew sending them home during the shift hurt the most, because nights when they knew they wouldn't be making snow they might get the chance to work some other job on the mountain during the day.

Joe expected the relieved crew to go home, but instead most of them hung out at the control desk, reveling to the beat of what Marty spewed, enjoying the only night life left in town. With one pump working, their laughter was louder than what Joe was accustomed to, which made it difficult for him to concentrate on crunching the numbers for snowmaking equipment that Warren had asked for. Finally, at three-thirty, he went to the control desk, which fell surprisingly silent upon his approach.

Al spoke up. "We just finished North Slope," he said. "I figured we'd start blowing some dry stuff in an hour."

Joe nodded. "Are we getting good coverage at the lifts? I got another message from ski patrol about it being thin."

Al shrugged his shoulders. "Yeah, I guess."

"For Christ Sakes, what the hell do they expect?" Marty asked.

Joe ignored him.

"The last message, and I just got it yesterday, says it's around and just above the triple, if that makes any sense."

"I bet," Al said, now seeming to understand, "that they mean that area under the chairs, you know, just above it, it's those god damn snow boarders that have been getting in there to jump, they're wiping it clean."

"Yeah, that sounds like it," Joe said.

"Well, the fixed guns don't reach that far. I don't know what kind of coverage we're getting there specifically."

"Hell," Marty said rocking back and forth in his chair, his hands clamped across his mid-section, "just tell them to rope the fucking thing off."

Joe was about to say that was not acceptable when Al spoke up.

"I'll buzz over and make sure we get some coverage there," he said, picking up his gear and walking out.

Joe was relieved that he had not been forced to make an issue over it. He hated to exercise his authority, especially when it was something simple that didn't require muscle.

"Hey, I got one for ya, you'll appreciate this, especially you, Joe," Marty said. "Remember Noah, the guy that used to work here back a few years, I don't remember his real name, but we called him Noah cause he had that big old boat in his backyard and he raised a bunch of farm animals, you remember, Joe, don't ya?"

Joe nodded. "I remember Noah, but I never saw the boat, I never go up that way."

"Oh shit yes, that thing was there for the longest time, he'd been keeping it for his cousin who was hiding it from the bank or some lending company, I don't know. Then when his kin ran off to Florida with his broad and her kid, it just sat there rotting away for years." Marty paused, repositioning the wad of tobacco in his mouth, enjoying the fact that he had a waiting audience.

"Well anyway, Noah's property just got bought by the state for preservation. I don't think anybody knew it, but he owned a couple-thousand acres up there."

"You mean where he lived?" John asked.

"Yeah, I read it in the paper. Apparently his acreage was part of some government land they want to protect, he got the going price for it, so he must have done okay. Can you imagine him living like that and working here owning that much land?"

"He must not have known he owned it," Andrew said.

John spoke up. "That place of his was a wreck. He started putting on that addition and never finished it, it's been ten years since he started it."

"Yeah, well, shit, his kids grew up, he don't need a fucking family room no more," Marty said, laughing at his assessment of the situation.

"So where is he moving to?" Joe asked.

"I don't know, but I bet…" Marty said, pausing when he heard the pump house door slam, a sound that never would have reached the control desk except that only one pump was working.

Johnny appeared around the corner. "Hey, what's this, a meeting?" he asked, surprised to find a group.

"Just killing a little time, what's up with you, Johnny?" Marty asked.

"I was hoping you guys had some coffee on, I'm dragging bad tonight," he answered walking toward the coffee pot. "We had a little get-together last night that didn't want to end."

"You don't want that motor oil," Marty boomed rising to his feet. "That shit has been there since I came in. We'll make a pot of fresh for ya."

Marty whistled as he made the coffee, but otherwise everybody was quiet, pretending to be watching the old black and white movie, even though the volume was turned down enough so you couldn't hear it.

Joe decided it was a good time to leave. He didn't like to hang around for very long, figuring it set a bad example. Even though there was nothing for the crew to do, he had work to do in his office and felt he should be doing it.

"Call me when the coffee is ready, will ya, Marty," he said as he walked away.

Putting aside the snowmaking equipment report, Joe filled out two purchase requests and approved a small pile of invoices for payment, enveloping them when he was done for delivery to Doris.

Twenty minutes later, he returned to the control desk.

"Oh, sorry, Joe, I forgot to call ya," Marty said.

"That's okay," Joe said, meaning his words. He had decided to go home.

The rest of the week went quickly. With perfect weather and a full crew, they were averaging ten tons of snow a night over virtually the entire mountain. With a season that had already exceeded any previous year in terms of the amount of snow produced and what was sure to be a record season in skier visits, Joe's innermost thoughts, which directly reflected his overall happiness, were positive.

CHAPTER 6

▼

THE ACCIDENT

It was just past one o'clock Saturday morning, fours days before Thanksgiving, when Joe's two-way radio crackled with an excited voice.

"510, pump house, we've got an accident on Infinity," the person said, "John's been hit by an air hose, he's hurt bad."

Joe recognized the voice as one of the new workers, Markie. John, he knew, was John Kelly, a veteran worker with a spotless record. The red flag for Joe was the dreaded words "hit by an air hose." The metal coupling on a loose fully charged hose had the power to deliver a blow that was equal to being whacked by a swinging baseball bat.

Joe snatched his gear from his guest chair and trotted down the hall to the control desk where Marty was answering Markie but not getting a reply. Why doesn't he answer, Joe thought, as Markie called in again, describing the situation.

Marty continued to answer Markie, mumbling something Joe couldn't understand between transmissions. But he might as well have been talking to himself, because Markie just kept saying the same thing.

"You'd better call ski patrol and an ambulance just in case. I'm on my way," Joe said.

Marty was already dialing the telephone as Joe dashed out of the building, jumped on his sled, shot across Go Between, roared through The Junction, and started up Infinity. He had made good time, having reached Infinity in just two minutes, but his sled slowed as he started up the steeper expert terrain. He was also in the deep ungroomed snow that had been blown that night. Each time he hit one of the so called whales, accumulations of snow generated by the guns in the shape of a whale, the sled seemed to pause as it fought to regain its power and break through. I just hope he had his helmet on, properly, Joe thought to himself as he gripped the throttle hard, squeezing out every last bit of power that the whining engine was capable of delivering.

Within a couple minutes he saw Markie's helmet light off to his right. He veered the sled across the trail, bringing it to a stop near where John was lying face up in six inches of new snow, not moving. Markie, who had been milling about, dashed toward the approaching sled and burst out yelling, answering an unasked question, "I don't know what happened," he said, "the hose was…"

"It's all right, Markie," Joe said, getting off the sled and kneeling down, never taking his eyes off John's still body. "Just take it easy."

Pulling off his gloves, Joe carefully flicked away bits of bloodied snow and ice from John's nose and mouth and lowered his ear to his face. Satisfied he was breathing, he lightly pressed three fingers into his neck and found a pulse. Despite Joe's apparent calm, he was well aware of the danger John faced. While the blow to his head, which appeared to be centered on his forehead above his left eyebrow, could have fractured his skull, there was also excessive blood loss, shock, and hypothermia to worry about, any of which could kill him under such conditions.

"Get me the emergency bag from under the seat of my sled," Joe yelled to Markie, who was roaming around, kicking snow, and muttering something Joe couldn't understand. Watching him fetch the bag like a clumsy bear, Joe radioed Marty with what they had. "John's been struck in the head pretty bad, he's unconscious."

"Ski patrol is on the way," Marty said, "they gave me a ten minute ETA here, then travel time to you from North Slope, and I'm on the land line now with the hospital, and I got a couple of groomers on their way from Abbott, they should be there shortly."

"Okay, thanks."

"You need anything else?" Marty asked after a long pause.

"Is Al coming?"

Before Marty could answer, Al broke in.

"503, 501, I'll be there in three minutes."

"10-4, thanks."

Joe had no medical training. None of the crew did. That was why ski patrol was required to have a team on call at all times. Joe knew that inside fifteen minutes he'd have two Emergency Medical Technicians, maybe even a paramedic or two, at John's side. Guys that treated injuries on the mountain during the day for a living and were well versed in mountain evacuation. But until they arrived, he needed to stop the bleeding. Being careful not to move John, he applied pressure to the gash on his head with a large piece of gauze from the emergency bag, which after several minutes he told Markie to hold in place. Next he opened a palm-sized package containing a shiny aluminum space blanket, shook it out, and covered John with it, knowing it would hold in his body heat and ward off the threat of hypothermia. He'd have tried to get it underneath John, but he'd heard somewhere that without a backboard and neck collar, a head injury victim shouldn't be moved.

By now the groomers had arrived, first one, then two more, and finally all four of them. Like pioneers circling their wagons to protect against Indian attack, they surrounded the scene with their Pisten Bullys. Now, with their powerful lights illuminating the dark mountainside, and the air filled with the soft humming of their perfectly tuned engines, there was a sense that everything was going to be okay. When Al arrived a few minutes later, Joe pulled him aside, out of earshot of the others. "It's not good," he said. "He's been out since I got here. He took it in the head, looks like it missed his helmet altogether."

They looked each other square in the eyes.

"Jesus, the poor bastard," Al said, plucking a cigarette from the pack in his shirt pocket.

Joe nodded and returned to John's side, kneeling in the trampled snow adjacent to his head. He was still sitting there, oblivious to the cold that had settled in his motionless body, when the first ski patrol sled arrived. It was Tom. Joe got up and backed away as Tom brushed by him, evaluated John, and talked on his radio.

When he was finished Joe spoke up. "Is there anything we can do, Tom?"

"There will be. You called an ambulance, right?"

"Yes, at the same time we called you."

"Good. Just sit tight then."

Three minutes later a second sled arrived with two patrollers on it and a toboggan in tow. Unneeded, Joe backed further away, surveying the scene. Should he go join Al and the groomers who were clustered together talking on the downhill side of John, or should he console Markie who sat twenty feet from John's legs on a raised section of water main, his ungloved hands flat on the cold rusted surface of pipe, his head bowed. Joe did neither. Something kept him still. He didn't know how much time had passed when Al was suddenly beside him, asking a question.

"What do you make of that," he said, flipping his head toward the still motionless Markie.

Joe's answer was immediate. "He's pretty upset, I don't blame him."

Al was indifferent to Markie's pain. "Did he say what happened?"

"He says he doesn't know what happened."

Al was skeptical. "He doesn't know?"

"That's what he said when I got here. I haven't taken it any further, yet."

"Well, ain't that great," Al mumbled as he walked back toward the groomers.

He was halfway there when Tom stood up. "We need lifting help," he shouted, beckoning everybody to John's side.

Joe moved quickly to the lower end of the backboard, where he figured his only responsibility would be lifting. Besides, he didn't particularly want to look at John's face.

But it didn't matter. Except for a tunneled slit above his eyes, John's head was draped snugly with a white thermal blanket that gave way to a neck collar that kept his head upright and tipped slightly back. Tom was definite about what to do.

"We'll pick him up on the count of three, one complete motion. Any questions?"

A few heads shook but nobody said anything as they searched for handholds and adjusted their stances. Finally, with three of them on each side, and two others holding the basket in place on the downhill side of the mountain, they lifted and lowered him easily, placing him into the metal cradle of the toboggan, strapping him tightly in with three belts—one just below his neck, one across his mid-section, and one over his legs between his knees and ankles.

Tom paused just long enough to thank the group. The groomers took it as a cue and started for their Pisten Bullys. Markie, who up till then hadn't moved, must have been watching things closer than Joe thought, because suddenly he slid off the pipe and headed toward them with slouched shoulders.

"How you doing?" Joe asked as he approached.

"Okay, I guess," he said, his voice flat.

They mounted their sleds in silence, with Markie behind Al, and waited while the patrollers made a final check before descent. Thirty seconds later they started down. The going was slow as the patrollers carefully choose their route on the bumpy unforgiving surface, stopping halfway down to check on John's condition. When they reached North Slope Lodge the ambulance wasn't tucked into its designated pick-up spot beside the building, so for the second time they rallied around John's still body, hoisted him up, and carried him into the warmth of the ski patrol receiving area, where they loosened the back-board straps and waited—the patrollers huddled around John while Joe, Al, and Markie stood outside. Nobody said much.

Ten minutes later Tom opened the door, disgusted with the smoke from Al's cigarette that was hanging in the air, trapped by the wide overhead deck. "How long has it been?" he asked.

Joe was embarrassed that he didn't know for sure. "At least 45 minutes. It's got to have been," he said. Then, lowering his head into the microphone clipped to his collar, he radioed the pump house. "Do we have an ETA on the ambulance?" he asked Marty.

"Negative," Marty replied. Then, in defense of himself, he added, "I called them right away."

"Do they know we're at North Slope?" Joe asked.

There was a pause before Marty answered. "I told'em," he said.

"Okay, thanks," Joe said. "I just wanted to make sure."

But there was still plenty of doubt in Joe's mind. Unlike during the day, when the ambulance almost always went directly to ski patrol, response to the mountain at night was usually for a specific location. Since Marty had no doubt told the dispatcher where he was calling from, he figured that maybe they had gone to Abbott. But Joe saw no reason to share his concern with Tom, at least not yet.

Five minutes later the red lights of the approaching ambulance came into sight on the connector road, escorted by Johnny, who had the Suburban 's green emergency lights going. I knew it, Joe thought to himself, they went to Abbott. The screw-up had probably cost them five minutes.

Joe poked his head in the door to announce the ambulance's arrival as Al snuffed out his second cigarette against the foundation, letting the butt fall to the pebble stones below. After John was loaded into the ambulance, Tom and the driver talked by the closed back doors of the rig for several minutes while the other attendant busied himself inside.

Suddenly Joe realized he hadn't been at John's side since they left the mountain. He edged closer to the ambulance, leaving Al and Markie and the two patrollers behind, trying to decide if he should interrupt what was going on inside the ambulance. But his hesitation cost him the chance. The driver nodded one last time and hopped into the cab.

Tom turned to Joe. "They're all set."

"Good," Joe said, still eyeing the lighted interior of the ambulance. His concern about not visiting with John one last time was deepening. It didn't matter if John was unconscious, he should have done it like any good boss would have.

"Well, thanks for your help, Joe," Tom said. Then, looking beyond Joe, he waved at the four others. "Good job, everybody." The two patrollers went back into the building while Al and Markie gravitated toward the sleds.

Joe was thinking clearly again. "So what's his condition?" he asked Tom, watching the ambulance cross the parking lot.

Tom raised his eyebrows. "I won't pull any punches with you. He's been unconsciousness for quite a while. That's not good."

"So?"

Tom yawned. "Excuse me," he said, smiling faintly. "I don't know. We'll just have to wait and see. We've done everything we can here. We did our best, all of us. Now if you don't mind, I'm going home. With any luck the sheets won't have cooled."

Joe managed a smile. "Thanks," he said, trudging up the incline that separated him from his sled. It was fifty feet he'd normally cross effortlessly, but all of a sudden he was tired and cold, and somewhere deep in the core of his torso was a sinking feeling. But he fought it off, at least for now, and picked up the pace. He was ten steps from his sled when Al exhaled a plume of smoke. "I'll head up and start that gun," he said, flicking away his cigarette.

Back at the pump house Joe and Markie went directly to the control desk to a waiting Marty who sported a rare look of concern. "Is he going to be okay?" he asked.

With his back to Markie, Joe rolled his eyes and frowned. "We'll see," he said, changing the subject quickly to snub out what he knew would be another question from Marty.

"Could you call his wife, tell her I'll be going to the hospital as soon as I get things squared away here, ask her if she needs anything, like a ride, somebody to watch the kids, whatever, we'll arrange it, and call Warren and let him know what happened. If he needs to talk to me, fine, but I really need to talk to Markie while things are fresh, and thank the groomers for their help, they were all there, all four of them."

Marty muttered something.

"We'll be in my office," Joe said, motioning for Markie to follow. "Oh, one more thing, could you make a pot of coffee, I'm going to need some."

Marty stood up. "Christ, anything else," he said. "Why don't you give me a broom and I'll stick it up my ass and sweep the fucking floor while I do everything else."

Like he had become accustomed to doing, Joe ignored the remark, which he figured Markie, who was several steps ahead of him, didn't hear.

Markie hesitated before entering the office, but Joe ushered him in and closed the door, something he rarely did. It was obvious to Joe that Markie was still upset. He sat upright in the chair in front of Joe's desk, his hands folded between his quivering legs, with a kind of wild look on his youthful face.

Joe sat down, pulled himself tight to the desk, and leaned forward on his forearms, trying to decide what to say and how to say it.

"How you doing?" Joe finally asked, trying his best to sound sympathetic.

Markie answered immediately. "Yeah, Mr. Littlefield, I'm okay."

"Good, then why don't we get started."

"Sure," Markie said, his beady eyes wandering the barren walls.

"So, what I need from you is what happened up there? I'll be taking notes so I can do the report."

It was customary to have the employee do a written statement, but Joe knew Markie couldn't write well, so instead of embarrassing him, he decided to take a verbal statement.

"Go ahead, tell me what happened," Joe said.

Markie snorted. "I don't know, I, well, one minute we were okay and then the thing just started. I did my best Mr. Littlefield."

"Markie, take it easy, this thing wasn't your fault," Joe said softly. "Now start at the beginning, I need to know everything. You and John were on Infinity, right? You came down from the top, then what?"

"Well, we'd done four or five, five I guess, you know, moving them, when all of a sudden the hose, the air hose on the fifth one come loose and started going all over the place. Next thing I knew John was pushing me out of the way."

"Okay, where were you, Markie?"

Markie wet his lips. "Right there."

"Where?"

"Like I said, I...I was behind him. Over near the hydrant. You know, where I was supposed to be." Markie pulled himself closer to the edge of the chair.

"So you were at the hydrant and he was at the gun then?" Joe asked.

"Sort of, I guess...I mean, yeah, like we're suppose to be."

"Markie, were you or weren't you at the hydrant?"

He wet his lips again. "I guess not."

"You guess not what, Markie?"

"I guess I wasn't, at the hydrant I mean."

Joe raised his eyebrows. "So where were you then?"

"I was taking a piss in the woods, Mr. Littlefield, you can fire me if you want. I wasn't there. I don't know what happened. When I come out of the woods the fucking thing was swinging everywhere, then I saw John in the snow. Like I say, fire me if you want."

Markie looked down, defeated by his own words, obviously on the verge of tears. Joe figured he probably ought to go over and comfort him, but that wasn't one of his strong suits. He'd have to handle it from across the desk. Almost a minute passed while Joe groped for what to say.

"Markie, listen to me, we're not here to assign blame. It's not your fault. I just need to know what happened and you're the only one that can tell me, you were the only one there besides John. Now just take it easy, take however much time you need, everything is going to be okay."

Slowly Markie raised his head, his eyes still hidden from where Joe sat.

"Okay then, you were in the woods when this happened, then what?"

Markie snorted and rubbed his eyes. "When I come out, out of the woods, I mean, I realized what had happened, so I shut the hydrant off as quick as I could."

"Okay, then what?"

"Well, I went to John, I rolled him over, he wasn't moving or nothing, that's when I called in."

"Okay. What was John doing when you went into the woods to go to the bathroom?"

Markie hesitated before he answered. "I don't know."

Joe did his best to conceal a growing feeling of impatience. "What do you mean you don't know, Markie? Where was he?"

"I don't remember, I think he was at the gun, yeah, he was at the gun."

"Which gun?"

Markie shrugged. "I don't remember. The same one, I guess."

"So when you came out of the woods the hose was loose and John was down, right?"

"Yeah. It all happened real fast."

Joe nodded. "So who moved the three or four guns above the one that got loose?"

"John did."

"Were they okay?"

"I guess, I mean yeah, sure they were, nothing happened."

"Okay then, that's good," Joe said. "How are you doing, all right?"

Markie nodded.

Joe had him go over it again to make sure he had it right, getting a lot of detail he hadn't got the first time through. When they were done Joe stood up.

"You go home, Markie. We'll sign you out at seven. Get some rest. Don't worry about anything. John will be okay."

"I sure hope so," Markie said getting up and starting for the door. Just as he reached it he turned around. For the first time Joe could see his eyes. They were moist and red.

"You know, Mr. Littlefield, I thought he was dead up there."

Joe's face softened. "I imagine. But don't you worry now, everything will be just fine."

Markie headed for the locker room to change. Joe sat down and pulled out a job injury report form from the top left drawer and laid it on the desk. He stared at it for the better part of a minute, watching out of the corner of his eye a stream of water on the floor that was flowing weakly toward the wall from a puddle that had formed from the snow and ice that had melted from Markie's pants and boots. After completing as much of the form as he could, Joe turned it over, tucked it under the corner of his blotter, and headed for the control desk.

"I see you sent him home," Marty said.

"Yeah, he's spent, the poor guy."

"Spent. I don't wonder. He must have fucking laryngitis for all the times he called me. Why the little bastard wouldn't answer me I don't know. He kept jabbering but he wouldn't answer for the longest time."

Joe nodded. "I got the whole story from him. That wasn't your fault," he said, helping himself to a cup of coffee that he cooled to gulping temperature with a generous dollop of cream.

"I know it wasn't my fault," Marty snapped. "So why didn't he just answer me normal like?"

"He panicked, Marty." Joe immediately regretted his choice of words. Wasn't he belittling Markie? "What I mean is you had to be there, John looked bad, real bad, and I guess he forgot about the radio at first, which of course John had, and when he remembered it, and got it from John's harness, he must have thought the volume was turned down because he turned it. 'Course, he was turning it down instead of turning it up, so he wasn't hearing it over the guns. That's why he kept calling you, he wasn't hearing you answer."

"So why did he finally hear me then?" Marty asked, obviously perplexed by Joe's version.

"He finally realized what was wrong and turned up the volume," Joe said, taking a mouthful of coffee.

"Yeah, well anyway, that wasn't all of it. When I called the hospital I got the emergency room usual like, and you know, I told the nurse we needed the ambulance cause one of the guys had been hit by a hose and was hurt pretty bad, and you know what she said, the stupid bitch, she asked me the extent of his injuries, well you know, I had radio traffic going, things to do, everything, so I told her, and I didn't mince my words none either, that we didn't know what was wrong yet, that he was unconscious, still on the mountain, and she needed to send the wagon. I figured that would be enough but is wasn't. She asked me to describe how his injuries occurred, almost like she was reading it from some fucking script she'd rehearsed. Well you know me, Joe, that did it, I told her 'look lady, we've got a man hurt on the mountain, I don't know what the hell is wrong with him, just send the god damn ambulance,' and I hung up the phone. I couldn't believe the run around I got from her."

Joe figured Marty was telling him just in case the hospital filed a complaint about his abrasive attitude, which Joe didn't doubt was bad. But that was the least of his worries.

"Everything okay?"

"Haven't heard that it isn't."

"What did John's wife say?"

Marty sighed. "Not much, but you could tell she was upset. They got a cousin living with them that could look after the kids so she left right off for the hospital."

"Good. Did you call Warren?"

"Yeah."

"What did he say?" Joe asked, finishing off his coffee.

"Nothing. He just listened and said okay."

"Where's Al?" Joe asked.

"I suppose he's still up on Infinity."

"Okay, I'm going to head up there."

Joe rinsed his empty cup, gathered his gear, and left the pump house. He was about to mount his sled when Al came blazing down Go Between and stopped two feet from where Joe stood, obviously anxious to share what was on his mind.

"You're not going to believe this," he said smirking, "but the two guns below the one that got John."

"Yeah."

"The ears were half open."

Joe closed his eyes and turned away. When he looked back a few seconds later his teeth were clenched behind thin lips. "On the two guns below?"

"Yeah."

"Both of them?"

Al nodded slowly. "Yeah, both of them."

"So you checked them?"

"Yeah."

"Why?"

Al looked surprised. "'Cause I had a feeling."

Joe nodded.

"What did Markie have to say?" Al asked.

"He says he was in the woods when it happened going to the bath-room."

"Figures. So he doesn't know anything then?"

Joe shook his head. "No."

"Well, they were on their second run. I'd say Markie left them open. It would be just like him."

Joe's response was immediate. "On three guns in a row?"

"What else could it have been?" Al asked.

Joe shrugged his shoulders. "I don't know," he said.

Al thought for a moment. "Well, you said Markie was in the woods taking a piss. Maybe he's lying. Maybe he was at the hydrant and maybe John had just flushed it and Markie touched off the air when John had the hose out. I mean, shit, that's happened plenty of times before."

Joe frowned. "Yeah. But what about the guns below?"

Al shrugged. "Markie opened them to cover his ass?"

Joe shook his head. "He didn't come across to me like he was covering anything up."

"Well, I'll admit I didn't think he was smart enough to come up with that, but it makes sense, him touching it off before John was ready I mean. He's always got his head up his ass."

"I suppose it's possible," Joe said.

"Damn right it is. Just last week he had the radio for some reason or other and he disappeared on John for the better part of half an hour. Now you tell me, what the hell would John have done if he had a problem."

"I didn't hear about that," Joe said.

"You wouldn't have. The guys think you favor him. Christ, John's the only one left that would work with him. He should have been shit canned after his first week."

"I favor him," Joe said. "How?"

"By keeping him and..." Al's voice trailed off.

Joe knew he'd regret showing his anger but he couldn't help it. "And what?"

"He's always getting the easier runs," Al blurted out.

Joe bite down hard on his lip. "That's not true and you know it."

Al didn't back down. "Maybe it is and maybe it isn't. But it's what the guys are thinking and if that's what they believe it's the same as being so."

Joe shook his head. "Anyway, how are things up there?"

"All buttoned up."

"So you put away the guns with the open ears?"

"Ya, we done the whole trail. Why?"

"It's all right. Don't worry about it."

"Any word on John?" Al asked.

"Nothing since he was taken to the hospital. I'm going to head there just as soon as the dust settles here."

They talked a while longer, revisiting Markie's culpability, lowering their voices each time somebody passed, which occurred frequently as the end of the shift approached. It was just before seven when they walked to the control desk where the last of the crew was gathering their things and leaving. Al had the sense to wait until they were gone before he told Marty about the open ears and started bad mouthing Markie.

"Wouldn't you say that if Markie screwed up he's capable of opening those ears to cover his butt?" Al asked Marty.

"I'll go along with Markie screwing off, but not the rest. He ain't swift enough to come up with that?"

Having his theory shot down for the second time, Al wasn't happy. Knowing that Marty and John were fishing and hunting buddies, Al decided to goad Marty. "Well besides that, the only other explanation is that they left them open on their first run."

"Well, I'll tell you one fucking thing," Marty wailed, "John didn't leave them open."

Al was unfazed. "It's one or the other and I still think Markie is lying. You got to account for those other two guns somehow."

Marty stretched out in his chair, shaking his head. "He ain't that smart, I'm telling ya. He's dumb as a post."

"I not saying he isn't. But maybe in a pinch he thought of it. I don't know."

Marty took his hands off the armrests of the chair and folded them across his mid-section. "Well the how of it ain't important, it won't change the fact that John's laid up, probably for a while. I don't know who's going to feed all those mouths of his."

With the subject changed, Joe spoke up. "I suppose we ought to be thinking about what we can do."

"I'll have my old lady talk to Carol, feel her out about things," Marty said.

Joe nodded. "Thanks."

Al said, "He'll be all right with workers comp, don't you think?"

"I think it's time to go home," Marty said as he got up and started down the hall. "See ya in church."

Al followed Marty, and Joe went to his office through the silent pump house, his mind free to think for the first time since the accident. When he called the hospital, they were unable to tell him anything since John was still in the emergency room being evaluated. Despite the fact he was exhausted, Joe headed for Rockwell, unable to shake the sight of John's spilled blood from his mind. Life was just too damn hard sometimes.

*   *   *   *

As he started down White Woods Road the night after the accident, Joe noticed Marty behind him, which he didn't like. Worse, Marty was right on his bumper, dropping back every few hundred feet to stick the nose of his truck into the opposite travel lane like he was going to pass even though sight distance and traffic made it impossible. When they reached the parking lot Marty sped around Joe and was parked and out of his truck before Joe had finished backing into his usual spot. Joe gathered up his lunch and the three extra packages of cigars he'd brought to replenish his desk drawer stash and got out, moving at his usual pace.

"Hey, Joe," Marty hollered from the pump house door where he had paused, "it looks like your fucking truck is on fire with all that smoke coming out the window," making reference to the cigar Joe was smoking.

"Yeah, whatever," Joe said catching up to him.

"Did you go to the hospital?" Marty asked.

"Yeah, I spent most of the morning there. He's got a severe concussion. But he did regain consciousness in the ER, which they said was a hopeful sign. They're going to be keeping him for a while for observation because his brain could still swell and he has to be woken up constantly to guard against him going into a coma."

"Coma. Jesus Christ, the poor guy."

"Yeah, it was a bad one, but let's face it, it could have been worse. Maybe the helmet absorbed some of it or maybe he was just plain lucky. I don't know."

"Damn right," Marty replied, "it could have caved his fucking skull in. So is he brain damaged or what?"

"Like I said, he's okay now, but these things take time. Who knows, he might come through it with nothing but a scar."

"Did you talk to him?"

"Yeah, for a few minutes."

"About what happened?"

Joe shook his head. "He doesn't remember a thing. At least not yet. The doctor said memory loss just before and after the accident is common but in time he'll probably remember things."

"By that time he'll have probably forgotten it," Marty said.

Whatever that means, Joe thought to himself.

"But if he does, remember that is, Markie will be screwed," Marty added.

"Listen, Marty. We can't be taking that position. That Markie is to blame, I mean. Did you give it any more thought, about what happened up there?"

Marty spit into the bushes. "Who the hell knows."

"I was thinking I'd talk to Markie again tonight."

"What else can you do."

"Nothing, I guess," Joe said. "Anyway, when the guys get their assignments tonight make sure you stress to them the importance of securing clutches and checking them on approach. We probably better have a shift meeting tonight, but for now make sure they all know it before they go out."

"Will do."

They parted ways in the pump house corridor. Joe had just gotten to his office when it suddenly occurred to him there was something he could do, something that would corroborate a piece of Markie's story. Grabbing his radio from the charger, he went to the control desk and plucked the keys to his sled off the board. "I'll be right back," he told Marty, not bothering to wait for a reply.

The quickest way to Infinity, his destination, was through The Junction, but that route would take him past the groomer yard, which would be a hotbed of activity at this hour. Afraid of getting waved down by a groomer, or worse, start them speculating about what he was up to, Joe turned off Go Between in the dimming light and started up Pipeline, saluting to the lone lift operator that was descending on the chair lift. Three quarters of the way up Pipeline, he leaned to the left and made a hard right onto Bail Out, shooting across Orbit and Thin Air, realizing afterwards that it was possible a lingering skier or two might still be on the mountain. When he reached Infinity he went left and squeezed the throttle.

Joe had no trouble remembering exactly where John had been struck down the night before. When he reached the place he stopped his sled, climbed off, jumped over the air and water mains, and surveyed the area, spotting the dual set of tracks that disappeared into the woods almost immediately. He followed them vertically across the mountain to where they ended behind a clump of small white pines where the snow was trampled. It was here, he assumed, that Markie had relieved himself. Deciding against probing the snow in search of tangible proof, he turned around, making note that from where he stood the trail wasn't visible. He traipsed back to his sled and returned to the pump house, convinced that Markie was telling the truth. When he walked by the control desk, intent on sharing his findings with Warren, Andrew came after him.

"I need to talk to you."

Joe turned around, walking slowly backwards toward his office. "Can it wait?"

Andrew was definite. "No."

Joe inhaled deeply and let it out, hoping his frustration wasn't noticeable. "Okay, come on then."

When they reached the office, Andrew spoke up before Joe was seated. "I know now I should have said something at the time, but it didn't seem important then." He paused. "Jim and I found a stretch of guns with open ears."

Joe perked up. "Really, when?"

"Last week."

"What night exactly?"

"I don't remember for sure, maybe Jim would."

"Where?" Joe asked.

"On Universe."

"How many were open?"

"Three or four I think, quite a few, all in a row."

"I really wish you had said something right off."

Andrew bowed his head. "I know, I know now I should have, but at the time it didn't seem to matter a whole lot."

Joe's voice was stern. "But, Andrew, you know better than most, that it does matter. You were there when Tuck lost his teeth a couple years back."

"Yeah, I know. But after what you did to Alan and Jason, I mean, I guess we figured we might get somebody fired or something."

"Or get somebody killed."

"I know now we should have reported it. I'm sorry. It won't happen again."

Joe nodded. Coming from anybody else he might have belabored the point, but Andrew was one of his best workers and there was no need to continue the lecture. He knew Andrew would be harder on himself than Joe could ever be.

"Okay. I'd like you to do a written statement. It doesn't have to be much, just give me the basics."

Andrew nodded. "Sure thing. I'll do it at break, if that's okay."

"Good. And by the way, Andrew, please don't share this with anybody else, a least not for the time being."

Andrew nodded and started to go but turned back almost immediately. "Again, I'm sorry about this."

"I understand," Joe said as Andrew plodded out of his office and down the hall.

Joe sank into his creaking chair, his mind reeling. That made three incidents of open ears on two trails, each one involving different snow-makers. Which probably meant none of them were accidents or negligence. He had reprimanded Alan and Jason unfairly and he had doubted Markie unnecessarily. But how could he have known? His mind searched for something, anything that would prove him wrong. An explanation that would reverse the sinking feeling he had about the ears having been willfully opened. But no explanation came forth.

Joe's thoughts turned briefly to John, lying in the hospital thirty miles away, his face permanently scarred, his family wrestling with the chance he might slip into a comma, or worse, a blood clot—what the doctors called a hematoma—would form.

Despite the fact Joe knew there was no time to waste if somebody had intentionally opened the ears, he couldn't bring himself to blow the whistle. At least not just yet. He went to the control desk where Marty was flipping channels on the silent television.

"Listen, I think we need to have a shift meeting tonight to talk about the accident."

Except for his response, Marty seemingly paid no attention to Joe. "Yeah, okay, are you asking me if we should or telling me we are?"

Marty's question was a simple one, but it made Joe angry. Marty had inferred that he was indecisive, which he wasn't, at least not any more. Early on in his years as chief he had perhaps been that way, but not anymore. His mind was spinning now like a whirlwind, a gamut of emotions at work. Was he the wishy-washy boss he so feared being, or was the pressure of the past few weeks taking its toll, or was it just that he couldn't think and talk straight when the pressure was on, particularly when it was somebody like Marty that was doing the pushing.

"Plan on a shift meeting tonight," Joe said. Without further comment, he walked back to his office. Like he often did when he was upset, he cleaned. Not the kind of cleaning he did at home, that wasn't necessary at the pump house. He did what he always did, swatted the tobacco laden cobwebs from the ceiling corners and rafters with the big rag he kept in his bottom desk drawer, swept the floor, and made neat stacks out of the piles of papers and literature that were on his desk and atop his filing cabinets.

The longer he stayed there the longer he wanted to stay. He didn't want to see anyone. Occasionally he would take the telephone off the hook for a few minutes, knowing Marty would see his extension light lit on the control desk console and think he was talking to somebody, as if that gave him an excuse to stay put.

Finally he settled in his chair, smoked two cigars back to back, something he rarely did, and read a bunch of junk mail, most of which he wouldn't have otherwise looked at. Mostly he sat there thinking.

With the whining of the pumps blocking out all other sound, creating a silence of their own making, it was a chance for him to collect his thoughts and soothe his resentment about what was happening. It was also an opportunity to wonder about who, and why. He didn't want to think about those things, but he knew he had to.

At six-twenty he emerged from his office to a nearly deserted pump house. Marty was at the control desk watching the six o'clock news with the volume too high as usual. Joe walked out the door into the sparsely lit parking lot and wandered around its huge cold emptiness. Except for the collection of vehicles owned by the snowmaking crew, mostly pick-ups trucks, which were parked near the pump house, there was only one small dark colored car covered with an even sprinkling of sparkling snow, probably manmade stuff carried to it by the wind from somewhere above.

He walked to the far end of the lot, where his view of the mountain was best. From where he stood he could see the lights of several groomers that appeared to be hung in the black sky high above him. Too bright to be stars, too slow to be planes, he watched them work their way down the mountain until they disappeared behind the trees.

He kept walking. After about ten minutes a car that had creep slowly up the access road and entered the parking lot interrupted his deep train of thought, its driver obviously lost. When its headlights picked up Joe, the car sped up and started toward him. An expensive-looking vehicle Joe couldn't put a name to pulled up beside him on the passenger's side as the window lowered. An attractive woman of forty or so, wearing a low cut dress and two strings of pearls smiled at him as the driver, a man of equal age, leaned toward the passenger's window, lowering his head and raising his eyes.

"Could you tell us where River Locks Condominiums are?" he asked.

Joe moved toward the window and stooped down, gladly drawing in the warm sweet smell that gushed from the car's interior.

"Sure, you just passed them, go back about a quarter of a mile, you'll see the sign on your right," Joe told them, eyeing a huge fruit basket draped in pink plastic that filled half the rear seat.

"Great, thanks," the man said.

The woman was still smiling as the window went up and the car crept away, its tires crunching softly on the gravel. Joe made note of the Massachusetts registration, wondering who they were and what had brought them to White Woods, when another vehicle entered the parking lot from the connector road. As it approached Joe recognized it as the resort's security Suburban. The vehicle made a wide circle in the parking lot, a maneuver that put the driver on Joe's side, and jerked to a stop, the green roof mounted emergency lights activating for a few seconds in greeting. It was Johnny.

"What are you doing working?" Joe asked.

Johnny cracked a big smile. "OT," he said. "It's harder to get than a greased pig, so I snapped it up. I'll be dragging in the morning, but I need the bucks. Quiet tonight, isn't it?"

"Yeah, well, it's a weeknight. It's early still."

Johnny pulled a pack of Big Red gum from his pocket and pulled out a stick that he unwrapped as he spoke. "Hey, I'm sorry about your guy that got hurt. What happened anyway?"

"It's still being investigated," Joe answered, offering no more.

"I heard it could have killed him," Johnny said, popping the gum into his mouth.

Joe nodded and changed the subject before Johnny could ask any more questions about it. "How's your job search going?"

"Same old. I've got a lot of apps and resumes out and I've been taking a zillion tests, but nothing definite. I guess I figured my Bachelors would give me an edge, but the competition is fierce."

Joe knew Johnny longed to be a police officer. The previous spring he had graduated from the state university with a four-year degree in criminology. Unable to get a full-time law enforcement position, he worked the summer as a reserve officer in a small police department on the southwest coast. While he wasn't one to admit it, he hadn't done much more than write parking tickets and gaze at scantly dressed woman along a mile and a half stretch of beach. At summer's end the regular job he hoped for still eluded him, so he took the security job at

White Woods, knowing he would leave in a heartbeat if something better came along. But as yet it hadn't.

Joe was about to ask if he had been looking for jobs out of state when Johnny's cellular telephone rang. Grabbing it on the first ring, he listened attentively for twenty seconds, said yes and yeah a couple times each, and hung up.

"Gotta go, Chief, I've got guests at Riverside locked out, see ya," he said, rolling his eyes. Joe watched until the vehicle disappeared and went back to the pump house. It was just before seven when he approached the control desk to the sound of Dan Rather finishing the news. Marty turned down the volume.

"There you are, Andrew has been looking for ya."

"What does he want?" Joe asked, realizing he'd forgotten to take his radio with him to the parking lot.

"Something about beefing up the base area at North Slope, we just did it but it keeps getting thin."

"If it's just the lift bases tell him to run the tower guns and let the groomers move it around. There isn't any sense in setting up over there for just the base."

"That's what we figured but we just wanted to be sure. I was going to put a pot on, you want some?"

"Yeah, thanks. Did you talk to everybody about checking the guns before they touch them?"

"Yeah."

For the next three hours Joe remained at the control desk with Marty talking, occasionally being joined by others who were on break. It wasn't like Joe to just hang around and not be productive, but for some reason he needed it.

Shortly after ten the crew started to trickle in—the first shift coming from the mountain and the second shift from home. By quarter of eleven the picnic table that sat in the middle of the locker room and the half dozen banged up metal chairs were full. The rest of the guys were standing, sitting on the floor, or squatting on top of their hard hats. Despite the fact some of them needed to change, nobody was trying to in the cramped quarters. The few who weren't being entertained by the usual slate of talkers sat quietly, held captive by peer pressure.

When Joe entered the locker room, Mike, who had the floor, stopped talking, which triggered a mix of snickering and nervous looks. Joe looked at his watch. Five past eleven. Time to start the meeting. Leaning up against an empty spot on the end of the picnic table that surprisingly hadn't been taken he spoke loudly, lowering his voice as the room slowly quieted.

"Okay, listen up. We might as well get started. Now, you all know we had an accident last night, a fairly bad one. John is doing okay, but he isn't out of the woods yet. There's a chance of complications, serious ones. So he's going to be there for a while and he can have visitors. He's at Valley Hospital in Rockwell, Room 305, which is on the third floor. If you can't get over there then consider a call or a card. I'm also taking donations to send him something, so if you want to kick in a dollar or two toward it that would be good. Any questions?"

Unfortunately, nobody said anything, which would have made it easier for Joe. Since shift meetings were few and far between, he was always nervous addressing the entire crew, and tonight was no exception.

"Okay, the accident itself is still under investigation. But the bottom line is this—you've got to check the ears on every gun before you touch it and I mean every one. Do it as you approach. I can't stress enough how important that is."

Again there was silence, which Joe interpreted as a bad thing. The guys were rarely quiet.

"Does everybody understand that?"

"Jesus Christ, Pete," Guy blurted out while rapidly waving his hand back and forth in front of his face. The room erupted into laughter that didn't subside for a full thirty seconds, kept going by Guy holding his gloves over his face.

"Guy," Joe said, staring at him.

"Well he's been farting like that all night, Joe."

There was more laughter.

Joe waited for it to stop and continued with his prepared presentation, telling them he was pleased with their performance so far. He mentioned the early start, how they had better than half the mountain open for Thanksgiving, and how they were on track, with a little help from Mother Nature, for 100 percent by Christmas. He also mentioned that if base depths on some of the summit trails continued to pile up at the same rate they would probably still be skiing in June. He hoped to end the meeting on a positive note, but he really wasn't surprised when it didn't happen.

Pete spoke up. "I'd like to know what's being done about making sure this don't happen again. I mean, why don't we just cut through the bullshit, Markie ain't here, so it don't matter."

It was what Joe had feared most. Why couldn't they just be satisfied until the dust settled. Until he figured things out. He knew he was in a no win situation.

"Like I said, I'm checking into it," he said. "All I ask is for you not to jump to conclusions. Just take the added precautions and do your job."

Joe knew his response was condescending, so he wasn't surprised when Pete, who was known to be abrasive, upped the ante.

"I don't know about anybody else, but I don't fancy the thought of my kids being fatherless because of a slacker."

Despite the fact that nobody voiced it, it was obvious to Joe that there was agreement in the room.

"We just need to stay focused and let things take their course," Joe said, wishing he could think of some way to change the subject without it being obvious.

"Well I want to know where he's worked. I don't want to be coming in without knowing. I mean, shit, think about it. It's dangerous enough out there without this bullshit. But then you wouldn't know, would ya," Pete said, lowering his voice and looking away.

Joe knew he couldn't ignore what he thought he heard.

"What was that?" Joe asked.

"I was just saying, you're not around much no more, you wouldn't necessarily know what we're up against."

Despite the fact that Pete had tempered his words the second time, Joe was furious. Not only was such a comment a low blow, but it was also the first time he was hearing it. Pete could have at least had the decency to tell him in private. He tried to make eye contact with Al in the back of the room, but he was looking down. Joe wasn't good at thinking on his feet, but he had to respond.

Ignoring Pete's pointed comment, he focused on the accident. "I know some of you think you've got this thing all figured out and maybe you do. But the bottom line is that noting has been proven yet. There is more to this than you know, more to it than I can share with you right now and some of you know what I'm talking about. But we can't be pointing fingers, we've got to stick together, take the precautions, get the job done."

"I guess I don't follow you," Pete said.

Several others grumbled their agreement.

"Are you saying it wasn't Markie's fault?" Pete asked.

"I'm saying you got to let me finish looking into it."

"Hey, I know who it was," Andrew yelled.

"Who?" somebody asked.

Andrew's answer was swift and sure. "Balloon Boy's ghost. The way we rode that poor bugger he's probably come back to haunt us."

They all laughed and continued to joke about Balloon Boy. It was something Joe was happy to let them do under the circumstances. A few minutes later he raised his hand.

"Okay, listen up."

Slowly the room quieted.

"If there isn't anything else, that's all I got. Just remember to check your guns on approach. All of them, every time."

Just as the noise level of the room started to increase Joe heard Pete get in the last word to a few others nearby. "I still say this place is fucked up, it's the blind leading the blind," he heard him say followed by something he couldn't make out. Joe ignored the comment, which from across the room he could do, and returned to his office, knowing he should have talked to Pete directly or at least stayed long enough for Pete to approach him. Disgusted with the meeting and everything else, he went home.

*   *   *   *

Joe had three-quarters of the kitchen wood box filled when the telephone rang. It was Doris. "Warren wants to meet with you as soon as possible about the accident last night," she said.

"Sure. You mean now."

"Yeah, the sooner you can get here the better. They're waiting for you."

Joe looked at the VCR's digital clock. "I can be there by...by three-thirty."

"I'll tell him, thanks."

Joe hung up the telephone thinking about how he hated to rush but neither did he want to keep Warren waiting, especially since it was rare for him to ask for a meeting. At least he'd already shaved and showered and eaten his dinner. Quickly, he brought in two more armloads of wood, got dressed, scribbled a note to his mother about going in early, and headed for White Woods, knowing that he'd regret not taking the time to pack something for lunch. When he walked into Warren's office at three twenty-seven by his watch, Dwight was there, lounging in a chair like he had been there for most of the afternoon.

"So what the hell is going on?" Warren asked from behind his desk.

"I don't know," Joe said, being direct about it. "I've been thinking about it, though, as a matter of fact, I haven't thought about anything but this, but I don't know, I don't have any answers, at least not yet."

Warren sneered. "Well we've got to do better than that for Christ sakes. We can't leave this fucking thing hanging. The insurance company will be taking a close look at this one not to mention the fact it's ripe with fucking liability. We better shit-can that little runt of yours, what's his name, Markie, that will at least cover our butts?"

Joe was blindsided by Warren saying he was going to fire Markie. He spoke before he should have, before his thoughts were collected.

"But we don't know what happened, we don't know it was Markie's fault. It isn't fair to blame him."

"Life isn't. But you haven't got shit to say it wasn't his fault and from what I hear he's a screw up anyway. I'll be damned if I'm going to give the insurance company any fodder on this one."

If he'd had time to think about it, Joe probably wouldn't have said anything more, but Warren and Dwight were looking at him with doubt or something that needed to be reckoned with. He had to strike back. Didn't he?

"But there's more," he said, baiting them.

"We're listening," Warren said impatiently.

Joe thought for a moment. "I was going to wait till I pulled it all together, but anyway, Andrew came to me last night. You know Andrew. To make a long story short, he found some ears open earlier in the week but didn't report it, and the week before I reprimanded Alan and Jason for leaving some open, so that makes three incidents. I've checked the logs and all three involved different guys, different trails. I don't think any of our guys were at fault, I mean, at least not incompetent or lazy or anything like that."

Dwight opened his mouth to speak but Warren beat him to it. "Why am I hearing about this for the first time?"

Joe squirmed in his chair.

"Because, like I said, with Alan and Jason it looked to be their fault, I mean, we've had that happen before, so I just handled it that way, and Andrew didn't come forward until last night, after the accident, that's when I checked the logs, that's when things fell into place."

Warren tapped his fingers on the desk while Joe waited patiently for him to speak.

"Different guys, different trails, huh?"

Joe nodded as Dwight's eyes darted between them.

"How many open each time?" Warren asked.

Joe annunciation was slow. "Three or four, always in a row."

Warren leaned back in his chair. "What do you think then?" he asked.

Joe said, "I didn't know what to think last night but now I think somebody did it. Why, I don't know. I can't believe it was one of the crew."

Warren's tapping got louder. He spoke to Dwight for the first time. "What do you think?"

"It's a mouthful, all right. But if we're sure these were malicious acts, then what about former employees, especially guys that worked for you, Joe, people that would know what to do and where, because heavens, I wouldn't have the slightest notion about what to do. I mean, I've clocked a bundle of years in this business—but the pipes, the hoses, the guns, the whole shooting match, it's all Greek to me."

Joe bit his lower lip to ward off an impending smile, the product of Dwight's way with words.

"You know we go through people almost as fast as water," Joe said, "no pun intended."

Dwight chuckled. "True enough. But the more I think about it the more it seems to have the classic marking of a disgruntled employee. Why don't I print out an employee list for, say, the last five years. I'll weed out those presently employed and those we know, that kind of thing, then we can go over what remains."

Joe wasn't sure the direction Dwight was intent on taking was the right one. He felt they should have fleshed out every possibility before putting on blinders and focusing on a single one. After all, there were many possibilities other than those that a computer would arrange in a neat list. But with Warren nodding his approval Joe wasn't about to meddle, particularly since Warren was in a cranky mood.

"Well then, I'll do the list and we can get together and go over it. It's bound to shed some light on things," Dwight said standing up. "Well, I've got a powwow with group sales at three, so I got to scoot. Thanks for coming in, Joe."

Joe watched Dwight leave out of the corner of his eye, turning his attention back to Warren when he disappeared.

"So you're pretty sure about this?" Warren asked, staring him down for the third time.

"What do you mean?" Joe asked.

"That we got some nut loose on the mountain that's pulling this shit."

Joe shrugged. "Like I said, the first time I didn't think too much about it. I blamed Alan and Jason, I gave them hell and I assumed that was the end of it. Even after the accident it didn't send up any red flags right off, but then Andrew came to me and, oh yeah, I forgot to tell you that Markie said he was in the woods going to the bathroom when John got hit, so last night I went to where he said he had been and sure enough, there was a set of tracks and a place where, where you know, so I think he's telling the truth. I've been doing this for fifteen years, nothing even close to this ever happened before. Like I said, we've had guys get careless, but it doesn't happen three times in a row in the span of a couple weeks with different guys and different trails. No, I'm sure, somebody did it intentionally. It's just who and why. That's where I'm stumped."

Warren nodded, unmoved by what Joe had said.

Joe continued. "I had a shift meeting last night and drove home the need for the guys to be checking every gun on approach, other than that I don't know what to do. I didn't let on much with them, which may or may not have been the right thing to do. What worries me is that by not telling them anything they're going to get at each other, you know, blame each other. One of them already went after Markie."

Warren nodded again but remained silent. Joe was wondering what to say next when Doris walked in.

"You told me to remind you about that call you need to make at four, it's ten of now."

Warren nodded again. Joe pulled himself to the edge of his chair.

"So what do you want to do then?" Joe asked.

"I assume you're writing all this up."

"Yes and I'm getting or I'll get statements from all the guys involved."

"Okay. For the time being let's finish up with that and let Dwight do his thing."

Joe's voice was tentative. "What about Markie?"

"What about him?" Warren shot back.

"Well, you said earlier that we needed…"

Warren interrupted. "Forget that for now."

Joe nodded, trying not to show how relieved he was, and stood up.

"Thanks for coming in early, Joseph, and by the way, you've done a nice job for Thanksgiving, things look good."

Joe left North Slope Lodge, turned on the pumps at Jordan, and got to the pump house just as the last of the crew was leaving for the mountain. Marty was quick to tell him the news. "Markie just called out again."

Joe rolled his eyes but didn't say anything.

"You know that ain't helping him none," Marty said. "It just makes the guys wonder all the more."

"He was more upset than you realize about what happened."

Marty wasn't buying it. "Guilty upset if you ask me," he muttered.

"Maybe I'll call him. How's the crew tonight?" Joe asked.

"Grumbling a little about working conditions like you'd expect. Mostly the rumor mill is grinding away. There's a heap of speculating going on."

Joe nodded. "That's what I was afraid of. Who do they suspect?"

"Anybody and everybody."

"Like who?"

"Guys that used to work here mostly, a few of them were saying it's another resort, and of course like I said, Pete and his group are still blaming Markie. But…"

Joe interrupted. "Who else?"

Marty shook his head. "That's about everybody, ain't it? I mean it's obviously somebody that's made snow before."

"Yeah, I suppose. Well I'm going to talk to Al when he comes in. We've got to get them to cool it on Markie and make sure they don't start suspecting each other any more than they are."

"Maybe the Markie thing will take care of itself. There was some talk that it would have been physically impossible for Markie to have anything to do with the other two because he was on other runs. Right?"

"Exactly, so if the word is out on that, that's good."

"But regardless, they'll say what they want, you know that."

"What do you think?"

Marty leaned back in his chair, stretching out his long legs. "None of the above."

"What do you mean?" Joe asked.

"Just what I said. I don't think it was any of our boys, past or present, and it sure as hell ain't another mountain."

"I agree with you on the latter, but why not a former employee?"

"'Cause it don't add up is all. Sure this place is a revolving door except for the guys that have been here a long time. But not a one of them would have reason to do something like this. I suppose it could be somebody with an ax to grind for something else and they just happened to work here once, but I just don't buy it."

"You never know these days what people will do. You can't rule out anything."

Marty wasn't convinced. "Sure. But whoever done this isn't bothered by hurting a guy."

With the crews reaching the tops of their runs the radio started to crackle, signaling an end to uninterrupted conversation. Joe stayed on the mountain until shift change, not because he wanted to but because he felt that given the increased danger the guys must have been feeling it was the right thing to do. When Al arrived he met with him briefly and spent the remainder of his shift writing and typing his report, which ended up being longer than he expected. But since there was no telling what was going to happen next or who might be responsible, he felt that documenting everything was the right thing to do. At least it made him feel like he was doing something. At two o'clock he headed home, kicking himself for not having eaten anything since lunch.

After a restless night, which he convinced himself was more the product of not eating than the events of the past several days, he got up a little earlier than usual to catch up on things around the house. But it didn't work. According to the message his mother had taken from Doris at eight forty-five, which was neatly printed on blue note paper, Warren wanted to see him before work or anytime after two. Knowing Warren the way he did, it was advisable for him to go earlier rather than later. Reluctantly, he did the essentials and made it to North Slope Lodge by two o'clock. Despite the absence of Warren's car, Joe went upstairs. Warren wasn't there, and not surprisingly, neither was Doris. If Art had been in his office he'd have hung out there, but the little marker board mounted on his door, which Art unfailingly kept up to date, stated he was at Abbot Lodge until three o'clock when he expected to be back in his office.

So instead, Joe went to the cafeteria and helped himself to a large coffee with extra cream, giving the clerk a hard time when she forgot to give him the employee discount. He was halfway through the coffee in the far corner of the seating area when Warren and Doris appeared, talking and laughing as they strolled down the corridor and disappeared up the third floor stairway. Joe waited a few minutes and followed. When he got there he breezed by Doris' empty desk and stepped into Warren's office.

"Joseph," Warren said as Joe closed the distance between himself and the desk, "I didn't expect you till later."

"I didn't want to keep you waiting, the message I got said anytime after two."

"Sure. This is fine. Get the door will you."

Joe closed the door and sat down, glad that Warren was in a good mood.

"What's new, anything?" Warren asked.

It was a question Joe had come prepared to answer. "Not really. I've got my report done and all the statements. It's at the office. If you want I'll get it after. I'm convinced it was intentional now. There isn't any other explanation."

Warren nodded. "I'm convinced of that also, but more importantly, I'm convinced I know who."

Joe perked up. "Really."

"Sure. It's obvious, so obvious in fact, that I didn't see it at first."

"I guess I don't understand," Joe said.

Warren sounded sure of himself. "It's the environmentalists."

Joe couldn't help the surprised look that took control of his face. "Yeah, yeah I guess. You mean because of the clear cutting ban?"

Warren hesitated before he answered. "No, I don't think that would be the force behind it. I know what you're saying. But that isn't it. It may have empowered them when it passed, maybe it fueled their passion and their plans, but it didn't trigger it."

"So what then?"

"Carter Peak."

"Carter Peak?"

"Absolutely. It's obvious. Shit like this doesn't happen in a vacuum. It's connected to something. I always look for controversy. Carter Peak is controversial. So you got to consider Carter as being the force behind it."

"Carter is really that controversial?"

"Do bears shit in the woods? Of course Carter is controversial, for Christ sakes. You'd never know it because the opposition isn't mainstream. But we've got a small group of people out there who are determined to stop it. To them Carter is a fucking shrine, their fucking shrine, it doesn't matter that they don't own it, it's five thousand unprotected acres to them, acres that are snuggled up against one of their crowned green zones and acres they know I intend to use down the road.

The picture is clearer now than it's ever been to me. You see, back a few years ago, before the greens here, or really anywhere, were organized and kicking in Maine, I spoke at Rotary in Waterford about White Woods. Foolishly I shared my vision with them, told them things that aren't even in the conceptual plan, like the golf course I want to build.

Well, surer than shit there were greens in that audience, or maybe family or friends of greens, or whatever, and they carried my every word back to their cohorts and that, I think, is what this is all about. Carter is a bud, she's about to blossom, and they know it. That's not to say it isn't just one of them, or maybe a few of them. The greens are the same as any group with a decisive issue. While they all have the same beliefs, they don't agree on how to tackle it, so they splinter."

Joe nodded, unable to constrain his interest in the golf course, which he was hearing about for the first time. "A golf course," he said.

"Absolutely," Warren said. "It would be our ticket to a four season resort."

Joe nodded again.

Warren continued. "Anyway, Carter would allow them to extend that green zone another mile which is what they want. It doesn't matter at what or whose expense that happens. I admit Carter is pristine, but to them it's more than that. Carter is symbolic. They get this notion that they got to take a stand on certain things or they've lost. Carter is one of those things."

"Yeah, I see what you mean," Joe said.

"And there's more to it than that. They can generate a shit load of press just by opposing us. No type of development gets more media attention than we do and they know that. They no doubt oppose Carter, but they would regardless because it helps them with fundraising and membership."

"So you think they'd do this kind of stuff?"

"Loosen those ears? Sure. They spike trees don't they, do you really think they would think twice about this shit. I don't think so. It would be just like them to do it, with all that's going on, I mean. Look at what they did up-country on that parkland that they didn't want logged. Christ, they tore down markings, sugared skidders. Finally they chained themselves to the trees, locks and all. Yeah, it'd be just like them to pull this shit."

Joe shook his head. "It just seems so bizarre. I guess I don't see how this accomplishes anything, I mean if it's them, it's not going to stop Carter. Right?"

"Right, but like I said, it gives them publicly. It also delivers a veiled message. Think about it in terms of your guys. I'm not saying they meant to hurt John, although I sure as hell wouldn't put that past them, but surer than shit they're trying to spook your crew, make them think twice about going out on the hill. At the very least they're trying to rattle them, which might be enough for them to retrench a little bit, which you and I know in this business can be a lot."

"Everything just seems so complicated," Joe said.

"Intertwined is probably a better word for it. But all we got to worry about is catching the bastards?"

Joe smiled. "I was wondering about what Dwight was doing on former employees, did that produce anything?"

"Yeah, an inch of useless green bar. Using just three years of data, he came up with a list of 2,200 names. I knew we had turnover, but Christ, I told him Doris must have had things fucked up with duplicates or something, but he said no."

"So that's a dead end then?"

"I told him not to bother with it, it's obvious to me who's doing it. But regardless, he was already about halfway through, and had over a hundred names in the possibility column. It would take two people a week of mind-work and a month of legwork to narrow it down. Forget that. I'm going to proceed on the assumption we know who, because we do, it's just a matter of catching them. Now, I've moved the second day security position to midnights on weekdays and authorized overtime for weekends, so we're going to have a second set of eyes and ears out there at night. They may ask you for a sled, it's all right to give them one as long as they wear helmets and know how to operate it. If they want to ride the lifts they can, as long as you know it and they stay clear of where you're blowing snow."

"Can I give them a lift operations sled, I only have two?"

"I don't gave a damn what sled you give them, I just want them going through you for everything so you know where they are. Those yahoos won't appreciate the dangers out there, especially that fat nitwit that works days."

Joe nodded.

"And tell your guys to keep their eyes peeled. Other than that, I don't know what else to do. I'd like to be able to keep a special watch on Jordan, but down there I don't see how we can."

"Me and Al could make some extra checks."

"Yeah, okay, if you got the time, but don't go out of your way, we got a good season shaping up and I don't want this to sidetrack us." Warren paused, then said, "Christ, now that I think of it, if it did, sidetrack us I mean, they'd be getting their way, wouldn't they?

Joe sighed. "Yeah, that's true."

Warren said, "Now, are your boys tearing each other up over this thing yet?"

"Yeah, a little anyway. I'm worried about that happening."

Warren nodded. "Well, I know this goes against your grain, Joe, but what you got to do is give them a target. If you don't they're liable to consume each other."

"I guess I don't understand."

"It's a favored organizational trick, particularly when you're dealing with a union, but it will work just as well here. People need to blame somebody or something, they need to be able to point at it and say that's the cause of our problem, otherwise they'll find something you might not like and land on it. It won't be hard in this case because it really is the environmentalists. All you need to do is start the rumor, they'll do the rest, probably in short order."

Joe's eyes narrowed. "Yeah, I guess."

"Like I said, Joe, I know this doesn't set too well with you, that it's not your way. But there isn't an alternative, at least not at this point. We need one hundred percent from your guys, especially this early in the season. If it were March it wouldn't matter. And we can't have them preoccupied out there wondering what's going to happen next. That's when the real accidents will start happening."

"That's for sure. I'm afraid they're going to get paranoid. I know I would."

Warren nodded. "Exactly. Furthermore, they might blame you."

Joe's face went blank. "Yeah, I guess."

"And with an unblemished track record you don't need that, Joe, particularly with Art's job on the horizon. In situations like this you've got to give them an enemy. You've got to identify their adversary. The greens are it."

Joe nodded.

"Anything else?" Warren asked.

Joe's mind was reeling. He hadn't finished processing the information, never mind adding to it or questioning it.

"No," he said.

"Oh, one more thing, did you report the accident to the police?"

Joe's face went blank for the second time. "No, I guess I didn't see the need."

"Well you've got to, given what we know now. Report all three incidents."

Joe nodded.

Warren rubbed his face. "Okay then. Hold the course and keep your guys safe. Besides this crap how is everything going?"

"Great."

"Good. I'm really pleased with your performance this season, Joe. We're way ahead of last year and you know how strong that was, you're doing a hell of a good job out there."

"Thanks, but it's the crew and the weather that's done it."

"Okay, Mr. Humble. So are you and your mother having Thanksgiving together as usual?" Warren asked.

"Yeah."

"What about your brother?"

Joe shook his head. "He isn't coming this year. I guess he hasn't got enough frequent flier miles," he said smiling. "He's coming for Christmas instead."

Warren nodded. "Good. I bet your mom will like that. Well listen, you have a good day and send my best to your mom."

Despite everything Warren had said, Joe felt surprisingly better by the time he reached the parking lot. Things didn't make any more sense to him than they had an hour before, but somehow Warren's declaration of who and why was reassuring and it was definitely worth pursuing. Now it was only a matter of proving it was the greens or catching them in the course of the next act.

Joe wasn't in the mood to go to work an hour early, and he wouldn't have gone if he didn't need to call the police, but he figured it was important to report the incidents without further delay. Joe plodded across the parking lot to the Reception Center, where security loosely based themselves, and left a message with a worker there to have the on-duty officer call or stop by the pump house as soon as he was free.

Joe turned on the pumps at Jordan and drove slowly back to the pump house, surprised to find the occupied security vehicle sitting out front. He pulled up beside the Suburban.

"Hey, Joe, what's up?" the plump middle-aged man sitting behind the wheel asked, popping a cheese ball into his mouth.

"Sorry to keep you waiting, I didn't think you'd get here this quick. I had to turn on the pumps at Jordan."

"I go off at four, and I've got paperwork to do," he said, almost like he was warning Joe not to hold him up.

"I just need to call the police and we're supposed to go through you."

The officer's resistance melted away. "Oh, sure. I've got the number right here," he said, displaying a surprising lack of interest in why Joe needed the police. The officer flipped down his visor with his left hand letting a laminated piece of paper drop into his right hand.

"Now let me see, yeah, here it is," he said, running his finger down a list of numbers. "Do you want me to call them for you?"

"Sure, thanks."

The officer tossed another cheese ball into his mouth, pulled the handset from between the seats and dialed. After a brief conversation he placed the handset back between the seats, and turned to Joe.

"He'll be along just as soon as he clears a dog bite call in Madison."

"Great, thanks," Joe said. "They don't need to know what's going on?"

The officer shrugged, flung another cheese ball into his mouth, and slid the Suburban into gear. "I'll be at the Reception Center if you need anything, Joe."

An hour and a half later a young impeccably dressed state trooper, who looked more like a drill sergeant than a cop, arrived. He made a few entries in a black memo book he pulled from his back pocket and seemed relieved when Joe told him they had no evidence to support their claim that the environmentalists were responsible.

Joe offered to take the trooper on the mountain. While he knew there was nothing much to look at or any evidence to collect, Joe felt the guy would benefit from seeing the area and the equipment. But the trooper abruptly declined, saying there was no need to do so.

The trooper hadn't been there more than three minutes when he stopped listening and started to question Joe, wanting to know why if they believed the accident to be intentional did they wait almost two days to report it. Joe explained the best he could that it was only after Andrew came forward, and he talked with his boss, that they had arrived at the conclusion that all three incidents were connected, and that it was the work of the environmentalists.

But the trooper wasn't buying it. He told Joe that he understood his concerns, but there was no evidence to support his assertion that there was any connection between the incidents, or that it was the greens that were responsible, or even that it had been done intentionally.

Joe patiently differed with him, citing his fifteen years experience during which nothing like this had ever happened. But the trooper kept shaking his Stetson clad head, explaining that the elements of a crime were simply not present for John's accident, which was the only matter he acknowledged as worthy of investigation.

In the end he mellowed slightly, assuring Joe that if anything changed or if anything else came up to let him know and maybe they'd have enough to do something, but until then he couldn't help.

When the officer returned to his cruiser ten minutes later, which he'd left running, Joe wasn't happy, but at least he'd done as Warren asked. When he got to the control desk Marty acted like he'd been waiting for him.

"What was that all about?"

Joe did his best to be nonchalant. "Nothing new, just the incidents."

"So you reported it to the cops then?"

"Yeah. Everything going okay?"

"Haven't heard that it isn't. What's he going to do about it, the cop I mean?"

Joe wasn't in the mood for Marty's prying. "What cops always do, investigate, hopefully arrest somebody." Joe paused. "Anything new with the crew?"

"Yeah, Pete backed down on Markie, like we thought, and it's good thing to, cause he showed up tonight."

"That's good. Anything else?"

"Nope."

"Have you heard any of the guys say anything about the environmentalists being responsible?" Joe asked.

"First I heard of that. Why?"

Joe couldn't help but feel like a heel to be doing what Warren had said was so necessary. It wasn't anything that Warren had said that was making him do it either. Joe felt that if he was going to succeed as Mountain Operations Manager he had to go along to get along more often and he might just as well get started.

So he told Marty everything, knowing full well it was like telling the whole crew. When he finished five minutes later he could see that Marty was surprised, either by what he had said, or the fact he had said it, or maybe both, but regardless, it was done. Joe figured it would take a couple days before he knew if they had taken the bait.

But when he got to work the next afternoon he could hear the crew in the locker room talking about it as he stood at the control desk listening to Marty complain about the new president of the River Locks Condominium Association who was intent on paying less for his firewood.

When the phone rang, Marty answered it. Almost immediately, he spun around in his chair, leaving his back to Joe, and lowered his voice, which gave Joe the chance to listen to the chatter that was coming fast and furious from the locker room. Although he felt like a heel to be eavesdropping, he had to know what they were thinking, and it wouldn't be long before the whining pumps would obliterate any conversations that didn't take place close by. By the time Marty finished his conversation a few minutes later, Joe was convinced by what he had heard that the greens were now the suspects of choice amongst the crew.

The evening went smooth and fast, so much so that Joe almost missed his intended rendezvous with Johnny. At eleven-thirty, purposely giving Johnny time to get settled, Joe tracked him down sitting in the security vehicle by North Slope Lodge reading a crumpled two-day-old edition of *USA Today*. If there was any chance they could lift fingerprints off the snow guns he wanted to know. But if Johnny knew, which Joe guessed he didn't, he avoided the question.

"Whoever did it would have worn gloves," he said.

Joe was embarrassed. Despite the fact the culprit might not have had gloves on, Joe hadn't thought about the likely possibility he would have.

"Yeah, I suppose," he mumbled.

Johnny changed the subject. "This thing really pisses me off, I'd love to catch the little bastards that did it so I could wrap a hose around their neck."

"I don't know why it should bother you, two thousand feet is a little out of your patrol area, don't you think?"

"True. But not for long. Did you hear about them transferring Chuck to nights? I'm going to have company."

Joe was surprised. "Word sure does get around fast."

Johnny ignored Joe's observation. "I'm hoping Chuck will let me take the sled on the mountain. That would be cool. There's a good chance he'll want to just take it easy in here, you know, like he does on days. Do you think the whole shift will be on a sled or will they break it up?"

"I don't know what they got planned. But the only thing that makes any sense to me is to use a sled and spend most of the time parked, maybe walk around a little. That's the only way you're going to spot somebody that don't want to be seen."

"Yeah I guess, well, I'd love to stay and talk, Chief, but I got to make some rounds. The hotel has been bitching they don't see enough of us."

"Oh."

"Yeah, they say we're not making enough appearances over that way. But," he said, flattening out his hand in a gesture of acceptance, "I don't let it bother me. I'll just make this miserable mug so familiar to them they'll wish they'd kept their little traps shut, if you know what I mean."

Joe went back to the pump house, coasted through the remainder of his shift, and went home in a decent mood, satisfied that they were doing everything they could about the open ears and content in the knowledge that White Woods had more terrain open for Thanksgiving than any other resort in the Northeast.

When he got up at eleven the next day, the house was filled with the smell of roasting turkey and the table was set with his mother's best dishes, stuff that rarely left the china closet. While fixing himself a cup of instant coffee in the kitchen, his mother enlisted his help pouring off the hot turkey drippings from the big blue roasting pan.

After dinner they took a leisurely ride to Rockwell, his mother's favorite pastime, returning through the rolling foothills, where farm after farm, their fields sowed with winter rye, had been tidied up for winter.

Back at home, Joe changed his clothes, wished his mother well, and left for work. The clouds that had been thickening and lowering all day started to spit big wet snowflakes as he turned from the state highway onto White Woods Road. A black Ford Bronco, it sides turned white with road salt, was parked near the store's front door, which had closed at noon for Thanksgiving.

Climbing the access road, the falling snow got decidedly drier. Snapping off his windshield wipers, Joe's eyes wandered into the overflow parking lots, which, surprisingly, were peppered with vehicles. We must still be pulling skiers from other resorts with limited open terrain, he thought, going out of his way to check the parking lots at North Slope which were chock full. With this many skiers and a forecast for decent weather through the weekend that would undoubtedly keep them skiing most of the day, he knew they'd be getting more ski patrol requests to tend to thin spots, which would slow the opening of new terrain. But Joe wasn't worried. With a decent chunk of the mountain open and being on track for full operation by Christmas, the bean counters in the corporate offices were adding up dollars now, not trails. He was off the hook, at least for the moment.

CHAPTER 7

▼

THE PLAN

They met at Stars, the best restaurant in town, a china and linen kind of place, not really what you'd expect to find in Cannon. Of course, it wouldn't have existed except for White Woods. Only a few of the locals had ever been there, and then only for those rare occasions like an anniversary or wedding.

"Good evening, Mr. Ainsworth," the maitre de said as Warren approached the elegant looking podium that graced the otherwise unpretentious lobby, which surprisingly was devoid of Yuletide decorations despite the fact Christmas was just three weeks away. Had the maitre de been somewhere else, attending to his other duties, Warren would have slipped into the bar for a drink or two while he waited, but the little man with the annoying high-pitched voice was already pulling a menu from the podium's side pocket and ushering Warren toward his usual table, a four person booth with a horseshoe shaped banquette. Flanked by the kitchen wall and door on one side and the butt end of the bar on the other, the one-of-a-kind table supplied almost total privacy in the otherwise poorly laid-out establishment.

Within minutes of Warren being seated Victor arrived. Almost immediately their waiter approached. "Good evening gentlemen," the young man said, his dark brown hair showing signs it had recently been spiked. "Can I get you a drink?"

They ordered Martinis, and Victor finished settling himself into the narrow bench seat, a process that usually took several minutes to complete. Victor, who was 50 pounds overweight, was wearing a suit that didn't fit, probably the result of another failed diet or exercise regime that had been somebody else's idea. His round friendly face, suffering from a drooping double chin, sported a pair of metal frame glasses that he was always taking off and cleaning, whether or not they needed it.

As Chief Executive Officer of National Pulp and Paper, a moderately sized mill located on the Salem River in Waterford, Victor and Warren had a lot in common, although not as much as years earlier when Victor had run the mill with an iron fist. Although he didn't talk about it, Victor had been stripped of his authority when the mill was purchased five years earlier by a group of foreign investors based in Japan. Known as The Nowacki Group, they owned a dozen pulp and paper mills around the world with National being their first venture into the American market. Victor was National's puppet, a person they kept for his historical knowledge and perspective, and his suave ability handling local people, from workers to politicians.

After placing their Martini's on white paper napkins with green tasseled borders, Warren shooed away the server that he had decided was probably a ski bum. Since he hadn't talked face to face with Victor in almost a month, he had his mind set on catching up on things, something you simply couldn't do with a plate of food in front of you. As usual Warren took the lead, delving into Carter.

"It really bothers me that I came up dry in New York."

"It didn't surprise me?" Victor said, sipping his Martini.

"Everybody is too damn cautious these days. You'd think we were having a fucking depression or something. In the eighties they were practically giving money away and now you can't sell your soul for it. It's like everything today, extremes."

"Amen," Victor said.

"I suppose we got to cycle through this period, but it pisses me off. We all get shafted, it doesn't matter what your track record or your project is."

"But you do have a lot tied up in condos, don't you?" Victor asked, cuddling his glass between his big hands.

"Condos that are selling, yes."

"But that's just it, Warren, a lot of what they got burned with was condos, you know that, not so much up here, but along the coast, particularly the southwest coast, there was a ton of speculative building down there, some of it was nothing but crap they threw together because they were afraid the bubble was going to burst."

"Yeah, I suppose, but they ought to judge a project on its merits. Besides, it's not like I had much of a choice."

"What do you mean?"

"Oh, I would have done Carter years ago, actually I had planned to, once I got the snowmaking system beefed up with 100 percent coverage, but I shelved it in favor of the condos."

"Which is a dirty word to a banker these days."

"But you don't have a choice, you've got to build beds if you want the vacation market. Christ, without it you're nothing but a day destination. When you get people for a week, you pick their pockets for a week, it's that simple."

"Sounds to me like a lot of debt."

"If you mean there isn't any net gain, you're wrong. Day skiers are focused entirely on skiing and travel time, I got both of those in the bag, I've got that market, been there, done that. But destination travelers are different, they want amenities, activities, an overall vacation experience, which means high-end lodging, like the hotel and the townhouses. But it's worth it because they generate much higher revenue than day skiers. You get a generous return, believe me."

Victor nodded. "If you get the money for Carter, what about environmental opposition? That's going to be your nemesis, isn't it?"

"Who the hell knows with things the way they are. I'm mostly worried about where they're going to drop that fucking green zone. Now that the bastards passed the clear cutting ban, they're going to go full steam ahead with that."

Cleaning his glasses with a white handkerchief he pulled from his jacket pocket, Victor said, "The truth is starting to come out about the ban. They passed it with a misleading media blitz, the voters were just pawns. And two-thirds of the money for the ads was raised out-of-state. Several of the national groups kicked in a lot, and there'll be more of that, mark my words."

"You must be feeling something from it."

Victor stopped polishing and looked up. "Are you kidding, they hadn't finished counting the ballots in half the state when I was feeling it. That kind of thing doesn't go unnoticed."

"So has it had any tangible effect on the mill yet?"

"Not yet, and it won't right off, but you can be sure Nowacki took notice, and with the excess production they got, and us being a marginal performer at best, you can be damn sure we're on the short list of mills to shed."

"I didn't realize it was that bad," Warren said, emptying his glass and looking around for the ski bum.

Victor sneered. "That ban has the dubious distinction of being the strongest in the country. It doesn't much matter from a distance whether it is or not, or if the projections of its effect could be skewed, or that we might not feel its full punch for years, or that it might be amended, appealed, or overturned. Perception is reality. Survival today can hinge on minuscule differences analyzed on paper in offices far removed from the real world by MBA's fresh from college that haven't got one iota of life experience. It sounds bleak, but it's a dog eat dog world, and something like that ban can cause you to lose."

"They're nothing but bastards."

"Well," Victor said, determined to keep the conversation constructive, "it's got to stop. They may think they're getting their way, but you know as well as I do it's just a game most of the time. We need to find middle ground, some way to work together. I don't expect them to be our business partner. Hell, I don't want them as business partners. But we've got to do something. Otherwise the extremes will just continue. I suppose they'd say the same about us, but it's like they're looking at a seesaw turned away from them by the weight of a 300 pound villain, so they get a 400 pound green barbarian to jump on it."

"Yeah, but remember," Warren said, "they're different. We've got businesses to run, we employ people, what the hell do they do, nothing. I'll be damned if I'm going to sit on my duff while they shove this crap down our throats."

Victor nodded. "I was talking with a buddy of mine over at Atlantic, the mill in Harrison, he's got a landowner talking about some crazy scheme to put huge tracks of his land into separate ownership—family members, friends, workers, whoever—of say 100 acres each, that way they can cut 50 acres off each plot. Does that make any sense?" Victor paused, but not long enough for Warren to answer. "It's crazy, we've got to have some moderation. After the ban passed, we were at a press conference in Augusta, an event arranged by the pulp and paper association, and you know what one of them said to me and another guy?"

"What?"

"Something to the effect that they aren't going to tolerate us clear cutting even 51 acres, you know, one acre more than the ban allows, and if we do they'll know about it and have us in court quicker than we can get the timber to the mill. We couldn't believe he was talking to us, the owners of the land, that way."

Warren nodded. "Well, it's got to come from the top. If we say anything or try to do anything they'll just say we're feathering our own nests. And you're right, it's not the message, it's the messenger, that's the problem. I mean, hell, I agree with a lot of the crap they stand for, we'd be crazy not to. At least in my business, people come here for what we got, nobody wants to ruin it. But we have to live here, do business here, god forbid, make some damn money. That's not a bad thing. You want another drink?"

"Yeah."

Warren motioned to their waiter who was idle near the bar and pointed at their empty glasses, then said, "Let's see if he can remember what we were drinking."

"I hope he can, I think we're the only table he's got," Victor said.

"You know, you mentioned moderation, there's something to be said for that. I attend all our town meetings and it always surprises me how that forum, that process, works."

Victor snickered. "Yeah, for you."

"What's that suppose to mean?"

"You know you've always gotten everything you wanted from the town."

"That wasn't my point. And I go to the meetings whether I'm on the agenda or not."

"Really?"

"Sure. I always have. It's a PR thing."

Victor laughed. "I bet it is."

"It is," Warren said, feeling the need to defend himself. "Rubbing elbows with the town's people doesn't do any harm. It's no different than the hobnobbing you do up your way."

"You've got it all figured out, don't you?"

"Christ, Victor, it's not like in Waterford with a council. All you do is kiss seven backsides and you're all set. In Cannon it's different, town meeting has the say on things, on everything really. Even if it's just paving a road or some petty thing like that. So it pays to be involved. Besides, it's only one Saturday morning in March and maybe a special meeting or two during the year. Well anyway, the point was moderation."

Warren paused while the waiter placed their drinks on the table and asked if they were ready to order. Without consulting Victor, Warren declined for the second time and continued the conversation.

"Those meetings can get controversial, darn right heated, and more often than not it's over something that people decided was more important than it really was. You'd be amazed at the things they do battle over. We had a special town meeting a couple months ago. There were two articles on the warrant, one to spend $50,000 on a new plow truck and the other to do with some minor adjustment to zoning. Well, they spent three and a half hours on one of those articles. Which do you suppose it was?"

Victor shrugged.

"The zoning of course, they spent $50,000 quicker than a jack rabbit, but they fought about that zoning adjustment for hours. There was a real heated exchange of words between people that were miles apart on the issue. But in that forum people come together, you know, face-to-face, they talk it out, and things get settled. People went home unhappy that night but they didn't feel slighted because they'd had their say and that's the trick to it. As a matter of fact, the ones that were sparring the worst that night were sucking up to each other on the way out."

"Aren't we philosophical this evening," Victor said.

Warren didn't speak. He was staring across the restaurant at two well-dressed thirty-something women who seemed to be alone.

"I wonder what B and B they're staying at?" he finally said.

"Maybe they're at your hotel," Victor said, craning his neck to get a glimpse of them.

"If they are, they're not skiers, not with clothes like that," Warren said, without relinquishing his gaze, an indulgence he could afford to take from across the room. "They're probably here for a conference." His eyes followed them till they disappeared into the foyer.

"Anyway, where was I?" he said, looking back at Victor.

"How people at town meeting go away happy."

"Oh yeah, and they do for the most part. But I suppose it can't work anywhere else. There are just too many people, scattered everywhere. Nobody has got the time to talk or they're unwilling to, or whatever, so they blindly advance their own agenda, even if that means fighting. When they finally come together it's usually in court, but hell, we aren't going to do anything about it, things are too far gone. You just have to protect your own turf, period."

Suddenly Warren was hungry. He motioned for the waiter who quickly appeared tableside. They ordered dinner and Warren requested a third drink which he was halfway through when Victor changed the subject. With a serious look on his face, he said, "Listen, we've got a problem over at the mill."

"What else is new."

Victor frowned. "Not that kind of problem," he said, his voice shaking with emotion.

"Christ, Victor, take it easy. Maybe you need another drink."

"No, this is different," Victor said, irritated that Warren hadn't taken him seriously. "This thing has been a living hell. Hear me out."

"Okay, okay," Warren said, suddenly remembering that Victor had labeled the meeting as urgent when they had talked on the telephone earlier in the day. Like a switch had been flipped, Warren's demeanor changed. "I'm all yours," he said. "What's going on?"

Victor looked around, lowered his voice, and said, "The day before yesterday there was a fire at the mill, in the treatment building, the water treatment building. It caused a lot of damage, mostly electrical, the control room got the worst of it."

"I didn't hear about it," Warren said softly, raising his eyebrows.

"Only a few people know. It happened on third shift, the area is secluded, and we have our own fire crew, so they handled it."

Warren nodded, but Peter Richardson, his attorney, who was approaching their table, had grabbed his attention.

"Well, here's an interesting pair," Peter said, stopping before them.

"What brings you in here?" Warren asked, knowing Victor didn't require an introduction. "I thought you were the all-American family man."

Peter smiled. "I was just over at town hall with a client on a zoning matter."

For the next ten minutes the threesome talked, mostly trying to out-do each other with playful jabs. Finally Peter excused himself, saying he needed to hook up with Jack at the bar.

Warren remembered exactly where they had left off. "So where does that leave you?" he asked.

"In a bad spot," Victor said, relieved to be discussing it again. "The early assessment from the engineers is that we can't operate until repairs are made which could take a while. Our primary and secondary treatment was shot to begin with. It's old stuff, half of it shouldn't have been in service, we can't replace it with what we had because it's obsolete. It's more complicated than that, but there are compatibility issues."

Like most business people, Warren's mind raced forward. "Does this mean a shutdown?" he said, raising his eyebrows again.

"It should," Victor said, lowering his voice and looking around to see if anyone was nearby, "but that would sound the death knell for us with Nowacki and or the greens."

"Well, if…"

Victor interrupted but fell silent when the ski bum appeared with their food, which he did a decent job of serving. With their water glasses full, their napkins in their laps, and their food salted and peppered, they ate, abandoning heavy talk for lighter dinner fare. When their plates were mostly empty, Victor plunged back into the mill conversation.

"So anyway, I've got an idea, a plan, if you will, that would be good for both of us, but I don't want to discuss it here."

Victor said it in such a definite way that Warren didn't even try to convince him to do otherwise.

"Okay," Warren said, wiping his green cloth napkin across his mouth. "Do you want another drink?"

Victor was looking at his plate, pushing around the fatty, uneaten edges of his steak with his fork, almost like he was trying to arrange them in a certain way. "I better not, I've got an early start tomorrow," he said.

"Well I'm going too," Warren said, looking around for the waiter. "Are you sure, just one more?"

"Okay, order me another," Victor said, as Warren gestured to the distant waiter. Victor got up and went to the bathroom, returning a few minutes later just as their last round of drinks were served. When they were finished, Warren paid on his credit card, collecting two twenties from Victor that he stuffed into his pocket. It was nine-thirty and snowing lightly when they left the almost deserted restaurant and walked across the street to their cars.

"Why don't we have lunch tomorrow," Victor suggested.

"Sounds good to me," Warren said, knowing there was no need to say where, because they always went to Stars. "One o'clock?"

"See you then."

Despite the suspense of what Victor was going to propose, it wasn't something Warren gave any thought to after they parted ways that evening. While he had a host of notable traits, curiosity was not one of them.

The next day Warren got to Stars at noon, sucking down two Martinis at the bar. He'd have had a third if Victor, surprisingly, hadn't been fifteen minutes early.

"What are you doing, having a liquid lunch?" Victor asked, eyeing Warren's empty glass.

They got seated, ate lunch, and left the restaurant without speaking a single word about the plan. It was two o'clock and a lot colder than it ought to be in early December when they climbed into Victor's late model white Lincoln Continental and headed out Route 62 that ran through the state park, a place that was sure to be desolate this time of year. Eight miles from Cannon and two miles into the park, Victor pulled into a scenic turnout and stopped. Leaving the car running for warmth, he turned off the radio and sat back.

"Well, first, let me just say that you need to hear me out before you decide anything, and second, what I've come up with isn't etched in granite."

"I'm listening," Warren said.

"Also, you should know that this didn't come to me easily. I've gone over and over it in my mind, piecing it together, and I've finally arrived at what I think will work, but it may still need to be changed."

"Okay."

"Well, like I was telling you last night, we can't shut down, we just can't. So we'll continue to operate, normally, without treatment, by discharging directly into the river."

Warren laughed. "You call that a plan."

"Hear me out," Victor said. "You know there isn't much distance between the mill and the Salem River Dam, right?"

Warren nodded.

"Well, my idea is to close the dam and store the discharged water there, where you can use it as your snowmaking source."

"That's it?" Warren asked.

"In a nutshell, yeah."

Bewildered, Warren shook his head and looked away. Almost a minute passed before he spoke. "But your discharge is bad shit. The Salem is a busy—what the hell are you doing, Victor, baking potatoes?" Warren said, reaching toward the heat duct on the floor. "Turn the fucking heat down will you." Annoyed, Victor snapped it off with two brisk movements.

"I had some concerns at first," Victor said, ignoring the episode with the heat, "but we're talking millions of gallons of water, the concentrations aren't that high."

Warren thought for a moment, then said, "But, if I remember correctly, that mill up in Washington County was fined three million dollars just a couple of years ago for what sounded like an accidental discharge. What about that?"

Victor avoided the question. "The stuff is harmless outside of the river bed, but regardless, once it's up there, on the mountain I mean, it will be filtered as it slowly melts and runs off."

"What about DEP, or whoever it is that regulates you?" Warren asked, thinking he had finally found something to hang his hat on.

"That's why it will work," Victor said. "You know the state hasn't got any money. DEP has lost a lot of people, and they've imposed severe travel restrictions on all their people. Field inspections are a thing of the past. They rarely leave their offices except in response to complaints or known spills. They're entirely reactive now. Everything is voluntary reporting and self-compliance, and the testing stations are all down river, below the Salem Dam."

Warren nodded.

"Besides," Victor continued, talking faster than usual, "we've got a Republican governor who's been doing a nice job of taking advantage of the fact the state is bankrupt and in a recession to boot. He's managed to get DEP to back off quite a bit. Business is claiming it can create more jobs with less regulation, and there's public support for that kind of thing."

"Yeah, today maybe, but that won't last and you know it," Warren said.

"No, it won't, but it will work in our favor right now, and right now is all I care about."

"What about the river flow below the dam?" Warren asked.

"Simple. We'll open the overflow dam at Jordan, which will replace most of the water that otherwise would travel down the Salem in winter which is the slow flow season. Because you won't be using it for snowmaking, Jordan will supply plenty of water."

"What makes you think we can pump it all, all the crappy water I mean?"

"Because our discharge isn't much more than your daily intake. But regardless, there's plenty of capacity behind the dam and we can use the spill pond at the mill for storage if we have to. We also control the river flow above the Salem Dam with the Johnson Dam, which is above the mill. Without close inspection, putting two and two together, the entire length of the river will appear normal to the untrained eye."

Warren didn't say anything.

"I know it's a lot to try and absorb right off, but I've thought it through, checked it out, I think it will work. The section of river we're talking about has only one exit tributary, which is nothing more than a small stream about a half-mile in length, which rejoins the Salem further down. Virtually all of the river we're talking about is not easily accessible. There isn't a single paved road that provides access that I know of."

"There must be access somewhere."

"There is, but all the roads are gravel. There are some mobile homes and shacks on them, but they're all dead ends because there aren't any bridges. At river's edge there are just summer cottages, fishing camps, that kind of thing, and they're all vacant in winter. I know this is all new to you, but I've given it a lot of thought, there's no reason it won't work."

"Yeah, on your end, maybe on the river, but what about the mountain, we don't know what might happen."

"Or not happen," Victor said, "it's volume, you know that, besides, you got to understand something. Up until the Clean Water Act we were discharging without treatment, so it's not a big deal."

"I know but—what did you say?"

"About what?"

"The Clean Water Act?"

"Oh, just that prior to it, which was the seventies, we didn't do any treatment, so it's not a big deal. The water will look and smell bad, but that's the extent of it."

Warren laughed. "So we wouldn't have two headed fish then?"

Victor frowned. "Hardly."

"Well that's a relief." Warren laughed again. "What about gigantic beavers?"

Victor sighed in disapproval.

"What's the matter, big boy?" Warren asked. "You seem a little tense?"

Victor shrugged. "I guess the difference for me is that this thing is real. It's not a joke."

Warren knew when Victor had had enough. "I need some new scenery," he said. "Let's hit the road."

Without hesitation Victor clamped his big hands around the steering wheel, pulled himself up, slid the car into gear, and headed west on Route 62. Leveling his speed off at forty-five, he licked his lips nervously, and began again.

"It's just that I didn't expect you, of all people, to care about the environment aspects of this thing. I suppose this is different though, considering it's your mountain, your livelihood, and not somebody else's."

"What the hell is that supposed to mean?"

"Okay, okay, I'm sorry about that. But this is a one time thing, Warren."

"I know that, but what about skiers, what about my guys?" Warren asked, referring to his snowmakers. "Christ, we don't even know what that snow will be like, kids eat the stuff, what about animals?" Warren knew he sounded like he was looking for a reason, any reason, not to do it.

There was a prolonged silence.

"I didn't think you'd be concerned about those things," Victor said. "I mean...I just figured you of all people wouldn't care."

Warren smiled. "I don't within reason. Hell, when the environmentalists were trying to stop us from building Jordan it was my idea to use our gray water as a snowmaking source. We would have had to do a lot of work to capture it all and it wouldn't have amounted to enough, but it sure as hell would have been an constant source."

Victor looked puzzled. "You mean bathing water?"

"Everything but the toilets."

Victor sighed. "Anyway, I didn't expect you would jump at this. I mean, heck, it's no great opportunity, but I need to come up with something and you need the money."

"How much?" Warren asked.

"Nowacki will be generous," he said, pausing for effect. "A month shutdown will run fifty million easy, probably more."

Warren smiled. "But there's more to this than avoiding a temporary shutdown, right?"

Victor sighed. "Well, of course there is. If we can't restart, they'll never sell a closed mill mired in problems. And even if we somehow stopped operating for repairs and got restarted, the shutdown would be a blemish that would cut deeply into the sale price, that is if there were any buyers interested in a mill with a green monkey on it's back. Nowacki paid too much for the mill back in the heydays. They could really loose their shirts if we don't do something. I don't want to say you can name it, but I bet you'll come close to doing Carter with it this summer."

"Does Nowacki know the plan?" Warren asked.

"Some of it," Victor said, tossing his head from side to side. "They're okay with discharge, they think we're in the middle of nowhere, and hell, it's a place they aren't too fond of anyway, they've got long memories, if you know what I mean."

"The middle of nowhere," Warren said. "What's that supposed to mean?"

"Put yourself in their shoes, when they visit we obviously don't fly them in. They get driven up from Portland, so by the time they get to the mill they're convinced it's nowhere, which it is to the civilized world."

"When you put it that way I see what you mean. So they don't know about the snowmaking?"

"Kind of. They know that you're going to help by using the water."

Again there was silence.

Then, with a sly smile, Warren said, "Well, all I can say, is that it's one hell of a scheme. Imagine, hiding, probably, I don't know, half a billion gallons of dirty water on the mountain. Christ, Victor, it's bizarre. I'd love to see it happen just to fuck the granolas. I'm curious though, where did you get the idea?"

"From a magazine, a trade magazine. There was this small article a few months back about how they were converting household sewerage to snow. I didn't pay too much attention to it, but it's what gave me the idea."

"It seems to me that Nowacki is taking a hell of a chance," Warren said.

"They are, but that's the way they've always operated, at least this mill. They got a lousy environmental record, and their safety record isn't much better, but we've managed to smooth it over and sweep it under the rug. Pay back will be you know what, but by then my daughters will be through college, and I'll be retired with a mild case of Alzheimer's, if you get my drift."

Warren laughed. "I didn't realize Nowacki was that screwed up."

"Oh yeah, that's why they need this deal so bad. Like I said, if we shut down we'll probably never start again. They'll point to the fire and say I told you so and they won't be wrong. We're not spending a dime up there that we don't have to. You just can't do that for very long without consequences. There's no doubt in my mind that the cause of the fire was substandard wiring or equipment or something we should have tended to. But regardless, a shutdown will invite all kinds of scrutiny, which we wouldn't survive, at least not unscathed."

"If the place is that bad, you'd think the workers would say something."

Victor smirked. "You know how that is, it must be the same for you in Cannon, you just don't cut off the hand that feeds you. We employ a thousand people up there, the pay is good, the benefits better. It takes a lot of corner cutting for someone to blow the whistle. And don't forget, Rockwell is small, we've got whole families working there."

"Still though, you'd think somebody would come forward sooner or later."

"Sometimes they do, but more often than not they get themselves labeled a squealer and it isn't too long before they forget what they were complaining about, if you know what I mean."

"Yeah, there's a lot of dependence there, no question about it. I guess you could go so far as to say it would be socially unacceptable to talk," Warren said.

"That's a good way of describing it."

Victor turned around in an abandoned gas station on the outskirts of Clifton and they headed back to town, continuing to discuss the plan. When they parted ways after a drink at Stars that Warren had talked Victor into having, it was close to five.

Warren went right home, remembering he had promised his wife he'd take her to a Christmas concert in Rockwell that was being put on by several organizations for which she did charitable work.

Sitting on a hard wooden seat in the drafty auditorium, he contemplated what Victor had said, as a parade of vocalists and people reading poems took their turns. By the time the concert ended at nine-twenty, he had prepared a lengthy mental list of things to ask about. Early the next morning he called Victor.

"I've got questions," he told him.

Admittedly, most of them were of the "what if" variety, which Warren generally had little tolerance for, but this was different.

"Oh sure, that's good," Victor said, sounding upbeat. "I've got a ten o'clock that won't last more than half an hour. I can be in town by eleven, maybe a little after."

"I'll pick you up at Stars," Warren told him.

Victor arrived closer to eleven-thirty. They took Warren's car and again headed out the state park highway.

"I know you've got questions, Warren, so fire away."

"That's an understatement."

Victor didn't say anything.

"All right, all right," Warren said, sensing that Victor was still touchy about things. "Where should I start, oh yeah, what about warm weather for a few days or even a week that would prevent snowmaking? If we can't pump from the river the dam would at some point have to be opened, or it would attract attention. It could even overflow, couldn't it?" He didn't wait for an answer. "How many gallons do you discharge in say, any given 24 hour period?"

"That's hard to say, ten million, maybe more, but if you're thinking you have to pump that, you don't. Like I said yesterday, there's a spill pond at the mill, it's designed to take accidental discharge, it's what we're using now to continue limited operations. We're doing the semi-annual cleaning now instead of next month when it was scheduled, that way we're producing very little discharge. Anyway, the holding capacity of the spill pond, the river, and the dam is, say, a hundred million gallons. That's why this works, we can regulate the flows and store when we need to."

Warren nodded.

Victor continued. "We control the mill, the pond, the river, the dams, and you control it from there. Think of the whole thing as one system, from discharge at the mill until you blow it as snow, think of it as all pipe, with valves, gates, and pumps that we control with reservoirs to hold the excess." Victor paused and smiled, shifting his big body in the seat to turn more toward Warren. "Yeah, that sounds good," he said, shaking his head. "Just consider it all like pipe. Why won't it work?"

I thought he was already convinced, Warren thought to himself as he wrapped his hands around the steering wheel and pushed back hard, burying his back into the soft leather seat. But it really did make more sense explained that way.

Victor changed the subject. "I meant to ask you, how many people on your end would know what's going on, if you agree to this, that is?"

It was something Warren hadn't given any thought to but he answered with what popped into his head.

"Nobody will know it all. The chief of snowmaking will know a lot, maybe everything if he asks, I don't know. But other than him, probably only the pump house operator and the foreman would know we're pumping from the river, and they aren't too bright. Beyond that, I don't know, I haven't really thought about it. How about at the mill?"

"More than that, but it depends. The environmental manager will know for sure and we'll have to intercept the lab reports at some point to doctor them. But we've got direct discharge capability, so it's really nothing more than closing some valves and opening others."

Warren squinted. "You keep mentioning direct discharge. You can discharge waste water directly to the river?"

"Yes. It's there as a measure of last resort, a life or limb kind of thing, but nevertheless, we got it."

"Outwardly it sounds like nobody will know what's going on."

"That's true, except for the foam."

"What do you mean, the foam?" Warren asked.

"When we discharge without treatment there's quite a bit of foam, brown foam. But it's nothing we have to worry about. Like I said yesterday the river below the point of discharge is sheltered and you can't really see it from the mill unless you go to it. It's surrounded by trees. You can only see it from a few windows and catwalks and then only from a distance. It's not a place that people go to."

Warren laughed. "So we don't have to worry about bird watchers then."

"Hardly."

They continued to talk, passing into New Hampshire. It was twelve-thirty when they came to a major north-south highway.

"Well," Warren said as they approached the intersection, "it's either Canada or home?"

"Why don't we head down to Ridgeway and get lunch."

Warren nodded, dropped his hand on the directional, and headed south. After a quick lunch of soup and sandwiches in a dinner-like place, they headed home a different way. Arriving back in Cannon, Victor said, "If we're going to do it, we need to start immediately, no more than a couple of days from now. We can't continue to stall operations any longer than that."

"What do you mean?"

"After the fire we slowly scaled back operations. We took one machine down ahead of schedule for an upgrade and we're alternating operations on the others while we clean."

"So you're not operating now?"

"We're only making paper with one machine, if that's what you mean, but everything else is normal."

Warren nodded.

"So in other words, you want my answer now?"

"No. Think about it over the weekend, but I'll have to know by Monday."

Warren dropped Victor off at Stars and went home, where the plan lingered on his mind all weekend. Nothing in recent years had consumed his thinking the way this did. There had to be something they hadn't thought of.

On Monday, with crunch time fast approaching, he woke up at four in the morning with the plan firmly on his mind. He went downstairs, had a glass of orange juice, and paced the front rooms of the house for close to ten minutes before returning to bed. Still unable to sleep, he lay on his back in the darkness for the better part of an hour watching the bright red numbers on the digital clock radio ascend as he tried to identify potential flaws in Victor's peerless plan.

Repeatedly he did a mental analysis of the whole process, from the mill to the mountain. But that wasn't what was really bothering him.

Was it? No, it was people, too many of them, all involved, some of them people he didn't even know. He'd done a slew of things in his life that could have landed him in jail or worse, but he had always been on his own. This was different. He closed his eyes and focused on what troubled him. Considering Dwight was his right hand man, he would have to know everything, but Warren wasn't worried about him. Warren never worried about Dwight. With a generous salary and liberal benefits package, which included a company car, an unencumbered expense account, and a subsidized twelve-room house with a heated in-ground swimming pool, Dwight was heavily in his corner, which wasn't likely to change, especially since his wife didn't work, their three children attended five-figure private schools, and their worldwide summer vacations for weeks at a time had become as much a part of their lives as anything else. It was opulence that flowed from a single source, making Dwight as dependent on Warren as a child was on his parents.

Joe on the other hand, wasn't quite as easy. His right and wrong, black and white view of the world could be a force to be reckoned with and his sheltered life had left him untested. He was smart, a thinker, that much Warren was sure of, so leaving him out of the loop altogether was out of the question, but he debated how much to tell him. Knowing Joe like he did, an unexplained switch from Jordan to the river would get him thinking. At the very least he'd start asking questions and at worst he'd start poking around, and he wasn't the type to let it go until he was satisfied.

But Warren finally silenced his concerns about Joe's loyalty, which he hadn't needed to breed up to this point, by deciding to dangle Mountain Operations Manager in front of him like a carrot, and make sure he knew that taking it away from him would be as easy as taking candy from a kid. Considering how much he wanted the job, it would keep him from flying the coop. Wouldn't it?

Beyond Joe, he wasn't really worried. Only Marty and Al would know they were pumping from the river, but they weren't likely to have much more than a passing interest. With turnover what it was, half the crew didn't even know where the water came from and the other half of them rarely went down there.

That left only Victor's people. They were the unknown. The object of his unsettled mind. No doubt that was what had awakened him in the first place. He'd have to ask Victor again who would be involved on his end and how he was going to be sure they wouldn't talk or screw things up.

Although the bedroom clock said five past five, the old wind up grandfather clock in the living room was striking five. Like people in the autumn years of their lives, it was slow, Warren thought, but surprisingly loud, at least in the quiet house. He knew he'd never get back to sleep now, and he wasn't about to lie there and think any longer, so he swung his legs to the floor and headed for the bathroom.

By six he was shaved, showered, dressed, and out the door. His wife hadn't spoken a word, she knew better than to question what he was doing. On the ride to the office he realized he and Victor hadn't set a time or place to meet. Lunch at Stars was out of the question. He wanted to get things settled early. He was tired of meetings, he was tired of questions and answers, and he was tired of speculating.

He made a mental note to get Victor's home phone number, which he knew was unlisted. It would have come in handy this morning to arrange a meeting, and he figured he might need it once the plan was in motion.

At the office he surprised himself by breezing through his usual work and tackling a few things he had been meaning to get done. It must be the morning quiet, he reasoned. Not knowing for sure what time Victor got in, he called his office just past eight, getting through to him almost immediately. Anxious to get together, Warren offered to pick him up, but Victor was dead set against it. They settled on Joey's Cafe, just beyond Waterford on Route 302, where they both bought a large coffee and set out in Victor's car. As they left the strip of stores and restaurants on the highway outside town, Victor speeded up, punched the cruise control and fell silent. His tenseness in anticipation of Warren's decision was written all over his plump face.

Eyeing Victor, Warren took a sip of coffee and spoke. "So how was your weekend?"

Victor's mouth tightened as he gripped the steering wheel harder.

"I was only kidding, Victor," Warren said, cracking a broad smile. "Don't be so damn serious all the time."

"It's just everything," Victor said.

Warren cleared his throat and spoke. "Okay then. I've thought this thing through and I don't like it. There are too many damn people involved. People we're going to have to depend on which I'm not used to doing. It seems to me that there are plenty of people who might hear something or see something or they might just suspect something and start poking around."

Victor stroked his forehead with his left hand a couple times. "There aren't that many people involved," he said, sounding disgusted. "We went through this. You just don't want to do it."

"Take it easy, big boy. I'm not saying no. I just want your assurance that you haven't left any stones unturned on your end, in terms of people, I mean."

Victor sighed. "Nobody will know everything. But you got to understand what the mill is like. I'd take you on a tour except for the timing. The complex is spread out, neither side of the mill has anything to do with the waste water, it's already left the buildings for treatment, that's where we're going to divert to direct discharge, outside, nothing is different but a few turned valves, nothing, trust me on that."

"What about the treatment facility people?"

"Three people, and they, like a few others, will be told we got a DEP permit for temporary direct discharge, which is plausible. But regardless, you got to understand these people, Warren. The mill has been putting food on their tables all their lives. I've said it before and I'll say it again, even if it sounds corny, you simply don't cut off the hand that feeds you. Besides, now that the clear cutting ban passed, these guys are running scared. Remember during the campaign, we fed the voters all that information about the number of jobs it would cut, well, most of it was hype, but we haven't backed off it and we won't, it still stands. And don't you think the workers don't know it, and that's how we want it, because we got contract negotiations next year, but it will also work nicely for us right now. There isn't a salaried, unsalaried, or contractual worker in that mill that isn't running scared."

Warren smiled. "You sly devil," he said. "I like that."

Victor grinned. "And that's not all, the grapevine has been doing a decent job getting the word out about our fragile position within the corporation. It's no secret Nowacki has excess production capability that they need to shed. I told you about that the other day, we're on the chopping block."

Warren was laughing. "Christ, how do you run a business with an atmosphere like that? Your morale must be shit if your employees know all that."

Victor was at ease now, the tenseness of earlier gone. "They know, because we feed it to them, not ourselves of course, but we make sure it gets out, if you know what I mean, and no, morale isn't a problem because we place the blame on Nowacki, the greens, whoever we can or need to."

"You know, Victor, did anybody ever tell you that you're a no good son of a bitch?"

"Not until now."

"Well you are."

"You're one to talk," Victor said. "You have to put out the lights when you pay your people."

Warren frowned but didn't say anything.

"Well you do, you pay darn near all of them minimum wage and nothing more, no benefits, no nothing, except that fabled season's pass which costs you squat. You use them half the year at best, and pretend that they and their families don't exist the rest of the time. They come and go, and you don't care, they're bodies to you, so don't talk to me about employee treatment issues."

Warren groaned but otherwise remained silent.

Victor continued. "Anyway, coming from Cannon I thought you'd understand that we're close in Waterford, it doesn't matter who you are. I don't mean that we keep company, but everybody understands what is important. I don't know that it's just the mill, maybe it's the isolation of the valley, the harsh weather, whatever. But we're not a hub, there is no metro area, no bedroom towns so to speak, we're a close-knit community. At the risk of being sacrilegious, you might say we all worship the same god which just so happens to be the mill." He paused. "So what about the plan?"

"There are a few things I still have to work out on my end, I need some time," Warren said.

Victor was annoyed. "I told you Friday we haven't got time, it's do or die. We only have one paper machine operating. I can't justify things any longer, I thought you understood that."

Warren slowly sucked down the last of his coffee and tucked the empty cup under his seat before he spoke. "I'm just not prepared to say yes right now. I need more time. But I promise you this, I'll go one way or the other very shortly, in a few days, by week's end at the latest."

Victor shook his head and sighed.

"What's your alternative?" Warren asked softly, trying not to provoke Victor with his loaded question.

"Just do me a favor, the sooner the better, okay?"

"I hear ya."

Victor had already turned off the highway onto a narrow back road that looped around the fringes of the state forest and rejoined the main road close to town. When they got back to Joey's Cafe, neither of them brought up the plan again. They were both satisfied with how it had been left and revisiting it might change that.

Warren unlatched his safety belt and climbed out. "I'll be in touch."

"See you later," Victor said, his farewell drowned out by the slamming door.

Immediately Victor pulled away and Warren ambled off across the small poorly plowed parking lot, fishing in his pants pockets for his keys, glad he hadn't agreed to anything. While Victor was obviously put out with Warren's noncommittal stance, it suited him just fine, at least for the time being.

CHAPTER 8

▼

THE FIRE

Anxious to train with Art, Joe took him up on his offer to start on the Tuesday after Thanksgiving. Prior to going home after a productive day together, Art suggested that they tentatively plan to get together every Tuesday, which Joe didn't like. With the string of expansion meetings and the trip to his mother's doctor, he was worried about setting a pattern of not being at work on Tuesdays. But Art said Mondays were out of the question because he needed time to catch up from the weekend, Wednesday was booked with staff meetings that consumed most of his day, and from Thursday on he was gearing up for the weekend.

So Joe was surprised when Art called him later in the week, saying he was going to be off-mountain the following Tuesday, but they could meet on Monday if Joe wanted to. He jumped at the chance, and followed the schedule he had carefully planned for Tuesday. He worked till five with Art, went home, took a four-hour nap, and went to work, intending to stay late.

When he got there a small group of second-shifters, who had arrived early, were hanging out around the control desk, where Marty was keeping them entertained with a steady barrage of tales.

"I was just saying before you came in, Joe, that Tim got himself a nice five point buck the other night."

"Oh," Joe said, aware that it wasn't deer hunting season. "You mean he hit it?"

"Damn square he did," Marty said laughing. "On purpose, you know."

Joe knew what he meant, but he didn't particularly want to know more. His usual concern about such situations must have shown, because Marty and Al were grinning like they always did when they were able to offend him, which wasn't too difficult to do considering Joe was straight as an arrow.

"Don't he know it's illegal to hunt with an F-150?" Al said, beaming from ear to ear.

Marty suddenly turned serious. "Hey, I don't blame him," he said, offering a warped justification. "He needs a couple of extras to feed that big tribe of his, especially with the holidays coming on and all. With that new asshole of a warden we got ourselves, there ain't no other way. Those bastards are even using decoys now."

"Yeah," Al said, obviously fired up by what Marty had said, "it's not like those flatlanders who come up here, doing it just for the sport of it, taking the thing home on the roof of their car like it were some frigin' trophy or something."

"I haven't seen one of them decoys yet myself," Marty said, determined to hold the floor, "but a fella I was talking to the other day said they got moving parts and all, you know, to look like the real thing. You'd think using them would be entrapment. 'Course, if the truth be known, anybody that shoots at one of them probably ain't too swift to begin with."

Before anyone could comment, Joe spoke up, knowing if he didn't they would continue hashing over the subject or move on to some other equally shallow topic that wasn't likely to interest him.

"Everything okay?" he asked, addressing Marty directly.

"Haven't heard that it isn't."

Joe nodded. "I'm going to head out then," he said, grabbing the keys to his sled.

At eleven-thirty, with top to bottom snow quality checks on the six trails they were making snow on completed, he returned to the pump house. Retrieving his lunch from the refrigerator and a day-old *Bangor Herald* from the locker room, he went to his office where he ate the dry Italian his mother had bought him that afternoon, pouring on all three packets of dressing she had packed. With Al on the mountain there wasn't much point in him going out so he didn't, opting instead to get caught up on paperwork. It was close to two-thirty when he plodded down the hallway to the control desk, feeling tired despite the nap he had risen from only a few hours earlier.

Marty was wide-awake. "I guess you're having a brain work night," he said.

Joe shrugged. "With Al doing the leg work, I might as well. How's the coffee?"

"It's shift change stuff, but probably not too bad. That maker seems to keep it fresher, or maybe it's that new grind we went to. Either way, it seems to last longer."

Joe poured a cup. "Everything going okay?" he asked, stirring in extra cream.

"Haven't heard that it isn't," Marty said.

Joe repositioned a chair, sat down, and sipped his coffee, running his eyes across the computer screens.

"That fishing show I like is coming on. You don't mind, do ya?" Marty asked.

"No, go ahead."

"They're reruns, but ya always pick up something you missed."

Marty pushed his big thumb down on the mute button and ran up the volume. Joe leaned back in his chair, pretending to be looking at the television, but mostly he stared at the computer screen, watching the gallons per minute data for the pumps fluctuate within their small self-established ranges. It was twenty minutes of three when an excited voice blared from the two-way radio speaker.

"507, pump house."

Unruffled, Marty muted the television and keyed the microphone, his eyes never leaving the television screen. "Pump house," he answered calmly, not intending to temper Pete's excitement, but nonetheless doing it.

"I'm coming down the triple and there's quite a glow coming up in the distance. It must be a fire. I can't tell where it is, it's beyond the buildings, beyond everything, but it's really going."

Marty glanced at Joe and keyed the microphone. "Where exactly are you?" he asked.

"I just loaded at mid-station," came the crackled reply, "it's off to the right of North Slope, in the dark, so I guess in the woods."

If Pete had it right, Joe figured it must be on the White Woods Road extension, the section of road that ran past the resort and dead-ended in rutted gravel about five miles out. Joe did a quick mental calculation and counted five houses along that stretch, three on the left and two on the right. Other than the youth wilderness camp, which had been shuttered since a week before Labor Day, there weren't any other buildings that Pete would be able to see from his mid-mountain vantage point.

"I'm going to head down there," Joe said to Marty. "You better call the fire department. I'll give you more when I have it."

Joe was out the door and almost to the truck when he realized he'd forgotten his two-way radio. Walking as fast as he could without running, he went to his office, yanked it from the charger, returned to the truck, and started down the access road. Despite the openness of the intersection and the absence of any other traffic, Joe came to a full stop at the access road stop sign.

He had just completed a left turn onto White Woods Road when a vehicle rounded the curve behind him and quickly closed the distance between them. Joe knew it was a responding firefighter even before he spotted the flashing red beacon on its dashboard. Whoever that is, he thought, must have been up watching television or something to have responded so quickly. Joe pulled to the right and slowed down, irritated with the firefighters high-beam headlights that were illuminating the cab of his truck. But the car didn't pass so he continued on, speeding up a little.

A quarter mile down on the right, the parking lot of the two-bay fire station that sat in the corner of a thirty-acre hay field was empty and the building was dark. Maybe my bumper mate will turn in there Joe thought to himself as he glided by. But he didn't. Which probably meant he was a lieutenant or captain. Joe knew it was customary for fire department officers to respond directly to the scene to access the situation and at least in theory, determine the level of response.

Bumping over the frost heaves and potholes that dotted the road, Joe turned his head left and right, his eyes searching the darkness for the source of the fire. His two-way radio, snapped into its chest harness, was squawking, but he didn't bother to pull his jacket aside and turn it up.

Almost to Reservoir Road, he suddenly caught a fleeting glimpse of the same glow that had excited Pete just minutes before. Slamming on the brakes he spun the wheel hard to the left, cursing under his breath as a thicket of low hanging white pine branches scraped across the truck's left front. His heart pounding, Joe straightened out the truck and accelerated, noticing in his rear view mirror that the firefighter hadn't made the corner and was backing up. Joe's radio was still squawking when he rounded the final curve and broke into the openness of Jordan Pond.

Somewhat weakened by a depleted fuel supply, the blazing pump house was still an ominous sight, particularly to Joe, who had been at that very spot a thousand times before, greeted only by the steady burn of the building's vandalism-proof lights that graced its four corners. His mind beset with a host of thoughts and his eyes fixed on the flames, Joe steered the truck to within fifty feet and jumped from the cab, leaving the door open, immediately feeling the heat of the fire wrinkle his face.

The bare hard-packed gravel that surrounded the building quelled Joe's fears of the fire spreading horizontally and the scorched limbs of the white pines that hung above the bed of fiery embers shivered only slightly in the dwindling rush of heated air that spiraled upward. Hoping for a glimpse of the pumps, he edged closer, changing his path several times to avoid the grayish white smoke that poured from the remains. But seconds later, with beads of sweat collecting on his forehead, he retreated toward his truck, driven away by the fire's searing heat. The firefighter, who had parked his car nose first into a thicket of evergreens, was leaning against his open trunk, pulling on hip boots. Joe ducked his head into the radio's microphone and called the pump house.

"Go ahead, Joe," Marty said.

Knowing that some of his crew and probably by now at least half the fire department was listening to his every word, Joe choose his words carefully and spoke calmly. "We've got a working structure fire at the Jordan Pond pump house. I'll be standing by."

"10-4, the fire department is on the way," Marty said.

As the lone firefighter, who looked to young to be an officer, finished dressing, Joe's thoughts turned to the mountain.

"501, pump house, what's the situation on the mountain?"

"I lost everything a few minutes ago all at once, just like a power outage," Marty said, his voice still unaffected by the situation. "We're shutting everything down, but the way the hill pressure dropped we're going to have a shit-load of frozen spaghetti up there for breakfast."

Despite the gravity of the situation, Joe shook his head and smiled. Had it not been for the fire, he would have to reprimand Marty later for swearing on the radio, a habit he had weaned him of years earlier, but under these conditions he knew he could ignore it.

"Okay then, do the best you can," he said. "I'm going to stand by here. Have you advised the fire department of the exact location?"

The radio crackled loudly. Joe couldn't tell if it was background noise at the control desk or interference, but with a parade of red lights winding its way along Reservoir Road he didn't bother to find out. Instead, he turned his truck around, putting about a hundred feet between him and the fire, and got out. The arriving vehicles, mostly pick-ups, parked on the fringes of the cleared area on both sides of the pump house, leaving the spots closest to the burned building for the fire apparatus, which entered in two waves.

First came the attack truck and pumper from the White Woods station and five minutes later, another of each and a ladder truck from central station. By now the area was congested with vehicles and firefighters yelling commands as they scrambled about connecting hoses. The flow of arriving cars and trucks had trickled almost to a stop when a clean shaven man in his forties, dressed in a white hat and jacket, approached Joe in a tizzy, apparently aware of who he was.

"Are there any hazardous materials in there," he said, tossing his head toward the pump house remains.

Joe was definite. "No, there's nothing but the pumps," he said. Then, as an afterthought, he added, "and they're electric."

With his radio letting loose a barrage of traffic, the officer in charge nodded and disappeared, leaving Joe alone again. After several minutes he climbed into his truck and started slowly out, bumping over a web of uncharged hoses, which had apparently been laid needlessly. He hadn't gone far when he was forced to stop by a flat-fronted fire truck that straddled the road, its driver halfway through a gear-grinding effort to get turned around.

"Clifton, what are they doing here?" Joe said out loud as his headlights picked up the reflective white lettering on the door of the cab. He would find out later that when the call was dispatched, only sketchy information about the exact location at White Woods was broadcast, which triggered an automatic mutual aid agreement that required Clifton and Dixfield, the two closest towns, to respond, a measure that had been taken because Cannon's fire fighting capability didn't match the size of the resort or the challenges it could present in an emergency.

A minute later the fire truck was underway and Joe followed, prepared for a slow ride out. But halfway to White Woods Road the fire truck pulled over, its red lights no longer flashing. Joe stopped, intending to wait, but the firefighter that jumped from the cab, his suspenders dangling mid-thigh, waved him on and turned his attention to the lighted control panel on the side of the truck. Joe squeezed by and continued on. As he turned from Reservoir Road back onto White Woods Road, he cut wide around the orange Mid-Maine Electric truck that was stopped waiting for him to exit.

"Darn," he said out loud, realizing he hadn't told Marty to call Warren. He looked at his watch. It was quarter of four.

"501, pump house," he said into the mike.

"Pump house."

"If you haven't already, could you give 500 a call and let him know what happened."

"Done," Marty said.

As Joe passed the brightly lit fire station, its two garage doors wide open, its bay's empty, he wondered if Marty meant he'd already done it or would be doing it.

Half the crew was milling around the pump house when he got there, where their ideas of what had started the fire flew around like leaves caught in a gust of wind. Al was among them, which irritated Joe.

Ignoring their conversation and not giving them the chance to question him, he turned to Al. "What's the situation on the hill?"

Al grunted loudly. "We got everything shut down, but with the cold and the pressure going like it did, we got a lot of hose to thaw."

Joe purposely avoided showing his displeasure that half the crew was idle with so much work to be done. Instead he told Al to clear the trails of equipment and pull down the hoses that were frozen, knowing that the emotionless act of telling Al what he obviously needed to be doing within earshot of the crew would serve as a subtle but effective warning.

Without waiting for an answer, Joe went to his office to call Warren himself, knowing that the situation not only justified a follow up, but Warren would no doubt be looking for more detail than Marty had offered. Warren mostly listened to what Joe had to say, finally instructing him to make a courtesy call to Dwight, which he had just finished doing when Marty buzzed him on the intercom.

"The fire chief says they're about wrapped up down there. He's got the fire marshal coming in this morning and he wants you or somebody there. He said it should be between eight and nine but it might be a bit later and they'd meet you there."

Joe was tired and didn't relish the idea of not getting to bed till ten or eleven, but he knew he had to stay.

He hung around the pump house till seven and went to the store for coffee. Ethel pestered him for information about the fire beyond what she had already been able to gather, which was a lot, but fortunately for Joe she was busy and had little time to fashion the kind of layered questions that would have allowed her to probe the matter deeply.

Joe drove slowly back to Jordan. The place was deserted now. Besides the charred ruins of the pump house and its unmistakable odor, the only evidence of the three-dozen men and vehicles that had clogged the area just three hours earlier was the fresh maze of tire tracks. Joe sipped his coffee, watching a few wisps of steam or smoke or maybe both curl up from the blackened boards that had been the pump house roof.

Bored and starting to feel a bit sluggish, he considered driving to the river for a change of scenery when the fire chief followed by the fire marshal arrived. The burly fire marshal interviewed Joe for twenty minutes, and then rummaged through his trunk, finally emerging with a camera that he used to take what must have been twenty photographs from every angle. Following that, he donned a pair of navy blue coveralls, and started picking through the remains.

Joe stayed close for about five minutes, in case they had questions. When they didn't seem to need him, he leaned up against his truck, his legs crossed at the ankles. Ten minutes later, both of them were still poking through the charred boards, when the fire chief glanced his way, spoke to the fire marshal, and then yelled to him.

"Hey, Joe, we're all set if you want to go. If we have questions we'll get ahold of ya."

"Okay then, if you're all set."

"Yeah, all set, thanks for coming down."

As he drove away Joe looked at his watch. Eight-thirty. Not bad he thought. If I skip breakfast and go right to bed I'll still get a decent sleep.

*   *   *   *

Warren went to his office early Tuesday morning and placed a call to Victor, waiting anxiously for it to be returned. At nine-thirty Doris announced that it had been. But when he picked up the telephone, June was on the other end.

"I'm sorry, Warren, Victor is tied up in a meeting. I didn't want you to be waiting, the girl said it was urgent."

"Yeah, I need to see him this morning."

"I'm sorry, Warren, but that won't be possible. Perhaps I can get him to give you a buzz."

"No, that won't work," Warren said impatiently. "What about lunch, what's he doing for lunch?"

June's pleasant tone of voice didn't change. "I don't know. Why don't I do this, I'll deliver a message to him personally right now, and I'm sure he'll contact you just as soon as possible. Will that be okay?"

"Sounds like it will have to be. Thanks, June," he said, hanging up the telephone.

An hour later, Warren was hanging out in Dwight's office engrossed in a deep discussion of mutual funds when Doris buzzed.

"June just called, Victor is going to meet you at Stars at eleven-thirty. I confirmed it, you wanted me to, right?"

"Yeah, good, thanks, Doris," Warren said without moving from Dwight's guest chair.

When Dwight left for a meeting twenty minutes later Warren gravitated back to his office, where he and Doris talked till she left for lunch. Waiting long enough so it wouldn't appear they were leaving together, he drove to Stars, and was halfway through his third martini when Victor showed up at twelve-fifteen with no less than four excuses, each of which he prefaced with an apology.

"You want to have lunch?" he finally asked Warren.

"I was planning on it," Warren said, pointing to the near empty basket of pretzels that sat on the bar, "but that was full when I got here."

Victor smiled. "Like I said…"

Warren interrupted him. "You've said enough, why don't we just take a ride, we can grab a sandwich somewhere later, if you want. You better drive though, I think I'm under the influence of salt."

They were barely out of Cannon when Warren confidently announced his intention of going forward with the plan.

"Really, that's great," Victor said. "What changed your mind?"

"Let's just say I found a way to take a few people out of the loop."

Warren betted that Victor was probably frothing at the bit to know what he meant, but didn't dare ask. Instead they worked out the details of implementation and returned to Stars, partings ways at one-thirty without having had lunch.

*   *   *   *

Joe's mother woke him up just past two o'clock with a message from Doris that Warren wanted to see him at his office at three o'clock. He rolled over, covering his head with blankets to defeat the sunlight that was streaming in around the shades, but it was no use. He was awake now. He shaved and showered, made a cup of instant coffee, declining his mother's offer for grilled cheese, and left the house just twenty minutes after he had rolled out of bed.

When he got to Warren's office he was surprised that Warren appeared to have been waiting for him. He couldn't remember an occasion when his presence had been that important. Showing a peculiar lack of interest in the fire, which Joe thought was odd, Warren got right to the point.

"Are you prepared to pump from the river tonight?" he asked.

The way Warren delivered the question, fast and direct, made Joe feel like a schoolboy. He tried not to show it, but he couldn't help stammering over his words.

"Yeah, I guess, I mean, yeah, we checked it out, you know, like we always do the start of the season, it should be all set, I can't think of any reason it wouldn't be."

Joe had no sooner answered when he realized that Warren had probably expected him to test the river pumps that morning, and maybe he should have, but with the inspection by the Fire Marshal, he never thought of it.

He was relieved when Warren didn't seem to care.

"Good, then do it, you know we can't afford to lose a single night this time of year. If you need some extra help, talk to Art or call some people in, whatever it takes. National has or will take care of the dams. I've already talked to them."

"Good," Joe said.

Warren nodded just as Dwight walked in, obviously anxious to share what was on his mind, but good mannered enough to greet Joe first.

"Hi, Joe, I didn't know you were here but I'm glad you are. It works out well. How are you?"

"Fine. A little tired from last night."

"Oh, I bet. Heavens, that was terrible. I've been thanking the Lord all day that we've got the river, we'd be stuck without it."

"Yeah, that's for sure."

Warren's telephone rang and he answered it, swiveling away from Joe and Dwight after several seconds of conversation.

"That reminds me," Dwight said to Joe, "you've got to leave things at the pump house as they are until the fire marshal wraps up his investigation, which shouldn't be long. Besides, it can't be cleaned up until the insurance adjuster takes a look. He couldn't get up from Portland today, but he should be here tomorrow or the day after at the latest. We saved quite a bit with this new carrier, but I'll tell you, when they were right in town it sure was easier to get an adjuster."

"Okay," Joe said. "I met with the fire chief and the fire marshal this morning."

"Yes, I know, and thank you for doing that, you must have been dragging."

Warren turned around and dropped the handset into the cradle. Joe waited for him to speak but Dwight was anxious to share what was on his mind. "I just talked with the fire marshal, and he's pretty sure the pump house fire was arson. He won't have anything definite until he gets the laboratory analysis back, but he seemed confident. The missing piece is the motive, which is where we come in, especially you, Joe."

Warren looked disgusted. "Sounds like he wants us to do his job."

Dwight was undeterred. "Not really. He recited a list of motives common to arson. Revenge, elimination of competition, insurance fraud, camouflaging other crimes, diversion, pyromania, and I think there was one other. But revenge seems to fit the best, so we agreed we should start there."

"I'll give you the motive in two words—Carter Peak," Warren said harshly, almost like he was challenging them to differ with him. When they didn't, he continued. "This has got the greens written all over it. When they didn't accomplish what they had hoped on the mountain, or maybe they figured we were on to them up there, or whatever, they obviously decided to go after our water source. That's the direction the fire marshal needs to be taking and he needs to be coordinating things with the sheriff."

Dwight nodded in agreement, despite the fact what Warren had said differed from what he had said only a minute before.

Warren looked at Joe. "By the way, what's happening with the investigation?"

"I'm not sure there is an investigation, at least not yet. The cop that came didn't seem to think it was anything other than an accident."

"Who'd you call?" Warren asked.

"The state police."

Warren frowned. "So it's beneath them to do anything about it."

Joe nodded. "It seemed that way."

"Well that's typical, those God damn troopers, they're nothing but highway cops, pinching decent people for ten over, and doing it like cowards from some hole they found. You should have called the sheriff."

"I didn't call them, security did."

"Why the hell did security call?" Warren asked.

Joe knew Warren was intent on finding fault with something, and the sooner he dropped anchor on it, the easier for him. "Because I called security. We're supposed to go through them before we call the police."

Warren sighed. "That policy is for Art's traffic and parking people, not you. Besides, I told you to call, that should have been good enough."

"Sorry. I just thought that was how it worked."

"Well, next time call the sheriff, for Christ Sakes, at least his deputies will follow through like they always do. And if they don't, he'll be doing it at his own peril, considering he's got an election to contend with next year. So the bottom line is that the state just took a report and nothing more."

Joe nodded. "Nothing that I'm aware of. I haven't heard boo from him since he took the report."

Always eager to please, Dwight piped up. "Why don't I talk with the marshal. He's a real nice fellow and he seems to be a go-getter. He can get with the trooper and they can compare notes, that kind of thing."

Warren nodded.

Dwight got up. "Okay then, that's what I'll do. But right now I've got to go, I've got a ton of things to do. We'll see you both later."

Dwight had barely cleared the door when Warren's telephone rang. He talked for a few minutes, mostly just saying yes and yeah. Joe was considering leaving when Warren placed his hand over the mouthpiece. "I'm going to be a while, Joe," he said, rolling his eyes. "Remember, if you need help, get it."

As Joe approached the Jordan Pond pump house on his way to the river he was surprised to see Mickey and a couple workers throwing charred timbers into one of the resort's dump trucks. Confused, he stopped, lowering his window.

"Hey, Mickey, what's up?"

Mickey sauntered over to the truck, pulling off elbow length gloves that he tucked under his left arm.

"Not much. This is a hell of a thing, though," he said, tossing his head toward the pump house remains.

"Yeah. Are you sure you're supposed to be cleaning up?"

Mickey's face remained expressionless. "Yeah, the boss said to pick it clean so the plumbers can get at it tomorrow to see what can be salvaged. Why?"

"I just saw Dwight, and he said the insurance adjuster had to see it before we did anything. When you say the boss, you mean Warren, right?"

"Yeah, the head honcho himself called me a couple hours ago."

"Really."

"Yeah, he said he wanted us to get right on it, so we dropped everything. You say Dwight said it shouldn't be done?"

Joe threw up his hands. "That's what he said and it does make sense."

"Imagine that. One hand doesn't know what the other is doing."

"Well anyway," Joe said.

"So you must be headed for the river, it's a damn good thing we got that, huh?"

"Yeah, except for what we could scrape up for rental pumps, we'd be out of business."

"Any word on what happened here?" Mickey asked.

"No, I haven't heard. I guess Dwight talked to the fire marshal, but I forgot to ask about it."

Mickey glanced at his crew, then leaned closer to the window. "What do you think sparked it?"

"I really haven't given it much thought. What about you?"

"I think it was set and that's the feeling on the mountain. At least with who I've talked to."

"Really."

"Sure. Think about it, Joe. What else? The electrical wasn't faulty, we don't store nothing in there, and it sure as hell wasn't struck by lightning."

"Yeah, I see what you mean."

Mickey narrowed the distance between them. "The buzz is that Warren ticked off the environmentalists with Carter Peak and this and all of your troubles is them kicking up their heels."

Joe was blasé. "Really."

"Yeah. Maybe it adds up and maybe it doesn't. But sure as hell somebody is up to something."

"No question," Joe said.

"What do you make of that?" Mickey asked, pointing to the Jordan Pond dam where a torrent of water poured through its concrete opening.

Joe raised his head and squinted. "Is that open?"

"Wide open. But it looks legit, the timbers are neatly stacked."

"They must have opened it when they closed the dam," Joe said.

"You mean the mill controls that to?"

Joe nodded. "Yeah, it's all the same watershed. When we built Jordan, the federal government made us agree to it being part of the water management for the whole area, which the mill controls. They adjust Jordan according to the dam flow, or at least that's how it's supposed to work."

"Sounds like a bunch of bullshit to me," Mickey said backing away from the truck with a smile. "I see you're still smoking them nasty weeds."

Joe held up the unlit cigar in his right hand. "Always. You want one?"

"No thanks, maybe another time. We'll see ya later."

Joe nodded and lightened his pressure on the brake, letting the truck pick up speed on its own. The road to the river had been well cleared, but the path to the pump house didn't look like it had been touched since the start of the season. Grabbing a shovel from the bed of his pickup, Joe shoveled a path, unlocked the padlock, opened the heavy wooden doors, and walked down the five metal slat steps to the poured concrete floor. He gave each of the four vertical pumps a quick once over, choosing not to start them. The only thing he couldn't check were the intakes, which were below water. Convinced that everything was ready to go he turned on the power, locked up the building, and headed for Jordan.

Since their three-thirty quitting time was close, Mickey and his crew had left, leaving behind the partially loaded dump truck. Joe closed the pond valve, opened the river one, and poked around the charred remains of the pump house for a few minutes, trying to get a look at the pumps which were still buried under debris. When he got back to the pump house Marty was already there, leaned back in his chair, watching a basketball game on television.

"Early for a game, isn't it?" Joe asked.

"It's a rerun, on one of them sports channels, I don't get it at home," Marty said as he lowered the volume.

"I just came from the river, we should be all set to pump from there tonight."

"Is there enough water in the river for that?"

"It might be tight tonight, but they've closed the dam so we should be okay after tonight."

Marty shrugged. "Any word on what caused the fire?"

"Nothing yet. But I was talking to Mickey, he's convinced it was set. Talk has it that the environmentalists did it," Joe said, wondering if he was spreading the rumor from another source or if Mickey's assertion was the original one that had gone full circle.

"Well if they done this then they done the other," Marty said. "But I think the jury is still out on who altogether. I ain't saying those no-nuke people didn't do it, only that nobody has proven to me that they did."

"Yeah, I know what you mean."

Marty tipped back his baseball cap and turned up the television. "Don't mind, do ya," he said, referring to the volume.

"No, go ahead."

Joe went to his office and was still there at six-thirty when Warren called for a status check. "Everything going okay?" he asked.

"Yeah, it's just like we were pumping from Jordan, there's really no difference."

"Good," he said. "I didn't really expect there would be, that setup at the river is identical. Have you been out on the mountain yet?"

"No, not yet," Joe said, looking at his watch and wondering why Warren had asked.

"Okay then, I just thought I'd check in with you. Call me if anything comes up."

"I will."

Joe hung up the handset and leaned back in his creaking chair, stretching his body. He didn't want to stay later than his usual quitting time, but somehow it seemed the right thing to do considering they were pumping from the river. So he stayed until five, expecting something to happen, a glitch of some type, but it never came to be.

The following night, with his pre-departure tasks done, he was primed to leave, but didn't. He split his time between the mountain and his office until four, when he struck up a fluid conversation with Marty at the control desk, which Johnny joined at first light. By the time it wound down the crew was already trickling in from the mountain. Because he didn't like the idea of leaving at shift's end, Joe stayed at the control desk, watching the weather on half a dozen channels that Marty bounced between using the remote control.

With a major snowstorm predicted, the crew was speculating about getting the night off. But Joe ignored the hoopla. Television forecasters often over-predicted snow, because unlike rain, snowfall was disruptive, particularly in urban areas. Which meant it often didn't come at all, or if it did, it arrived later than expected.

Joe preferred to hang his hat on what Northern faxed in daily, a report that talked to professionals like him, and didn't have to be concerned with the public. In the final analysis, knowing only Republicans were more conservative than the weather service, Joe waited for a Winter Storm Warning to be issued, which, unlike a watch, wasn't posted until the storm couldn't miss.

In this case, he didn't expect that to happen until the huge low pressure system that was grinding its way east transferred its energy across the Appalachians and re-developed off the North Carolina coast, where it was expected to intensify as it churned slowly northeast, stalling in the Gulf of Maine, where it would spin around, depositing huge quantities of dry snow over the region's interior snow belt, of which White Woods was a part.

CHAPTER 9

▼

CARTER PEAK PROCEEDS

As soon as Warren got to his office Thursday morning he called Victor to let him know that things were going okay. While he had his doubts about how much of the dirty water they were actually using at that point, Victor had assured him that based on the river's flow of around 100 cubic feet per second, it would be behind the dam in twenty-four hours. Regardless, Warren had his doubts, hence the call.

As usual, Victor wasn't available. June did her usual good job of making Warren feel important, while simultaneously providing him with a variety of generic responses she had culled from years of knowing what Victor expected. Unfortunately, they were also what Warren expected, which meant they had lost their ability to placate him. But June's soft enunciation of the well-versed words that weren't hers soothed him, and he didn't take his frustration out on her, at least not so she noticed. Warren's shortcomings were legendary, nonetheless, he wasn't about to be a tyrant with those whose strings he had no right to pull, at least not two weeks before Christmas.

"I'll have him call you the minute the meeting breaks," June concluded. But much to Warren's displeasure, Victor hadn't returned his call by mid-afternoon. By then Warren was irritated enough to scold him, but didn't.

"Meet me at Stars at five," he told him, purposely not giving him any input.

With better than four inches of snow on the ground and two feet in the forecast, the restaurant was almost deserted when Warren got there ahead of Victor just after five.

He sat at the bar. Halfway through his second drink Victor arrived, still huffing and puffing from his trudge through the snow.

"Looks like this one is going to be bad," he said, brushing snow off his coat's generous fur collar and stamping his big feet on the carpeted floor, briefly turning it white.

"Yeah, that's what they're saying."

Warren was ready to dive into the business at hand, but it took Victor the better part of three minutes to get settled, insisting on hanging his coat, hat, scarf, and mittens in the unattended cloak room rather than laying them on one of the tables that had little chance of being used. When he finally hoisted himself onto a barstool and ordered a drink from the waiting bar tender, Warren spoke softly.

"Everything was fine this morning, that is, if we're using your crap."

Victor had his handkerchief out, drying his glasses. "You are if you're pumping from the river. That's good, I'm not surprised, everything on my end is fine as well."

The bar tender served Victor his drink.

"Put it on my tab," Warren told him, a hint of resentment in his voice.

"Thanks," Victor said, taking a sip.

"You know," Warren said leaning toward Victor's left ear, "this snow we're getting is good just in case, the more natural stuff the better, you know that don't you?"

Victor nodded, taking a second sip of his drink. "That's true," he said. "I didn't think of that, but the timing is perfect, isn't it?"

"Darn right, for that and the holiday period. We'll be a hundred percent with this. We sure as hell deserve a decent Christmas considering the meager ones we've had in recent years. It's been a bitch. Feast or famine takes on a whole new meaning in my business, a literal god damn meaning, if you know what I mean."

"It's a fickle economy for all of us right now, but I think it's improving. We're due for a cycle that's in our favor."

Warren was annoyed. "I guess you don't understand what I meant. People write letters, read newspapers, and pull toilet paper off the roll at about the same clip year round, your market is constant. We do or die in three weeks a year."

"When you put it that way you sound like the retailers. Always squawking about how bad you got it. That you only got one chance to make any money."

"Obviously you still haven't grasped the seasonal nature of the skiing industry. I suppose I ought to excuse you since you don't come from it, although it occurs to me we've discussed it before. A full quarter of our business comes from just three weeks of the year—Christmas and Presidents' Day. If the weather sucks, or Wall Street is in a nosedive, or some global conflict like a war happens to capture the attention of mainstream America, we suffer to some extent. Your business is different. We both have the competitive challenge, but you're unaffected by the kind of external events that can suck profit margins dryer than summertime in the Mojave Desert."

"But you aren't affected by imports."

"What do you mean by that?"

"International trade. Countries that pay their employees twenty bucks a month and give Sunday off as a benefit, try dealing with that."

"You're not making shoes," Warren said.

"That's not the point, you have regional, national competition at best, we're in a global marketplace."

"Everything is relative."

"Whatever."

Warren changed the subject. "Anyway, like I was saying, everything this morning was fine. You don't have any problems on your end?"

"No, nothing, we went back to full production sometime Tuesday night or early Wednesday morning without a hitch or a raised eyebrow. It's like I told you more than once, nobody knows everything and even if they did they wouldn't care."

Warren suddenly realized they were discussing things in public for the first time. But even if somebody had happened to take it all in, which they hadn't, and decipher it, it would still be so far out of context that it wouldn't make sense.

"That reminds me," Warren said, "next time we're in the car we've got to talk about a transfer."

"Okay."

The bartender, a clean shaven middle-aged man with neatly cropped hair, stopped polishing the counter with the damp white cloth he seemed to be inseparable with, switched the television to *The Weather Channel* and drifted toward them, commenting on the forecast that predicted two feet of snow by morning.

"Looks like we're going to get walloped," he said, inviting them to respond.

For the next hour the three of them talked, the conversation going from the weather to sports, to the vicissitudes of seasonal business, which Victor got chided about for not understanding.

"I suppose," Warren said, feeling good now that he had passed his five drink tolerance "that we ought to get our butts home before it's too late. What do you think, Victor?"

"I'm ready."

Warren got up, scanned the restaurant, and proclaimed it to be empty even though he couldn't see the no smoking section at the far end.

"This is going to hurt our reputations," he said.

"What do you mean?" Victor asked as he retrieved his overcoat and other belongings from the cloakroom rack.

"Closing the place," he said with a smile. "Everybody and his brother will be saying tomorrow that we closed the place, not exactly a favored distinction, you know."

The bartender smiled from across the room.

"You want a ride home?" Victor asked Warren, as he draped his knitted gray scarf around his neck for the third time.

Warren looked at Victor, then at the bartender, knowing he was probably answering them both.

"Hell no, in eight inches of snow you got three things going for you. First, the cops really aren't out there, second, nobody else is, and third you got an excuse for driving bad. Besides, that new Town Car I bought drives itself, it knows where I live, it's like a pet dog, it'll find its way home."

Victor and the bartender smiled nervously but didn't say anything.

A blinding burst of snow buffeted Warren and Victor as they stepped onto the sidewalk and parted ways. Victor was across the street, bundled like an Eskimo, clearing his car of snow, when Warren drove off, satisfied with the two arched tunnels of visibility his windshield wipers had made.

$$*\qquad*\qquad*\qquad*$$

Joe went to bed exhausted Thursday morning but managed to get only a couple hours sleep before the excitement of the storm woke him and lured him to the television, which he kept muted for fear of waking his mother, who was taking a nap twenty feet away behind the balsa wood door that separated her bedroom from the living room.

With pressures rapidly dropping over the Delmarva Peninsula, the warning was up and he headed for the mountain, stopping for coffee at the store, which was buzzing with storm talk and activity.

"Mother Nature is gonna give ya a helping hand tonight, Joe," Ethel hollered from behind the counter as her frail fingers danced over the cash register keys.

"Yeah, looks like a bad one," Joe said, maneuvering his way behind the six-deep line of customers at the check out.

"You don't need to tell me, milks gone and the bread is darn near."

"Really."

"Yep," she said, pulling bills from the till as Joe disappeared from sight to get his coffee.

Back up front, Joe waited in line behind a heavyset man with two bottles of Diet Coke and a box of Little Debbie brownies. When the man reached the counter he asked for five packs of Camels and took a checkbook from his hip pocket. Ethel laid the cigarettes on the counter and reached forward, extending her open hand toward Joe who dropped fifty-five cents into her palm.

"Thanks," he said.

"Take it easy now, Joe," she said, dropping the coins into the till.

"I will, you too," Joe said, heading for the door.

When he got to the pump house Marty was at the control desk.

"They're looking for a loader operator for morning," he said.

"Oh," Joe said, his eyes glued to the television that Marty had tuned to *The Weather Channel*.

"Yeah, Herb's sick."

"You interested?" Joe asked with a smile, knowing Marty would say no like he always did.

"Hell no, you know I ain't."

"Did you call Al?" Joe asked, knowing he was the only other one qualified to operate the loaders.

"Not my place to," Marty said.

"Okay, I'll call him."

"Got a lot of calls to make, don't ya?"

"Yeah, sure do," Joe said as he turned and walked toward his office.

Joe breezed through the list. At four o'clock, with Marty gone, he locked up the pump house and headed home. A steady snow was falling and three inches had already piled up.

Joe went to bed early and got six hours sleep before the howling wind that was beating snow against his window woke him. He lay there in the darkness, listening to the rattle of a loose pane of glass that was loud even from across the room, thinking about how he'd like to be out in the storm, maybe plowing snow. He tried to get back to sleep, but the raging storm called him from the warmth of his electric blanket. Sitting on the ottoman in front of the living room television with *The Weather Channel* on but muted, he learned the storm was going to be true to its prediction. He stood at the backdoor, with the floodlight on, watching the storm for a few minutes, before returning to bed. At six-thirty, he got up, dressed, and quietly slipped out of the house, knowing his mother would almost immediately rise and watch him go from the dark kitchen window. Clicking the front wheel hubs to four-wheel drive, he left, grateful he didn't have a drift to contend with at the end of the driveway.

The truck labored along the unplowed Johnson Road, its undercarriage forced to part snow despite its sixteen-inch clearance. He scarcely made it through the huge drift the plows had made at the edge of the state road, where a lane and a half at best had been cleared, but not recently. White Woods Road was nothing but a path, a pure white roofless tunnel really, and the access road wasn't any better.

The snow removal crews, confronted with snowfall rates of an inch or two an hour, resigned themselves to keeping things open, even if that was nothing more than a single passageway. Cresting the hill into the parking lot at Abbott Lodge he followed the two-hour old path of the plow—a sweeping noose-like pattern that brought him facing out, a hundred feet from the pump house door. He parked the truck and waded through the thigh-deep snow littered with twigs and branches, his body buffeted by a howling wind that whistled through barren branches and distant utility lines. When he reached the entrance, he unlocked the door and pulled hard, barely able to squeeze through the small opening.

The cool pump house air felt surprisingly warm against the exposed skin of his face. He stamped his boots on the concrete floor and kicked them against the cinder block wall, shedding them of snow. Then, walking briskly down the hall, he shook his head like a dog, shaking away more snow. At the control desk he turned on the two-way radio and switched to the groomer frequency, which the snow removal crew used. Next, he powered up the computer and clicked his way to the data for the North Slope weather station. Barometric pressure 29.19 and steady, temperature 15 degrees Fahrenheit, wind north-northeast at 37 miles per hour with gusts to 51. A few more mouse clicks took him to the summit station data, which was reporting wind gusts in excess 70 miles an hour.

He exited the program and shut down the computer. Anxious to be outside again where he could be a part of the storm, he shoveled the pump house walkway as a chorus of back-up alarms rose and sank in intensity on the sound of the howling wind as a fleet of diesel-powered machinery worked feverishly at North Slope clearing away what Mother Nature had left.

He had just finished when he heard the steady roar of a ten-ton truck as it climbed the hill, its plow and wing grinding against the pavement, spewing a stream of sparks, as it pushed mounds of snow to its right. Unable to stop on the uphill grade with a ton of snow on its two blades, the truck swung wide through the empty parking lot and veered sharply to the right where it deposited its load at lot's edge, its flashing amber lights piercing the night, illuminating the falling snow that swirled in every direction. Briefly the wind subsided, and a beeping sound filled the cold night air as the truck shot backwards and the plows upward. On course again, the plows dropped in unison with a thud as the truck lurched forward with a roar and crept slowly ahead on the level surface. Rejoining its previous path, the truck slowed to a crawl and stopped.

Joe stood near the door, leaning on the shovel, waiting to see who would emerge from the dark snow encased cab. He was happy when he saw it was Buck.

"What brings you in so early?" Buck asked.

"Oh, I couldn't sleep, you know how it is. Looks like we got plenty of work."

"Oh hell yes, it's coming down like blazes, but I guess we don't have to worry about getting things ready for morning. With the wind blowing like it is I don't suspect we'll be opening anytime soon. What do you think?"

"No, no way. I checked the summit station when I got here, it's gusting over 70. Besides, I don't know how the day-trip people would get here if they wanted to; the highway is a lane and a half at best. You want coffee, I'll make some?"

"Yeah, that would be good."

Joe threw the shovel like a javelin into the larger of the two piles of snow he had made. With Buck close behind he headed for the control desk.

"You got the radio on? Case they're looking for me," Buck asked.

"Yeah."

Buck stretched himself out in a chair while Joe fixed the coffee in silence. When he finished, he noticed Buck's eyes were closed. "You asleep?" he asked.

Buck opened his eyes immediately and smiled. "No, just resting my eyes is all. It gets to be hell out there after a while, trying to see where you're going. If I ever needed a wing man it's tonight."

Joe tipped his head. "That's right," he said, "where's your partner?"

Buck shook his head. "They got him doing clean up because Eddy had to run the loader."

"Oh," Joe said.

Buck sat up straight, massaged his bull neck a couple times, and said, "Is pumping from the river going okay for ya?"

Joe nodded. "So far so good."

For the next five minutes they hashed over the troubles that had beset the snowmaking crew, a conversation Joe was tired of having. So he was relieved when Buck looked at the coffee pot and said, "Is that one of those jobs you can pour from in progress?"

"Yeah, but it might be a bit strong."

Buck got up. "The stronger the better for me. I got to be going. If I don't wipe out the condos we won't be getting in there with anything but the loader, especially with it blowing like it is. There's a section toward the top of Lockwood that drifts in worse than a sand storm. I'll be right back, I've got to get my cup from the truck."

When he got back, Buck filled his oversized travel mug to the rim, forgoing any additions to it, thanked Joe for the coffee, and left. When the pot gurgled its finish a few minutes later Joe keyed the control desk microphone. "Coffee's on," he said to no one in particular, knowing the base station's powerful signal and his distinctive voice would serve to tell them where.

White Woods didn't open that morning. Despite the demand, and admittedly the temptation of some employees to open with a mountain buried in snow, the wind, still gusting in excess of 70 miles an hour at the summit, was simply too fierce to safely operate lifts. While dozens of red laminated signs, posted at the ticket concourse and on the doors of the lodges, announced a wind delay, the weather service did not expect the winds to go down until the sun did.

Joe milled around the pump house all morning, entertaining the snow removal crews with coffee and cigars and keeping abreast of things via the two-way radio.

At noon, with the wind still howling and an updated forecast calling for it to continue through the night, Joe canceled the crew, cleared another three inches of snow from the pump house walkway, and left.

The roads were better as he drove home, but by no means good. The top of the thirty inch red plastic snow fence in the hundred acre hay field halfway down White Woods Road was barely visible as he passed, which meant its effectiveness would soon diminish, requiring the road be plowed every few hours until the wind went down. The state highway was in decent shape, but The Johnson Road and Joe's driveway had only been punched out. Still, it was enough to get him home.

He spent a quiet afternoon in the house, doing chores and watching television. At six o'clock his mother served a dinner that was every bit as good as her usual fare despite her assertion that it would be meager because she hadn't been able to get to the store. Exhausted, Joe went to bed and slept soundly despite the wind that continued to howl.

When he got up early Saturday morning to check the weather, he wasn't surprised to hear the storm had stalled. When he got to the mountain just before ten, the parking lots were almost empty. While the sheltered runs at North Slope were open, the hordes of skiers who had arrived that morning to partake of the conditions that were nothing short of superb had left.

Joe hung around the pump house and North Slope Lodge most of the day, keeping abreast of the weather. At three o'clock, the wind hadn't diminished, nor was it predicted to, so with Warren's blessing, Joe canceled the crew for a third night and went home, spending a quiet evening with his mother.

When he got up Sunday morning at seven-thirty, the sky was a mix of sun and clouds and the worst of the wind was gone. Joe wolfed down the fried eggs, bacon, and buttered toast his mother made, bundled himself from top to bottom, and went to the yard, where he shoveled for three hours—clearing the walkway, mailbox, clothes line, and a Y shaped path two feet wide to his mother's bird feeders. By noon the broken sky had yielded to a solid gray overcast and when Joe left for the mountain a three-thirty, the light snow that had been falling for two hours had succeeded in summoning the tired snow removal crews from their homes, adding to the 27 inches that had officially fallen since two o'clock Thursday afternoon.

With all seventy-three trails open top to bottom, White Woods was mobbed. The sides of the access road were lined with cars and every parking area, including the distant overflow lot, were jammed with mostly out-of-state vehicles. Joe weaved through them all, taking in a sight rarely seen during a pre-Christmas non-vacation period, absorbing what it meant to him and his crew. Although it wouldn't be spoken, the pressure was off. Now they only had to concentrate on building base depths and laying down the layers of fresh powder that White Woods skiers had come to expect each time the sun rose.

If there were no new incidents, the cases of open ears and the burned pump house, which at one point was on the tip of everybody's tongue, would soon be forgotten.

When he arrived at the pump house, Joe was in a decent mood. But it didn't last. He'd barely set foot at the control desk area when Marty started complaining.

"We've got to do something about the parking, Joe, put up some more signs or something, they got half our spots."

Joe hated to be pounced on the minute he arrived. He did his best not to show it.

"I know, it's a busy day."

"Well that don't excuse it, every one of them spots are marked plain as day, it's those frigin Mass-holes. If I catch'em I'm gonna chew them out good."

Joe was stowing his lunch in the refrigerator. "Don't do that," he said, shaking his head.

"Why the hell not?" Marty asked.

"Because your job and mine depend on those people. You know darn well that half our weekend skiers come from Massachusetts."

"Well that don't make it right."

Joe smiled.

"Well," Marty said, refusing to back down, "I'm gonna at least run them out."

Joe knew he had to offer something. "I'll look into getting some cones to mark it off on busy days. More signs aren't going to help if you ask me."

"'Course not, cause they don't care. We ought to tow the bastards, but what do I know."

Joe didn't say anything as he finished making coffee, which Marty had forgotten to do.

"So what do you think about Carter?" Marty asked changing the subject.

"What do you mean?" Joe asked, dreading the answer.

"Didn't you hear? They're saying Carter is a sure thing."

Joe was embarrassed. Embarrassed that he hadn't been told through official channels like he figured he ought to have been. He could ask Marty who told him, but decided against it, since it was probably Doris who had dropped the ball and that was a battle not worth fighting. At least they had been alone when he found out. It would have been worse to hear it in front of the crew.

"So where do you suppose he got the money from?" Marty asked.

"That I don't know," Joe said, shaking his head. "Last I knew it didn't look good."

"So I suppose this means they're going to want me to work this summer."

"Well, the opportunity will surely be there," Joe said, knowing Marty preferred to have his summer for cutting wood and fishing.

"Yeah, well, we'll see," Marty said, clicking on the television, which he quickly muted.

Joe started for his office, not bothering to wait for the coffee to finish. For the early part of the shift he was quiet and kept to himself as much as possible. He didn't fare well when blind-sided, especially when it was something important like Carter. Even if he wasn't the chief of snowmaking, he had gone out of his way to attend the expansion meetings and generate the cost data for Warren and Dwight. It wasn't right that he hadn't been told properly. It was just past nine when Joe jumped at the sound of a voice.

"Hey, Chief, you got a minute?" It was Jim.

"Oh, you scared me," Joe said, trying not to show just how much it had frightened him.

"I'm sorry, I didn't mean to, it's the noise, I guess," Jim said, motioning toward the pump room with his right hand that held a bottle of spring water.

Joe knew Jim must have come in early to talk with him, so he knew he had to give him his full attention.

"It's okay, it happens all the time. What can I do for you?"

Jim was tentative. "Well, if you're busy, it can wait, I just wanted to talk, but I don't want to bother you."

Joe laid down his pen. "It's no bother, have a seat, Jim."

"I was wondering," Jim said, settling himself in the chair, "what you think about all the stuff that has been happening?"

Joe's eyes narrowed. "In what way?"

Jim cleared his throat. "I realize it isn't any of my business, but it just seems like nothing is being done about it."

"What do you mean?"

"As you know, I haven't been working here very long, but it seems to me that you people have taken what's happened in stride."

Joe frowned. "Not at all, but we can't do any more about it than we have. We've done some investigating on our own, we've called the police, we shifted a security position to nights. What more can we do?"

"Are you aware of the common denominators?" Jim asked.

"The what?"

"Like I said, it's none of my business, but there are certain things that the investigators seem to have missed, I mean, it doesn't take a scholar to figure out we got a pattern here."

Joe smiled. "Or an MIT graduate. What do you mean by a pattern?"

"Okay, as far as I know, and please, correct me if I'm wrong, there have been three gun incidents and the pump house fire. Right?"

Joe nodded. "Yeah, that's right."

"Well, all three gun incidents occurred on White Peak, above, say, 3,000 feet. The pump house fire wasn't even on the mountain. Here, let me show you."

Jim got up, pulled a trail map from his jacket pocket, unfolded it, and laid it on Joe's desk. A thick black line was drawn across the top third of the mountain, with three bright red X's, the size of quarters, above the line. A fourth X, at the very bottom of the map, had an arrow pointing off the paper.

"Now look, everything happened from here up except the pump house fire, which was way down here," Jim said, fingering each X as he spoke. "It's almost two miles between the pump house and the closest incident."

Joe pretended to be studying the map while he collected his thoughts.

"Do you see what I mean?" Jim asked.

Joe nodded and leaned back in his chair. "Yeah, it's interesting," he said, "but what does it mean?"

"I think it's obvious, the pump house fire had nothing to do with everything else. Look at the concentration of the incidents," he said, again fingering the three red X's on the mountain, "they're clustered together, two of them not more than a stones-throw apart and the third in the same ballpark, and like I said, all of them on White Peak above 3,000 feet. So why would the person responsible for all this suddenly end up two miles away torching your pump house?"

Joe thought for a moment. "I see what you mean, and you're right, nobody has put that together that I know of, but I'm not sure it means anything. Maybe we just scared whoever it is off the mountain. They had to know we were watching for them and we did put on extra security. Who have you shared this with?"

"Nobody, it's not my place to do that. I've taken it as far as I can with what I know."

Joe nodded. "Well, I appreciate your interest. Any thoughts on who?"

Jim was prepared for the question. "Well, first, I'd discount the fire. It could have been a malfunction of some sort, and if it was suspicious, it might have been a coincidence that it happened when it did. Anyway, I'd focus on the open ears. We know they were malicious acts that basically involved the same thing being done all three times in the same general area. Assuming you agree with that, then I think you need to be looking for somebody with a grudge against the resort and I wouldn't be quick to buy into the disgruntled employee idea or the failed litigation thing. Neither would I hang my hat on the greens, which, in case you don't know it, is presently the explanation of choice amongst your crew. No, whoever is doing this high elevation stuff is not your ordinary guy. It strikes me as being somebody that is used to this terrain, somebody who knows how to get around without being seen. If you want my opinion, you got yourself a mountain man."

From the look on Jim's face and the passion in his youthful voice, Joe was convinced he was sincere. Regardless, he still felt he needed to be aloof, so he smiled. "A mountain man, I don't know, what about a high altitude beast of some sort."

Jim snapped his fingers. "That thrives in thin air? Maybe."

They laughed.

"Why not the greens?" Joe asked.

Jim's answer was immediate. "Because it isn't their style. We had our share of them in school, they can be fanatics, no doubt about that, but they're organized, consistent. This doesn't fit them at all. They're more in the open, they want you to know it's them, this guy doesn't."

"I don't know. I hear they have people that splinter from the main group. People that aren't satisfied with how things are going."

There was no swaying Jim. "That's true, but highly improbable in this situation. I mean, what do you think, they're climbing 3,000 feet above sea level, which equates to better than a 1,000 feet of vertical, in the dark, with temperatures that routinely hover around zero, to take out your guys. I don't think so."

Joe massaged his chin. "You certainly have done your homework."

"I'm just trying to help," Jim said.

Joe nodded. "Anything else?"

"Yeah, I know you've reported these incidents to the police, but I bet nobody has looked at the big picture, like doing this," Jim said, motioning to the map that still laid spread out on Joe's desk.

"I'll definitely pass it on. It's good work on your part, no doubt about that."

"I just thought it might help," Jim said standing up.

"Well listen, Jim, I really appreciate you sharing this with me and don't hesitate to let me know if you come up with anything else. Can I keep the map?"

"Oh sure, Crayola and I can make another in two minutes."

After Jim left, Joe folded up the map, tucked it under his blotter, and leaned back in his chair, thinking about what Jim had said. It was still on his mind the following night when he heard most of the first shift arranging to take their meal break at their favorite haunt—the ski patrol shack on the summit of White Peak, a run down wooden building not much bigger than a small bedroom.

When Joe got there at eight-thirty most of the crew was there. As usual, they were all sitting on the floor so they could tilt back and stretch their legs, a welcome position after hours of leaning over and lifting. Except for the loud hissing of the propane heater, which was turned to high, the room was quiet when Joe entered. A couple of the crew stared at him with puzzled looks, probably wondering why he was there. Everybody was eating except Andrew, who was cutting pieces of cheese off a big block with a jack knife and placing then on two pieces of white bread that were lying on his legs.

Why doesn't he just use regular pieces of cheese, Joe thought to himself as he made his way to the back of the room and sat down on the bench beside Al. "How's Universe look?" he asked.

"Good," Al said, popping a potato chip in his mouth.

"How about North Slope, I got another message from ski patrol that the snow boarders are wiping it clean, they're apparently running the edges enough that they're pushing snow into the gullies and woods where the groomers can't get it."

"It looked okay. We're getting decent coverage tonight all over, definitely a lot of bang for the buck."

Looking around the room, Joe's eyes settled on Andrew, who had finished making the sandwiches. Joe watched him fish a couple pieces of well-used aluminum foil from his lunch pail and smooth it out with his hands on the wooden floor. Next he placed a sandwich in each piece, wrapped them up, and put them on top of the metal guard of the heater. Then, turning to Joe, he smiled and said, "Grilled cheese."

Joe raised his eyebrows and nodded.

Pete spoke up from across the room. "Cook me one of those babies, will ya."

"I will for the right price, three bucks apiece," Andrew shot back with a laugh, almost like he had rehearsed it.

"Yeah," Pete said, taking a bite from his bulging tuna fish sandwich, "you'll make somebody a good wife."

Joe wished he hadn't come. Being there didn't feel right. He was eyeing the open path to the door, thinking about leaving, when a snowmaker sitting in the corner spoke for the first time since Joe had arrived.

"Why don't you use a fork," he said to Jason who was eating pasta salad out a bowl with his fingers, apparently unaware of the dressing that dribbled on his jacket with every loaded pass.

"Fingers existed before forks," Jason said, hoping to shut him up with a snappy reply.

"Not yours," Jim said.

"Maybe I like eating with my fingers, so what."

"Well it *ain't* proper," Jim said, mocking Jason's crudeness.

Jason reached for the bowl's cover, snapped it on, and slapped the top of it hard to be sure it was sealed. "Why don't you mind your own frigin business," he said.

"Fuck you."

"Is that the best you can do?" Jason said. "I really expected better from you, being a graduate of NIT and all."

"It's MIT," Jim said, the fight gone from his voice.

Despite the fact he was curious how well propane heaters cooked grilled cheese sandwiches, Joe had had enough.

"It's a cold one tonight, guys," he said as he got up and walked across the room toward the door, "take your time, but no sleeping."

Nobody said anything. Probably because nobody had been spoken to directly. But Joe figured it differently. Maybe the guys were upset with him, maybe things were worse than he imagined. Maybe he should have stayed longer, or at least made a better exit.

The cold air felt good against his exposed skin as he walked slowly to his sled and sat down, gazing back at the shack. Except for occasional glimmers of light that showed through all but the hinged side of the door, you'd never have guessed anyone was inside.

He sat there, feeling sorry for himself, as the cold from the vinyl seat penetrated his layers of clothing. He had made this visit with the best of intentions, hoping to find out how the crew was feeling. But somehow he felt he had done more harm than good.

It would have been better not to come at all, he concluded, as he pushed the ignition button on his sled. The powerful engine roared to life, breaking the stillness. He knew they could hear it. I bet they're talking about me now, about me coming and why, he thought to himself as he gently pushed his thumb into the throttle, narrowing the distance between it and the handle bar.

He hadn't traveled a dozen feet when the door opened. Instinctively, Joe released the throttle and the sled slowed to a stop. It was Jim, and he was heading right for Joe.

"I'm sorry to bother you, Chief, but I need to talk to you if you got a minute."

Joe silenced the engine. "Sure, Jim, what's up?"

"I was just wondering about…about the talk we had last night. I think you might have misunderstood me."

Joe leaned back, resting the palms of his hands on the edges of the seat.

"How so?"

"I didn't mean to imply that I was a know-it-all."

"Who said you were?"

"Nobody, it's just that, well, these guys see things differently," Jim said, gesturing back toward the shack. "They've pinned this thing on the greens and the word is that everybody has, including Mr. Ainsworth, and maybe it is them, who knows, it's not my place to say otherwise, but in my opinion it isn't them. But regardless, if they're your only suspects, if they're the sole focus of your investigation, the real culprits have free reign."

"What are you trying to say, Jim?"

"Just that something more than a political statement is being made here. I just don't think it's them…that's all."

"Why?"

Jim's answer was immediate. "Like I said last night, it doesn't fit, at least not in this case. I'm not saying there aren't some thugs in the environmental movement because there are, but they aren't all that typical of it, you know. The average environmentalist doesn't condone this kind of thing, they don't know what the radicals are doing anymore than the average German knew what was going on in the SS. Like I said last night, we had more than our share of environmentalists in school, they can be fanatics, no doubt about that, but they wouldn't do what you're convinced they did."

Joe was in a no-nonsense mood. "So why couldn't it be the fanatics?"

"It could be, but in my opinion it's highly unlikely. First of all, tree spiking, and I mention that because it seems to get the most play around here, is directly related to cutting trees, which is what they are opposed to. With what we got here, there is no direct connection between what you're doing and what there're trying to stop. Sure, they're no doubt opposed to you gobbling up Carter Peak, but these incidents are far removed from the eventuality of Carter Peak being developed. I'm not saying they couldn't have thought of this approach, but think about it, would they?"

Joe nodded, giving Jim the cue to continue.

"Like I said, spiking trees is different. It's part and parcel to stopping logging, not only for the guy with the chain saw but at the sawmill as well. There are books out there with detailed instructions on how to spike trees, drawings and all. Spiking trees is common knowledge. You want to slow down speeders you install speed bumps, you want to slow down loggers, you pound spikes. But in this case it's different. Nobody except somebody in this business would know to do this. Think about it."

Joe nodded again.

"Another way to look at it would be that if you really had somebody out there that was opposed to Carter, they wouldn't do something like this. It may sound harsh, but the most they can hope for is maiming or killing one of your guys. The kind of people we're taking about are radicals, people who believe this is a war, and they would strike you where it hurts, like destroying some of your lifts."

"Burning down the pump house is just as bad. If we hadn't had the river, which they wouldn't necessarily have known about, we'd have been out of business."

Jim smiled. "True, but like I said last night, the greens doing the pump house still doesn't fit."

"Why?"

"Because they're more in the open, the greens I mean, they most often claim responsibility, they want you to know it's them. Your guy doesn't. Anything is possible and again, it's none of my business, but based on my knowledge of them, it's not them."

Joe raised his eyebrows. "What do you mean when you say your knowledge?"

Jim sighed, then smiled. "This was the last place I ever expected to be dealing with this. I came here to get away from this crap, to clear my mind of the cobwebs of a life long gone and past. But I guess you just can't escape it, can you? Your past, I mean. But anyway, you don't spend four years at MIT without things…without getting involved in things. I've added my name to every petition they circulated, lent it to every press release they mass produced, and inserted it in plenty of HTML pages. I've marched with the best of them and chained myself to the worst of them. I've lived and breathed their lifestyles, sometimes for a week at a time in D. C. I know these people, that's all."

"I didn't realize how close you were to it, I mean…"

Jim nodded.

"But still, I don't know, their opposition to Carter is substantial, and they…" Joe stopped, interrupted by a glimpse of Pete, who was on the bottom step of the ski patrol shack, lighting a cigarette. Neither he nor Jim had heard the door open so neither of them knew how long Pete had been standing there, possibly within earshot. Well aware that ending the conversation now would look bad, Joe lowered his voice and continued. "From what I've been told they'd do anything to stop Carter Peak from being developed."

But it was obvious that Pete's appearance had taken the wind out of Jim's sails. "Yeah, I guess," he said pushing around a mound of snow with the toe of his right boot.

Deciding the conversation was over, Joe said, "Well anyway, I appreciate your thoughts. I need to hear it, you know."

Jim nodded.

Joe started the sled. "Be safe," he said, creeping away.

Discouraged, Joe decided to take the long way back to the pump house. Going faster than he should along a trail that was for sleds only, he dodged a half dozen trees and an outcropping of ledge, emerging into the openness of Abbot Peak, where half the summit was a smooth corduroy like surface, the telltale mark of fresh grooming.

Like a performer taking center stage in a dark concert hall, he sped to the center of the opening, and turned his sled toward Starburst, the expert trail that dropped suddenly before him, and stopped. If it were possible to go straight, he'd be heading directly for the stars.

Several hundred feet below the powerful light of a grooming machine ascended steadily toward him. Realizing he was in the groomer's path, Joe turned sharply to the left and sped to where the groomer had already been. A minute later the Pisten Bully reached the summit, and despite the distance and darkness, Joe could make out Buck's stocky silhouette behind the wheel. The groomer made a wide U turn, and slowed to a stop a few feet from where Joe sat. Buck leaned over and opened the passenger's side door.

"Hey, Joe," he said, gesturing to the empty seat. "Jump in."

Joe left his sled running and climbed into the warmth of the groomer.

"What brings you out here?" Buck asked.

"I was just checking on the crew and I figured I'd take the long way back."

"So how you been?" Buck asked, not waiting for an answer. "I see you survived the storm."

Joe smiled. "Oh yeah. It sure was a blessing to get that much so early. How's everything going with you?"

"Good. Working a bit more than I'd like, we're running short with George out on disability. 'Course, they never replaced Harry either, so we got two less guys this season. If these things weren't such jewels I'd say the hell with it and work days year-round on the skidders."

"Do you make more doing that?" Joe asked.

"Yeah, a little, but the cold is a bitch in winter. The skidders are open...well, you know how they are. 'Course, your crew does it and at night no less, so they got it worse. I respect what your guys do, even the ones with the crabby attitudes."

Joe was about to answer when the radio crackled.

"Three to One."

Buck keyed the microphone in its metal perch and answered loudly. "One. Go ahead."

"Yeah, Buck, I'm going in for lunch, you coming?"

"Shortly. I've got a few more passes here and I'll be done."

Joe figured he was holding up Buck. "Well, I better be going," he said reaching for the door handle, "maybe I'll ride with you for a few hours when I get off some night, you know, like old times."

"Anytime," Buck answered as Joe stepped out of the cab onto the wide track. Carefully closing the door, he jumped down to the firmly packed snow and flipped the rusted chains on his sled's front skis onto the snow just as the groomer's power tiller roared to life and Buck started slowly down.

Sitting as still as a statue, deep in thought, Joe kept his eyes glued on the groomer until it dipped out of sight several hundred yards down. As he started his descent, depending on the chains to control his forward speed on the steep rolling grade, Joe couldn't help but feel that things were slipping away from him. Not all at once, but slowly. As horrible as it sounded to him, he no longer felt he had control.

Back at the pump house he stowed his gear in his office, hung the key to his sled on the hook by the control desk, and announced his departure to Marty who looked ready to doze off.

Marty twirled around in his chair. "You calling it a night?" he asked. Joe nodded.

"See ya in church," Marty said.

The gist of what Jim told him didn't sink in until well after Joe got home. Jim was a green, or at least he had been, which didn't matter to Joe anymore than if he was gay or something like that. What concerned him was whether or not Pete had heard their conversation, and if so, had he heard enough to label Jim, which would surely complicate things and potentially put Jim at risk. If that happened, wasn't it his fault for not having the strength to reject Warren's slick way of doing business? He'd compromised himself to get the job he coveted, and now he was in the middle of a tangled mess that sickened him.

Following a restless night, Joe got up early Tuesday and made it to Art's office just before nine. Several times during the day he considered bringing up his woes, that seemed to weigh more heavily on him with each passing hour, but it didn't feel right, so he didn't.

He still despised the idea of missing work to train with Art, but by the time he left North Slope Lodge at six o'clock, he was exhausted, so he scraped the idea of going to the pump house and went home, where he fixed himself a modest meal and went to bed. He got up at ten Wednesday morning and used the extra time to fill the wood box, chop a bunch of kindling, hang a wreath on the front door, and a bag of suet in a backyard tree. He left for work a little early, talked longer than normal at the store, and arrived at the pump house after Marty.

"How'd last night go?" Joe asked.

"It went," Marty scoffed, not taking his eyes off the computer screen.

Joe took a deep breath and gritted his teeth, but it wasn't enough to keep his temper at bay. "Can't you just answer a question for once," he snapped, almost immediately regretting his words.

Marty spun around in his chair and looked Joe in the eyes. "For Christ sakes, what's eating you?"

"Well?" Joe said.

"Nothing, it was quiet all around."

Joe nodded and went to his office. A half hour later he gathered up his equipment and spent the entire evening checking snow quality. When Al arrived for work just past ten, Joe was at the control desk, eating his lunch and trying to soothe things over from earlier despite the fact that Marty had probably already forgotten his outburst.

"What do you know about Jim?" Al asked pouring a cup of coffee from a fresh batch Marty had just made.

"Just that's he's as queer as a three dollar bill," Marty shot back, sounding sure of himself.

"Really."

Marty nodded. "Oh sure, he's a royal pain in the ass, always asking questions or poking his nose where it don't belong."

"Really," Al said again.

"Oh, Yeah," Marty continued. "He's an aggravating little cuss. I'm surprised you haven't noticed. He's got an engineering degree from one of those fancy ivy schools so I guess he thinks he's smarter than the rest of us. If you ask me, he's got too much interest in things. It just don't seem right, but what do I know."

Al laughed. "Not a hell of a lot."

"Fuck you," Marty shot back.

Joe suspected the worse. "Why do you ask, Al, about Jim I mean?"

Al took a sip of coffee. "Well, you know how the guys are blaming the environmentalists for the stuff that's happened with the guns?"

"Yeah."

"They're saying Jim is an environmentalist."

Although he felt bad doing it, Joe did his best to seem surprised. "One of them?"

"Yeah, and they're convinced of it. Pete says he heard Jim say it."

Joe's heart sank. So Pete had overheard his conversation with Jim.

"Jesus Christ, that's a mouthful ain't it," Marty said.

"What's that supposed to mean?" Al asked.

"Well if he's one of them, who knows what he's been up to," Marty said.

Joe quickly realized Marty had given him the opening he needed. "I know what you're thinking, Marty, and it can't be. He was on the hill when the fire started and I'd have to check but I bet he was accounted for during the other incidents, at least some of them."

"But that don't mean he ain't feeding them with what they need to know to pull this shit, like a kind of plant, you know, the kind you hear about. Sure, that makes sense, he gets hired on here to give them somebody on the inside. It happens all the time."

"Yeah, in the movies," Joe snapped. "I don't buy it."

"You're just partial to him because he's clean cut and tucks in his shirts."

Joe rolled his eyes.

"Well it's true ain't it?" Marty said.

Joe shook his head. "No. No, it isn't true. He's a good worker and you know it."

"Well that might be so, but it don't change things one iota if he's one of them."

Joe shook his head. "There's two different things here guys. If Jim is or maybe was an environmentalist that doesn't mean he had anything to do with the guns being tampered with. You've got to separate the two. There's a lot of environmentalists around. Just being one doesn't mean anything."

"Sounds like he is, then," Marty mumbled.

"What was that?" Joe asked.

"I said, it sounds like you know he is one of them."

Joe forced a smile. What should he do? Lie? Expound on what Jim had told him? "I'm not saying he is or he isn't," he finally said. "I'm just saying that if he is one of them it doesn't necessarily have anything to do with what's been happening. Like I said, there's environmentalists everywhere. There's a lot of them right in Cannon."

Marty sighed as he leaned back in his creaking chair, massaging the stubble on his chin.

Well, anyway," Al said, rejoining the conversation. "I brought it up 'cause I thought it might create a problem with the guys. It really don't matter who Jim is or what he has or hasn't done. If the guys are thinking this stuff, it's the same thing. Ain't it?"

Joe nodded. "That's true. So what do we do about it?"

There was a short silence. Joe was about to rephrase the question when Alan strolled in, eyeing the coffee pot.

"Hi, Alan," Joe said, concealing his displeasure at having to end their conversation.

"Hi," Alan replied sleepily as he grabbed a plastic mug from beside the coffee maker and filled it to the brim.

Marty turned to Al. "What did you think about them Celts last night?" he asked.

Joe hung around for a few minutes, listening to their conversation, which Alan joined, before announcing his intentions.

"I'm going to White Peak," he said. Marty and Al nodded and picked up their conversation where they had left off. Joe went to his office, gathered his equipment and headed out to check snow quality on Orbit and Pipeline. When he finished an hour and a half later he considered finding Al to finish their discussion, but for some reason he had cooled to the idea of bringing him into the fold. He needed to talk with Warren first.

Chapter 10

▼

Suspicion Mounts

Joe hadn't bothered to call ahead for an appointment with Warren like he knew he should have. As he approached Doris' office, which was plastered with tacky Christmas decorations she had probably hung in lieu of doing her job, he could see that Warren's door was closed.

"Hi, Doris," he said faintly.

"Oh, hi, Joe."

"I guess Warren is busy, huh?"

"No, he's just talking to Art, go ahead in if you want."

Joe turned to leave. "I better not, I'll wait downstairs," he said, knowing he had no intention of waiting with Doris. Despite the fact that her romance with the boss had been going on for years, Joe still felt uncomfortable around her. Most everybody did. Their affair was so open and intense that Doris had achieved some undeserving status of nobility that made people feel uneasy. And lately things had gotten worse. Joe was certain that Warren was pampering Doris more than ever, allowing her to come and go as she pleased and to shed responsibilities that had been a part of her position for as long as he could remember. On top of that, her recent inclusion in management issues, which Warren made easy by her light workload, left those in the upper echelon wondering where they stood with her.

"Joe," Doris said in a condescending voice.

Joe turned around to see her punching buttons on the telephone with one hand and motioning him back with the other, a snide smile on her make-up laden face.

Warren's unmistakable voice came over the speakerphone.

"Yes," he said.

"Warren, Joe is here, he needs to talk to you."

There was a slight pause.

"Send him in," Warren said.

"Will do," she said hitting a button on the telephone and smiling at Joe like she had just accomplished some great feat. I bet she thinks she earned her pay for the day Joe thought to himself as she continued to beam.

"Thanks," he managed to say softly as he headed for the closed door. Joe hated interrupting meetings and he despised entering rooms when his arrival had just been announced. It was okay if there was only one person, but two or more made him feel uncomfortable, particularly when they were superior to him. Like entering a classroom during a mid-term examination, he would become the center of attention, and worse, he might be put on the spot about what he had come for at a moment that was not right for bringing it up.

Before he was through the door Warren spoke up from behind his desk. "Come in, Joe, sit down."

Joe could feel their eyes on him as he crossed the room, passed between them, and seated himself.

"We were just talking about what a pain in the ass this job you want is," Warren said smiling.

"Oh," Joe said.

"You're damn right, why do you think they call it M-O-M. It's because you've got to be a fucking mother to hundreds of mostly college age kids who are living their dreams by working here for a season's pass."

"That's about it," Art said, "with a few notable exceptions."

"Like me?" Joe said.

Art's face went blank. "Excuse me?"

Joe abandoned his feeble attempt at humor and changed the subject. "I don't think your people are all that bad, I suppose..."

Warren interrupted. "Most of them are nothing but ski bums. They don't know what work is, which your guys do."

Joe didn't say anything, nonetheless pleased that Warren still remembered that snowmaking was a tough job.

"Anyway, are you two spending some time together?" Warren asked.

Joe looked at Art, giving him the opportunity to answer.

"Ah, yeah, we've been getting some time in, but it's tough right now with everything that has been happening. Once things slow down a little we'll have more time. Well, I've got to be on my way," Art said, rising to his feet, "see you gentlemen later."

Warren watched him go, turning to Joe when he disappeared. "So what's up, Joseph?"

"Well, I'm worried about how things are going."

"What do you mean? Everything looks okay to me."

"And it is. But...but one of the new guys, he's a graduate of MIT, he...he and I talked a couple of times recently, he told me he's convinced that the pump house fire hasn't got anything to do with the other incidents."

Warren's demeanor changed instantly. "So what. Who the hell is he? What the hell does he know?"

"Maybe nothing, I just thought..."

Warren interrupted. "Well then, what's the problem? He's got an opinion, everybody does. Is that it?"

"Not really."

"What then?"

"Well, you know how you wanted the environmentalists to be blamed for things, or at least for it to look that way, well, that worked, I guess, but the other night I was talking to Jim about…"

Warren interrupted again. "Who's Jim?"

"Jim? He's the one I'm talking about, the MIT graduate. He replaced a guy that quit the second night. I was talking to him, and I guess one of the other guys overheard us. Jim didn't come right out and say it but he said enough so you'd think he was one of them, an environmentalist I mean, and now there isn't anybody over there that doesn't know it and as I'm sure you can imagine it's causing quite a problem with the crew because they were already convinced the environmentalists were responsible because that's what we decided to do."

"Well is he or isn't he?" Warren asked.

"What?"

"An environmentalist."

"Oh, yeah, I guess he was, once anyway, back at MIT."

"Well that figures, those fucking Massachusetts colleges are nothing but bastions of liberalism. They're breeding grounds for wealthy offspring that have the time and money to devote to causes they don't understand."

"Like I said, he didn't come right out and say it, and I'm pretty sure he doesn't have anything to do with them now, but I guess he was fairly active years ago."

Warren laughed. "Good God, Joe, those fucking bastards are like the Ku Klux Klan. You can't brainwash them into not believing. Fire him while the firing is good."

Joe starred at Warren to see if he was serious but his face remained expressionless.

"Are you sure?" Joe asked, wishing he hadn't mentioned Jim at all.

"Sure I'm serious, why the hell not."

"I'm not sure that would be best, firing him I mean. We were just talking, he's really a pretty good kid, and I'm sure…"

Warren interrupted a fourth time. "Look, Joe, if he's got an agenda which he obviously does, and he's poking his nose into our business, which he obviously is, we simply don't need him. Show him the door. Let him keep his season's pass if you want, but we don't need the likes of him in our midst. We just don't need his type, that's all." Warren paused, cleared his throat and continued. "What I mean, Joe, is that if Jim is at the point where he thinks he knows how to do things better than we do, then it's best for all of us that he be let go. If he's just graduated from MIT then let's face it, he's got a head full of ideas that we just can't afford to contend with right now."

"But it's not really that," Joe said, trying to sound sincere. "I mean, he was trying to help us by talking with me about the incidents, and like I said, I'm pretty sure he doesn't have anything to do with the greens now. It might be to our benefit to have him around, at least until this thing plays itself out."

Warren was getting angry. "Look, Joe, we don't need him, period. You're a capable man, and I'm convinced you're going to make one hell of a Mountains Operations Manager, but you can't be so damn realistic all the time. It sounds like this guy meddled in our business and got himself labeled in the process, which is nothing less than irreversible. You got a problem with the crew courtesy this guy, you said so yourself. The needs of the many outweigh the needs of one. Show him the door."

Joe wasn't happy but he knew better than to argue with Warren. Silently he blamed himself. He never should have told Warren about Jim's noble attempt to upright things.

"Christ, what a day this has been," Warren said opening his bottom desk drawer and taking out a fifth of Dewar's Vodka. Joe concealed his surprise. Is this what it's coming to, he thought?

"You want some?" Warren asked, waving the bottle.

Joe smiled. "No thanks."

Joe knew Warren was a heavy social drinker. Everybody did. Barely a night passed when he didn't have at least a couple of drinks. But keeping a bottle in his desk was new to Joe. He watched Warren pour a couple of ounces into his coffee cup and take a large swallow.

"Ah, ice coffee vodka," he said with a faint smile as he screwed the cap on the bottle and put it back into the drawer.

"Yeah," Joe said trying to think of something to say that would change the subject.

Warren took another generous swallow and spoke.

"So how bad is the problem with the crew?" he asked, being more direct than Joe would have liked.

Joe tipped his head. "It's hard to say. There's a lot of talk right now. I think most of the guys are still pretty wound up by the open ears. It leaves them wondering all the time, if you know what I mean."

"Christ, you'd think they would have settled down by now. It's almost been a month, hasn't it?"

Joe couldn't help his candor. "A month. What do you mean? The pump house burned just last week."

"Yeah, yeah, that's what I meant, a week. So how's it looking for Christmas?"

"Good, real good in fact. We should be a hundred percent, easy. Considering everything that's happened we're lucky, 'course the big storm helped. That reminds me, I was wondering when Jordan will be rebuilt."

Warren pushed his chair several feet away from his desk and leaned back, taking the cup with him, holding it between his legs with both hands.

"Soon," he said.

"What's the hold up, the pumps? I can't imagine it being anything else."

Warren glared at him. "What's the problem with the river, it's an identical set up."

"Oh nothing. There really isn't a difference except the extra mile. I just figured we should have both of them operational. If we hadn't had them both when Jordan burned we'd have been out of business."

"Let me worry about that. Anything else?"

"No."

Warren took another swallow from his cup. "Let me know if you need anything."

"I will, thanks," Joe said getting up.

Warren nodded and took another swig from the cup, emptying it.

Joe turned and left the office without another word being said. As he walked down the stairs he had a feeling that things were going to hell and the worst was yet to come. Not knowing what to do, he went to the store, got a coffee, traded barbs with a couple old timers and small talk with Ethel, and left, arriving at the pump house early. All evening he kept expecting something to happen—the product of his uneasiness—but nothing did.

By the time he left at one o'clock he had arrived at the conclusion that it was only what he knew that made him think things were so very different. Nevertheless he went home with a sinking feeling, wolfed down the meal his mother had left, and went to bed without turning on the television.

*   *   *   *

At eight-thirty the next morning Warren was halfway back from the cafeteria with two toasted bagels, five packets of cream cheese, and a plastic knife, when he realized his instructions to Joe about not using Jim was the wrong thing to do. You keep your friends close and your enemies closer was the thought that popped into his head. Afraid that Joe might have already talked with Jim he decided to call him at home.

Having just returned from the bathroom, Joe was trying to get back to sleep when his mother tapped on his bedroom door and announced the mountain was on the telephone. By the time Joe got to the living room extension he was convinced it was Art calling, so he was surprised to hear Warren's voice.

"Listen, Joe," Warren said, "did you talk to that kid last night about not using him?"

Joe's mind raced. Was Warren going to be angry he hadn't told Jim?

"No, I was going to do it…"

Warren interrupted. "Good, I want you to keep using him, right to the end of the season."

Joe was perplexed by the sudden change and didn't immediately say anything.

"That's not a problem, is it?" Warren asked.

"Oh no, that's fine," Joe said.

"Good. Rest easy."

Joe hung up the telephone. "What the hell," he said softly, rubbing sleep from his eyes. Why would Warren call me at home, which he rarely did, to tell me something that petty?

"Did you say something," his mother called from the kitchen.

"No, nothing."

As he shuffled back to his bedroom in his loose fitting slippers, Joe pondered Warren's instructions, searching for an explanation. But nothing came forth. Climbing back into bed, he expected Warren's change of heart to keep him awake, but it didn't.

*   *   *   *

National Pulp and Paper had fired Dickie after sixteen years on the job. He had been a good worker, but his alcoholism had increasingly taken its toll in recent years. While he knew better than to show up drunk, he kept calling out sick, depleting his available sick leave.

The mill, with a strong employee assistance program in place, stood by him for a long time, trying everything to help him, but he refused, saying he didn't have a problem. While the union initially defended him, he continued to call in sick at the eleventh hour, forcing his coworkers to take overtime they didn't want, or work shorthanded. The mill's personnel director and his few remaining friends did their best to save his pension, but his persistent denial that he had a problem prevented the treatment that an extended leave of absence required. With a continued abuse of sick time, he was fired. Too drunk to show up for his hearing, the termination was validated.

With no job and no skills to get one, Dickie went on general assistance and became increasingly bitter toward the mill, a situation made worse by his continued drinking. He spent his days around town, bad-mouthing National every chance he got. Knowing he had an ax to grind, most people in town didn't pay much attention to him, or they just figured he was drunk or that the booze had affected his mind in a way that made for his crazy talk.

One day while he was at the local garage, a favorite place for those with time on their hands, he was carrying on about the mill to an uninspired audience. Two elderly men sat motionless in metal frame chairs and a third younger man was leaning up against the wall, his legs crossed at the ankles, his hands deep in the pockets of his faded blue jeans. A greasy mechanic, on break, leaned against the door to the shop area drinking a Coke. The owner, an overweight middle-aged man with a kind face, was behind the counter writing out a repair bill. When Doug walked in to pay for the twelve dollars-worth of regular gas he had just pumped at the self-service island, everybody except the owner eyed him while Dickie kept talking.

"Those bastards kept that fire quiet, but surer than shit, it did a lot of damage, more than people know. The plant ain't working right, they're not treating the discharge, least not right, 'course them Jap owners never were ones to do much of anything right. I'm telling you, the place is just fucked up. I don't hold no grudges, but wrong is wrong."

Dickie paused. But since he wasn't talking to anyone in particular, nobody said anything.

"People think I'm just out to get them, but I worked there sixteen fucking years, and I'll tell you, after it got bought things went to hell."

"If you ask me," the mechanic said slowly, "there ought to be a law against them buying up everything, it's a damn shame we're being forced to work for them. Then them running the place into the ground to boot. It just ain't right."

The mechanic's interjection roused Dickie. "That's right, hell, yes," he said, turning toward one of the older men, "you know, you were there, you know what they're like. I mean, hell, they shot us in the back."

Doug pocketed his change and turned toward Dickie. "Are you talking about the mill in Waterford?"

Dickie got defensive. "Yeah, why? You work there or something, mister?"

"Oh no," Doug replied, shaking his head, "I was just," he paused, "curious, thank you just the same."

Doug had wanted to know more but he felt awkward in the setting, and not knowing who the other people were he figured it was best to keep quiet. But as he got into his car and drove off, he found himself wishing he hadn't left so quickly. Maybe the next time he was at the garage he would ask the owner who the guy was.

*   *   *   *

On Friday Joe trained with Art. It wasn't that Art wouldn't be working on Tuesday, because he would be, but Art had said that getting a taste of final preparations for the long Christmas holiday period was more important. After a hectic day that Art said went smoothly, Joe dropped in at the pump house, touched bases with Marty, went home, ate, and was in bed by eight-thirty. He had no idea what time it was when he heard the timid knocking of his mother on the bedroom door. Disoriented, he sat up.

"What?" he called into the darkness.

"Joe, the telephone was just ringing for the second time, I thought it might be the mountain."

Still confused, he pushed the paperback book that was blocking the illuminated numbers on his bedside clock out of the way. Three thirty-seven.

"Okay, I'll call them," he said, groping for the light switch.

By the time he got to his bedroom door, his mother was gone. Dragging himself down the hallway to the living room, he slumped into his mother's big upholstered chair, snapped on the table light, grabbed the Caller ID, and scrolled backwards through its memory. Sure enough, the last two calls were from White Woods. He dialed the pump house. Marty answered.

"Marty, this is Joe, what's up?"

"Yeah, I tried to get you. There really ain't any reason to call, to wake you up I mean, but we figured you needed to know."

"Know what Marty?"

"The fucking phantom got us again."

Joe was irritated Marty wasn't being forthright. "What do you mean?"

"I mean that Pete damn near got himself stiffed. We had more open ears up on Infinity just like before. Same fucking thing all over again. No difference."

Joe leaned back in the big green chair, shivering in the cold that had firmly established itself in the five hours since the last stick of hard-wood had been put on the fire.

"What exactly happened?" Joe asked, trying not to let the hopeless-ness that was consuming him show.

"I don't know the particulars, you'll have to talk to Pete, all I know is that it come loose and he kissed snow. Al's up there with them now talking about it. You want me to see how long he's going to be?"

"No. I'll be right in."

"Well, like I said, there's really no reason. We just figured you needed to know. I'll have Al call you with the particulars if you want."

Joe was definite. "No. I'll be there shortly."

"Suit yourself. I'll tell the boys you're on your way in."

Joe hung up the telephone slowly. "Shit, shit, shit," he said softly as he pushed himself up and went to his bedroom to get dressed, returning to the living room where he put on his boots. Despite his best effort to walk softly, he knew his mother could hear the sound of his heavy boots on the hardwood floor and would start worrying about what was going on. Regardless, he wasn't about to bother her. It was almost five minutes of four when he quietly pulled the door shut and walked to his truck in the still night air.

Arriving at the pump house he found Al and Pete at the control desk talking with Marty. As soon as Joe rounded the corner the trio fell silent, their eyes riveted on him.

"You all right?" he asked Pete, although he was fairly sure of the answer.

"Oh yeah, I dove for it, and Eddie was right at the hydrant. He got it shut down right off."

"Where is Eddie?" Joe asked.

Al answered. "I sent him to help with Leader of the Pack, then the three of them are going to finish Infinity. I figured you'd want to talk with Pete."

Joe nodded. "Yeah, actually, what I need is a written statement. But first tell me what happened."

"Well, we were coming down Infinity, getting good coverage so I probably hadn't moved a gun in the last three or four, we were right on that wide bend, you know, where it's hard to get coverage, so I went to pull the gun out a little further and that's when it happened. Like I said, Eddie was right there, I don't think it was loose more than fifteen, maybe twenty seconds."

"So how many others were affected?"

"Rigged you mean?" Pete said. "The two above, none below."

"So you didn't notice they were open then?"

Pete was defensive. "No, I didn't notice, there was snow on the guns."

"Was that your third run?" Joe asked.

"Second."

Joe frowned. "And those guns were okay the first time down?"

"Al already asked us that. We don't remember."

Joe nodded and looked at Al. "So nobody saw anything then?"

Al shook his head.

"Okay. If you want to come down to my office, Pete, you can do the statement there."

In his office, Joe cleared the corner of the desk nearest his guest chair and laid out a couple statement forms and a stick pen.

"Why don't you get started," Joe said motioning toward the paperwork. "I'll be at the control desk."

Pete sat down on the edge of the chair and fingered the two blank forms. "You want me to do both of these?" he asked.

"If one sheet is enough that's fine but it needs to be detailed."

Pete nodded, picked up the pen, and started writing.

Back at the control desk, Joe looked first at Al, then at Marty. "So what do you think?" he asked.

Al didn't mince his words. "I think we're in deep shit, that's what I think."

"How so?" Joe asked.

"Obviously we got some nut doing this crap, and there ain't much we can do about it."

Joe was still sluggish from the deep sleep he had been roused from just forty minutes earlier. "I don't know about that."

Al frowned. "How do you figure? We got 200, 300 guns going out there at any given time spread out over, what, I don't know, 2,000 acres. This is for your ears only, but we're sitting ducks out there. I don't care how careful we are, if this guy wants to nail us he's going to do it, and I don't see how we can do a damn thing about it."

Joe turned to Marty. "Is that how you see it?"

"That and then some, yeah."

Joe knew he was on the spot. He knew he needed to be decisive and announce his battle plan. But his mind was blank.

"Well, I'll talk to Warren. We'll have to do something," Joe said softly.

"And soon," Al chimed in.

Joe changed the subject. "Are you all set then?" he asked, eyeing the computer screens.

"Yeah, sure. I'll head out," Al said, gathering up his equipment.

Joe returned to his office just as Pete was finishing the statement. He took it from him, not bothering to read it. "You can go home if you want, I won't dock you for it."

Pete shook his head. "Thanks, but I'd just as soon stay, if you don't mind."

"Fine with me."

Silently they walked back to the control desk. Pete passed by Marty without a word, picked up his equipment, and was out the door before Joe spoke.

"I'm going home," he said, not in the mood to talk.

"See ya in church," Marty said, his eyes glued to the TV screen.

*   *   *   *

Doug realized he had made a mistake not to follow up on what he heard at the garage. He decided to go back the next day.

"That was Dickie Short," the garage owner told him.

"If you don't mind me asking, why was he talking about the paper mill in Waterford?"

"Because Dickie is always talking about the mill in Waterford. He worked up there for fifteen, maybe twenty years. They let him go a while back, from what I hear because they had to, but regardless, there's no love lost there, that's for sure."

"He was talking about a fire at the mill. Do you know anything about that?"

"Nope. I didn't hear nothing about that, but you got to consider the source."

The bell rang twice as a late-model Volvo with colorful out of state plates pulled up to the full-serve pumps. The owner headed for the door.

"I wouldn't put to much stock in what Dickie says, he's got an ax to grind," he said as he walked out of the building with Doug close behind.

"Thanks," Doug called after him. Doug didn't want to be a bother or make it seem like he was prying, but neither did he want to leave without finding out everything this time, so he stood on the curbing in front of the station acting as causal as he could. After squeezing an extra dollars-worth of gas into the Volvo's tank, writing up the credit card slip, and giving the driver a confusing set of directions to Ridgeway, the owner went back into the station, seemingly oblivious to Doug's presence. Doug waited for a moment and went in.

"Do you know where I could find Dickie?" he asked.

The owner stopped what he was doing and looked Doug in the eyes for the first time, apparently trying to size up the situation.

Hoping to alleviate the obvious concern the garage owner had about his purpose, Doug said, "I'd just like to chat with him, that's all."

"Yeah, sure, I don't see why not. He's probably over at Doc's having a beer...or two. I bet if you offer to buy him one, he'll tell you whatever it is that you want to know."

"Thanks, I appreciate it."

Doug returned to his car, surprised at how the owner had seemed to go from protecting Dickie to exposing him in one sentence.

Doc's was a small tavern located in the basement of Cannon's lone Laundromat, accessible by a single door near the rear of the building. Except for a small metal sign over the door that was in the shape of a triangle that said Doc's Tavern in faded red paint and a neon Budweiser sign in a side stairwell window, you'd never have known it was there. Doug hesitated to go in. He knew it was where all the locals went, almost like a club, he thought. Wouldn't he feel out of place? He could take off his round wire-rimmed glasses, but his cashmere sweater, creased khaki pants, and shiny loafers were sure to look out of place, and his mannerisms, amplified by awkwardness, would undoubtedly call attention to him.

So he sat in the parking lot at the rear of the building trying to summons the nerve to go in. He tried to convince himself it didn't matter that most every vehicle he could attribute to the tavern's customers was a pick-up truck of some kind, a third of them with snowplows hydraulically hung in mid-air.

Ten minutes had passed when Doug decided if he was going to talk with Dickie he'd have to go in, he'd have to muster the courage to descend the flight of steps that would undoubtedly drop him into surroundings that nothing but his passion for the environment could get him to do.

He was relieved to find it was not as bad as he thought. Other than a few casual looks, nobody paid much attention to him as his feet hit the unpolished tile floor, where he paused, scanning the room for Dickie. When he spotted him at a table in the back talking with two men, he crossed the room to the bar and ordered a draft beer. Halfway through it he approached the man whose words had struck a chord with him 24 hours earlier. At this point, there was no hesitancy in his step or words.

"Excuse me," he said looking at Dickie. "I was at the garage the other day and you were talking about the mill in Waterford."

Dickie looked surprised. "Yeah, so."

"I was wondering if we could talk about what you were saying."

Unfortunately, Dickie seemed to take Doug's inquiry as a goad of some sort, something he had to rise to, probably because of the presence of his buddies.

"What's your interest, you writing a book or something?"

Dickie and the two men laughed loudly, like they could dispel his query by discrediting it.

Doug smiled. "No, I'm interested in…" He hesitated, concerned about mentioning it in front of the others. "I'd just like to talk with you privately."

The two men started to leave and Dickie didn't stop them. The larger of the two, sitting on a bench against the wall, wiggled himself out from behind the rickety table. "They've found out about you Dickie, but don't you worry none, we'll bail you out," he said, righting himself. Clutching their drinks, they left laughing.

Doug sat down. "Can I buy you a beer?" he asked.

With his hands cupping his almost empty beer mug, Dickie squirmed in his chair. "What's this all about?" he said in an irritated voice, eyeing the departure of his friends.

Doug decided to back up and start from the beginning, regretting he hadn't handled it better to begin with.

"I'm Doug Andrews, I live here in town, here in Cannon, and I'm on the Natural Environmental Council. When I was at the garage last week you were talking about how they were discharging untreated water at the mill, at National, that's what I'm interested in, nothing more. This has nothing to do with you personally, nothing, I'm only interested in the mill."

Dickie's demeanor changed immediately, so much so that Doug kicked himself for not being straightforward in the first place. Doug had not considered that the bony little man before him was probably on unemployment or worker's compensation and he thought that Doug was the investigator sent to prove he was unworthy to receive his next check. Even though he knew better, he hadn't put himself in Dickie's shoes, something every investigator was a fool not to do.

"Well, ya," Dickie said, "a lot went on up there that nobody knows about, I could tell you stories you wouldn't believe."

For the better part of an hour Doug picked Dickie's brain. While it took some effort to keep him from rambling, Doug got far more information that he figured on. Even if only half of it was right, he had a lot. As he drove home he thought about how his curiosity had paid off. If it was big enough, and it might just be, it would help him win the seat on the council board of directors that he was vying for. If it was blatant enough the national organization might be called in. Not bad, Doug thought, for an afternoon's work and the cost of three beers.

*   *   *   *

Things were starting to wear Joe down. He no longer enjoyed being at work. His last date with Brenda had been weeks ago, and despite the fact she had called him three times, he hadn't returned her calls, which bothered him. But for some reason he just couldn't bring himself to do anything but the basics. It was the same at home. His mother knew when to keep her distance, but with his share of the chores mostly undone, she couldn't help but complain, which only made things worse. Increasingly, Joe found himself biting his lip, a nervous habit he had kicked years before. Mostly he nibbled on it, like he used to, but every now and then he'd latch onto a sizable chuck of skin and bite it out, grimacing from the pain and the taste of his own blood. But somehow, he kept going, hoping his state of mind didn't show, expecting things to get better. But they didn't. When he got to work Saturday afternoon Joe was surprised to find Marty already there.

"What brings you in early?" Joe asked, expecting Marty to say he had been delivering firewood and finished up ahead of time.

"I wanted to fill you in on things before anybody got here."

"Oh?"

"Yeah. The thing last night and the other stuff has got the guys up in arms. It's not good."

Joe frowned. "I can't say I blame them, but what can we do about it that we're not doing. Suspend operations?"

"It ain't that simple, Joe, it's more than that, they don't figure you're doing anything about it, and I can't fault them for feeling the way they do. Some of them think maybe you've forgotten what it's like to be out on the mountain."

Joe held his tongue and clenched his teeth, grinding them together harder than he ought to. What Marty said hit home. Joe's pride and joy was being on the mountain, and he went to great lengths to avoid being tagged with the very thing Marty just pinned on him.

"They don't mean no disrespect or nothing," Marty continued, obviously enjoying the chance to belittle Joe. "But it ain't no god damn secret that you're fancying to be Mountain Operations Manager. The guys haven't been taking too kindly to you spending so much time with that fellow, I mean, it'd be one thing if everything was going slick, but it ain't."

"You mean the crew thinks there is a connection between me…"

Marty interrupted. "It don't matter if there is or not, Joe, that's what they're thinking."

"That me not being here a day or two a week is to blame?" Joe couldn't help the sarcasm in his voice. He wanted to tell Marty that his small number of absences had more to do with expansion meetings and personal matters than training with Art, but something held him back. Probably that he couldn't blame the crew for thinking there was a connection. After all, his sudden absences, which in previous years would have been unheard of, had coincided with the flurry of incidents that had transformed the season into a mess.

"They're not saying you not being here is the cause. What I heard them saying was that you ain't paying attention to things."

"Like what?"

"Just everything. The guys think if you hadn't blamed Alan and Jason the first time, Andrew would have come forward sooner and maybe there would have been something to go on. Then when John got hurt and it was obviously an intentional thing, and all you did was a report but nothing else…"

Joe held up his hand, interrupting Marty. He didn't like defending himself, but he felt he had to. "A lot more than that was done and you know it. We reported the incidents to the police, we got one of the day-shift security officers, and we put a lot of effort into identifying who and why, it just didn't produce anything that's all. What else is bothering them?"

"Well, you yourself fingered the greens for it, and you know damn well that little runt with the earring is one of them. I don't believe for a minute that he had anything to do with it, but some of the guys do. Regardless, they think you favor him."

The pump house door slammed, signaling an end to their conversation.

"We'll talk later," Joe said, as he started for his office, not bothering to wait and see who had just arrived.

Despite what Marty said, the evening progressed normally. If things were so bad, the crew certainly was doing a good job of hiding it. But by nine o'clock Joe had reached the conclusion that if there was animosity toward him, it was likely coming from the second shift. When Al arrived Joe called him to his office before he had time to talk with Marty.

"What's going on with the crew? I understand they're not happy."

If Al was surprised by Joe's inquiry, he didn't show it. "Yeah, the guys are really down about things, especially after last night. If you want to know the truth, they're getting on your case."

"Yeah?"

"They don't think you're doing your job, right or wrong, Joe, the guys are blaming you, talking about a vote of no confidence, that kind of thing."

Joe was speechless. A vote of no confidence. That was what the faculty at Waterford High School had done to the principal last fall. By second semester he was gone.

Al was talking again. "I know they don't understand, but put yourself in their shoes, the whole damn season has been screwed up. They're worried, maybe scared would be a better word for it. They know John ain't never going to be right again. They got families to think about."

Joe wished he felt angry or challenged or sad. Those were active emotions that could be dealt with. But he felt drained, like an empty shell drifting into darkness.

"Don't worry about it," he somehow managed to say. Then, rising to his feet, he said, "I've got things to do."

"Sure," Al said as he got up and left.

Joe closed the door and sat down at his desk. Al, and Marty for that matter, were right. He couldn't blame the crew after everything they had been through, but neither were things his fault.

What if they take a vote of no confidence? I'd be finished, he reasoned. Warren would never let me handle the hundreds of employees that Mountain Operations Manager is responsible for if I can't manage the snowmaking crew. With his elbows propped on the desk, he buried his face in his big hands, lightly brushing his eyebrows with the tips of his fingers. Maybe he should give up on becoming Mountain Operations Manager. Just the thought of it gave him a sinking feeling, but maybe it was the only way. He couldn't let things continue the way they were. He couldn't risk things getting worse. He had to do something. The crew needed to know he was taking care of things. Before something else happened, he had to take decisive action.

*   *   *   *

Of all the things Dickie said about the mill, it was what he first mentioned at the garage—the fire and apparent discharge of untreated wastewater—that interested Doug most. He planned to talk it over with Kay on their way to the state council meeting, held the third Sunday of every month. In deference to Christmas, most everybody had argued for a December recess, but the chair insisted there was too much going on to skip a meeting, and since nobody had called for a vote, the meeting was taking place as scheduled.

After a quick stop at the store for coffee and a box of powdered donuts, Doug started for Bangor, not worried about drinking and eating on what was sure to be a deserted highway.

Doug had already told Kay the gist of his conversation with Dickie, but he relished the idea of discussing it at length, doing what Kay called beating it to death. Despite the fact they had fifty-five miles to travel, he wasted no time bringing it up.

"So what do you think about the mill?" he asked, not waiting for an answer. "I can't imagine them doing it."

"I can," she said, "who'd know? Remember what they said at the council meeting last fall, I think it was the October meeting, they were saying the state has cut back so much that they don't do any inspections or anything, the mills are self-reporting now."

"Yeah," Doug said.

Kay continued. "I suppose they'd have to alter the records, but think about it, if the state is depending only on what they supply, there aren't any checks and balances, nothing."

"You're right, it's like the clear cutting ban, what good is it if there isn't any enforcement? That's why I keep advocating for monitors. We need to organize that. If we don't ensure compliance, who will?"

"True."

"Do you want another donut?" Doug asked as they sped by the town line marker.

"No thanks, I've had enough."

Doug wasn't convinced the mill was up to no good, which Kay sensed.

"Don't forget the Backyard Theory," she said. "These companies are always doing stuff wrong, and it's always in somebody's backyard, but people often don't look there. This time it may be in ours."

Doug knew she was right, but something made him leery of getting involved, which wasn't like him. It must be Dickie he thought. If somebody else, maybe a council member, had told him about it, wouldn't he believe it? Of course he would.

"Honey, your coffee is getting cold," Kay said.

"Yeah."

"And you've got some sugar on your pants."

Doug rubbed it away. "You know, I bet my interest in this is waning because of Dickie, I mean, he did get fired for alcoholism. You got to be really bad to get fired for that today. Maybe he's not credible. Other than what he says, there's nothing you know."

"Which is exactly why you need to work on it, to find out if there is anything there. Maybe there is and maybe there isn't, but it's surely worth following through on."

"Yeah, I'm going to talk with some of the guys at the meeting, get their angle on it."

When Kay changed the subject, commenting on the stacks of unsold Christmas trees at a roadside farm stand, Doug didn't bring up the mill again.

By one o'clock the meeting was over and they headed home.

"I don't know if you noticed, but I was disgusted with the discussion at the end. I was ready to walk out," Doug said.

"You mean the North Woods thing?"

"What else," Doug said.

"What exactly is it anyway?"

Doug looked at Kay and smiled. "Fantasy," he said, pausing before he continued. "Essentially they want to prohibit new development, which means building of any kind, in an area north and west of Bangor, about five million acres total."

Kay nodded. "I see what you mean, that is rather significant."

"You're darn right it is. And Patrick, Joan, The Rivards, they're obviously preparing to lead another radical shove-it-down-their-throats type campaign, and this one," he paused, "this one I don't even support. It's crazy. I mean it's nothing more than a taking of private land. But what bothers me most is that we'll lose, lose the cause and lose long term. We're going to get labeled as extremists and that won't get us anything."

Kay smiled. "Aren't *we* on a soap box this afternoon."

"It's just that the extreme stuff gets to me. There has to be middle ground, to some extent, otherwise it's just another battle that nobody wins. Don't you think people will take up arms over the pact?"

"Oh, sure they will, and I agree with you about them, but they think it's the only way."

Doug sighed. "If we want to achieve anything we've got to be willing to work within the system, this all or nothing stuff is pointless."

"But you've got to be able to show at least a majority of them that we aren't compromising ourselves, that we aren't accepting something less than definitive structural change. They're leery of anything short of that. They don't buy into the installment approach."

"But it's the only way to get anything done. You have to nibble at these things and be satisfied. It doesn't mean you're any less committed to taking big bites."

"But it's more than that, honey. Don't you think it's ideology?"

Doug sighed again. "I suppose."

"It's the same old story. Take recycling, we've got friends who think establishing a recycling center is a major accomplishment, and we've got friends who would rather be working to eliminate wasteful packaging. As far as I'm concerned, both are worthy."

Doug shook his head, switching hands on the steering wheel. "I won't budge on the need for moderation. Anytime you propose something extreme, there's a backlash and that's when people organize and fight you and nothing gets done, nothing. We simply aren't in a position not to care about people, jobs, communities, and yes, even private landowner rights. If we seem apathetic to those things we lose mainstream public support. We get labeled as uncaring."

"You should talk like this at a meeting."

"Yeah, right."

"No, I mean it, you should. I know we've discussed this before, but they need to hear it. If they understood you, I bet more than a handful would come your way."

"Maybe." Doug thought for a moment before he spoke, "You know, twenty years ago it was socially acceptable to drive drunk and smoke anywhere you happened to be. Look at how things have changed today. That change was the product of widespread acceptance that those things were bad. That's what has to happen for meaningful change that lasts, most all of us have to sign on. If we had tried twenty years ago to make alcohol illegal to deal with the menace of drunk drivers, wouldn't we have failed like we did in prohibition? Well, in my opinion that's what the pact is, prohibition. It just won't work."

"Well said. I wish I had a tape recorder."

Doug shook his head. "Right."

"Like I said, you need to be heard."

"Yeah, but that requires a pulpit. We'll see."

Anxious to change the subject, Doug had an idea. "Why don't we take a ride past the mill and see if we can get a look at the river."

"Good idea."

Doug wasn't too familiar with the area, but he was fairly sure that Route 202 went to Waterford. He was right. An hour later they passed by the fringes of downtown Waterford and stopped for a red traffic signal at the intersection of Route 2, where they studied the mill's sprawling complex that was spread before them. A minute later, they were jolted by a short, loud horn blast. Doug's eyes darted from the traffic signal, which was green, to the rear view mirror. Despite the sunglasses the woman driver behind him wore, he could see annoyance in her face. Quickly, he snapped on the directional and turned right, waving his hand in apology, a gesture he knew she might take as derogatory, which was why Doug was relieved when she turned left.

Above the mill a green two lane suspended bridge carried Route 2 traffic across the Salem River, where a cluster of aging homes and businesses, most of which hugged the highway, quickly faded, giving way to rolling hills and thick forest. Doug turned around and drove back to the bridge, stopping halfway across. The river was fairly wide here, probably forty feet across; its steep banks thick with bushes and vines. Three hundred yards down, it made a sweeping left turn, and disappeared. Doug estimated the mill was probably a quarter mile further down river. For the second time that afternoon, a horn sounded behind them.

"Honey," Kay said.

Doug glanced in the rear view mirror, purposely not seeking out a face, and accelerated hard. Passing the main entrance of the mill a minute later, Doug looked in the rear view mirror again, hoping the car behind him would turn in. It did.

With the road to himself again, Doug slowed down, bumping over the set of railroad tracks that crisscrossed the highway, his eyes scanning the outskirts of the mill's yard, hoping for a glimpse of the river. But there was nothing but endless piles of debarked wood logs stacked end to end and dark brown box cars loaded with rolls of paper, all of which ended abruptly at a ten foot high chain link fence.

Doug kept driving and they both kept looking, but the modest homes and businesses that lined Route 2 along its right side were on shallow lots, their rear property lines thickly forested. Two miles out, where he figured there was little chance of finding access to the river within sight of the mill, he made a tight Y turn on a straight-away and started back.

"Unless there's a road in from the other side, which doesn't look to be the case," Doug said, "I don't see how we can get a look at the river at the point of discharge, or even below it for that matter."

Kay nodded.

"Short of trespassing on foot that is," Doug added.

"I think you're right."

Back at the intersection of Route 202, Doug pulled into the empty parking lot of The Mill Diner.

"What do you say we eat here?" he said, motioning toward the diner with his head.

"I'm game if you are."

"You make it sound like we'll be taking a chance."

"No. Being right here they probably do a lot of business, and it's well maintained."

Doug nodded. "Let's do it."

They sat in a small booth at one end of the mostly deserted diner. The waitress, who was the only employee in sight, was talkative. She explained to them that staying open Sunday afternoons and evenings was something new they were trying.

"We're open seven days a week for breakfast and lunch, we open up at four in the morning," she said, almost like she was proud of it. "We've always closed at two, but we figured we should see if folks were interested in Sunday dinner, so anyway, here we are."

"How's it going?" Doug asked.

"Well, you can see, but it's only been a couple of weeks, maybe word hasn't got around yet. Anyway, it's nice to see you folks, what can I get for ya, the meat loaf is on special."

"Why don't we just have coffee and look at the menu," Doug said.

"Oh sure," she said smiling. "I guess I need to change gears doing this Sunday stuff. The guys from the mill just want to dig in. Two coffees it is."

As she marched off Doug and Kay looked at each other and grinned.

They had hardly read half the menu when she was back, placing steaming unmatched mugs of coffee before them, and unloading a half dozen containers of cream from her apron pocket that she deposited in the center of the table.

"You folks from around here?" she asked.

"No, we're up from Cannon," Doug said.

"Oh, skiers?" she asked, backing slightly away from the table.

"No, we live there," Doug answered.

"So what brings ya up this neck of the woods? Sunday driving?"

She was obviously lonely. She would tell them later that she wasn't used to not having customers to talk to, and Bob, who was her husband and the cook, was watching a football game in the kitchen.

"Kind of," Kay answered, looking at Doug.

"Actually we came up to check out the mill," Doug said.

"You fixing on working there or something?" the waitress asked.

Doug gave her a warm smile. "No, nothing like that. You've been here a long time, right?"

"Twenty years next summer," she said proudly.

"If you don't mind then, what's your opinion of the new owners of the mill?" Doug asked, purposely fielding an open question.

The waitress had her answer on the tip of her tongue. "Just that it's a crying shame it ever sold. The people who work there are scared, real scared. They're not putting anything much back into it which makes ya wonder. But heck, we ain't nothing more than a pebble on the beach to that company. They don't care about the mill, they don't care about this town."

"So that's pretty much what bothers people then, that it might close?" Doug asked.

"I think the worst of it is, you don't know what they're going to do. It's the not knowing that bothers folks the most."

Doug nodded. "So they're not putting anything back into the plant?"

"That's right. Most of us feel they're running the place into the ground."

"Which must create a lot of problems."

"Sure it does."

"What about a fire over there recently?"

The waitress thought for a moment. "Yeah, there was one the beginning of the month. They were mopping up when we opened."

"Where in the plant was it?" Doug asked.

The waitress frowned. "That I don't know. But I don't think it caused much damage. The boys were talking it up as another example of their corner-cutting way of running that place."

"So you don't remember anything else about it?" Doug asked.

"The fire. No, can't say that I do. But like I said, it couldn't have amounted to much."

"That's interesting, thank you," Doug said, sitting up in his seat. Then, turning to Kay he asked, "are you ready to order, dear?"

"Yes, I'm going to have the meat loaf." Kay said.

"I'll have the same."

"Good choice, it's my favorite," the waitress said.

Doug hoped to talk to her again about the mill, but she didn't return to their table until she served their meals, and by then she was busy with two other tables—a family of five and an old man who didn't look like he could afford to be there.

It was just past three o'clock when they finished eating, paid the bill, left a three-dollar tip, and headed for home. Three miles down Route 2 Doug braked hard and made a right turn onto a side road.

"What's wrong?" Kay asked, surprised by the sudden change in direction.

Doug shook his head. "Nothing, I just thought I might be able to get a look at the river down here."

Doug didn't know where the road would take them, but he knew that if he headed generally west they were likely to find the river. Two miles in, the road got narrow and bumpy and the mostly shoddy looking trailers disappeared, leaving only tin-roofed farm houses with peeling paint and sagging barns every mile or so.

They came to a four corners and kept going. The road was gravel now, but that didn't concern Doug. Lots of roads weren't paved and Doug loved exploring them, especially when he had a purpose like he did today.

Nothing much bothered Doug about these roads except mud. He had traveled enough of them in his 47 years to have a good idea of what laid ahead. Like signs on a highway, there were signs on these roads too, if you knew how to read them.

If it stayed wide, at least a lane and a half in most places, and the grass and trees that lined its sides didn't encroach on the shoulders too much, it was usually worth staying on, especially if there were a lot of lines on the utility poles. Of course, if there weren't any poles you could figure there wasn't much of anything civilized in your path and you probably ought to be turning around. But none of that mattered in winter. If it was plowed, then it went somewhere. This road was plowed well, its banks winged back, which probably meant it was a public way. So Doug sailed along, occasionally eyeing Kay, enjoying the countryside, thinking about what the waitress had said. They were three miles from the four corners when Doug eased the BMW to a stop several feet shy of a big pile of snow, emblazoned with the outline of a snowplow, that sat across the road.

"Well, we're not going to get to the river this way, now are we."

Kay laughed. "I guess not. Talk about dead ends."

Doug sat upright in his seat, pulling on the steering wheel with his left hand to raise himself higher. "Looks like it keeps going for a while, but there's probably only summer camps beyond here," he said, making note that the utility poles supported only two wires, one telephone and one electrical.

Doug turned around in the ample area made by the plow and headed back.

"You know," he said, "it's possible there isn't winter access to the river. I can't think of a bridge between here and Madison. It's hard to believe, but I can't place one."

Kay ignored Doug's comment. "I know, why don't we ski in sometime, it'd be fun."

"You mean to the river...yeah, that's a good idea," Doug said. "We could take a lunch, make a day of it. We haven't taken a long cross country trip for a while."

"With Christmas coming up we ought to try to have the shop open every day, so I don't know when." Kay meant what she said about keeping the shop open, but also, selfishly, she wanted the trip to be after Christmas. Doug's big present was a new cross country ski outfit she just knew he was going to love, and the trip would be a perfect time to try it out.

"I suppose, although we never seem to do much business before Christmas."

"I know, but if the skiing conditions aren't good, people gravitate to town, you know how it is. I guess we'll have to do it after vacation."

"I'd rather not wait that long. What about Christmas day? The afternoon is always so dull."

"Fine with me. So it's a date then?" Kay said smiling.

Since high school, saying that had come to symbolize the time Doug had first asked Kay on a date. They were just 15. Doug had finally collected the nerve to ask her to the movies, and despite his uneasiness he had done okay. She had agreed to Friday at seven at her house. But instead of saying something like "see you then," Doug blurted out, "so it's a date then?" in a questioning tone of voice.

"It's a date," Doug replied.

Chapter 11

▼

The Past

By the time Joe got to work Sunday afternoon, he had made up his mind to call Warren, but it was nine o'clock before he got up the nerve to do it. Warren's pleasant-sounding wife answered the telephone on the second ring.

"I'm sorry to bother you so late, but I was wondering if Warren was available."

"Oh, it's no bother, Joe. Let me get him for you, hold on."

Joe heard the telephone handset being laid down, and faintly he could hear her footsteps as she walked to get Warren. As he waited, Joe thought to himself that maybe he should have put off talking to Warren until tomorrow, after all, what did he have that couldn't wait? But just as he started to cool to the idea of having called, his concerns rushed back to the forefront, and he felt himself getting angry.

"Hi, Joseph, what's up? Have we got a problem?"

"No, everything is fine. I'm sorry to bother you at home, but I need to discuss some things with you."

The fact that Joe hadn't called for a specific reason immediately agitated Warren, particularly since he was half way through his fifth martini of the evening. His tone of voice made Joe want to hang up. "Like what?"

"Well, we had another incident of open ears Friday night, a hose got loose, and just missed one of the guys."

Warren didn't say anything, so Joe spoke again. "Maybe I should have waited until tomorrow, but I'm worried about another accident. I mean, who knows what might happen. The liability would be enormous for us, for all of us."

Joe hoped that his mention of liability would get Warren's attention, but it didn't.

"Is that it?" he asked.

"Yeah, and everything that's been happening lately, we could be headed for trouble, things just aren't good. The crew is getting real antsy."

Joe wasn't satisfied with what he had said. It was too vague. He realized it had been a mistake to call, but decided not to back down now. Warren remained silent. Joe thought he could hear him breathing.

"I just thought you needed to know how bad things have gotten," he added.

"Be in my office at nine, no, that wouldn't be good for you would it, make it two tomorrow, we'll see you then."

"Okay," Joe said as the line went dead.

Although he felt a little better, Joe regretted calling Warren. Maybe he had come on too strong. He knew how much Warren valued loyalty and despised those who didn't practice it. But he hadn't betrayed him, had he? What if Warren didn't see it that way? Too often, Joe knew, he left his thoughts, his feelings, his intentions, unspoken, and was surprised later when people didn't know about them. Maybe he should have explained himself better. But it was too late now.

Disgusted, he planned to leave work early. At quarter of twelve he started his truck to warm it up, and left ten minutes later, lighting the cigar he had prepared earlier. Because the long Christmas holiday period was in full swing, the mountain was buzzing with activity. Joe had intended to go home, but instead he drove through town, marveling at the cars that lined the streets and filled the parking lots of the restaurants and bars.

No matter how many times he bore witness to the winter transformation of Cannon, he was always charmed by it. Which wasn't true of everybody. Most people, Joe knew, were barely tolerant of the town being taken away from them during ski season. Like living with the smell of a paper mill for its economic benefits, the 1,238 citizens of Cannon were forced to accept traffic delays and long lines, which, by their standards, were considerable.

But to Joe, variety was the spice of life. Hence, he didn't mind the metamorphosis. After cruising the downtown area, taking some streets twice to hit them all, he headed out of town on the state road, planning on doubling back on the Gore Road. The Gore Road had no street lights, and most of the houses were set back into the woods, so it was pretty much eleven miles of darkness, a perfect time for Joe to figure things out, maybe to think of what it was that he needed to do, indeed, should be doing, to hold all that was dear to him together.

He wasn't the top dog, the buck stops here kind of boss, but he was in a divisional leadership position. If things were going awry he felt he should be able to do something about it, irrespective of others. It was his duty and it was his desire. Sucking on a half smoked unlit cigar, with the truck rattling over pot holes and frost heaves, he went over the incidents as he remembered them and racked his brain for what he must be missing. But the stop sign that signaled his arrival back at the state road made him realize that maybe the solution, if there was one, wasn't in the cards he had been dealt, at least not yet.

As he approached home, the eternal optimism that always seemed to take precedence over him kicked in and he smiled, sure of only one thing. Whatever he had once was damn near gone. He stayed up late that evening watching a three-hour movie he'd seen twice before. After a restless night of tossing and turning, he got up at noon, and headed for the mountain. When he walked into Warren's office, Dwight was there.

Warren motioned to an empty chair. "Sit down, Joseph. Considering what you said last night, I've asked Dwight to join us."

Joe's mind reeled. What had he said last night that was so bad? "I guess I don't understand," he managed to say.

"You made some statements about liability. Under the circumstances I need a witness," Warren said as Dwight got up and quietly closed the door.

Joe didn't know what to say. Should he act normal, appearing not to be care about Dwight's presence, or should he refuse the meeting at this point? There was no time to debate it; Warren was looking right at him, like a deer caught in headlights.

"It's just that I've been worried lately, real worried about the way things have been going," he said, trying to sound causal. "Like I told you on the telephone, we had another incident Friday night, Pete came close to getting hit. It just doesn't seem to me that anybody is doing a darn thing about it. It's obvious we got a problem. That's all I meant about liability."

Joe paused. He was sure there was hostility in the squinted blue eyes that looked back at him from across the cluttered desk. He didn't dare look toward Dwight, he was too close for that kind of eye contact. He figured they were letting him get things off his chest, letting him have his say. It made sense to keep talking. The words came easier now.

"I just think we ought to be pulling out all the stops to get whoever is doing this, but it doesn't seem to me that we've done anything to speak of. I'm the one that's getting blamed, but I can't do anything more than I've already done."

He was talking too fast now. Anything worth saying was worth saying well, and that meant breathing. But he had to get it out so they understood. This was his chance to be heard, so he went on despite the fact his thoughts weren't collected.

"I know that them blaming me doesn't mean anything, they got to blame somebody. I think they're just scared and afraid to admit it, and I don't blame them one bit, being scared I mean, considering what has happened and still could. I guess that's the whole problem, it would be different if it was over, but it isn't, and I just don't want to sit around and wait for another guy to get crippled. John was a decent guy, and look at him now, he'll never be right again. He's lost some of the things he loved most in life—hunting, fishing—at least for the time being. He didn't deserve that, it shouldn't have happened, it just shouldn't have." Joe paused, unable to continue, his voice cracking with emotion. He could feel his eyes getting moist. "I'm sorry, it just bothers me," he added, resisting the temptation to wipe his eyes.

The anger that had been behind each word only a minute before had slipped away now, and Joe fell silent, knowing he had to hold himself together no matter how strongly he felt, no matter how much it ripped him apart inside.

Warren shifted slightly in his big chair, cleared his throat, and spoke, unmoved by what Joe had said. "It's Art's job that is really bothering you, that's what this is all about, isn't it, Joe?"

Joe tried to maintain eye contact with Warren but he couldn't, so he substituted Warren's nose for his eyes, which made it seem like Joe was looking at him. "No, it's not that," Joe said, feeling a little angry again at not being understood. "I've considered giving…" His voice trailed off, unable to recite his thoughts about forsaking the job of Mountain Operations Manager. "You know we haven't done enough about this."

"Don't tell me what I know," Warren shot back.

"I just meant that…"

Warren interrupted him. "We've had years of unprecedented growth here, we're on the verge of one of the largest expansions ever, and revenues this season are far ahead of last, you tell me what the hell is wrong with that."

Joe couldn't believe what Warren had said. "Well, if that's all you care about, then there isn't much sense in me being here," he said, twisting the ring on his finger.

Dwight spoke for the first time, before either of them could.

"Excuse me, Joe, I don't mean to interrupt, but you don't have a sole proprietorship on caring about our employees, the mountain, and the like. We're all interested in those things. What it sounds to me like, sitting here listening to you, is that you've let things build up inside you a bit too much and now it's all coming out. You have expectations, Joe, which I'll be the first to admit haven't been fulfilled this season, but let's put things into perspective."

What Dwight said made sense, but Joe still felt a need to defend himself. "I know my expectations are higher than most, but nothing has gone right this year, nobody seems to care about John."

Dwight's tone of voice became decidedly compassionate. "It was very unfortunate what happened to John and we're all deeply concerned about his future just as we are about the safety of all your people. We're frustrated just like you about this thing. I was talking to Warren about it just the other day, but honestly, I don't think we can do anything that we haven't already. It's one of those things that just has to run its course and it will. Do you have any suggestions of what we might do?"

Joe shrugged his shoulders.

Dwight continued in earnest, inspired that his mediation was working. "It sounds to me like we've got a bit of a blame game going and you've unfairly taken the brunt of it, Joe. Couple that with your high standard of care, which is something we all value very much, and you have the ingredients for feeling pretty horrible."

"I suppose," Joe said, not really meaning it. Any other time what Dwight had said would have satisfied him, but not this time. He didn't know what it was inside him that remained fed up, but he knew full well that no combination of sympathetic words were going to fix it, not now anyway. He didn't say anything more. There was no need.

"We must stick together on this thing and see it through," Dwight said. "If you have any ideas on how to proceed don't hesitate to give me a ring, Joe, anytime, even at the house. And feel free to call just to talk if you need to."

Joe nodded.

"Perhaps we've talked enough for one day," Warren said, forcing a smile at Joe. "Think about things and for Christ sakes don't burn any bridges."

Like Warren, Joe put on a smile before he left, not wanting to box himself into any set course in the future. He knew he was in the midst of a volatile situation that could change at any moment.

The brevity of the meeting left Joe with more than an hour to kill so he headed for the store. Joe was aware he was slowly falling apart, but what he didn't realize was that Ethel had known it for sometime. When he dragged himself into the store that afternoon, wearing a tired, troubled face, she brought it up just as soon as he got to the counter with his coffee.

"You just don't seem to be yourself, Joe. Is something bothering ya?"

"No. I guess I'm just tired."

"It's more than that, Joe, ain't it?" she said, handing him a quarter and two dimes.

Joe knew the store was empty so he could talk if he wanted to. But it wasn't like him to share his personal life, certainly not his personal problems, with anyone. You kept things like that in the family.

"Not really."

But Ethel was persistent. "I'm not one to pry, Joe, you know that, but you've been acting different lately. If you don't mind me saying so, I'm worried about you, naturally I didn't say anything right off, but it's been going on a while now."

Joe was avoiding eye contact when he knew he shouldn't, pouring his change from palm to palm. "I'm okay, really," he finally managed to say.

Ethel knew better. "I watched you grow up from behind this counter, Joe. You were two weeks old when your mum brought you in for the first time. I remember her carting you around while she did her shopping, singing to ya. She always boasted that you took your first step in the canned goods aisle," she said, waving toward the side of the store. Ethel was smiling now, taken with her own reminiscing. Leaning into the counter, she continued. "I remember after church you and your brother, all done up in Sunday best, would come in for a coke and candy bar. Every Sunday, year in and year out. It was just the sweetest thing."

Joe could feel himself blushing. He was at a loss for words. So he pocketed the coins for something to do.

"I'm just trying to say, Joe, that I know ya well enough to know something is tugging at ya."

Joe took a deep breath. "There's just a lot of things going on right now," he said, fishing a few tidbits of waste paper from the penny cup and rolling them into a little ball between his fingers.

"At the risk of prying, I know it's the mountain that's got you blue, and heaven knows, with what's been happening up there you got every right, but it don't do an old lady no good to see you like this. I'm fit to be tied, Joe, so I'm gonna tell ya something, something I think ya need to know."

His interest piqued, Joe looked at Ethel with raised eyebrows.

"I think maybe it might make sense to talk to Buck about the old days," she said slowly.

Confused, Joe remained silent.

"It's probably nothing, but I've racked my brain and it's all I can think of. I've always felt that things happen for a reason. You probably don't know it, but White Woods had a colorful past, which might shed some light on what's been going on. Like I said, it's probably nothing, but it's worth a try." Ethel's tone of voice was solemn now, her eyes penetrating. "And if you want to talk about things, I'm all ears," she added. "I ain't done nothing much with my life except tend store, so I don't reckon I got too many answers for ya, but I'm a good listener."

"Yeah, I appreciate that," Joe said.

"I mean it. And talk to Buck."

"I will. Well, I better get going," Joe said.

Ethel leaned over the wide wooden counter, something she rarely did, and clamped here wrinkled hand down on the smooth blue nylon of Joe's bulky coat sleeve and squeezed hard enough so he really felt it. "Just remember, Joe, snow made that mountain, and you made the snow."

Joe smiled faintly and nodded, holding still until she let go. "Thanks," he said.

Then, without another word, he turned away and walked out. It was obvious from the way Ethel talked that things were worse than he knew at the mountain, but despite that, he felt better, a lot better. Maybe things weren't insurmountable. After all, he wasn't the one at fault, and he had to stop acting like he was.

Joe was anxious to get out on the mountain and find Buck, who had been transferred to first shift, but he didn't want it to look like he had a mission, so he hung around the pump house until quarter of five and set out on his sled to locate him, foregoing the use of the radio that would only arouse interest amongst his crew and Buck's.

He got lucky, finding him almost immediately halfway up Starburst. Joe pulled up parallel to him on the steep incline, slowing down to match Buck's tilling speed. He could barely see him in the cab motioning but Joe knew what he meant. He didn't want to stop on the grade. Joe shook his head and raced off to a level area a couple hundred yards up and stopped. Swinging his feet to one side, he fished a cigar out of his inside jacket pocket and waited. A minute later the groomer crested the rise and the tiller went silent as the machine crawled to a stop. Buck threw open his door.

"Hey, Joe, what's up?" he bellowed, beaming from ear to ear.

Joe was off his sled and walking toward the groomer.

"I need to talk to you about something, it may take a while if that's all right."

"Sounds serious," Buck said. "Sure, hop in." Buck turned and reached across the cab, pushing open the passenger's side door. Joe pulled himself across the groomer's wide track and hoisted himself into the seat, flinging the cigar onto Buck's lap as he slammed the door shut.

"Hey, thanks," Buck said, tucking the cigar lengthwise under the lip of the visor. "I'll have it after my supper."

"Sure, anytime," Joe said.

"So what's on your mind?" Buck asked.

"Well, I need to talk to you about things that happened years ago," Joe said softly, not knowing what kind of response to expect.

"So you've been talking to Ethel about the old days?"

"Yes, kind of, I mean, it came up."

"The past has a way of doing that, don't it?"

"Yeah, I guess."

"No good ever comes of it getting dredged up, you know."

Joe shrugged, unsure of what to say. "Ethel didn't say much, just that I should talk to you about it."

"Yeah, well, there ain't too many people still here that remember that, but those of us who are still around, like Ethel, certainly were in the thick of it, no question about that. I'm curious, though, why she would mention it to you?"

Joe didn't figure he should pull any punches with Buck. "Just regarding how it might relate to things right now."

There was a long pause before Buck spoke. "I think I know what you mean, Joe, without putting you on the spot that is."

Joe wondered what he meant, but decided not to ask. "So you don't mind sharing it with me then?"

Buck's lips tightened. Again there was a prolonged silence. "I'll tell you about it, Joe, if you think it will help ya. Where do you want me to start?"

Joe shrugged. "I wouldn't know, all Ethel said was the old days."

"Well then, did you ever notice anything about the trees on Carter?" Buck said, pointing to his right.

A look of bewilderment spread across Joe's face. "No, not really."

"How you got places where the growth isn't near as mature as the rest, smaller stuff?"

"Oh yeah, I've noticed that, there are places that look like they've been logged."

"Right, or a fire went through there, but neither of them things happened, Joe," Buck said, shaking his head. "If you look close, especially if you got the right angle, and the light is just so, and you let your eyes wander a bit, you'll see that those places look darn like ski trails, because that's what they were going to be. There's quite a story behind that, Joe. I suspect that's what Ethel was talking about."

"Really. Ski trails, huh?"

Buck nodded.

"How many?" Joe asked.

"Oh," Buck said, raising his head in thought, "I think there were a dozen altogether."

"When were they cut?" Joe asked.

"Why don't I start at the beginning and tell you the whole story," he said. "I'll probably catch hell from the boys for not pulling my share, but I suppose with both of us being bosses we can chalk it up to something official."

Joe nodded, eager for what Buck had to say.

"Anyway," Buck said, "this place, which has always been called White Woods, was started after the war, in 1947, back when a lot of ski areas were getting started. It was just a speck of a place then, ten trails and a couple T-bars. Mostly locals and the like frequented it. Well anyway, in 56', the guy that owned it decided, quite correctly I might add, that people liked to ski, that the sport was gonna grow, so he decided to expand.

He'd just acquired the whole of Carter Peak, everything from the road on up, for back taxes. That was something folks did back them. 'Course, he was a selectman, for a time anyway, so he was privy to the way of doing it and what was available.

Anyway, in the late spring of that year, 56', as soon as the mud was out, he hired a bunch of us from town, yours truly included, to cut trails on Carter. Now mind you, I said trails. It wasn't like it is today with these wide-open slopes. Then it was just narrow trails, some of them more like hiking paths. That was just fine with us, making them no wider than they had to be I mean, because it was hard work. It was also before designing things on paper ahead of time became the way. Back then you just cut down the fall line. The turns came from avoiding cliffs or a big outcropping of ledge or from a lazy chopper who could see a stand of oak in his path. You with me so far?"

Joe nodded. "Yeah, but it's hard to believe all that took place on Carter."

Buck smiled broadly. "Oh, it gets better. Around mid-summer, I think it was late July or early August, after we'd pretty much finished the cutting and only had the timber to move, the owner came into a real bad time. He was a successful businessman, a real hard worker, and he had the money to show for it, but he had two weaknesses in the world—woman and vodka. For whatever reason, his drinking got real bad. He'd always been a heavy drinker, but this was different. He wasn't tending to his family or minding his business, having those blackouts they're always talking about. Well, one night, he was drunker than any man ought to allow himself to get, holed up in his office, which he had been getting in the habit of doing. When he didn't come home nobody went after him, his wife had tired of doing that. She figured they'd find him there in the morning, like they had become accustomed to. Well, anyway, sometime that night, nobody quite knows when, he got into his pickup truck and drove up to Carter. Nobody ever knew why. He hit a sharp incline, the truck rolled over, he come out of the truck, the truck rolled over him. His wife found him there in the morning when she came to fetch him for church, crushed to death. Some say he was flat as a pancake, but I suspect that's just legend, the truck wouldn't have done that to him. We, the other choppers and I, would have found him if it hadn't been Sunday, that was the only day we didn't cut."

Joe interrupted, his face a sea of doubt. "When she didn't find him in the office I wonder what led her to the mountain, I mean, it just seems strange she'd go up there."

Buck thought for a moment. "I don't know, a woman's intuition maybe."

"It would have made sense if the truck was there, at the office I mean, but with it gone, he could have been anywhere. Could she have seen where the accident happened from down below?"

Buck shook his head. "I don't know that."

Joe shrugged. "It doesn't matter. I'm sure there's an explanation."

"So anyway," Buck said, continuing with the story, "his wife, who was weaker than watered whiskey, went all to pieces, which for her wasn't hard to do. When she finally got straightened away, she sold everything she could convert to cash money and went home to Connecticut, leaving the lawyers to bankrupt White Woods. Needless to say, White Woods didn't operate that year, 56' and 57'. By spring there was a new owner. He either didn't have the money, or maybe he didn't share the vision for Carter, whatever, it was left alone, to grow back like you see it now."

"So it was never touched again?"

"Nope. The executor of his estate must of sold the timber because it disappeared, but other than that it wasn't touched."

"So the new owner started operating the following fall?" Joe asked.

"Yep."

Joe thought for a moment. "So what does that have to do with today?"

Buck shrugged. "Probably nothing, but the owner?"

"Yeah."

"His name was Warren."

Joe's face went blank. "I don't understand?" he said slowly, cocking his head to one side.

"I'm not saying there is anything to understand, Joe, but Warren, the old owner, he had a son named Warren."

"Oh, I see what you mean."

"Yeah, he just adored that boy too. Before his drinking got the best of him, those two were inseparable, particularly when it came to skiing. He taught his boy how to ski as good as any pro. Damn, that kid could ski."

"Well what about the last name, was it the same?" Joe asked.

"Well no," Buck said sarcastically, "they're different. It wouldn't be a mystery if they weren't, would it?"

Joe was embarrassed. "Yeah, I guess," he said, changing the subject. "How old was the boy when you remember him, when you were cutting Carter?"

Buck nodded and raised his bushy eyebrows. "He was twelve when his dad died, so he'd be about Warren's age now."

"So you think that our Warren is the son?"

"I didn't say that."

"But it's possible? I mean, it fits, doesn't it?"

Buck didn't say anything right away.

"Look, it was a long time ago, Joe, Ethel was young, I was younger, you just don't remember things like that. Other people in town don't remember either."

"Does he look like him?"

Buck threw up his hands. "Some say he was a spitting image, others say no, me, I don't know, it's hard to remember that far back."

"So why are you even mentioning this, what's the relevance?"

"You asked, Joe, remember."

Joe nodded. "Okay then, what makes you, or anybody, think there is a connection?"

"I don't necessarily think there is a connection, I just got a hunch there is."

"And this hunch, you've discussed it with Ethel?"

"Yeah, she's family, Joe, or didn't you know that?"

"Yeah, I mean, no, I didn't know that."

"Look, Joe, when a man does this every night," Buck said, sweeping his large arm across the console of the groomer, "you think a lot. Yeah, I got a fancy radio and the latest model CD player, but I don't use them. I think. When Warren, our Warren, proposed Carter, was when it hit me, particularly since he is so adamant about doing it. I'm no expert mind you, but you don't do this half a lifetime without learning something. Carter is a tough cookie, sure it's great terrain, but you got to have vision to see it for what it can be. And then, well, I heard it might not be right for the kind of terrain you got to have today."

"I see, so you think," Joe paused, "you think that Warren is finishing what his father started."

"One possibility."

"Does our Warren look like him?"

"I told you, I don't remember. Regardless, the old Warren was an alcoholic in his last years, and looked like it. I don't remember him before, maybe Ethel would, but you know how it is, you remember people how you last knew them."

"But you've been around here forever, all the way back. Right?"

"I've been here every year of my life except for a stint in Korea."

"Exactly, so don't people wonder about this?"

"Wonder? Yeah, sure, they did, but not so much anymore. Everybody speculated when the new Warren popped onto the scene in 77', a few people tried to find out, but back then how would you go about it? People forget, Joe, either because they do or because they want to, but it's the same thing. And now that he's going ahead with Carter full steam, people are talking again, only this time there's just a handful of people who remember."

"But you're pretty sure about this, aren't you?"

"Pretty sure, no," Buck said shaking his head. "But look at it like this, Carter was that guy's dream. That was one thing we did know. I suspect he went up there the night he died because it meant so much to him, there wasn't any other reason. I'm just guessing, but he had to know he was in trouble, he had to know he was losing control, he had to know the end was near. I figure he went there because it meant so much to him. Like maybe it would help him find his way."

"So you think maybe the present day Warren is just seeing his dad's dream through?"

"When you consider everything it's a big coincidence."

"I suppose, but why did Warren wait until now to do Carter? I mean he's tripled the terrain here since he came and built more condos than he can sell. It doesn't make sense that he hasn't touched it up till now."

"I don't know," Buck said. "I just don't know."

Joe looked away, out the passenger's side window, at the twinkling lights below, trying to make sense of things. When he finally looked back there was a sarcastic grin on Buck's face. "There is one way we might be able to find out."

"What's that?" Joe asked eagerly.

"Well, the boy, I told you he was a great skier, he was so fast that he got himself a nickname that most everybody knew him by."

"Oh?"

"Yeah, everybody used to call him Bomber."

Joe thought for a moment and smirked. "So I'm supposed to walk up to Warren tomorrow and call him 'Bomber', is that it?"

Buck shrugged. "Not if you want Art's job."

"What about newspapers or records?"

Buck took a deep breath. "There wasn't a local paper back then. If the paper in Bangor had a story, I doubt it would tell you much. As far as records go, why would there by any around? The place went bankrupt, it was sold."

"Historical records maybe, there must be something, somewhere. I mean it was a going business."

Buck hunched his wide shoulders. "Who knows."

"Well I appreciate you sharing this with me, if it's true, I mean, I know it's true, but if it relates to things now it might explain some things."

"I know what you mean and I know you got a full plate right now, Joe. I don't envy you, not one bit, but if we're right about this, would it make a difference?"

Joe thought for a moment. "I don't know, it might. Something has got to explain all that's happened. The whole season has been nothing but one thing happening after another and I think they're related, like a chain reaction."

Buck nodded, his lips pressed together.

"Well, I've got to be going, thanks again, Buck." Joe opened the door and climbed out, raising his voice over the purring of the groomer. "If you think of anything else let me know."

"I will."

On the way back to the pump house Joe went over in his mind what Buck had said. It was interesting stuff, but what did it mean? Maybe Buck was right, he reasoned, even if the two Warrens were father and son what difference would that make? Warren's motivation for doing Carter was not in question. Whether it was simply to be bigger like he said or being done in the name of his dead father or for some other reason, what difference did it make? As he approached the pump house he realized that he had turned off his portable radio halfway through the conversation with Buck. He turned it on, wondering what, if anything, he had missed.

"Everything quiet?" he asked Marty when he got to the control desk.

Leaned back in his chair, his feet planted on the desk, his eyes fixed on the television, only Marty's mouth moved. "Haven't heard that it isn't."

Joe stood there for a moment, watching the muted half-time show while he silently contemplated a cup of coffee. But his mind wandered. He was thinking about what Buck had said. He decided he needed to talk with Art and the easiest way to do that would be to work with him. It meant getting up early but this was important.

He puttered around the pump house till after shift change. With everybody settled he told Marty he was leaving and headed home, finding it difficult to fall asleep after what had been a short and mostly passive shift. He dragged himself out of bed at eight the next morning, skipped a shave and shower, and made it to Art's office by nine.

"Good morning, Joe," Art said as he walked in. "I didn't know you were coming in today."

"Yeah, I'm sorry. I know we had last Friday. It's all right isn't it?"

"Sure, I told you, anytime."

"If it's okay with you, there is something I need to talk to you about."

Art put down the pencil he was holding and leaned slightly back in his chair. "Sure, what's up?"

Joe lowered his voice and glanced toward the open door. "I'd rather not talk here, it's kind of, well, shall we say involved."

"Oh, one of those hush-hush kind of things, huh?" Art said raising his bushy eyebrows a couple of times in rapid succession.

Joe nodded. It was easier to agree.

"Well then, I've got some paperwork to do for an hour or so, stuff we've already gone over, so if you want to just hang out till ten, we could take a ride and talk."

"Sounds good to me," Joe said getting up. "I'll be back around ten."

Joe got a coffee from the cafeteria, made small talk with a couple parking attendants on their way to lift duty, and bought a copy of *USA Today* from the corridor vending box, which he read in the far corner of the lodge seating area where he blended in with the other people who had claimed their stake for the day. At precisely ten o'clock he was back in Art's office. Joe offered his truck, but Art was set on taking one of the resorts five Jeep Cherokees, which had been supplied under some generous promotional plan by the manufacturer.

"So what's up?" Art asked as they started down the access road.

Joe wasn't one to beat around the bush, particularly when he was the one that needed help. "I was wondering what you might know about Warren's past?"

Art glanced at Joe. "What do you want to know?"

"Anything."

"That's kind of a broad subject."

"Considering everything that has happened, without going into it, I need to know more about Warren's past, it might shed some light on things."

"You know he recruited me, right?"

"Yeah."

"Well, there's more to the story than that. Warren and I go back a few years. We worked at Shapleigh together from '76 till '78, when he jumped at the chance to manage this place. It was about 80 acres then, 25 trails, four lifts—three of them surface—and a small base lodge, all of it on White Peak except for a T-bar and a couple trails on Abbott. In a good year they barely did 20,000 visits. He ran the place the best he could, but he could see it wasn't going anywhere the way it was."

"You've got a good memory," Joe said, relieved that Art seemed to be talking freely. Then, to make it seem like his interest wasn't limited to Warren, he asked, "what about snowmaking?"

"Some, but it wasn't much, nobody had much then. Anyway, we used to talk on the telephone, Warren and I, he was frustrated because they wouldn't put a dime into the place and anything they made they took to expand Shapleigh, which is why Shapleigh is so damn big today. Anyway, to make a long story short, he decided to buy White Woods in '80. He hawked everything he had and got some help from his in-laws and finally came up with a down payment. The parent of Shapleigh, called Alpine Adventures, liked the idea of unloading it because they wanted cash for Shapleigh, so he got a decent deal."

"Is Alpine Adventures still in business?"

"Oh yeah, sure they are, they transformed Shapleigh into the monster it is today, and they've bought two other resorts in the east and one in the west, they've done well for themselves. The only thing they misjudged was White Woods. I don't know why they couldn't see it, maybe because they were only looking at it on paper, but White Woods had all the potential Warren told them it had, only they weren't listening."

"Now you said that Warren jumped at the chance to manage White Woods."

"Yeah, like a fly on shit, he couldn't wait to get over here. I figured he was having trouble with the brass at Shapleigh and wanted to be his own boss, which is something I can relate to."

Joe nodded. "Then what happened?"

"Well, Warren was still wet behind the ears when he rushed out and got conceptual approval for a big expansion, which included, first and foremost, Carter Peak. Talk about biting off more than you can chew. But he couldn't do a thing because he didn't have any money. He was mortgaged to the limit. But that didn't stop him from growing the place. The first year he cut two new trails from the summit of White Peak and kept adding a little more every year. Whether he knew what he was doing or whether he was just plain lucky, I don't know, but he made all the right moves. While some of the other notables were building condos he was cutting trails, installing lifts, and laying pipe, which turned out to be the right thing. Unlike Shapleigh, he put every penny of profit back into the place and in '82 he built the lodge at Abbott and put in a triple over there. I kind of lost track after that, you know how it is, you mean to stay in touch but it's hard to find the time. But hell, you know the rest anyway, you came in, what, '83, right?"

"Yeah, late '82."

"Well then."

Art turned into the almost deserted state rest area on the highway and stopped. Only a mid-sized red car was at the opposite end, its owner walking slowly across the parking lot preceded by a small well-groomed dog.

"So you know Warren fairly well then?" Joe asked as Art adjusted his sitting position so he could face Joe.

"Better than most, I guess."

"Hey, you want a cigar?" Joe asked, remembering that Art had shared one with him in the past.

"Yeah, I'll have one," Art said.

Joe reached into his jacket pocket and pulled out two cigars by the top, extending them in a V shape toward Art who took the one closest to him. Silently, they unwrapped their cigars, cut the ends, lit them, and cracked their windows.

"You know Warren isn't well-liked around here," Art said.

Joe was surprised. "Really. I guess I thought it was just the opposite, I mean, with what he's done for Cannon and everything."

Art took a long drag, exhaling the smoke toward his open window. "Working nights you probably don't hear much," he finally said. "But Warren is a case study in this town. Sure, he's been good for Cannon, good as gold for the economy. He's created more jobs here than there are people, which has meant a sense of well being that hasn't existed since the sawmills folded up about forty years ago. When he came here, I guess the very year he came, there was talk about relinquishing municipal government, letting the state take over. Whether it would have become an Unorganized Territory or not, who knows, but the point is Warren's success put an end to that talk. But you've got to realize that he's everything Cannon isn't. They know about his unethical ways of doing business, his lifestyle. Not too many people don't know about him and Doris. I may be from away, but I like to think I understand this town. They may be behind the times a bit, but they're decent people with little tolerance for those who aren't and Warren," Art paused for effect, "isn't."

Joe was getting more than he expected. Art was knocking Warren off his pedestal and he didn't know why. He didn't say anything as an awkward feeling started taking hold of him. It just didn't feel right to be talking about Warren this way. But Art had more to say and Joe wasn't about to stop him from saying it.

"But," Art said, poking the air with his cigar, "their dislike of him, disdain really, is held at bay by his success. Nothing will change as long as things stay the same. If Warren fails, this town fails, it's that simple, so that breeds a lot of forbearance, it represses people's feelings, even strong ones, but they're there just the same, ready and waiting to be unleashed when the time is right."

"You make it sound pretty bad," Joe remarked.

"It's just the way it is, you know me, I call a spade a spade. You're probably thinking because I'm leaving I can afford to talk this way, but that isn't it. If you had asked me last year or the year before I'd have answered the same."

Joe changed the subject. "What do you know about Warren prior to, when was it, '75?"

"'76. Nothing really. Why do you ask?"

"Well, I thought maybe all the stuff that's been happening might be rooted in the past somehow."

"I figured that's what this was all about," Art said, puffing his cigar a few times to keep it lit. "And I thought of that, how the past may figure in all the shit that's been going on, but I never considered anything that far back."

"Yeah," Joe said.

"But you're thinking that far back, huh?"

Joe thought for a moment, deciding not to delve into what Art was clearly ignorant about.

"I've just been wracking my brain for anything," he said. Then to change the subject he asked, "What about Dwight, do you think I should talk to him?"

Art chuckled softly. "I wouldn't," he said, shaking his head. "He's nothing but a kiss ass. Whatever Warren wants he just goes along with and why wouldn't he? He's got a tit to suck on that won't go dry as long as he remains the yes man he is."

"I've always felt he was a decent person."

"He is. He's one of the nicest people here, but he knows which side his bread is buttered on. He's gotten good at looking the other way. At first it was probably hard for him, but the more you do something the easier it gets."

"I just think that if he knew everything, he wouldn't go along with it. Especially when you consider what happened to John and that it could happen again. This isn't a case of my guys' livelihood or anything like that. We're talking about getting maimed or even killed."

Art puffed his cigar. "Yeah, I know, but people rationalize these things. At some point I'm sure he wouldn't go along, it just depends on what he knows and what he figures lies ahead. You know what they say, a guy will follow you to the edge, but he won't go over with you. But I bet dollars to donuts that Dwight figures the edge isn't even in sight, never mind going over it."

They talked for a while longer and went back to White Woods. The day passed quickly, with nothing further said about Warren or Dwight. At five-thirty Joe left Art in his office, dropped in at the pump house, and headed for home, stopping at the store on his way for a few things his mother had asked him to get. With the commuter hour over, the store was empty. Ethel was behind the counter with the Bangor paper spread out across it.

"Hi, Joe, coming or going?" she asked, not waiting for an answer. "I have to ask you these days, used to be you were always going, now I never know."

"Yeah, heading home, I worked with Art today, training for the new job."

"Good for you," she said neatly folding up the paper and putting it back in the stack.

"I talked to Buck," Joe said.

"Oh, good. Was it worth it?"

"What he told me was really interesting, it might mean something, but it might not, who knows, things are such a mess. I suspect I'm missing something, I just don't know what.

"Oh."

"Yeah, it's a real puzzle."

The door opened and a young man with a full head of unkempt hair and baggy clothes strolled over to the counter, which Joe quickly relinquished with a nod. The man bought two packs of Marlboros from the counter display and left without speaking a single word.

"So things are still a mystery, huh?"

Joe rolled his eyes. "As much as ever. I wouldn't care except that I'm afraid of what might happen next. If I knew we were in the clear, I'd just forget it. But who knows what's next. I'm worried about somebody else getting hurt."

Ethel stared back at Joe for a moment, then looked away, through the aging plate glass window, across the parking lot to the other side of the road, where a grove of young maples, illuminated by a street light, swayed gently in the wind.

"What's the matter?" Joe asked warily, afraid it was something he had said. She didn't answer.

"Are you all right?" Joe asked. Ethel raised her hand, which to Joe meant she needed time to regain her composure before facing him, which only served to heighten his concern. What had he said? Feeling uneasy, Joe leaned back from the counter and shoved his hands in his pockets, his mind groping for what had triggered Ethel's pain. Finally, she turned back, looking a whole lot older than she had a minute before.

"I guess I ought to tell you something, Joe," she said meekly, "something nobody else knows."

Joe raised his eyebrows and nodded.

Ethel's voice turned bitter. "Something I ain't the least bit proud of. But it might help."

"What is it?"

She hesitated. "What did Buck tell you?" she asked.

"About the other Warren, how he tried to develop Carter, how he died, how the place went bankrupt."

A big woman, half as wide as she was tall, with bushy hair that flowed halfway down her back entered the store, calling attention to herself even before the door slammed.

"Hey, Ethel," she bellowed from the entryway, "have I got one for you."

She waddled toward the counter, continuing to spout off, oblivious to the fact that Ethel and Joe had been talking. Joe considered holding his ground, which for him would have been unusual, but when two boisterous men, who were apparently following in the fat lady's wake entered, intent on settling a score with her, Joe backed away, smiling because it was the polite thing to, and let them go at it.

When they didn't stop after a couple of minutes he went to the back to the store, where he could still hear them clearly, and got himself a coffee, putting extra cream in to lighten what must have been brewed hours before. Any other time he'd have gone up the aisle nearest the counter so Ethel would see him coming, emerge with the correct change in his hand, drop it into Ethel's outreached palm, and leave, waving as he went. But today was different. He wanted, really needed, to finish his conversation with Ethel. He'd just have to wait them out.

He puttered around the aisle he had come down, making note of the cans and boxes that had dust on them and those that didn't, trying to decide the relevance of that. The door slammed and it was quieter. The only thing Joe could hear was the big woman's voice. Joe went back to the front of the store, milling around ten steps from the counter, smiling at the fat lady when she turned to look at him. She must have figured out that he was waiting to talk to Ethel.

"Oh heavens to Betsy," she said looking at her watch, "I promised Anna I'd be at the church fifteen minutes ago and I can't even remember what I came in for, that's a sure sign of old age." She laughed at her own joke. Joe took a sip of coffee so he wouldn't have to.

Ethel spoke up. "You ain't bad off till you can't remember what you did, not what you were supposed to do."

"Well just give me a couple packs of smokes," the woman said, taking her wallet from her pocket book that was resting on the counter.

Without the woman saying anything more, Ethel's hand disappeared behind the overhead rack and returned with two packs of Newport Menthol cigarettes, which she laid on the counter, giving them a little shove in the direction of the woman. Falling silent for the first time, the woman paid with four one dollar bills, putting the change in a small coin pouch in her wallet, which she plunged deep into her pocket book.

"These things are going to be my New Year's resolution," she said, shaking the cigarettes in her hand before dropping them in her pocketbook. "I suppose I should do the diet thing again. I made it almost to February last year. I trimmed down some, course I gained it all back now. Lloyd says I should quit drinking and I suppose he's right, the booze isn't any good for you, and it's full of calories. Did I tell you, Ethel, that that foolish daughter of mine, you know, the one in Texas, she's talking getting married again, I couldn't believe it, I mean, I never even met her first husband. I told her to come home to mama and we'd settle her down, but she wouldn't hear of it. I don't see what keeps her there. It's hot and those killer bees are getting closer all the time, mostly though I think people down there haven't got any roots. Oh heavens, I got to go, ciao everybody." She walked away faster than she had come, leaving Joe and Ethel smirking.

The door slammed and the store was silent again. Afraid they'd be interrupted, Joe wasted no time restarting their conversation.

"So what were you going to tell me?"

"Where were we, oh yes," she said, briefly looking away which she rarely did. "Buck told you about the previous owner of White Woods, well, I used to help out in his office. He was a handsome man and...and I was young, pretty, it was just one of those things that happened. Like I said, I never told this to no one before, there was no reason. Anyway, when he died, I had to clean out his office. There were a lot of papers about Carter. I didn't read them mind you, there was no reason, but they had to do with it all right."

"Really, like what?"

"Papers and the like—letters, reports, maps, drawings—all kinds of stuff, enough to fill three, maybe four cardboard boxes."

"Where are they now?" Joe asked.

"I have no idea," she said, shaking her head. "I boxed the stuff up with everything else and left it there. Because things weren't settled legally it's all we could do. I never saw it again."

"But you're sure the stuff was about Carter?"

"Yeah, most of it anyway. I didn't look at everything, but it was stacked separate. If you think it might help, there is one thing you could try. Warren's lawyer was Herbert Thistle, he's dead now of course, but his widow still lives over on Parsons Street, the big white place just beyond the monument. Herbert took care of all Warren's business, including the bankruptcy, his probate, everything."

"Yeah, I know the house you mean. Do you think it would be all right if I went over there and talked to her? I mean I don't want to cause her any hardship."

The door slammed. They both looked over. A young couple, clad in neon-colored ski clothing, were talking and giggling as they walked side by side out of sight down the frozen food aisle.

"I doubt you would be," Ethel said, lowering her voice. "Harold has been dead for, oh, going on seven, maybe eight years now, and she's a good woman, from good stock, she'll do the right thing."

"I think I'll give it a try then," Joe said. "At this point I'll try anything."

The ski couple was back at the front of the store asking about aspirin. Joe wanted Ethel to know that he appreciated what she had told him. It didn't seem right to take in that kind of information and then leave, but the skiers were loud, and they had more questions.

"See you later," Joe said waving as he walked toward the door.

"See ya, Joe," she hollered.

At first he had no intention of going over to the Thistle woman's house. But the more he thought about it, the more he realized that if he was going to get himself out of the hole he was in he was going to have to do it himself. So he cut a decisive U turn on the highway and headed for Parsons Street. He knocked lightly on the door on the chance the elderly woman was in bed, purposely not using the over-sized brass knocker. Maybe he shouldn't have come, he thought to himself as he stood there shivering in the darkness. He didn't know why, but he was always colder when he was tired. Even if she was up, she might not want to open the door. He was about to leave when a frail voice asked who it was.

"Ah, my name is Joe Littlefield, you don't know me, Ethel Cole from the store sent me," he said, frustrated to be talking through the door, particularly because he didn't even know if she could hear him. "Do you want me to come back tomorrow? It's no problem."

There was no answer but Joe could hear the sound of bolts and chains. Slowly the thick wooden door opened, and he was face to face with a feeble-looking woman with a wrinkled face, clad in a white nightgown that touched the floor. She shouldn't have opened the door, Joe thought to himself, I could be anybody.

"Hi, I'm Joe Littlefield, like I was saying, Ethel Cole from the store sent me over. I guess your husband was Warren Taylor's lawyer, the guy who owned White Woods back in the 50's? Well, we're trying to locate some old records that he, that Mr. Taylor, had in his office when he died, and Ethel said your husband had them, and she thought they might still be around."

"Oh goodness," the old woman said, standing up straight and cupping her hands together in front of her chest. "I don't know. Herbert's things are in the carriage shed, but I don't know what's there, and there isn't a lamp in there. Who did you say you were?"

"My name is Joe Littlefield. I work at White Woods."

"Oh, I see."

"Do you think there might be something, I mean, did he keep the records of his clients?"

"Oh, I wouldn't know that, dear," she said in an apologetic tone of voice while shaking her head. "But there are a lot of boxes in there, up on the loft. I just don't know what's there, I haven't been able to get around for years."

"Would you mind if I came back when it was light and looked? I mean if that would be okay, I wouldn't look at anything else."

"You'd be welcome to come, young man, but like I said, you'd have to help yourself, these legs of mine don't carry me far these days. But you can come anytime and I'll give you the key."

"Oh, good then, that's what I'll do. Well, thank you and I'm sorry to have bothered you."

"No bother a-tall, goodnight."

As Joe walked down the carefully shoveled path he could hear the woman locking the door. He drove slowly home, feeling really tired. It's just as well there was no light in the carriage shed, he thought, I'm spent anyway, and besides, he had absorbed enough information in the last 24 hours to keep his mind busy for a week.

Following his mother's four-course dinner, exhaustion quickly consumed him. He knew better than to go to bed on a full stomach, but his eyelids were heavy, and besides, he'd have been lousy company.

*   *   *   *

It was just past noon on Christmas day when Doug and Kay finished putting on their cross country ski gear and set out toward the river from the same place they had turned around earlier in the week, leaving their BMW parked as much out of the way as they could get it, with the alarm set.

Doug carried the knapsack full of liverwurst, cheese, crackers, peaches, and hot tea. He didn't know it, but Kay had slipped a half liter of white wine and two plastic wine glasses in the bottom of the pack, things she had purchased the day before on her way home from Jenny's house.

Side by side, they followed the almost straight road, arriving at the river in less than an hour. Except for the upper end of a good-sized pine tree that laid square across the road, almost like it had been put there to prevent passage, they had no trouble getting there.

Just as Doug thought, a cluster of aging cabins, sitting on concrete blocks, dotted the riverbank, their doors and windows shuttered with coverings made of knotty pine boards. While each of them was slightly different they were all small, a bedroom or two at most, each with an ample wrap-around porch with large empty windows.

The area around the cabins was cleared of everything but the largest trees, and even those were trimmed to a height of ten to fifteen feet, higher above the cabins. Considering their closeness, their similarity, and the single dock that lay on shore, Doug was fairly sure that the same person owned them all.

"Why don't we ski a while," Doug suggested, motioning down river, "and then we can come back here for lunch."

"Sounds fine, dear," Kay answered, waiting for Doug to take the lead.

They hadn't gone more than a couple hundred yards when they encountered a thicket of brush that made further passage impossible. Afraid that the ice alongside the river's edge wouldn't support their weight, they turned back and tried the other direction with similar results.

Returning to the where the cabins were, Doug stepped out of his skis, descended the nicely-sloped river bank, and advanced cautiously onto the snow covered ice, bobbing his lean body up and down after each step, listening intently for the cracking sound that would signal his retreat. Twelve feet from shore, at a place where he knew he had to be above water, he cleared snow from a small area with his feet, then, using the hard plastic toe of his boot he began thrashing the surface, spewing shards of ice into the air. Thirty seconds later, gasping for breath, he stopped.

"I guess I should have brought something to break through with," he yelled to Kay who was watching him from shore.

"Maybe I can find a rock under one of the cabins," she offered, peering into the darkness under the building closest to her.

Doug shook his head and started for land. "Never mind. It's probably not a good idea anyway. I'm liable to fall in."

When he reached the shore he traipsed up the banking and sat down on the snow-covered dock, where he undid the laces of his right boot, redoing them to a tightness that pleased him.

"You know, I should have borrowed Ed's gas powered auger," he said. "It would have been perfect for this. Then I could have checked the water."

Kay frowned. "You could have gotten it in here?" she asked.

Doug nodded. "Oh yeah," he said, pulling tightly on a bowknot.

Kay watched silently as Doug did his other boot, and then got up, brushing snow from his backside.

"There," he said "that's better. I think I'll walk back down river and see if I can get a little further on foot."

Kay looked worried. "You're not going to try the ice again, are you, dear?"

Doug smiled. "No, I'm just going to poke around along the shore, I won't be gone long."

While Doug walked the riverbank Kay sunned herself against the trunk of a huge oak tree that stood close to the river. Twenty minutes later Doug was back with nothing new to report. Together they went to the porch of the largest cottage, where Doug had shed the knapsack an hour earlier, and settled themselves on the dry pine floorboards, their backs squarely flanking the cabin's front door.

They ate the lunch Kay had carefully prepared and lingered there in the warm sun, nibbling on sesame seed crackers and sipping white wine. As their conversation slowly ebbed, Kay drifted off to sleep, an attribute Doug envied. Why couldn't he catnap he wondered, eyeing her head which seemed to slump a little more with each passing moment.

Instead, he sat motionless, his eyes fixed on a large black butterfly fastener directly in front of him, thinking about how it wouldn't be long before it was once again helping to hold one of the porch's big screens in place, screens that allowed summer breezes to flow freely while keeping bugs at bay.

His thoughts turned to Dickie. Beyond what the waitress had said, Doug hadn't been able to corroborate his story, and he was beginning to feel that the reason he couldn't was because it wasn't true. Or was it that he wasn't trying hard enough?

He'd just have to think of something more he could do. The land use issues that had dominated his life in Dracut had been simple compared to what was on his plate now. Even if he was somehow able to root out the problem and prove its existence beyond a reasonable doubt—a self imposed standard—there was no agenda waiting for him to weight in on, no panel of civilized people that would listen to him late into the night from behind a long wide table strewn with papers and sweating soda cans.

Things were different now, and he knew it. Here, deep in the Western Mountains, Doug was on his own, and being from away, which was akin to being an outsider, he knew that even when he had enough to make a case, he wasn't likely to be listened to or understood, at least not by local officials. But the opportunity to single-handedly prove that profitable environmental evils, committed by and for the very industry that defined existence here, kept him motivated. It was a coup he'd relish having under his belt.

When Doug finally looked at his watch, it was close to three.

"Heavens," he said loudly, rising to his feet.

Kay groaned.

"It's almost three," Doug said.

Kay groaned again. "Really," she said without moving. "I could stay here forever."

"We'd better get going, dear, it'll be getting dark in an hour," Doug said, adjusting his clothing. "As soon as we lose the heat of the sun, you'll wish we were home."

"I suppose," she said, getting up slowly and taking a big stretch.

They put their trash in the backpack, strapped on their skis, and left.

*   *   *   *

Christmas was cold at White Woods, but the worst was yet to come. Each day that followed, the temperature dropped, until it was well below zero by Sunday. The crew struggled to stay warm as they battled a multitude of freeze ups that slowed the amount of snow they produced. Normally Joe would have cursed the weather and hoped for a relative warming trend, but with all that had happened lately, the dome of frigid arctic air, that had modified little before spreading over the Northeast, was a welcome diversion for the crew.

Despite the fact that he stayed until almost four Monday morning lending moral support to the crew, he got up early. Moving his coveted schedule slightly ahead, he shaved, bathed, ate lunch, did a few chores, and got ready for work, managing to leave the house early enough to stop at the Thistle house.

He had checked what must have been fifty boxes when he finally found the documents from White Woods that Ethel had remembered. Carefully, he sorted through the yellowed papers, most of which were faded and brittle, brushing and blowing away scores of dead moths and spiders that seemed to occupy every layer. The contents of the boxes turned out to be useless, a concoction of materials about the ski industry and ski area construction. A lot of the literature tracked the growth of skiing nationwide—the areas that were opening, the lifts they were installing, the advances in ski equipment and clothing. That which had to do with Carter specifically was nothing more than rough sketches, contractor estimates, and timber quotes.

In retrospect Joe should have known it was a wild goose chase. What he was looking for probably wouldn't be written down anywhere except in a diary. Warren's dreams for Carter, his motivations for pursuing it, the hardships he had faced, weren't things he'd find here. So he put everything back the way it had been and left the building, making sure the shed door was properly locked, which Mrs. Thistle had made a condition of his visit. It didn't seen right to be leaving without checking with her, but she told him not to because she was going to lie down in the back room.

As soon as he got to the pump house he quietly eased his office door shut and called Brenda. She was at her desk. The sound of her cheerful voice quickly relieved the uneasy feeling he had about conducting personal business on company time. He was also pleased that she apparently held no ill feelings about the calls he hadn't returned to her, which now numbered four.

With the small talk dispensed with, Joe delved into the matter at hand. "I was wondering, you have the old editions of the newspaper, right?"

"Oh sure, we have something like forty or fifty year's worth on micro film. Why?"

"Well, I've found out some things about White Woods' past, it might be nothing, but it sounds fairly colorful. I think maybe there might have been some coverage of it."

Brenda thought for a moment before answering. "It would be worth a try, I guess. What year was it?"

"56."

"1956, well…if it had been here in the city we'd have a much better chance of finding it. I don't know how well things over that way got covered back then. It would really come down to how news-worthy it was, you know, how important."

"But you have that year, right?"

"Oh sure, we got it, that stuff gets accessed more often than you'd think, if not by us, by somebody. When can you make it over?"

"Well, afternoons are always best for me, say around one, so I wouldn't be late getting here."

"Ah, let me see, I've got a busy morning tomorrow, so I should be in the office writing all afternoon."

"That works for me," Joe said, knowing Art had planned to skip their get together on December 30.

"Good, I'll see you then."

Feeling uneasy that his request was the sole purpose of the call, Joe quickly added, "I'd like to get together sometime if you want."

"That would be nice," Brenda said, her tone of voice suddenly cool.

Joe figured he knew why. As a friend she didn't mind him popping into her life for a favor, but if it was going to be more than that, she expected more. He decided to do some fence mending. "I know I didn't return your calls and...and that I haven't been around, but things here aren't good, it isn't you, it's just that things are kind of messed up right now. I know I sound like I'm just making excuses, but really, I would like to get together."

She didn't make it easy for him. "Well, you have my number."

"Yeah, and I really do want to get together and do something. Well, anyway, tomorrow at one then."

"Yes, just come right up. You don't need to stop at reception, nobody else does."

"Okay, see you then."

The handset hadn't been in the cradle ten seconds when Marty buzzed Joe. Fingering the hands-free button, Joe spoke loudly. "Yes."

"Coffee's fresh," Marty bellowed back.

"Okay, thanks. I'll be right out."

By the time Joe was halfway to the control desk he had managed to put Brenda and the investigation out of his mind, something that only the job he loved could do for him. Despite the upheavals that had seemed to mark more shifts than not, this one was uneventful, almost like the old days. Joe checked snow quality on the mountain, crossed paths with the crew, checked the river pump house regularly, and chatted with Marty while keeping a watchful eye on the computer screens that delivered a steady stream of data. Leaving work at the usual time, Joe got a decent night's sleep, and departed for Bangor the next morning at eleven, knowing he would rather kill time than be late.

By one fifteen he and Brenda were sitting side-by-side, closer than they had ever sat, in the cool basement of the newspaper building, surrounded by a century's worth of publishing. Brenda fast-forwarded halfway through the July 1956 spool of microfilm, where she began the methodical process of checking each edition. The film ran smoothly through the machine as Brenda accelerated, slowed, stopped, looked, and at times reversed.

"Being so far away, I doubt this would have been front page news. Is that going to make it tough to find?" Joe asked.

"Yeah, but to pin down the date, I'm checking the obituaries. There's an index on the front page."

When the take-up spool was nearly full Brenda pushed the reverse button "It must have been in August," she said, raising her voice above the noisy rewind speed.

Joe rubbed his hand across his clammy forehead. "Jeeze, that thing makes you feel funny, doesn't it?"

"Oh, I'm sorry," she said, turning toward him. "I should have warned you, it will do that, give you motion sickness, I mean. You can't watch it, at least not up close. You okay?"

"Oh yeah, fine, it just makes me feel nauseous."

Brenda smiled. "Like a hangover?"

"Yeah, I guess."

With the August roll on and threaded, she continued to search while Joe quietly watched, afraid that conversation might distract her.

A couple minutes passed when Brenda said, "I think this is it." Then, fiddling with a mechanism near the lens, she added, "let me enlarge and focus it."

With the small fuzzy print of the death notice in the August 10 edition filling most of the screen, Joe read aloud the first paragraph, which confirmed it was the right one. "Warren V. Taylor of Cannon, formerly of Mystic, Connecticut, died unexpectedly Sunday at White Woods Skiway, of which he was the owner"

Resisting the temptation to skim the notice, Joe read every word. When he was finished he spoke slowly. "Wow, that's it all right, it's so strange. What about the picture?"

"Yeah, let me print this first," she said, pushing a button on the left side of the machine which triggered a series of groans. When the glossy copy dropped into a bin on the machine's right side, Brenda pulled down the picture and focused again.

"Damn," Joe said. "That's him, that's Warren."

"You mean it looks like Warren Ainsworth, because this is Warren Taylor."

"Yeah, right."

"But I suppose there's a good chance they're father and son if there's a resemblance with it this blurry."

Brenda printed the picture and Joe took both copies from the bin, holding them in his lap, studying them.

While Joe reread the notice from the beginning, hoping to find something more in it, Brenda searched seven editions before and after August 10, looking for a news story about the accident, but found nothing.

"I'm not surprised," she said. "Being so far away, I suppose we're lucky we found an obit."

Joe wasn't listening. "Do you have the original of this picture?"

"Now that's asking a lot, and I doubt it, I think this is the record," she said, pointing to the copied picture that still laid in his lap. "But we can check."

"It would really help. There's something in this picture, something that would clinch it if I could see it better."

Brenda was on her feet, putting the two rolls of film back into the cabinet drawer. "Sounds intriguing," she said. "Let's go talk to the photo lab people."

Joe stood up, folding the two pieces of paper in half. "Where are they?" he asked.

"Top floor," Brenda said.

They took the elevator, which was noisy but surprisingly fast, to the fourth floor, and stepped out into what looked like an empty warehouse. Joe followed Brenda to the left, toward a solid windowless wall, constructed of plywood, than ran the width of the building, and through a door, that led into a small lobby with a service counter. Gently, Joe closed the door behind them, speaking for the first time since they left the basement.

"This seems more like a separate operation than part of the newspaper."

"We own and operate it," Brenda replied, "but it's not just for us. There are quite a few contractual users like other newspapers, advertising and modeling agencies, even a few police departments."

Joe nodded. "That makes sense."

Not a minute had passed when a little man with glasses wearing a pure white lab coat appeared. Since Brenda hadn't rung a service bell or pressed any buttons Joe figured there was probably an announcer on the door, which had summonsed the little man to the counter. Brenda bantered with him for a while before stating the purpose of her visit.

The little man shook his head. "1956, no, not here, we don't go that far back. If we got it at all, it would be in the archives."

Brenda wasn't about to be put off. "Where are the archives?"

"At the historical society, across town."

Brenda nodded, but didn't say anything.

"We send all the old stuff over there," the little man said, suddenly sounding apologetic. "They supposedly have the expertise and the environment for preservation. But it's still accessible, at least it's supposed to be under the terms of transfer. We never really give it to them if you know what I mean, they become the depository for it, provided they maintain it properly and in a way that allows it to be accessed. If you go there and give them the date, they should be able to find it for you if it's there."

"What about giving them a call first?" Brenda asked. "To see if they've got it."

The little man shook his head. "The archive people only accept walk-ins. You'll have to go over there."

"Well then, I guess that's what we'll do," Brenda said with a smile. "Thanks."

"Anytime," the little man said.

They left the photo lab and started for the elevator.

"If they have it, will they have the negative?" Joe asked.

Brenda thought for a moment. "Probably not," she said, fingering the elevator's call button, "but it depends on where it came from. If it was a file photo they'll probably have the negative. But considering there isn't a news story, I'd have to say we didn't cover it, which probably means the family supplied the picture, and if they did, it could have been returned."

"So there's no way of knowing then?"

Brenda shook her head. "No. Do you want to go over there and give it a try?"

"Yeah, if it's not too much trouble."

"No, it's fine. We can take my car."

An hour later they had the picture. It took some doing to convince the youthful curator that they would have it copied and returned by day's end, but Brenda's press credentials swayed him. As soon as they exited the dimly lit historical building, Joe pulled the picture from the manila envelope, his eyes going directly to the upper right corner. Sure enough. There they were. While the backdrop scenery was still a bit blurry the pair of ski shaped bookends that he had looked at a thousand times before while sitting in Warren's office were plainly evident.

"Well," Brenda asked, "is it any help?"

"Yeah, yeah it is," Joe replied, putting it back in the envelope.

"Good," Brenda said as she unlocked the passenger's door and started for the driver's side. Joe got in quickly and unlocked her door, hoping she wouldn't ask what it was that had sparked his interest in the picture. She didn't. They grabbed a quick lunch, went back to the Herald office, and had the photo lab copy the picture, which was ready in twenty minutes.

As they left the building for the second time that day, it occurred to Joe there was no need to take any more of Brenda's time. "Why don't I return this on my way home," he suggested.

They stopped on the sidewalk.

"Are you sure? I don't want you to get lost."

Joe nodded. "I'm sure, it's not a problem."

They said goodbye, with Joe promising to call her soon, and parted company.

Twenty minutes later, with the picture returned long before the Historical Society's self-imposed deadline of closing, Joe drove quickly back to Cannon, pleased that he ended up arriving at the pump house a few minutes early. He stashed the picture in the bottom right drawer of his desk between two file folders. Not only would it be safe and flat there, but also nobody was likely to stumble across it. Despite the fact that the picture had already served its purpose, he needed to keep it handy just in case somebody disputed his claim.

For the first half of the shift, Joe was convinced he had accomplished something that afternoon by proving, at least to himself, that Warren was the son of the previous owner. But by ten o'clock his mind, like it was inclined to do, had taken a complete reversal. Even if they were father and son, what did it prove?

CHAPTER 12

▼

FALSE HOPE

When Doug arrived home from the dentist Kay met him on the back-yard walkway, wiping her hands on a green-checkered dishcloth.

"Did you see that guy out front?" she asked.

Doug's face went blank. "No. Who?"

"Oh, maybe he's gone then. Some raunchy-looking guy drinking beer came into the shop looking for you. I think it might be that guy from the mill you talked with."

"Oh. Well if it is, it's bad timing," Doug said, holding his jaw and rolling his eyes. "He pulled that tooth that was bothering me, I'm all numbed up with Novocain."

Kay ignored what Doug had said, assuming the man was still out front and Doug just hadn't seen him. "He said he was going to wait out front for you. I got worried and locked the shop door. Come on, let's go look."

Doug followed her inside, to the living room door, and paused. Kay walked to the center of the room, looked out the side window toward the shop, and nodded, beckoning him to join her. Doug stood behind Kay and looked out the window over her shoulder. Sure enough, there was Dickie, sitting on the ground next to the shop door, his back against the building, his arms draped loosely across his arched knees, his right hand holding what looked like a can of beer in a crumpled brown paper bag.

"Yeah, that's Dickie," he whispered into Kay's ear. "He's quite a sight, huh?"

Kay sidestepped away from the window, her voice hushed.

"I don't mind you pursuing this thing, dear, but that guy gave me the willies, he's so seedy looking."

Doug stepped out of the window and smiled. "Sorry, I had no idea he'd come here, I didn't even know he knew where I lived."

"That's my point, it's unsettling that he's here."

Doug nodded. Though he wasn't genuinely concerned about Dickie's presence, you'd never have known it from his reply. "I understand, honey, I'll tend to it. But don't worry, he's okay, a bit rough looking, yes, but otherwise harmless."

Kay frowned.

"You know," Doug said, staring out the window again, "looking like he does and sitting there silhouetted against the weathered shingles of the shop like that, he reminds me of a Norman Rockwell painting. Don't you think?"

Kay shook her head. "Spare me that one, no matter how much I like Rockwell's."

Doug laughed. "I'll go tend to him," he said, heading for the shop door.

"Hi, Dickie," Doug said, hanging his head out. "What's up, guy?"

Dickie got slowly to his feet. "Well, I got some more information about things at the mill, you know, ya told me to let you know if I heard anything."

"Yes," Doug said. "Do you want to come in?"

"That would be okay I guess."

Doug backed up and Dickie stepped inside, pulling the door closed.

"Have you been waiting long?" Doug asked.

Dickie shrugged his shoulders. "Not too long. Don't matter though. Time I got."

Doug nodded. "So you have some new information."

"Yeah. Quite a bit of stuff."

"Well then, why don't we go inside where we'll be comfortable."

In the kitchen Doug introduced Dickie to Kay, who was preparing a pound of beef for her special meat loaf. "Yes, we kind of met in the shop," she said, continuing to mix the ingredients, which Doug knew was her excuse not to shake hands.

"Dickie has some more information about the mill," Doug said.

"Oh, that's good."

"Sure is a nice place you folks have got here," Dickie said, his eyes wandering across the furnishings of the spacious kitchen.

"Thank you," Doug said pausing, wondering if he'd made the right decision to invite Dickie in. After all, he'd only met him once before. Normally he would have taken a guest to the den, but that didn't feel right. At the risk of disturbing Kay's dinner preparation, he decided it was best to talk, at least for the time being, at the kitchen table.

"Well, have a seat," Doug said.

They sat down across from each other.

"Can we get you something to drink—water, juice, something stronger perhaps?"

"Oh, a glass of water would be okay I guess."

Doug got up to get it but Kay shooed him back. "I'll get it, honey, you want one?"

"No, I'm not supposed to be drinking, remember," he said, patting his cheek.

"Oh, that's right."

Doug sat back down. "So, Dickie, you've heard from somebody at the mill?"

"Yeah, that's right. I still got me some friends up there, guys that are still working there."

Doug waited while Kay put a tall glass of water in front of Dickie.

"Thanks," he said, reaching for the glass.

Kay smiled faintly. "You're welcome."

Dickie took a long drink, slurping it louder than was polite, and wiping his face with the back of his hand. "Gee whiz, that's good water. Nice and cold."

"Purified," Doug said. "We bought the works just in case."

"Well, I don't blame you for not drinking the water around here, considering what's going on."

"What do you mean by that?" Doug asked, intrigued by Dickie's words.

"Well, it's like I said, like I told ya before, the mill don't care, they were always cutting corners, but since the fire they've been discharging right into the river, no treatment, no nothing. People think I got a grudge, but it's not that, I know what they're doing, you don't work in a place for as many years as I did and not know what's going on." Dickie paused, his eyes drifting around the room. "Do you suppose I could use the head?"

Doug got up. "Oh sure, it's down the hall to the left," he said, pointing him in the right direction. As soon as he disappeared Doug looked at Kay and smiled, hunching his shoulders. "Would you mind if he stayed for dinner?" he asked in what was almost a whisper.

Kay tipped her head back and rolled her eyes without saying anything.

"I know, I know," Doug said, "but I'd like to pick his brain. He's all I've got to go on."

Kay nodded her approval.

A minute later Dickie was back at the table.

"Would you like to stay for dinner?" Doug asked.

"No," Dickie said, "you weren't planning on me."

"No, really," Doug said, touching the fingers of his right hand to the right side of his face, "I had a tooth pulled this afternoon, I won't be eating much. Regardless, we'd like you to stay."

"Okay then," Dickie said. "Thanks."

"Well, why don't we go to the den," Doug said, knowing that Kay would prefer to have the kitchen to herself.

They both got up and Dickie turned from the table without taking his glass.

"Don't you want your water?" Doug asked.

"Oh, yeah," Dickie said, turning to pick it up.

"You sure you don't want a beer? I think we've got some Rolling Rock."

"Well, ya, that would be okay I guess," he said, putting the glass back down.

Doug went to the refrigerator and got out a bottle.

"Do you need a glass?" he asked, holding up the bottle for Dickie to see from across the room.

"No, that's okay."

For the next half hour Doug and Dickie talked in the den, uninterrupted by Kay.

"So your buddy at the mill has told you this, right?"

"Yeah, his name is Amos Bird."

"I don't need to know names, at least not at this point, the important thing is what he said. Where does he work?"

"Amos, he's maintenance, so pretty much all over."

"You mean all over the mill?"

"Yeah, you know, they go to wherever they're needed, they got themselves a shop, but they go everywhere carting what they need for a job."

"So what exactly did he tell you?"

"Well, he knows the place good like I do, after working there for as long as we have ya know things. He said after the fire, you know, the next day like, they started using direct discharge."

"What do you mean by direct discharge?" Doug asked.

"Well, every mill, I guess every mill, they got the means to discharge waste water direct, without treatment. It's not something they got a right to do, but they can do it if things get really bad."

"Discharge directly to the river you mean?" Doug asked, straightening up in his chair.

"That's right, people don't know it, I didn't even know till Amos told me," Dickie said, taking a swallow of beer and wiping his mouth with the back of his hand. "They got the means to do it, but they're not allowed to use it except in a life-threatening kinda deal, but see, the way it's rigged, nobody knows where it's going, with all the pipes, underground and all."

"But, if the fire was in the control room, what about the pumps, I mean, you'd still have to have pumps even for direct discharge, wouldn't you?"

"That's how Amos knows, he did some of the work that allowed them to run the pumps from another spot."

"So the pumps weren't damaged in the fire?"

Dickie looked surprised. "No, it was the control room. You don't know the layout, but they ain't near each other, not these pumps."

Doug felt he needed some kind of independent verification, aside from what Amos was saying. "Besides what Amos told you and what you've heard before, is there any other way of knowing for sure that they're doing direct discharge? In other words, not treating the water?"

Dickie didn't hesitate to answer, almost like he was just waiting to be asked the question. "Sure, that's a cinch, the foam."

"The foam?"

"Yeah, there's always some foam in the discharge, but when you don't treat it, there's more, a lot more."

"Foam, huh?"

Dickie nodded.

Doug thought for a moment. "But I guess that doesn't do us any good right now with the river frozen over."

"Well it ain't froze over where they discharge, it never does because the water is something like a hundred degrees."

"How far down is it open?"

"I don't know, not far, maybe a couple hundred feet."

Doug shifted in his chair. "But that area isn't accessible. At least not to you and I. I've checked it out. From what I can tell, the only way you can get a look at the river behind the mill would be to hike in, maybe from the Route 2 bridge, but I bet you'd be trespassing and it may even be fenced. Are there any other ways you can think of to verify what they're doing?"

"Just foam in the discharge," Dickie said, repeating himself. In fact, Dickie kept repeating himself, although he usually included something new each time, so Doug felt it was best to just let him talk. Fifteen minutes later Kay poked her head into the den.

"Dinner is ready," she said with a smile, immediately turning and walking out.

Doug followed Dickie to the dining area and was surprised to find the table beautifully set, and their best serving dishes on the counter. But when he thought about it, he realized that was Kay. It didn't matter who Dickie was, he was a guest, and he got just what any guest of theirs would get. They sat down while Kay placed the steaming serving bowls on the table.

"It's family style," she said for the benefit of Dickie, so just help yourself. "What would you like to drink?"

"Oh, the water is just fine," he said, pointing to the big glassful that was in front of him.

They served themselves, with Doug taking nothing but a heap of mashed potatoes that he covered in gravy.

"I boiled the carrots extra long to soften them, dear," Kay said.

"Thanks."

When Dickie had a plate full of food he started eating like a deprived man, shoveling down mouthfuls of meatloaf and potatoes with his salad fork that he held like an ice pick. You either felt sorry for him or despised his manners. Doug's reaction was mixed but he didn't show it. Twenty minutes later they were done, the mostly empty serving bowls in a circle around Dickie's empty plate, his cloth napkin untouched.

"That was one fine meal, ma'am, just like a Sunday dinner," he said, wiping his hands together and taking a swallow of water from his glass that Kay had just refilled.

"Thank you, I'm glad you enjoyed it," Kay said.

Doug was contemplating what to do next when Dickie decided for him.

"Well, I don't like to eat and run," he said, snickering at his own words, "but I really got to get going if you don't mind."

They all stood up.

"Do you want a ride home?" Doug asked, wondering where home was.

"No, no, I'm all set, I reckon these two feet got me here, they can get me back."

"Are you sure?" Doug asked, "I could..."

Dickie interrupted, waving his hands back and forth. "I'm all set, really, but thanks."

With the Novocain starting to wear off and feeling a bit tired, Doug wasn't about to press the issue. Besides, he reasoned, Dickie was probably going to Doc's Tavern, which was just down the street, the place he had no doubt come from.

Doug did his best to sound upbeat. "Well, thanks for coming and sharing that information with me, if you hear anything new, let me know, no matter what it is. Even if it seems insignificant to you, sometimes it's just the piece I need to finish the puzzle, if you know what I mean."

But Dickie didn't seem to know what he meant, at least he didn't show it as he edged toward the kitchen door. "Sure thing, good bye, ma'am," he said, waving to Kay across the room.

Kay smiled back. "Nice to have met you. Good night."

Dickie opened the door, stepped outside, and turned back. "Thanks again for the supper," he said, closing the door firmly without waiting for a reply.

Doug went to the dark living room, arriving at the window just in time to see Dickie poking along the sidewalk in the direction of Doc's. Doug watched him till he disappeared into the darkness and returned to the kitchen.

"Well, I'm glad that's over with," he announced as he entered.

Kay, who was wiping the already cleared table, stood up straight and smiled. "It wasn't so bad," she said. "He tried his best. Did you find out anything worthwhile from him?"

"Yes and no. He told me a lot of new stuff, but it doesn't really help because it's still coming from him. Without the benefit of some type of independent verification, it's useless. Well, not useless, but for me, I need a third party or…or something tangible."

Kay had gone back to wiping the table. "I thought I heard him say he had talked to somebody at the mill."

"He did, but it's still coming from him. You think I should try to talk to the guy directly?"

"I suppose it's one option," Kay answered, walking to the sink where she shook the cloth into the basin.

Doug shook his head. "I don't know. I'd have to get Dickie's permission and…and the guy he mentioned is working there now, I don't see him talking to me. Dickie is one thing, but I doubt this guy would give me the time of day."

"Well I'm sure you'll think of something, dear," Kay said, raising her voice above the running water and the clanging dishes.

Doug sighed. "Yeah, I suppose," he said, cradling his right cheek in the palm of his hand. "If you don't mind, dear, I'm going to pass on wiping tonight, I'm pooped."

Kay pulled her hands from the sink, grabbed a towel, and spun around. "Of course, honey. Go lie down. Do you need anything?"

"No, I'm all set," he said, as he ambled toward the den.

*   *   *   *

After a restless night Joe left for work early, knowing that the store tended to be in its afternoon lull between lunch and three-thirty or so, when the first shift mill workers started stopping by on their way home. When he got there the store was empty, so he passed up getting coffee, taking advantage of the quiet. With his two hands planted on the edge of the counter he addressed Ethel directly.

"You're up to date on things at White Woods, right?"

Ethel's wrinkled face went blank, prompting Joe to continue.

"I mean everything that has happened this season."

"I guess," she said looking confused. "There ain't much I miss from this perch."

"What do you make of it all, I mean what…?" His voice trailed off.

Ethel curled in her lips and looked at the ceiling, staring at nothing in particular, while she collected her thoughts. "Well, I guess I'd say that most folks don't know what to make of it. It's six of one and half a dozen of another, 'course, they don't know the all of it either, mostly it's bits and pieces they've heard."

Joe saw the opening he was looking for and seized it. "But that's what I mean, that's why I wanted to talk with you, between what we've talked about and all that you hear, I need to know your take on it."

Ethel massaged her chin a couple times and shook her head slowly. "Can't help ya there, Joe. I only know the what of it, not the why. I've tried to take stock of it like everybody else, but it ain't something you can put your finger on. You know that. It's kind of like the plague the way it's been spreading. One thing after another and all. If I had to point to any one thing I'd say it's probably political, maybe the environmentalists, maybe Warren pushed one of them too far, somebody with the grit, maybe the wherewithal to push back. You don't know these days. Ya just don't know."

"I suppose," Joe said, just as two chattering woman walked in, stealing the floor from him with their bubbling enthusiasm about their shopping trip to Bangor which they were anxious to share with Ethel.

Joe smiled and backed out of the conversation. He got coffee, counted out the right change, and returned to the counter, where he dropped it into Ethel's outstretched hand and left without a word. Surprisingly, he wasn't disappointed about his chat with her. For some reason, as he was inclined to do, he expected her to know more than he did.

Following an uneventful evening, Joe was in his office, finishing off the turkey Italian his mother had bought for his dinner when a flurry of radio traffic hit the airwaves a half hour into second shift.

"510, 512, where are you?"

"Just below mid-station. Why?"

"Nothing, disregard. 510, 515."

"515."

"Are you still on Supply Side?"

"Yeah."

"502, 510, what's going on?" Al asked.

"I don't know. We're on Thin Air right at Bail Out and we could have sworn we saw somebody on Universe walking down."

"On Universe?"

"Yeah, you know, by that straight stretch where you can see all the way."

"You sure it wasn't just an animal."

"On two legs!"

"Okay. How long ago?"

"Just now, when we called 512."

"Where are you now, can you still see him?" Al asked.

"We're just getting to Universe now, hold-on."

Joe had heard enough. If somebody was on the mountain, it was unusual, particularly at this hour and at that elevation. The person 510 saw might just be their saboteur. Without using air time that Al and the others might need, Joe trotted down the hall past the control desk, yelling to Marty that he was heading for Universe, and flew out the door, jacking up the volume on his radio as the crew's play-by-play continued.

"Okay, 510, 502."

"Go ahead," Al replied.

"We're on Universe, we can just barely make him out in the dark, but it's a person all right. There ain't no question about that."

Joe's heart started to pound. This might be the break he so desperately needed.

"You're sure?" Al asked.

"Positive."

"Okay. Where exactly is he?"

"Just below where we put those new tower guns in last summer, but he's gone from sight now. Either he ducked into the woods when he saw our lights, or he dropped down below the head wall. We can't see him anymore."

"Okay, there's a groomer in The Junction, he's going to watch for the guy from there."

"Okay. What do you want us to do?"

There was a pause before Al answered. "Just stay put, for now anyway."

As Joe sped along Go Between he decided to call Al. "501, 502."

"502, go ahead, Joe."

"Where are you?"

"Coming down the triple. Are you at the pump house?"

"Negative. I'm headed for Universe."

"Okay, did you hear everything, Joe?"

"I think so. I'm going to head for The Junction and go up from there. You said there's a groomer in The Junction, right?"

"Yeah, Greg's right there, he said he'd keep his eyes peeled, but if this is our man he's probably going to steer clear of him and you. He's probably long gone."

"Maybe…501, pump house."

"Pump house."

"Would you advise Johnny what we got, the guy will probably go cross country, but if by chance we flush him out it will be to North Slope."

"10-4," Marty said.

Joe found Greg sitting in his dark idle groomer in a hollow just above the North Slope lift shacks with the door open smoking a cigarette. Easing his sled to a stop beside him, Joe shut off his engine.

"Nothing, huh?" he asked.

Greg shook his head. "I haven't see hide nor hair of anybody. I set up here just as soon as Al called, but he must have gotten by me. Either that or he took to the woods."

Joe nodded. "If he did that, he'd have to have snow shoes."

Greg dragged on his cigarette, flipping it away as he exhaled. "I suppose. You think it was a star gazer, or somebody up to no good?"

Joe eyes narrowed. "One guy alone this far above the condos at this hour. Seems to me it was somebody up to no good."

Greg nodded, fishing another cigarette out of the pack in his shirt pocket. "Well, I've got to get moving. I'll let ya know if I see anything, Joe," he said, sticking the cigarette into his mouth as he reached for the door.

"Good, thanks for your help."

Greg nodded and closed the door.

Joe checked every trail on North Slope, zigzagging often so his light lit up the woods. Finding nothing, he passed through The Junction and directly up Universe, where he found Pete and his partner hunkered down several hundred feet below Bail Out. After questioning them about what they had seen and speculating with them about who it might have been, he sent them back to Thin Air, descended Universe, took another pass on North Slope, and returned to the pump house where he found Al waiting for him at the control desk.

"What do you think?" Al asked.

Joe shrugged. "I don't know, I'd say it was probably our man. I mean, who else?"

Al nodded. "I'd sure like to get my hands on him, whoever he is."

Joe turned to Marty. "Did you get ahold of Johnny?"

"Sure did, he said he'd 'trol the area."

After a few minutes speculating about the situation, Joe went back to his office and Al returned to checking snow quality on Supply Side. At quarter of one, Joe was back at the control desk talking to Marty when the telephone rang. Marty plucked it from the cradle and barked his usual greeting into the mouthpiece.

Almost immediately he lowered the handset. "It's Johnny," he said, without a hint of excitement. "Somebody was just in the tunnel at North Slope and they ran on him."

Joe sprang to his feet. "Tell him I'm on the way," he said, snatching his helmet and gloves from where he had shed them earlier and racing from the building. Two minutes later, halfway down the middle trail of North Slope, he snapped off the sled's light and slowed to a crawl, scanning the darkness, knowing his best bet of seeing somebody was silhouetted against the brightly lit buildings that lay below.

A hundred feet from the lodge, a powerful light appeared from the second level deck, bathing Joe in its beam and momentarily blinding him. Irritated, he lurched the sled slightly forward to escape the glare. When the light went dark, Joe squinted at where it had been just in time to see Johnny bounding down the deck steps two at a time, which was testimony to his age, and run toward where Joe had stopped.

"Hey, Chief," he said, winded only slightly by the pack-and-a-half a day that he smoked, "I was lying low, hoping to see him again. I don't know who it is, but I bet it was the guy that was up above earlier. It's weird this late, even for a weekend."

"What was he doing?" Joe asked coldly, still bothered by Johnny's tactless method of signaling him.

"I first saw him from the car. He was on the other end of the tunnel then," Johnny said, pointing to the walkway that went under the lodge. "He saw me, I mean, I guess he did, 'cause he disappeared real fast-like. When I got out here he was gone, and he shouldn't have been, not if he was walking normal."

Joe decided to play devil's advocate. "You think maybe he was just after something from a vending machine, like a soda or maybe a newspaper, and he doubled back to his condo? Sounds crazy at this hour, but you know how people are."

Johnny was skeptical. "I don't think so. I don't think this was kosher. Something wasn't right. I bet it was that guy from earlier. I bet it's got something to do with everything that's been happening."

Joe nodded. "Jump on, we'll have a look around."

"Cool," Johnny said as he hopped over the back of the sled and settled down onto the ample vinyl seat behind Joe.

They circled the two lift shacks and slowly cruised a couple hundred yards of tree line on both sides of the four slopes that gently climbed from the North Slope base area. Johnny occasionally turned on his seven-cell flashlight, panning it through the sparsely wooded trail sides. Back in front of the lodge Joe eased the sled to a stop, and Johnny got off.

"Well anyway, thanks for coming down, Chief," he said, passing his flashlight from hand to hand.

"Sure, anytime," Joe said smiling.

"You know, it's a hell of a thing," Johnny said. "We ran with the extra guy for what, almost a month, and nothing happens, and now this."

Joe shrugged.

"I suppose they couldn't afford to do it forever," Johnny added.

"I heard it wasn't the money, they just needed day shift coverage, was all."

Johnny thought for a moment. "Yeah, sure, to do all that public relations crap that ain't our job anyway. Don't that take the cake, using security like that, I mean. I'm telling you, one of these days it's going to be pay back time. A lot of shit happens around here." He paused. "Well, anyway, thanks again, Chief."

"Don't hesitate to call if you need anything, I mean it," Joe replied, moving away.

Johnny raised his voice to compensate for the throttled engine and the distance that had suddenly developed between them. "I won't, see ya."

Joe was halfway back to the pump house via the lodge connector when Marty radioed, telling him Johnny had called again to say he had the guy. Barely making a tight U-turn on the narrow connector trail, Joe gunned the sled and headed back toward North Slope, quietly chiding himself for not staying longer.

As he descended the final hundred feet before the lodge, he saw two figures moving across the long wide deck of the ski school building, located adjacent to the lodge. He aimed the sled for them and accelerated again, stopping inches from the deck. Holding a rusted double barrel shotgun upright in his left hand, Johnny was using his right hand to guide from behind a handcuffed man of at least sixty-five. Except for his head, which sported a dirty crumpled Celtics cap, the old man was dressed warmly. At his collar, Joe counted at least four upper body garments, and the size and tightness of his pant legs were telltale of multiple layers.

Joe silenced the sled's engine and rose to his feet, meeting them on the deck's steps. Purposely, Joe didn't say anything, preferring to let Johnny take the lead on what was clearly beyond Joe's authority to be involved with.

"I found him in the alley between the buildings," Johnny proudly announced, beaming from ear to ear. He paused and held up the shotgun. "With this," he concluded.

Joe nodded, unsure of what to say.

"I'm going to walk him back to the Suburban and wait for the sheriff, I already called them, they got a deputy in Franklin they're sending down A-S-A-P."

Apparently believing Joe was Johnny's supervisor, or somebody else he wasn't, the old man spoke as he passed by, pushing his face close to Joe's. "You're making a big mistake, you got no right," he declared.

Neither Joe nor Johnny said anything. Johnny just pushed the old man along a little faster toward the tunnel, the flashlight in his back pocket flopping back and forth to the cadence of his stride. Joe had an uneasy feeling about the situation. Hadn't Johnny overstepped his authority by handcuffing the old man? Joe wasn't sure of the law, but didn't criminal trespass require signs or fences?

Certainly the row of vending machines that lined the sides of the tunnel, the ATM's that straddled its entrance, and the myriad of wall-mounted literature racks that dotted the walls between the ticket windows weren't off limits at any hour, particularly since late lodging arrivals would often partake of their offerings. Joe figured Johnny was probably okay since the old man was in the alley and carrying a shotgun, but he silently wished Johnny had waited until the deputy arrived.

In any event, he knew that leaving Johnny alone till the deputy got there was a bad idea, so he pulled the key from his sled and followed, jogging to catch up. When he got to the Suburban the old man was sitting on the step of the vehicle's open passenger door whining about how tight the handcuffs were.

"The more you move the tighter they'll get," Johnny said, standing in front of him inspecting the shotgun. With the breach open, Joe could see it wasn't loaded. Johnny looked at Joe and tossed his head in the direction of the old man as he walked to the vehicle's back doors where he stowed the weapon.

"You got no right screwing with me," the old man said when Johnny returned. "I wasn't bothering nobody."

Johnny's response was immediate. "So what were you doing then?"

"Like I already told you twice before, I was hunting coons," the old man said fiercely.

"Yeah, right, we have a lot of people doing that here. In case you didn't notice this is a ski resort."

The old man took a deep breath. "I'm telling you I was hunting coons over on Carter Peak. I was just heading home."

"So where's your car then?" Johnny asked.

"I don't have no car," he snarled.

Johnny shook his head in disgust and scanned the parking lot. "The deputy ought to be here anytime now," he said, addressing Joe directly.

"Good." Joe knew better than to get involved, but he felt they ought to at least hear what the old man had to say. He knew he was letting his curiosity get the best of him, but he needed to know more. "So you live nearby?" he asked the old man.

"Yeah, last place in on the Valley Road, lived there all my life."

Joe knew Valley Road was the original name for White Woods Road before Warren had gotten the town to change it. But Johnny didn't.

"Valley Road?" he said.

"That's the name of it, least it was before they came along, stealing and changing things to suit their needs."

"So you were walking home then?" Joe said, hoping the sincerity of his tone would draw out the old man. It did.

"That's right," he said, his attention now directed solely at Joe. "I often loop up around, I'm telling ya, I wasn't doing nothing I haven't done a hundred times before. 'Course it's just like the fucking bastard son of Taylor to have me hauled in." The old man dropped his head, seemingly defeated by his own words.

Standing as still as a fence post, his eyes fixed on the old man, Joe was silent while he repeated to himself the six words he had just heard. "The fucking bastard son of Taylor." If there was any doubt about Warren Ainsworth being the son of Warren Taylor, the old man had just spontaneously put it to rest. Joe's minded raced forward. Who is this guy? What else does he know?

"Hello," Johnny said, invading Joe's body space with his hand that he waved rapidly in front of his face. "Are you there?"

Joe took a small step backwards and smiled at Johnny. "Yeah, sure."

"I thought I'd lost you there for a minute," Johnny said, oblivious to the old man's claim.

"Just thinking," Joe said causally, turning his attention back to the old man who was still hunched over, not moving. Against his better judgment he continued the conversation, opening with a harmless question that he hoped would get the old man talking again.

"Were you up on Universe, up on the mountain earlier tonight?"

The old man slowly raised his head. "Yeah, so what if I was. Sometimes I go back that way. There ain't no harm in it. I wasn't bothering nobody."

"I didn't say you were, but it's not like we have people out on the mountain at night."

The man grunted just as a pair of headlights crested the access road hill and started across the parking lot.

Darn, Joe thought to himself, I need to talk to this guy some more.

Johnny met the Deputy, who didn't look to be much older than he was, at the cruiser. The two of them talked for a few minutes, a conversation Joe couldn't hear. He was tempted to continue questioning the old man, but felt uneasy talking to him in the absence of Johnny. After all, he was under arrest, wasn't he?

It was close to three o'clock when the deputy loaded the man into the caged back seat of his aging cruiser, transferred the shotgun to his trunk, and roared off. Johnny thanked Joe for staying, locked up the Suburban, and hurried off to the Reception Center to do his report, which he said the deputy would need the next morning in court if the old man didn't make bail. Joe watched him lumber away, the otherwise smooth nylon of his navy coat wrinkling with each broad step he took.

Back at the pump house, Marty, who was halfway through a crusted uncut sandwich with a paper-thin filling of peanut butter, insisted on all the details. Joe talked freely about what had happened, but he purposely held back on what the old man said about Warren and Warren being father and son and the grudge he apparently had against them.

When Joe turned to look at the clock on the wall he was surprised to find it was after four. Where had the last hour gone?

Joe stood up, stretched, and was about to tell Marty he was calling it a night when Johnny burst into the control desk area, his youthful enthusiasm still bubbling forth from earlier.

"Thanks for your help, Chief. I couldn't have done it without you. You too, Marty, thanks."

"You did just fine," Joe said.

"Yeah, well, I guess, but the worst part of it is he's already made bail. The deputy said he wasn't back in his patrol area before the guy was being released, it sure makes you wonder, don't it?"

"He already made bail?" Joe asked despite the fact he had clearly heard Johnny say so.

"Yeah. The deputy just called me so I wouldn't do a rush job on my report, but it's all done anyway. Crazy isn't it, him making bail, I mean."

Joe nodded. "Yeah, I guess. So when will he appear in court?"

Johnny face went blank. "I don't know."

"Probably never," Marty chimed in. "Warren won't let them prosecute him. He wouldn't have let you pinch him if he'd had a say."

Johnny looked at Joe then back at Marty. "I don't know about that," he finally said. "I filled the deputy in on what's been happening here. He said he was going to read the reports and talk with their detective and…" Johnny's voice trailed off.

"Ah," Marty said waving his left hand at Johnny while the other one fingered the channel button on the remote.

Joe watched the television as Marty flipped through the channels, bypassing some of them without stopping long enough for the picture to settle. Prior to Johnny's arrival, Joe had decided that he needed to talk with the old man again, and soon. It was possible that the old man held the key to all that was eluding him. But if the sheriff's department detective was going to get involved, wouldn't he be meddling in a criminal investigation? Joe was about to feel out Johnny on the subject when he spoke. "Well, I better go make some rounds," he said. "We'll see you guys later and thanks again for the help."

"Anytime, Johnny," Joe said. Marty was still grazing channels when Joe left the control desk a few minutes later. He ought to go home, but something was gnawing at him. He left the pump house, intending to walk the perimeter of the parking lot when the resort's pick-up caught his eye. If the keys are in it, I'll take a ride down to the river he thought.

He climbed into the cab and pulled down the visor. The keys fell into his lap. Halfway down the access road, it occurred to him that nobody knew where he was going and his radio was sitting in its charger in his office.

Instead of turning around, he eased the truck to a stop and lit up a cigar, taking a couple of deep drags before he lightened the pressure of his foot on the brake and let the truck slowly gain speed. He spent close to half an hour in the truck, making a pass at the river just to say he had. When he got back to the pump house Marty was engrossed in a basketball game that he was bringing to life with his special brand of spectator narration.

Joe stood behind him just long enough to peruse the computer screens, which looked normal. Then he said, "I'm going home."

"See ya in church," Marty replied without changing his relaxed position in the chair.

At home, Joe ate the three-course meal his mother had left for him in the refrigerator, which required only heating, and watched the last half hour of a movie he had seen twice before, which relaxed him enough to get to sleep.

The next day Joe left for work at the usual time, the action of the previous night no longer at the forefront of his thoughts. But it didn't stay that way. When Joe walked into the store for coffee, Ethel wasted no time motioning him over to the counter.

There was excitement in her voice. "I almost called you at home, Joe, when I heard about Henry Pike getting himself arrested on the mountain last night. I'd forgotten all about him, I mean, why would I have remembered, but maybe things make sense now, Joe. I feel so bad for not seeing it before, if I'm right, that is."

Having been out of bed only a couple hours, Joe was grumpy. "I guess I don't understand," he said, doing his best to conceal the fact he was irritated.

There was no dampening Ethel's exuberance. "Henry grew up here in Cannon, on a cow farm, over on the other side of town. After the war he married and built a modest place, out in the pucker brush on nothing more than a speck of land alongside the river on what's now White Woods Road, all the way to the end, where it's nothing but rutted gravel. He went to work at National as a custodian, where he made a decent living but nothing more. Not too long after that, his wife got a big chunk of inheritance money. People expected them to move but they stayed put. About a year later they bought Carter Peak and the land in the valley below it, probably four or five thousand acres all together."

"He owned Carter Peak?" Joe asked not waiting for an answer. "Are we talking about the same guy, because, because..." His voice trailed off when a customer entered the store.

"Hi, Mabel," Ethel said, waving back at the stooped-over woman who was wrestling with two hand baskets, trying to separate them. Ethel lowered her voice and continued. "He did then, own Carter Peak I mean, and that's what I'm getting at. Anyway, it wasn't long before his wife got sick, first one thing then another, complications I guess, she'd never been well. Henry cherished that woman, and when she got sick he bought her the best care money could buy. So it wasn't long before their savings were used up, and they were strapped for cash. What you'd call land-poor. They fell behind paying their bills, including the taxes on the land, and never got caught up, you now how it is. In, oh, it must have been the mid-fifties, Warren came along, and he snapped up Carter Peak for back taxes. I suppose he had his mind set on expanding even then, because he bought up some other land adjacent to White Woods. But…how you doing, Mabel," Ethel said as the old woman passed slowly behind Joe to the next aisle.

"Not bad for an old lady."

As she turned the corner, Joe was close to her, closer than he would have liked, considering from her looks she probably had body odor. Her gray unkempt hair, showing signs of having been laid on, fell loosely around her large wrinkled neck. Her bulky white overcoat was dirty, and dotted with enough dull-colored stains of various shapes and sizes it was safe to say most of them had probably been there a while.

Joe raised his eyebrows. Ethel returned a smile and continued.

"Where was I, oh yeah, Henry's wife, she kept getting worse and she needed more than he could do at home, but by then they were broke. There wasn't any Medicare, nothing like that. Folks were expected to pay their own way back then. They tended to her, but back then the good care went to those who could pay for it. She died sometime later and…you all set, Mabel?" Ethel reached for the old woman's basket as Joe backed away, trying to conceal his irritation. Interruptions had a way of rubbing him the wrong way. Without a word he fixed himself a coffee at the back of the store, lingering there till he heard the door slam a few minutes later.

"Where are ya, Joe?" Ethel hollered, as he quickened his pace up the aisle trying not to slop his coffee.

"Right here," he said, rounding the corner, amused at how intent Ethel was to tell this story, which was unusual for her. She plunged right back in.

"So like I was saying, after his wife died, Henry got as bitter as a man can. He swore his wife would have lived if he'd had Carter to sell or maybe use the stumpage as collateral for a loan. He claimed that Warren stole his land and killed his wife, pure and simple."

"Would she have?" Joe asked, taking a sip of his coffee. "Lived that is?"

Ethel shrugged her shoulders. "Who knows, probably not, but the thing was he thought so. It was one of those things that got worse over time, not better. Over the years he became a hermit, and to tell ya the truth that's probably why I had forgotten all about him. We wouldn't see hide nor hair of him for weeks, even months at a time. If the truth be known, I bet he did all his trading over in Chesterfield, just to avoid people he knew."

Joe nodded. "So he blamed the old Warren for his wife's death?"

"He did. 'Course when Warren died, on Carter Peak of all places, it was the talk of the town that Henry had gotten him. They said it was an accident. But I bet they never even talked to Henry. Things were different then. If it looked like an accident, it was an accident."

"So you think maybe Henry killed Warren."

Ethel shook her head. "Who knows. But I never thought so. All Warren had done up to that point was get Henry's land, which he did legally of course. Henry's wife didn't die till a year or so after Warren did, so you might say he didn't have enough reason to do him in. Besides..." Her voice trailed off.

"What?"

Ethel looked away. "Nothing."

Joe wasn't one to pry, but being in the midst of trouble himself, he came on a little stronger than he otherwise would have.

"I'd appreciate you telling me," he said.

Ethel turned back toward Joe, her face stiff. "Warren didn't need any help dying," she said. "He was a heavy drinker and his drinking then was as bad as he ever allowed it to be. It would have been just like the damn fool to get tanked and drive up Carter Peak like he did, he was that way."

"But I wonder, how would Henry have known that Warren and Warren were father and son, I mean, we only proved that recently."

"I don't know, maybe some legal wrangling or something like that brought them together, or maybe Warren tried to buy him out in recent years. His place abutted Warren's land. Or maybe he only suspected it like most of us."

Joe shook his head. "No, he knows it. Last night he said it."

Ethel looked surprised. "So you were there then?"

"Oh yeah. Johnny, the security officer, needed help, so I went over."

"So you saw Henry then?"

"I talked with him," Joe said.

"What'd he say?"

"Well, he mentioned that Warren was the…that he was the son of Warren Taylor," Joe said, avoiding the use of the word bastard.

"So he said that right out?"

Joe raised his eyebrows and nodded. "Yeah, no question about it."

"That adds credence to it then, all of it. I reckon he heard about Carter being developed and he wasn't going to stand for it. I bet he got all fired up, which would explain a heap of things."

"It does make sense."

"'Course it does. I bet he did nothing for thirty years cause nobody tried to do nothing with Carter. As far as I know, nobody ever set foot in there except him. Henry was a real ridge-runner, and word had it he used that land like it was his, hunting and the like, so I bet when he heard about Warren's plans for Carter he probably snapped quicker than a pine twig underfoot."

Two other customers had come in back to back and Joe knew it wouldn't be long before they'd be at the counter. Besides, he had enough to think about.

"Well, I've got to get going."

Ethel nodded. "Think about it, Joe, and I'll do the same."

"I will," Joe said, backing toward the door. "And thanks for your help."

"I just hope it explains things and gets ya backs on an even keel up there."

Whenever Joe left a conversation with Ethel he felt good. He figured it was the chemical thing that some people have between them. His mother was always saying it existed. In any event, Joe's hope for normalcy seemed to be within reach. If Henry had done everything, or even most everything, the mess that had consumed his life might be cleared up soon. No longer would his days and nights be filled with notions of what might happen, could happen. The constant supply of what ifs that his brain seemed to mass-produce would be gone. Wouldn't they? However, the more he thought about it, the less likely that seemed. How could such a simplistic event wash away all his troubles? I just need some quiet time to piece everything together he thought as he backed into his usual parking spot beside the pump house. But it wasn't to be. The rickety pair of snowshoes leaning against the wall across from the control desk caught his eye immediately.

"What are these?" he asked Marty.

"Ski patrol brought them in first thing when I got here, somebody found them up on Universe alongside the trail and figured they belonged to us. I tried to tell them they didn't, but the guy that brought them over left them anyway."

Joe picked them up. "They're old. You say they were found on Universe?"

"No, I didn't, the patroller did."

"Did he say when he found them?"

"I don't remember if he did."

"Do you remember who it was that brought them?"

"I haven't got the foggiest."

"Okay, thanks."

"Sorry, Joe, I didn't know you'd be interested in them or I'd have paid him more attention."

"That's okay, I'll take care of it. Everything else okay?"

"Haven't heard that is isn't."

Joe nodded and started for his office, taking the snowshoes with him. He figured ski patrol was probably already closed, but he knew that if they had an injury or two late in the day they might still be there, waiting for transportation. He punched their three-digit number in and waited. A young voice answered on the fifth ring.

"Yeah, this is Joe Littlefield from snowmaking."

"Yes, sir."

"Somebody from over there brought in a pair of snowshoes, are you familiar with that?"

"Yeah, that was me."

"Oh, did you find them?"

"No, Juston did. But he's gone."

"Do you know where they were? We heard they were on Universe, is that what Juston said?"

"Yeah. He said he'd seen them there since morning, and when they were still there toward the end of the day, he brought them in. Tom told me to bring them to you. We figured they were yours."

"Okay, thanks."

Joe slowly hung up the handset, his mind racing ahead. It was already too dark to go looking for tracks on Universe. If only he hadn't talked with Ethel so long. But that had been important too, hadn't it? He carefully slid the snowshoes between the wall and his filing cabinet where they would be out of sight, and went back to the control desk, where he helped himself to a coffee.

"Have one of them chocolate chip cookies my wife made, they're good, real chewy," Marty said.

Joe sat down, running his eyes across the computer screens. "No thanks," he said.

"Good thing you weren't around at starting time. It was hell getting the boys out there, they had their minds made up to talk."

"Yeah, well, there's a lot to talk about."

Marty repositioned his hat. "You know, I don't remember him, but you got a good look at him, how old would you say he was?"

"I think I heard Johnny tell the deputy he was 69."

"69, huh. He's only got ten years on me, seems I should remember him. So I suppose this clears things up then?"

Joe didn't feel he should speculate with Marty. Doing so would be like sharing it with the entire crew.

"Jury's still out on that, don't you think?"

"How so?"

"We'll see. Sometimes these things never get cleared up for sure. Well, I got things to do," Joe said, walking away, mostly interested in putting an end to the conversation.

✳   ✳   ✳   ✳

On Friday, the day after New Year's, Doug telephoned the Department of Environmental Protection. It was by no means the first time he had called state or federal environmental authorities, so he was prepared for the endless transfers and the time he'd have to spend on hold. When his call finally funneled to the right person, he wasn't surprised to get their voice mail. After all, with New Year's Day falling on a Thursday, a lot of people had taken off the day after. He passed at the opportunity to leave a message and hung up.

On Monday, he called back, escaping the network maze by asking for the person he had been referred to on Friday.

"Alex Stone," the man said, sounding so informal that Doug wondered if he knew he was on an outside line and not on the intercom.

"Good morning, my name is Doug Andrews."

"What can I do for you, Mr. Andrews?"

"I understand you're the pulp and paper mill expert."

"Yeah, that's one of my fortes. How can I help you?"

"What can you tell me about National Pulp and Paper in Waterford?"

There was a slight pause. "As it relates to what?"

"Just generally."

"Well, it's a medium sized mill by Maine standards. A foreign company that as yet hasn't delivered on its promise to spend some badly needed money on upgrades purchased it not too long ago, but overall it's a good clean operation. Was there something specific?"

"So you're not aware of any problems, environmental problems I mean?"

"No. We had a couple of spills up there years ago, but they were ruled accidental and their post-spill response was good, real good as I recall, other than that, nothing."

"What about those spills?"

"Like I said, they happened, oh, it must have been two or three years ago. They were accidental, both of them, and they voluntarily did what they needed to do to prevent future occurrences. There's no consent decree at National, nothing pending. They're closed cases."

"I see. Now they discharge their waste water to the Salem River, correct?"

"Yes, that's right."

"What can you tell me about the water quality of the Salem River?"

"The Salem," he said, hesitating to make a point, "is a clean river. We're not aware of any problems at this point in time. Was there something, maybe somewhere specific that was of interest to you?"

"I've got some concerns about the paper mill's discharge."

"You mean National?"

"Yes. Why? Is there another one?"

"Yeah, there's Saint Louis in Rockwell, 30 miles to the south. It's one of the state's largest mills."

"Oh, I didn't know that. Right in Rockwell, huh."

"Yes."

"Well the one I'm interested in is National."

"We're not aware of any problems on the river from National, if there..."

Doug interrupted. "You say from National, does that mean that there are problems with the river from another source?"

"Oh no, that isn't what I meant, not at all, we're not aware of any problems on the Salem period. Are you familiar with the Clean Water Act?"

"Not very."

"Well, industries, like National, that discharge their waste into a surface water body, like the Salem, are called point sources of pollution, and they have to be licensed. They have to obtain a permit from the EPA, and a discharge license from us."

"They have to have both then?"

"In Maine they do, because we haven't sought permit deregulation from the EPA."

"Oh."

"Anyway, National has to regularly monitor their effluent and report the results to the EPA and us. Like I said, we have a separate permitting procedure, but the EPA shares the compliance information and the discharge monitoring reports with us."

"So they do their own monitoring then?"

"That's right. They do pH, BOD, the simple tests. The complex tests like Dioxin are done by a private lab that has to have a DEP and a EPA certification."

"So the mill reports the simple tests to you and the private lab sends their results."

"Actually, the lab reports to the mill and the mill reports to us."

"How would I access the monitoring data?" Doug asked.

"Just ask to see it, it's all public stuff."

"So I can just waltz into your offices and ask to see it then?"

"Yeah, you can. Obviously we'd prefer to know you're coming so we can best serve you. We don't get much call for that stuff."

Doug laughed. "So they're not beating a trail to your door then?"

"Hardly. No, really, anything we have is public, available for public inspection, except for enforcement records, those are off limits. But everything else is open to the public. But regardless, if for some reason you weren't getting what you wanted you could file a Freedom of Information Act request for it. But I can't think of any circumstance where you'd have to."

Doug figured that Alex probably wanted to end the conversation there, but he wasn't finished. "Could you tell me about your testing stations?"

"Sure," Alex said, his tone of voice remaining steady, "but they're not ours, they're owned and operated by United States Geological Survey, they…"

"Who?"

"United States Geological Survey, or USGS for short, they're the principal water-data collector for the country. They have tens of thousands of sites nationwide that do water quality and quantitative water measurement."

"I never heard of them."

"I'm not surprised, they're not exactly a consumer type agency, but they've been doing it a long time. They go back to the 1800's. Anyway, for the mills, they do temperature, pH, specific conductance, and dissolved oxygen. They monitor constantly and download their data in real time, so we would detect anything out of the ordinary immediately and react to it immediately."

"So they download to your offices?"

"No, it goes to USGS. They share the data with us."

"Oh. Where are they?"

"They have an office in Augusta."

"So the information is received there?"

"That I don't know, maybe, but in any event it's shared with us regularly."

"How many testing stations are there?"

"In Maine we got one located downstream from each of the ten mills."

"So there are only ten of them total?"

"Yes."

"Which means there are two on the Salem, right?"

"That's right, one below National and one below Saint Louis."

"Where exactly are they located?"

"That I don't know."

"Is it public?"

"Oh sure, you can know, I just don't happen to, you'd have to call USGS. I can give you the number if you want. I'm not sure if it's toll free, though."

"What about test results?"

"You mean recent data?"

"Whatever," Doug said, knowing he wouldn't be satisfied with any information he received over the telephone from some guy whose only interest was seeing the clock strike five.

"Well, we analyze it on a regular basis. If any irregularities had been identified, they would have been reported."

"I see."

Doug was beginning to feel the frustration that had become so familiar in Dracut. Alex was obviously giving him the standard bureaucratic run around. He knew he could ask him to define regular, explain what he meant by irregularities, and disclose who they would report to, but he knew that would only serve to satisfy his ego.

"But I can assure you there is no reason to worry, Mr. Andrews. National is in compliance as far as we're concerned. I talk with their environmental manager two or three times a week. You may not know it, but unlike years ago the environmental manager is on equal footing today with everybody else in authority. The standards are in place, the checks and balances are there, and if anything was wrong we'd be addressing it."

"When was the last time you or one of your colleagues visited National?"

A slight pause preceded Alex's response. "You mean the last inspection?"

"No, I mean the last time somebody from your office was physically there on-site. You've alluded to receiving test data daily and talking on the phone with them two or three times a week, but when was the last time you or somebody from DEP was actually there?"

"I'd have to check on that. This is a big office, there's land, water, and air quality, hazardous waste, then it would depend on whether it was permitting, compliance, enforcement, I wouldn't have any way of knowing, really."

"So you can't give me a ballpark figure?"

"No, there is no way I could...like I said, we have..."

Doug interrupted. "Okay then, when was the last time you were there personally?"

Again there was a pause. "September...I guess...but really, Mr. Andrews, rest assured, the protocols are there. We appreciate your interest, actually we depend on people like you to be our eyes and ears. I'll double check things up there, but I'm sure there is no need for concern, not in their case. If you hear about something specific, definitely let us know and we'll send an inspector immediately, usually the same day we receive the complaint."

Doug didn't mind being pushy. "And what would that entail?"

"A site visit, beyond that, it depends on the nature of the complaint. If we suspected a waste water treatment problem, the first thing we'd probably do is split a water sample with them and conduct our own tests."

"I see. And you'd do that upon receipt of a complaint?"

"Yes, definitely, if you have something specific. That's what we're here for."

"Okay then, one more thing."

"Sure."

"Do you have or does the agency have a map of the Salem River?"

"I assume you mean in the area of National."

"Yeah."

"No, we got...yeah, yeah the mill's on it, we've got a map of the watershed. I don't know what you want it for, but it will probably work for you."

"Do you have what I'll call a plot plan of the mill?"

"Yes."

"Would it be possible to get a copy of that?"

"Yes and no. It depends on what you're looking for in terms of detail. I think we got a reduced layout version on eleven by seventeen and a half I can send you, but it doesn't show much of anything besides buildings and landmarks."

"Does it show the river in relation to the mill?"

"Yeah, I think it does. It really isn't much, though."

"What about something that would show the path of waste water discharge, from the mill to the treatment facility to the river, that kind of thing."

"That's what I meant when I asked what you were looking for. We've got dozens of rolled close-ups but they all show different things. I think I know what you're looking for though. I've got a small set that might be helpful, it doesn't show much and it's not to scale, but it might be something you could use."

"Could you mail that and the map to me then?"

"Sure, give me your name again and your mailing address. I'll get it out to you today, the mail room willing."

Doug gave Alex the information, said goodbye, and hung up feeling frustrated. Granted he hadn't given Alex anything specific, he wasn't ready to do that just yet, but nonetheless, Alex hadn't shown any interest, he hadn't tried to corner Doug's concern by pushing him about the purpose of his call. At first Doug dismissed Alex's bureaucrat sweet talk as nothing more than a government official who was too comfortable in his job to say or do anything that rocked the boat. A person who accepted the status quo because anything else meant more work. But the more he thought about it, the more it seemed to him that he had hit a wall with Alex, and he couldn't help but feel that Alex's programmed responses had to do with his past.

Kay told him he was silly. "Maine may be a small state, honey, but a DEP staff in Augusta isn't likely to remember a year-old newspaper article, that is if he happened to read it in the first place. You know how these people are, they always talk like that."

"I'm not so sure this time. That article was something they would talk about, something that somebody probably clipped out of the newspaper and hung up somewhere."

"You're being paranoid," she said.

"I don't think so. You got to figure that DEP people need to be aware of who might be looking over their shoulders, maybe you've forgotten, but that story was strong, stronger than it should have been."

Kay couldn't argue with that. It had been strong and slanted. Published in the Sunday paper which had a statewide circulation of 170,000, as part of a front page series on Maine's future, the article featured Kay and Doug as people from away who relocated to Maine for all it offered, but who were now trying to close the door on others who might follow by stymieing development. The article also showcased their active membership in the Natural Environmental Council, the group that had planted a bull's-eye on every pulp and paper mill in Maine, threatening the state's best paying jobs.

Ignoring the main stream anti-growth work Doug had done in Dracut, the article portrayed him as a radical by focusing almost exclusively on his early days of activism, mentioning he had been arrested many times at various demonstrations, including protesting the construction of Seabrook in 1977.

"I know it was," she said, obviously irritated they were talking about it again, like they had for months following its publication.

"You know, people probably think I'm ashamed of my past, but that isn't it. It's just that times change, people change, I've changed. I'm no less committed or determined, you know that, in a lot of ways I'm more dedicated, but it's how we go about it. We used to think getting in their face was the only way, now we know we've got to create a consensus, work with society at large. I mean, our mission at Seabrook was simple, to halt construction. That approach was right then, but today, it would be crazy. That doesn't make it any less noble, it's just how things have changed. But that article labeled me a radical, ignoring the past ten years of my life." Doug paused. "That reminds me, did

I tell you that Warren Ainsworth, you know, the owner of White Woods, brought up Seabrook when I met with him, kind of threw it in my face in a nice sort of way."

"No, you didn't tell me that."

"Yeah," Doug said frowning. "Like I said, he did it nicely, but I know what he was trying to do. Anyway, you're probably right, that guy at DEP probably didn't know me from a hole in the ground, but he sure said a whole lot without really saying anything, almost like he knew, like he needed to be standoffish with me."

"But that's par for the course, isn't it, dear?"

Doug nodded. "Yeah, I guess."

"Well, I've got laundry to do," Kay said.

Doug nodded. Then, smiling, he said, "If this thing at National pans out the way I think it might it won't matter about my past, it won't matter one bit."

*　　　*　　　*　　　*

Joe enjoyed the evening with Brenda—dinner, shopping, and a late movie—but mostly he treasured the talk they had in the car with the engine running and the headlights on in the parking lot of a dimly lit lounge they hadn't patronized. It had started innocently enough, with him mentioning that things at work weren't going good. Like a cue he hadn't intended, she picked up on it.

"What do you mean? I can't imagine you having problems at work."

"No?"

"No."

Joe shrugged.

Brenda seemed sure of herself. "I was there, I didn't notice anything."

"That was before."

"Before what?"

Joe turned away and looked out the driver's side window, his eyes settling on the changing shades of light that filled a row of little windows on the lounge's rear roofline.

"I'm sorry, Joe, I didn't mean to pry."

Joe looked at her. "You didn't. It's just that things haven't been going good with the crew, that's all, and I'm to blame whether it's my fault or not. But I get dealt my hand, I'm stuck with what others do or don't do, that kind of thing. I know that's my greatest weakness, expecting things to be right in what's an imperfect world. But things could be right if only people would do what's right, you know, care, care about things that matter. But I don't know, it's just the way things are I guess."

"What exactly is it?" Brenda asked softly.

"Oh," Joe said smirking, "don't mind me. It's just everything and...and nothing."

Brenda nodded slowly. "I think I know where you're coming from. I don't mean to sound like I know much about it, but to me it's like we all have a little circle around us and we control only what is within that circle. You hope for the best for things outside it, but you have to accept what's there. Does that make any sense?"

"Yeah, yeah it does."

"That's what I've always tried to do. Like when I write what I think is a really good story and my editor cuts it all to pieces. I don't want to say it doesn't bother me, because it does, but I've learned that the research, the interviews, the writing of the story, maybe even the idea for it, were all within my circle, but once I push that send button on my keyboard it's gone, it's left my circle."

Joe nodded. "I like that. But really, I didn't mean to delve this deeply into it. I just don't like it when my personal best doesn't seem to matter because there are all these elements you can't control that feed into how well you do. But like I said, I didn't mean to burden you with it."

"Oh, I don't mind, really," Brenda said. "It's kind of like something I've been meaning to mention to you but haven't." She paused. "You mentioned about doing right. But sometimes there are two things that are right."

"What do you mean?"

"Well, I wasn't going to bring it up, and I probably shouldn't."

Joe turned to her and locked his eyes on hers. "What is it? You can't hold back now."

Brenda looked straight forward, then back at Joe. "Well...I'm only human and it's kind of been eating at me, if you know what I mean, but I just wish it...I don't want it to be an issue with us. Do you promise you'll understand?"

Joe shrugged. "Sure."

Brenda took a deep breath. "Well, you mentioned that things aren't good at White Woods. I think we've gotten some information about that."

Joe couldn't help his startled look. "Like what?"

"Well, let me preface it with the fact it was anonymous, all three times. We've tried to identify the source but we can't."

Joe was impatient. "So what is it?"

"A lot. The accidents with the snow guns, the fire at the pump house, the old guy that was arrested."

"So you know about that stuff, huh?"

Brenda nodded. "Yes, and I've been working at it feverishly, but we keep coming up empty. My editor doesn't know about our friendship, I can't tell him, because he'd want me to use you to get the story, but I refuse to do it, which isn't really fair to the paper. And I've held it back from you, which wasn't right either. I've really been torn by it. I guess in one way I feel I've been working behind your back, even though I really haven't, and in another way I feel I'm doing a disservice to my editor, not so much because I won't use you to get the story, but because I can't bring myself to tell him about us."

Joe exhaled loudly through his lips. "I see what you mean. So you haven't done any stories yet, right?"

"There isn't anything to print, at least not for us. The resort maintains the snow gun incidents were accidents, nothing more, and..."

Joe interrupted. "But we reported those to the police."

Brenda nodded. "I know. I've talked with them. But the owner maintains they were accidents. And the pump house fire, although ruled suspicious, hasn't got anything to do with the accidents and the guy that was arrested hasn't been tied to anything either. It's nothing unless we can show a connection, which we can't, at least not at this point."

"So you don't know who it came from then?"

"No. Not a clue. Actually, we get a lot of stuff like that, but this seems to be something, and of course with me knowing you it's taken on special meaning. My editor is pushing, because ski stories are always good copy, and this one, if it's anything, would probably be a blockbuster."

Joe tipped his head back, resting it on the seat. "I wonder who it is. It's so strange they'd call you. Was it the same person all three times?"

"We think so. But somebody different talked to him each time."

"So it was a man then?"

"Yes."

"How old would you say?"

"Older, we think, but it's hard to say. So you don't have any idea who it might have been?" Brenda asked.

Joe shrugged. "No, nobody comes to mind right off. I see what you mean though, about me."

Brenda nodded. "Exactly. I didn't plan on saying anything tonight, even though it's been bothering me something terrible, but it seems to relate to what you were saying. You should know, though, that I would never use our friendship in that way."

Joe decided to be forthright. "But if I tell you anything that would be okay, right?"

"Oh sure, and it could be anonymous."

"Even from me?"

"Oh sure. As long as my editor and I know the source is credible, we can run with it."

Joe could tell that Brenda desperately wanted him to offer something, even if it was off the record, but he needed time to think before he did that.

"I'll think about it then, and let you know. Well, we better get going," he said.

"Sure," Brenda said, looking disappointed.

Joe eased the truck out of the parking lot, yielding to two carloads of people that turned in faster than they should have, no doubt hurrying to make last call at the lounge, and headed for the city's west side, where Brenda lived.

Joe was quiet, thinking about what he said to Brenda and wondering if he was going to regret it. A few minutes later he turned off Bangor Boulevard, and was relieved when Brenda began giving him directions through the web of streets that led to her apartment. It had only been six hours since he had followed her home from the newspaper building, where he'd met her right after work, but he hadn't been paying attention.

Her navigational commands were frequent enough to prevent conversation, so Joe concentrated on trying to memorize the way, at least some of it, but any hope of that was dashed when they had to detour around a city snow removal crew that had their intended route completely blocked, mostly by mounds of dirty snow they had pushed from both curbs into the middle of the street.

When Brenda gathered her things together on the floor and brought them to her lap, Joe knew they must be close to where she lived, despite the fact he still didn't recognize anything. But a minute later, when she said, "here it is," Joe recognized her little blue car across the street.

Joe stopped the truck and turned to her.

"Well, I had a wonderful evening," she said.

Joe smiled. "Me too."

"I'll think about what you said, about the crew, but I wouldn't worry about it. If they're not happy you can't fix that, if you know what I mean."

"I guess," Joe said. The night was over and he couldn't very well plunge back into that conversation again. "I'll think about…about the news thing, and let you know. And I'll call you soon, so we can get together, you know I can't really say when, it's mostly dependent on the weather, but I had a good time tonight."

Brenda smiled widely as her right hand pulled the door handle toward her. "So did I, so please call me, either here or at work, it doesn't really matter. If I'm out, there's plenty of tape to listen to you."

Joe smiled. "Great."

Brenda climbed out, hesitated like she was going to say something, and slammed the door shut. Like a child leaving a school bus, she crossed in front of the truck, smiling and waving in the vehicle's headlights as she hurried across the deserted street.

Joe was tempted to pull away immediately, but he knew that was nothing more than an impulse to end the evening smoothly. Instead he sat there, watching her slip between her car and a Toyota pick-up, cross the sidewalk, and climb the steps to the door. When she reached it, she turned and waved, still smiling. Despite the fact she wasn't safely inside, Joe figured her wave was his signal to leave, so he crept away, his eyes glued to the truck's outside mirror. Fifty yards later, Brenda disappeared into the building and Joe turned his attention back to the road and sped up, realizing that while Brenda had guided him to wherever he was, he had forgotten to ask for directions out. With his mind still stuck on the job related dialogue of earlier, he took a left onto what seemed to be more than a side street, and drove straight forward, cruising through a green traffic signal and stopping for two red ones. Slowly the consecutively placed three decker apartment buildings gave way to single family homes surrounded by big yards and two-car garages, and the road ended at a T intersection.

If it hadn't been for the sweeping vista before him, he'd have been lost. But far away in the darkness he could see the brightly lit interchange, and beyond it, the freeway. He headed for it, picked up Route 302, and started the long journey home, hoping his mind would be diverted by the easy listening FM station he had turned up louder that usual.

∗   ∗   ∗   ∗

Warren called Victor early, so early in fact, that he got the mill's control room instead of the corporate offices. The young technician he talked with was polite, offering to take a message, which Warren left. Half an hour later he called again, this time reaching the main switchboard. Victor's secretary was not available, so he was told what he figured was the packaged response of the morning.

"Mr. Doucette is in a meeting, he's not expected in the office until mid-day. May I take a message?"

Warren wasn't satisfied. "I need to talk with his secretary, is she in?" he asked in a no-nonsense kind of way.

"I'm sorry, sir, but she isn't available at the moment, may I take a message?"

"Listen," Warren said sharply, "I need to speak with June, put her on please."

"One moment, sir," the pleasant sounding woman said, followed by a click and an earful of elevator music that had become all too familiar. He hadn't waited more than a minute when he heard what he knew was June's voice on the other end.

"June, this is Warren, Christ, what a run-a-round to get to you."

"Oh, hi, Warren. I'm sorry, I was downstairs and it's early, you must be looking for Victor?"

"Yes. I need to talk with him this morning."

"He should be out of the meeting by eleven at the latest. I'll have him call you, Warren. Are you at the office?"

"Yes, but can't you interrupt him? It's really important."

Warren had no sooner said it than he realized it was out of character for him to be so pushy. But that was what this thing was doing to him.

"I'd rather not, but if you insist, Warren, I will."

"No, forget it then, just have him call me as soon as possible."

Warren spent the next half hour unproductively bouncing between offices, talking with Doris, Dwight, and Art. Finally at quarter of nine as he was heading for the cafeteria to snare a chef's salad before the lunch crowd got them all, Victor called.

"Sorry to keep you waiting, but I was in a meeting."

"Yeah, so I was told. Anyway, how are things going?"

"What do you mean?"

Warren sighed. "It's coming up on a month, how much longer?" he asked, frustrated by the need to talk in general terms.

"Not long, things look…everything is pretty much on schedule."

"Okay, I hope so, it really needs to be."

They talked for a few minutes longer and hung up without arranging a meeting.

CHAPTER 13

▼

HIGH WATER ALARM

When Joe got up Sunday afternoon a heavy blanket of low gray clouds and a forecast that packed rain for the foreseeable future greeted him. A large juicy low-pressure system, laden with tropical moisture captured from the Gulf of Mexico, was expected to crawl across the Great Lakes and along the Saint Lawrence Seaway, drawing in warmth from the south as it skirted the northerly edge of the Maritimes. Everything to the east of the storm's center would get rain, White Woods included.

Joe drove to work to cancel the crew, completed a methodical march down the roster, and lingered in his office smoking a cigar. It was going on eight when he snapped out his office light and locked the pump house door. A burst of balmy air tossed his hair as he walked at his usual pace to his truck, making no attempt to shield himself from the steady rain that was falling. As he turned onto the access road, already washed clean by the rain, he could see the roadside drainage ditches were full and fast. Further on, Bubble Brook, which got its start on the mountain and ended at Jordan Pond, was running hard, close to its spring run off mark.

Stopping the truck in the travel lane he got out, leaving the door open. On the mountain side of the road the brownish water was far above the two-foot culvert creating a sucking whirlpool—on the other side water poured from the galvanized steel pipe with a deafening roar, careening down the hillside into the darkness. He knew that if the rain kept up until morning as predicted, at least ten nights work would slip under the road by dawn.

Back in the truck the wipers slapped nosily back and forth as he drove slowly home in the thick fog that hugged the surface of the roadside snow banks, thinking about how there was good in everything. Despite the snow loss and the depressing state of mind that rain in winter seemed to bring, it would give him a day or two off to do chores around the house and get caught up on a bunch of things he had been forced to ignore. He also knew the crew was cranky, ready for some time off.

With the house quiet, he slept late Saturday, courtesy of his mother's consideration and the rain that continued to fall steadily. Hungry, he ate a big lunch and was enjoying his second cup of coffee and a cigar when the weather on the noon news confirmed his suspicion. The storm had stalled west of the Maritimes, which meant more rain. Worse, it was blocking the eastward movement of the cold front that was draped across the Province of Ontario and the Great Lakes from James Bay to Missouri. Until the front swept east of White Woods, pulling its huge bubble of arctic air into New England, there would be no snowmaking.

Joe filled the wood box, cleaned the fireplace, tended to the recycling, and helped his mother hang the new bird feeder he had given her for Christmas and shore up the old one that had seen better days.

At three o'clock he headed for the mountain, surprised at the number of skiers, donned in clear plastic, that dotted the mountain, outwardly oblivious to the rain that still pelted the area, turning the slopes into a wet cement-like surface and creating deep puddles of slush in the base areas.

With the crew canceled for a second night, Joe called Brenda collect at home, hoping she might want to get together now that he was free.

He could hear her voice on the answering machine in the background as the operator apologized. He'd have liked to have left a message, and briefly considered calling back by charging the call to his home phone, but he didn't. Instead he called his mother, telling her he would be there for dinner, taking advantage of a loose arrangement they had for when his plans changed.

Sunday morning he got up to a still house, so quiet in fact, that he knew his mother had left for church early even before he got downstairs and found her neatly printed note that said she was attending a meeting of the church elders.

It wasn't raining, and by noon the solid overcast that had started the day was breaking nicely, but the temperatures remained balmy on a southwest wind all day. The stalled storm, which by now had ballooned into a monster, continued to block the cold front, which remained glued over the Great Lakes. For the third night, Joe canceled the crew.

Knowing that driving to Bangor on a night when Brenda had to work the next day wouldn't be worth it, Joe spent another quiet evening with his mother and went to bed.

*   *   *   *

It was close to seven Sunday evening when Doug and Kay returned from a long weekend getaway in Stowe, Vermont. They hadn't wanted to leave the shop for three days, but the price they got on a cross-country skiing package was hard to pass up, and because they hadn't been away since moving to Maine, they were anxious to go. Jenny's offer to keep the shop open Saturday and Sunday afternoon clinched it.

Because they left before the mail came on Friday, there was quite a stack of it waiting for them. As he often did, Doug went right to it. Like a postal employee with a grid of empty mail slots before him, he sorted the pieces into four piles—his, hers, theirs, and that destined for the trash.

The big official looking manila envelope from DEP, which was on the bottom of the stack, caught his eye halfway through the pile. He was anxious to get to it, but nonetheless finished his sorting job, leaving the four neat stacks on the kitchen counter.

Grabbing the scissors from the drawer, he took the envelope from DEP to the table, carefully cut the top off, pulled out the contents, and leafed through it. He knew better than to think he could delve into it now having just arrived home, but he was anxious to see what they had sent. He sifted through the dozen or so pages of discharge pipe plans, quickly determining that they were likely going to be useless, and picked up the folded map that somebody, probably Alex, had labeled National/Salem River watershed. Carefully he unfolded it. Spread out, it nearly covered the kitchen table.

"What's that?" Kay said, returning from the bedroom where she had been emptying suitcases.

"The stuff from DEP."

"Oh. Is there anything left in the car?"

"Yeah, I'll get it in a minute," Doug said, studying the map.

Better than ten minutes had passed when Doug called to Kay. "Honey, come here please," he said. When Kay joined him at the table he could tell she was annoyed he hadn't finished cleaning out the car, but she didn't say anything.

"Look," he said, jabbing his finger down near the top of the map, "that's the mill, now…" He paused, realizing she probably had no idea what he was talking about. So he started over. "This is the Salem River watershed," he said, looking at her blank face while he ran his right hand across the entire map, "and that's the mill." His manicured index finger pointed to the same spot as before. "Now, this is the river, quite a bit of it anyway, and from what I can tell, if I'm reading this thing right, there isn't any access, just like we thought."

"Would it show a road to the river?" Kay asked.

"Yeah, yeah I think it would, because it shows roads. Let me see if I can find the one we went in on."

Doug continued to study the map as Kay moved away from the table.

"I'm going to call Jenny and let her know we're home. Do you want to pick up Sam or should I?"

"The kennel is closed, isn't it?" Doug asked, his eyes still glued to the map.

"No, well yes, but they live right there. I'll do it."

Doug was still studying the DEP materials when Kay got back fifteen minutes later.

"I tied Sam outside, after being cooped up in that cage for four days he needs the fresh air. I'll bring him in soon."

"Oh good. How is he?"

"Seems fine, he was happy to see me, his tail hasn't stopped flapping yet."

Doug folded up the map and put everything back into the envelope, aware that he'd better save the rest for later.

"I don't know about you," he said, "but I'm hungry. That Chinese food we had for lunch just hasn't stood by me, as usual."

"Me either. A snack would be nice."

With nothing fresh in the house they settled for crackers and deviled ham. Tried from a full day, and anxious for a good night's sleep in their own beds, they retired early, forgoing their usual bedtime reading.

*   *   *   *

It was eleven-ten Sunday night when Warren got the call at home, swearing when the telephone rang because he didn't want to miss the news. It was Victor.

"I just got a call from the Chief Engineer. The high water alarm at the dam has activated," he said, an obvious degree of distress in his voice.

Warren and Victor had established a simple but necessary procedure if the water rose too high behind the dam. The control room operators had a memo instructing them to call the Chief Engineer who in turn would call Victor. They had set it up that way to insulate Victor. If the control room operators were required to call Victor directly they no doubt would consider it suspicious to be bothering the CEO about something that was generally a minor problem and normally required only a flow control adjustment.

"Yeah?" Warren said.

"Well, what are we going to do?"

Warren ignored Victor's question. "It's the damn rain, we've had two or three inches, maybe more, and we haven't pumped a gallon for two days, what the hell do you expect."

Warren knew he was letting the booze do his talking but he didn't care. He was sick of Victor, sick of the mill, and he was definitely sick of the dam.

"We've got to do what we talked about, right?"

"I suppose we don't have much of a choice, unless you just want to say fuck it and open the gates."

Victor didn't say anything.

"No, I'll call Joe, how much time do we have?" Warren said, muting the television. He figured Victor was probably feeling some relief, now that he was responding the way Victor thought he should.

"That's the problem, none," Victor said solemnly. "I got it sec-ond-hand of course, but from the sound of things the second shift operator kept silencing the alarm and didn't call. When the third shift operator came on he immediately followed through, but it's been four, maybe five hours and with the rain and the runoff…" He paused. "Damn, this isn't good, is it?"

Warren was amused. He'd never heard Victor swear before. He cleared his throat and was about to speak when Victor started in again.

"Now that I think about it, those alarms are advisory only, they aren't set for a closed dam, they assume a flow and an immediate discharge as a response, we could have a problem already."

Warren remained blasé. "Yeah, okay, I'll have Joe get right over there."

"Good, because we really need to do something, the reservoir on that dam is small, relatively speaking that is. That reminds me, they might have had to increase the flow on the Johnson Dam, that's the one north of the mill, which could be another problem. Gee, I don't like this, I can just see the water going over the top."

Victor rambled on for another minute until Warren interrupted him.

"I bet you're cleaning your glasses," he said in jest.

"What?"

"Never mind."

"Well anyway," Victor said, "I don't think that dam has ever been closed, at least I don't remember it, so who knows how much it will take, but if it goes over, then...I just don't know."

"Victor, take it easy. I'll get Joe on it, I'll call you later, see ya."

Warren called Joe, who he knew was at home because of the rainy weather. "I don't know if I mentioned this to you or not, but the high water alarm at the dam went off, we've got to dump some water."

Joe's mind whirled. Dump some water? That didn't sound right. Having been woken from a sound sleep, he must not be thinking straight. "Ah, I guess I don't understand."

"Then I guess I didn't tell you," Warren said, realizing Joe was about to ask why they didn't just open the gates. "I can't explain it now, it's complicated, but regardless, the mill needs us to suck a couple million gallons of water out of the river."

Joe stretched out in the living room chair and tried to make sense of what Warren was saying. The only thing that had clicked so far was the part about dumping water. That was a procedure they would use occasionally to flush debris out of a line.

Warren spoke again. "We don't have a lot of time for this, Joe, so you'll have to go full tilt."

"For how long?"

Warren's answer was immediate. "As long as it takes."

As long as it takes Joe thought to himself. What does that mean? "I guess I don't understand," he said a second time.

"The dam is closed, Joe, and they can't get it open. We've got to suck every gallon we can out of the river. Is that so hard to understand?" Warren didn't particularly like to be blunt, but he knew if he beat around the bush any longer Joe would keep asking questions, questions that he didn't want to answer.

"Yeah," Joe replied, opting to say no more. He was slowly getting the picture and he didn't like it. With the pumps at full tilt, all the hydrants closed, and all the end valves open, they could, a least in theory, unload better than 12,000 gallons of water a minute onto the mountain. But doing that was risky. If they failed to build pressure they could exceed the rated RPM on the pumps and burn them out. But that was something Warren would have little tolerance for. A 'what if' scenario. Regardless, Joe was all too aware that while they often let loose a single main, he was certain they had never had them all open at once.

"I hate to ask at this hour, Joe, but you're going to have to do it. You can do it alone, right?"

"Yeah," Joe said. "But it will take some time. I'll have to manually open the gates."

"How long?"

"Before we start pumping," Joe said, looking at the red numbers on the VCR clock. "Probably close to two hours, opening the gates will take a while, and..."

"We need to start pumping right away, so work as fast as you can."

"I can be out of here in five minutes," Joe said, always eager to please.

"Good," Warren said.

Again, Joe's mind raced ahead to the thought of dumping so much water on the mountain. What about the run offs that were close to trails? Too much water dumped there could cause washouts that people might notice. Feeling he should at least hint at his concerns, he said, "That's a lot of water, and with the ground frozen…I mean…I just don't see where it's going to go. How long did you say we need to do this for?"

"I didn't. I'll see you in the morning," Warren said, knowing Joe would have to stay all night if the pumps were running.

"Okay then, I'll head right out."

"Good, call me if you need anything and make sure when you go to open the gates that security knows where you'll be."

"I will. See you in the morning."

Warren hung up the telephone and looked at the clock, it was almost eleven-thirty. With the television muted he sat listening to the rain pounding on the roof, thinking about how wet weather was always trouble. His mind drifted back to his early years of ownership of White Woods, when he would worry for hours on end about how much snow they would lose to rain and how long it would take to recover from it. Times when they were operating at or near a hundred percent with pretty much top to bottom powder, and in twelve hours it was gone, annihilated by weather that just wasn't supposed to happen in winter. Snatched by a fickle low-pressure system that just as easily could have tracked a hundred miles east. It was hardest to sallow when Mother Nature took away what she hadn't created. Actually, it was damn cruel.

Then there were those times the mountains would be spared, but heavy rain in the asphalt jungles to the south would clear basketball and tennis courts, and as the storm system responsible moved away it would set up a southerly flow of warm sunny weather that would entice the city dwellers to shoot hoops and exchange volleys rather than ski. How could you compete with that? But that was another time, and this was tonight, when the rain meant something different.

A pudgy standup comic he didn't recognize was on the screen, a poor substitute for the Late Show, which was a staple of his television diet. He watched the speechless figure parade across the screen, his mouth in motion, his arms fluttering. The remote laid on the armrest of the chair, but Warren made no move toward the mute button. The audience was clapping. Only ice cubes remained in his glass.

Maybe the rain didn't mean something different. Tonight it was water stacking up behind some godforsaken dam that wasn't his, which he shouldn't have to be worrying about. But regardless, it was still about money. Money he needed for Carter Peak.

The grandfather clock in the vestibule was striking twelve when Warren picked up the telephone handset and dialed Victor's number. He answered on the first ring.

"What the hell, were you waiting for this call or what?"

"Yes, I mean no, what's wrong?"

Warren laughed. "I got Joe heading for the mountain, but it's going to take more than an hour before he can start pumping."

Victor let out a long sigh.

Warren said, "Well shit, it takes time to open all the gates and start the pumps."

"I suppose," Victor said, obviously on edge. "It's just that I don't know the structural limits on that dam. I don't know how bad it is. And like I said, if they had to open…"

Warren laughed again. "Christ, Victor, an hour ago it was going to overflow, now it's the whole dam you're whining about."

"I just don't know how fast it might be piling up. If they've been getting this rain north of us then I'm almost sure the Johnson Dam would have had to be opened some by now which only makes things worse for us. I just don't know. I'd call the mill but that would raise more than a few eyebrows."

"Well, big guy, how about if I come over and pick you up and we go and take a look?"

"You'd do that?"

"Why the hell not? I've only had six martinis, or was it seven?"

Warren was hiding the fact he wanted to go to the mountain by making it like he was doing Victor a favor. But Victor didn't catch on and he either didn't hear or ignored what Warren had said about his consumption of alcohol. Either way, Warren didn't really give a shit. Not tonight anyway.

"I'll leave right away, watch for me, so I don't have to wake up the whole damn neighborhood blowing my horn, because if you don't come right out, that's exactly what I'm going to do, blow the horn, because I don't care if I wake up those elitist bastards you call neighbors." Warren paused. "So you'll be ready when I get there, right?"

"Yes."

"Okay. See you in a little while."

Warren had second thoughts about driving the fifteen miles to Victor's house once he got on the road and realized how poor conditions were. The rain was still coming down hard and coupled with the ground fog, the going was slow. When he finally pulled up in front of Victor's house it was close to one. Immediately, Victor came running out the open garage door, trying in vain to stay dry. Panting, he plopped himself into the passenger's seat as Warren pulled away.

"Wait," Victor cried, making a frantic search through his pockets for the garage door control as Warren stopped the car halfway into the road. When he found the control Victor fingered the big round button in the center of the device and craned his neck, catching a glimpse of the door descending. "Okay, all set," Victor said, still breathless, as he made several moves to settle his large body into a comfortable position. When Warren started up for the second time, Victor, who was still struggling with his seat belt, started to speculate.

"While I was waiting I was thinking, there is a fairly elaborate Emergency Action Plan for the dam, there're all required to have one. I don't have a copy of course, it's at the mill, but I'm pretty sure we're required to notify EMA of high water."

Breaking his silence, Warren turned toward Victor and laughed, taking his eyes off the road longer than he should have with the low visibility. "For Christ sakes, Victor, we're not going to call EMA. I suppose if it was up to you you'd call the Army Corps of Engineers too?"

Victor was obviously offended by Warren's words, but he did what he always did. Ignored it. "I just want to make sure we're doing everything we can. It may be worse than we know. If only the second shift operator had done what he was supposed to do."

"If I was you I'd be firing that boy first thing in the morning."

"Yeah, well, it won't change anything tonight."

Warren bowed his head. "Regardless."

They rode in silence for several miles before Victor spoke, bringing up another protocol issue. "I had to notify Mid-Maine Power that the dam was off line, that it wouldn't be producing any power, so they know it's closed," he said.

"Yeah?"

Victor shrugged. "I just thought I'd tell you that."

"You mean like you might tell your shrink."

Victor ignored the insult. "You should know what's going on."

"Why?"

"Because we're in this together."

"No," Warren said, shaking his head. "Why did you tell MMP?"

"Because these dams are regulated."

"So you reported to them that you closed the dam?"

"Yes, I wasn't going to lie, it's closed isn't it."

"Shit, I'd have lied," Warren said with a sneer.

"It just would have shown up in reports, I told you, these dams are regulated, there's a lot of planning and reporting we have to do."

"And you're not doctoring reports now?"

"I just hope we're not too late," Victor said, avoiding the question by changing the subject.

"Jesus, Victor, it's not some fucking earthen dam a bunch of hapless homesteaders built to water their corn. You told me so yourself, it's a new dam that's as tight as a drum, to use your very own words," Warren said, glancing at Victor who was looking straight ahead.

"It's not your hide if this thing goes bad," Victor said softly.

"You're damn right it's not," Warren snapped back, "but I didn't realize you knew that. All I've done is pump from the river, which I got a permit for. I could deny everything. Then I'd sue the shit out of Nowacki for polluting the river. By the time I was done with them I'd own the fucking mill and anything else the pricks hadn't sheltered."

Victor was silent, continuing to stare straight ahead.

Warren thought for a moment. "You're too damn soft, you worry more than a mother hen," he said with a smile, bumping Victor on the shoulder with his right hand in the form of a fist.

"I just don't think you realize what we're up against. It's not just the integrity of the dam. If we lose any water here, Saint Louis will pick it up. It's not just the testing station, either. Saint Louis runs a tight ship. They've always gone the extra mile with their in-house program. We've always made fun of them for doing what we call the daily double. They test twice a day whether or not it needs it. Some of us in the association have always said their board is composed of 51 percent greens. But regardless, if anything slips past the dam they'll detect it quicker than a shark does blood, and they'll blow the whistle on us at the drop of a hat to cover themselves."

Abruptly, Warren slowed down to a crawl and stared at Victor until he turned toward him. With eye contact established, Warren said, "Now you're telling me this."

Victor immediately looked away. "It didn't seem important before."

Warren sighed and sped up. "Before what?" he asked.

Victor shrugged.

They were quiet the rest of the way to the dam, breaking silence only once to briefly discuss the poor driving conditions. As they started down the road to the dam Victor spoke.

"So this is the way, I never would have said it was."

"You mean you've never been out here before?"

"No, not this one. I've been to some of them for one reason or another, but never this one."

"If you've never been here how the hell did you cook up this scheme?"

Victor shrugged. "I told you how I came up with the idea, then I checked the maps and asked the right questions, it wasn't that difficult. After you bought into it I was sure I had everything right."

"I suppose."

Warren dodged the legion of puddles that had formed in the tire ruts of the road as the car continually bumped up and down, occasionally bottoming out with a dull-sounding thud. As they passed Jordan Pond, Warren was surprised how high it was but didn't say anything. He didn't want to be an alarmist in the event the river wasn't as bad.

"The fog is worse in here," Victor said.

"Yeah, the snow banks are closer."

"From the sound of it, so isn't the road."

"That's for sure. But at least it stopped raining, for now anyway."

They were approaching the dam and Warren was trying to get a glimpse of the water level, but everything was gray and murky. Then he realized what was wrong. He was looking too low.

"Holy shit, it is high," he said loudly.

Victor groaned.

Warren stopped the car in the road, about a hundred yards shy of the dam, and they got out, pausing by the front bumper.

"What do you think?" Warren asked from across the hood.

"Well, it's up to the spillway," Victor observed.

"Yeah."

"I just don't know, if we can't bring it down, I mean, it'd be better to open the spillway than have something else happen. Wouldn't it?"

Warren shook his head. "Victor, we can pump 12,000 gallons a minute, do the fucking math, by dawn we'll have sucked three millions gallons out of here." Then, without waiting for a reply, Warren walked to the river, climbed onto the dam, and went to the chain link fence.

From where he stood, Warren could see the dark water lapping at the smooth concrete below, which looked to be about five feet above the spillway and two feet below the dam's top. Warren swung himself around the end of the fence, easily reaching the opposite side.

"I don't think you should go out there," Victor yelled from where he was standing ten yards from the dam.

Warren waved his arm at him without turning around, and kept going. When he looked back from the middle of the dam, Victor was still standing motionless where he had left him, his hands jammed deep into the pockets of his trench coat. Warren walked to the far side of the dam and was a third of the way back when he heard the horn blowing. What the hell is he doing that for, he thought to himself. More curious than concerned, Warren trotted back to the fence as Victor walked briskly back to where he had been standing.

"What's the matter?" Warren yelled when he got close enough.

"Are the pumps down here remote-start?" Victor asked, not bothering to wait for an answer. "I think they're running, either that or the dam is letting go, I hear something."

"Is that all you wanted," Warren said, easing himself around the fence and jumping off the dam. "Yeah, that's them, Joe must have just started them."

"Good," Victor said. "I'd swear it's risen since we got here."

"Who the hell knows, maybe it has."

They got back into the car, turned around, and headed out.

"By the way, the homesteaders didn't build dams, they drilled artesian wells," Victor said as they were passing Jordan.

"Fuck you."

As they approached the pump house Joe was walking toward the door from his truck. Dressed from head to toe in yellow rubber rain gear, he reminded Warren of a statue of a fisherman that he had once seen at the entrance to some harbor Downeast. Warren eased the car along side him and lowered the window.

Joe held up a five pack of cigars. "I was just getting these," he said, trying to justify being at his truck. "Everything is done, we should be all set."

"Good, that's good, Joe," Warren said. "This is Victor, he's the CEO up at National, this is Joe Littlefield, my snowmaking chief."

Joe leaned down, Victor leaned over, and they shook hands.

"We just came from the dam," Warren said shutting off the car and getting out. "What do you think?"

Joe shrugged. "I don't know, I've never seen it that high, but it's a dam."

Warren nodded. "I suppose. Well, anyway, this weather is just what we need coming into the holiday." Then turning to Victor, he said, "The Martin Luther King weekend is second now to Christmas and February vacation for visits, it's even surpassed our big events, like the Olympic trials."

Joe smiled. "We've still got time to turn it around," he said.

"I hope the hell so," Warren said.

Joe led them to the control desk and did his best to make them comfortable. He'd have entertained them in his office except that he needed to watch the computer screens. For the next several hours they sat there, drinking the pot of coffee Joe had made and smoking his cigars. Despite the fact they were an unlikely trio, conversation came easily. It was well past three when Warren and Victor left, going to Waterford, where they ate breakfast at the Mill Diner before heading home for a couple hours sleep.

CHAPTER 14

▼

GETTING CLOSE

Early Monday morning, with Kay busy in the shop, Doug spread out the map again and studied it. It was difficult to tell where any given section was located because it contained few reference points. It was clearly meant for displaying the watershed and not intended to get you around like most maps. Finally, Doug's attention was drawn toward the bottom of the map, an area that appeared to be adjacent to Cannon. It was there that he located a large pond and what appeared to be a dam on the river. Despite having lived in Cannon for five years and having spent plenty of time in the woods that surrounded it, the pond and dam were new to him. He suspected that the pond, which was labeled simply Jordan, was the snowmaking source for White Woods. It was certainly in the right place.

According to the map, a small winding road, that seemed to originate near White Woods, gave access to both the pond and the dam. He knew his next step would be to find that unnamed road and he was tempted to go right then. But the long list of chores he had to do and his promise to help Kay get caught up in the shop convinced him otherwise.

So early Tuesday morning, with Sam along for the ride, Doug set out to find the road that led to the dam. It didn't take him long to locate the road, called Reservoir Road, but getting to the dam wasn't meant to be.

A hundred yards in, on a fairly sharp bend, he met a dull gray utility truck. For a moment it seemed he was face to face with the two bulky figures that filled the front seat of the truck. Without the least bit of hesitation he threw his car in reverse and sped backwards. When he reached White Woods Road he turned his BMW sharply to the right, backing further down than he needed to, and waited, hoping the utility truck would go the other way.

The trucked emerged slowly from the road, rolling through the stop sign, and took a left onto White Woods Road. Relieved, Doug crept slowly along the left shoulder of the road until the truck disappeared. But for some reason, when he reached Reservoir Road, he didn't turn down it. Instead, he accelerated hard, throwing Sam against the back of the seat. Catching up to the truck just as it passed the entrance to White Woods, Doug slowed down and established a safe following distance.

The truck turned left at the end of White Woods Road and picked up speed fast on the well-maintained highway, reaching almost sixty miles an hour before it leveled off. By the time they reached the outskirts of Waterford, Doug was having second thoughts about following the truck. He was about to turn around when he caught a quick glimpse of steam spewing from the stacks at National. "Of course," he said out loud, drumming the steering wheel with his right fist. The truck is from the mill. Who else in these parts would have a specialty vehicle that looked like it belonged to a fleet.

Three minutes later, Doug watched as the truck turned into the mill's main entrance, which was aligned with the traffic signal at the intersection of Route 202. Passing by the entrance, Doug turned his head just in time to see the utility truck being waved through the gate by a security guard. He sped up, crossed the bridge, turned around, and pulled into the parking lot of the Mill Diner, where he swung the BMW around so he faced the mill.

So what does National have going in Cannon, he thought, as he scanned the sprawling complex, turning his head to take it all in. Doug didn't want to leave, as if staying there was going to shed some light on things. But he knew he couldn't find out any more even if he went into the mill, which was out of the question.

He surveyed the complex one last time, and returned to Reservoir Road. Once again, without any degree of hesitation, he started in the narrow rough-looking road. After a half mile of slow going, with the undercarriage of his BMW dragging more times than he would have liked, he came to Jordan. It was obviously man-made. Nearest the road a huge contoured banking, that resembled an earthen dam, formed a semi-circle that stretched several hundred yards. Judging from the looks of the vegetation, it hadn't been long since the bulldozers had made it.

Doug left his car in the road, got out, and walked to the pond's outlet, a concrete dam, where a torrent of water rushed between its seven-foot-opening into a rock bed spillway in the shape of a half pipe. From there, the churning white water, gently rocked by its semi-circle trough, entered a ten foot galvanized steel culvert that ran under the road and disappeared out of sight into a stand of trees.

Returning to his car, Doug continued on. The clearing around the pond gave way to woods and the road got worse. Over and over the BMW bottomed out, but despite how protective he was of it, he never considered turning around.

He traveled another mile, weaving from side to side, trying to find the best path. Once again he broke out into a clearing, and what lay before him was what he had expected—the river and the dam. He drove to where the road dead-ended and shut off the car. He wanted to think he wasn't concerned about where he was, but he knew he was probably trespassing, although he hadn't noticed any signs driving in. Opening his door, he surveyed the area.

Deciding it probably wasn't a good idea to let Sam out of the car, Doug reached into the back seat, patted his head, and headed for the dam. When he reached the clear dry concrete surface, he boosted himself onto it and sat for a few minutes to catch his breath. He thought it odd that the dam surface was clear and dry, assuming the sun and wind must have been responsible. For the first time he looked back toward his car, and was surprised at how fully he could see the winding white trails of White Woods. Like the pictures he had seen in their glossy advertising brochures, the snow-covered slopes cascaded out from its two peaks, and broadened into a maze of brilliant white as they wound their way down, disappearing below the tree line.

Rested, he jumped to his feet and went to the shoulder-height chain link fence, planting his forearms on its top while he surveyed the forbidden territory beyond the barrier. Then, ignoring the aluminum signs attached to it that warned against trespassing, he grasped the metal lattice and easily swung himself around. When he reached the middle of the dam, where the snow-covered river stretched out above and below him for a quarter mile in each direction, he looked back at White Woods, noticing that the roof tops of the buildings that dotted the base areas were now visible.

He stood there, surveying the entire area, trying to take in all he could see. A good-sized fast-running stream that came from the direction of the pond poured its contents into the river a hundred feet below the dam. While the ice and snow cover of the river prevented him from seeing exactly what was happening, it appeared no water was passing through the dam. Was it closed? Jockeying himself into a better position close to the edge by holding onto a rusty iron rod that protruded from the concrete, he was able to see the area directly below—a mass of ragged snow, ice, and mud, devoid of water.

Returning to the safety of the dam's middle, he looked toward the mountain again, his head still, his eyes wandering.

"Oh my God," he said out loud, surprising himself that he had used the Lord's name in vain, something he rarely did. Without realizing it, he started nodding his head as he scanned the area again and again.

Ten minutes later he was back in the car, driving past the pond, anxious to talk with Kay about what he'd found, and more importantly, what he suspected. But the further he drove toward home the less convinced he became that his theory made any sense. He needed more information.

The parking lot of the Cannon Free Library was empty, but he pulled in anyway on the chance it was open. It wasn't. The posted hours, hand-printed on a small piece of light brown cardboard, said it would open at ten o'clock. Since it was nine-thirty, he decided to stay, despite the fact its size made him wonder if it was worth waiting. While the library was an attractive brick building that was nicely maintained and beautifully landscaped, it was very small. A couple of rooms, maybe three, he thought. He knew Kay always returned from her weekly library trips with an armful of new releases she shared with him, but they probably wouldn't have what he wanted, whatever that was.

He went to the store and bought a coffee and newspaper. Back at the library he parked across the street, leaving the car running for heat. At about ten minutes of ten a big old dark-colored Buick crept into the parking lot. An old woman, nicely dressed, got out and walked slowly to the front door, unlocked it, and disappeared inside. Doug waited until about ten-past-ten before he followed. The woman was sitting behind a desk in a small corralled area surrounded by a counter covered with books in piles of varying height, some of them with pieces of paper taped on top.

Doug slowly crossed the room, which was very cold, walking over the large metal grate that made up half the surface he covered.

Almost like the woman read his mind, she spoke. "Cold in here, isn't it?" she said in a friendly voice. "The heat is on though, the blower will start any minute and warm it up nicely."

"That's all right," Doug said, not really meaning his words. He didn't mind the cold when you might expect it, like when he was cross-country skiing, but being cold in a building like this one just wasn't right. Why do they turn the heat down so much, he wondered.

Again, the woman seemingly read his mind. "Our budget is so small," she said, "we can't afford the heat unless we're here. We keep it set to 50 at night. Well," she said, with a kind smile, "you didn't come to listen to me, what can I do for you?"

Not knowing what he was searching for in particular, he would have preferred to look himself, but it didn't seem to be that kind of place. Involving her seemed to be the right thing to do.

"Do you have any books about paper mills, paper making?" Doug asked, a tinge of doubt in his voice.

"Oh dear," she said, almost like he had said something wrong.

He spoke again. "You know, how paper is made, the process."

"Oh yes, paper making. Let's check…" she said, flashing a look of understanding, almost like he had said something remarkably different. He couldn't make out the last of what she said because the blower had come on.

She spoke again louder, obviously used to having herself interrupted, "Let's check the card catalog."

It took a full minute for her to even find the right drawer. Doug had spotted it right away, but he didn't want to embarrass her, so he didn't say anything. She fumbled through the cards, having difficulty going one at a time. "Oh dear," she said, obviously not satisfied with her own ability, "my arthritis is bad this morning."

There was no book about papermaking. The only thing they found was a local history of papermaking that she said was mostly about the mill in Waterford. Unfortunately it was a reference book, something that Doug could not take with him. With the room getting warm and not wanting to insult the woman's offering, he decided to look through it.

He scanned the pages, struggling to keep himself from reading what wasn't relevant. The blower had turned off and on a dozen times and the room got so warm he wondered what the thermostat was set at. Ten minutes later, anxious to get home, Doug returned the book to the counter, noticing for the first time a new-looking computer in an alcove at the back to the building.

"Is the computer for public use?" Doug asked.

"Excuse me?" the woman said, turning her good ear toward him.

Doug pointed toward the alcove. "The computer, is that for public use?"

The woman stood up. "No, it's for interlibrary loans. It's tied into the university system somehow or other, they gave it to us, every library in the state got one."

"I see. Could we check it for books about paper making?"

The woman gave a definite answer. "Oh no, I don't have the slightest notion about how to work it. You'd have to see Carol, the head librarian, about that."

"When will she be available?" Doug asked.

"Well let me see, today is Tuesday, so tomorrow is Wednesday, so Carol will be here at ten tomorrow."

Doug thanked the woman for her help and left. As he pulled into his driveway he realized he had been so deep in thought about the river and dam he didn't even remember driving home. He never liked the feeling associated with having done that. Kay was in the shop with a customer, a short middle-aged man who must have weighed at least 300 pounds. That's strange, Doug thought. He hadn't noticed a car out front and this guy sure wasn't the type to be walking.

Doug fastened Sam's collar to his tether in the yard, got a glass of apple juice from the kitchen, and returned to the shop. Kay was still taking with the man, something about New York. Doug went into the back room and started looking over two big boxes of items they had just purchased from a local woman. She had come into the shop with the stuff saying she desperately needed to sell the items to raise some money. She talked about how sick her husband had been and the high cost of his prescriptions. It was obvious she didn't want to part with the stuff. In the end Kay talked her into taking back several pieces that she had described as having sentimental value, and gave her more than a fair price for what remained.

About ten minutes into his inspection of the lot, the over-the-door bell rang, signaling the departure of the big man. Kay appeared in the back room doorway.

"Who was that?" Doug asked.

"He owns several shops in New York, one of them right in Manhattan, he's up here on a buying trip."

"But apparently not buying."

"No, he said he's already bought a lot."

"Of what, food."

"Honey," Kay scolded.

Doug beamed back a sheepish grin. "Well."

"He's looking for certain stuff, you know, looking for pieces he already has buyers for."

Doug grunted. "More likely he's looking for unsuspecting, gullible natives. People who don't know what they've got."

"Well, aren't we in a bad mood?"

"No, but you know what I mean, take this stuff, for example," he said, sweeping his hand across the two boxes of items he had been inspecting. "We treated that woman right. Do you think he would have?"

"I don't know, maybe, not everybody from New York is a complete jerk, you know."

Doug smiled. "That's true, what's the name of the guy that isn't."

Kay didn't say anything and Doug could see she had had enough of a conversation that obviously wasn't going anywhere. He was about to change the subject when she did.

"So how'd it go for you?"

Doug stopped what he was doing and leaned up against the worn workbench, pleased she had asked. "I've got an idea about what might be happening, maybe what happened. Let's go in the house."

Kay smiled. "Must be good."

Halfway into the house the telephone rang, and Kay shot off like a rabbit to get it, saying she was waiting for a call from the doctor. Doug continued inside, finding Kay at the kitchen sink filling the teakettle.

"Who was it?" Doug asked.

"Wrong number. I'm making tea, it'll just be a minute."

Doug took the trash and recycling out to the garage while he waited, visiting briefly with a tethered Sam on his second trip back in. A few minutes later they were sitting at the kitchen table with steaming cups of tea. Doug started from the beginning.

"Let's assume there was a fire at the mill, which I'm convinced there was, and let's assume it caused a lot of damage to their waste water treatment system, or at least their ability to operate it. So they make temporary repairs and keep operating, because they are operating, but, for whatever reason, and there are a lot of them, they find they have to replace the whole system or something like that, you know, a major job, that would probably require a shutdown."

"But we don't know for sure…"

Doug interrupted her. "Hear me out first. Since a shutdown would cost them millions, maybe tens of millions if it was long enough, they decide to discharge directly into the river. Now, here's where it gets bizarre, and granted, I haven't necessarily thought this all the way through, well, let me back up, do you agree that everything to this point makes sense?"

"I suppose, but we really don't know much for sure," Kay said, taking a sip of tea.

Excited, Doug stood up and raised his index finger. "But it's possible. Right?"

Kay nodded. "I guess."

Doug cleared a space on the table above their cups, using his right arm to push away the contents of his pockets he had a habit of unloading on the table whenever he got home. Picking up the saltshaker, he placed it to the far left of the cleared area. "Suppose this is the mill, and this is White Woods," he said, placing the peppershaker to the far right. "Now as you know, the river passes very close to both the mill and White Woods…wait a minute, forget that," he said, jumping to his feet and disappearing into the den, returning a minute later with the map from DEP which he spread out, putting back the salt and pepper shakers in their appropriate places on the river.

"Now, suppose the mill discharges its waste water untreated into the Salem, it flows down the river and is stopped here by the dam, which, I might add, the mill owns and operates," Doug said, plucking his gold Cross pen from his shirt pocket and laying it across the river just below the pepper shaker. "Anyway, there is a building on the river, just behind the dam, that looks to be a pump house. Suppose it is, a pump house I mean, which, if it is, it's probably for snowmaking at White Woods."

"What makes you think it is?" Kay asked.

Doug held up his right hand, shaking it back and forth. "Please, let me finish. So White Woods uses the water stored behind the closed dam as its snowmaking source while they replace the river flow from the pond. What do you think?"

When Kay didn't say anything Doug spoke again. "Sounds crazy, I know, but it's all there—the closed dam, the out flow from the pond…"

"Hold on a minute," Kay said, "what do you mean the outflow from the pond?"

"Oh, I didn't tell you that did I. When you go in the road…it's called Reservoir Road, we've passed it before on the way to that hiking trail at Kenny Mountain. You know where I mean, right?"

Kay shook her head.

"If you take White Woods Road and instead of bearing to the left and going up the access road you continue on, it's a half a mile or so down on the right. I never noticed it before, but it's there. Anyway, about a mile in on Reservoir Road from White Woods Road is Jordan Pond. It's a big pond they must have made for snowmaking. The outflow from the pond is a small concrete dam, which is wide open. It flows into the Salem just below the dam."

Kay nodded. "I see."

"But, huh…"

"What?"

Doug scratched his head. "It's just that…I don't remember seeing a pump house at the pond, I mean…there must be one."

Kay shrugged. "Yeah."

"Maybe I missed it, because it would seem to me they would have the ability to pump from the pond. When you consider how important snowmaking is it would only figure they'd do that."

"And why would there be a reservoir if they didn't pump from there."

"It could be there for water management purposes, but I don't think so."

Kay thought for a moment. "So anyway, there could be a pump house at the pond, there is one at the river, the pond outflow is open, and the dam is closed."

"Right."

"And you think they're pumping the dirty water from the mill out of the river and using it to make snow?"

"Right again."

Kay threw up her hands and shrugged. "And so what if they are?"

Doug's face dropped.

Kay smiled. "I'm only kidding dear."

"I know it sounds crazy," Doug said. "But it's not like I came up with this thing from the White Woods end and now I'm trying to trace it somewhere. We're sure there was a fire at the mill, we know the mill is operating, and if you believe Dickie, there has to be an explanation."

"What exactly are they getting away with?" Kay asked.

"A lot, that is if they're discharging in violation of their permits. I talked with some of the guys on the council about it. They'd be facing serious penalties. Civilly it can be up to $10,000 per day. For criminal violations, which would be for knowingly violating permit conditions, making false statements, that kind of thing, it can be up to $50,000 per day and up to a year in prison."

"What about the environmental considerations?"

"Oh, well, mostly it would deplete the oxygen in the river, killing the fish, there's more to it than that, but it's complicated."

"So why would they do it?"

Doug smiled. "Money of course. Like I said, a shutdown could cost them tens of millions. But that's not all. When I talked with Frank he said the spotlight they'd be in if they shut down would be worse, especially with their record. But you know, if I got this thing right, I mean if it is as I see it, there are a couple of big things that don't make sense."

"What?"

"Well, there would obviously have to be a lot of falsified reporting and lying at the mill, that kind of thing, which I think is doable, but what I can't figure out is what they did to the testing station on the Salem below the mill, which they would have had to deal with in some fashion for this to work. Frank says altering things at the mill would be a bigger task than dealing with the testing station, but I don't agree. It's one thing for them to fiddle with things in-house and weave a web of deception, but quite another to venture several miles down river and tamper with federal property, that is, if that's what they did."

Kay nodded.

"And the other thing I can't figure out is why the owner of White Woods would shit in his own bed?"

Kay's face changed from cheerful to sour in an instant. "Doug," she blurted out.

"Sorry, it's just a figure of speech, but think about it, it's true."

Kay looked at her watch. "I've got to start dinner, honey, and you haven't touched your tea." Kay rose to her feet, lifted her cup off the table and wiped her napkin across where it had sat. "You just might have it right, but you're going to need proof," she said, walking to the kitchen sink.

"Yeah, I know."

Doug folded up the map and put it back in the growing stack of materials in the den. Walking back into the kitchen where Kay was loading dishes into the dishwasher he spoke from across the room. "You know, if the mill was still offering tours, like they did years ago, I'd take one."

"Oh," Kay said, turning around, a glass in her hands, "I didn't know they used to do that."

"Oh yeah, before it changed hands. It was a public relations thing, but it sure would come in handy now."

"Well that in itself seems suspicious, the fact they stopped the tours, I mean," Kay said.

"Ah, I don't know for sure, but I heard they stopped them because there were so many environmentalists taking them, they were talking about it at a council meeting back when they were stopped. The tours were every Wednesday, from May till September, and our little splinter group, you know who I mean, they were attending every time, or somebody was. I suppose they were hoping to see something wrong, or catch them doing something, whatever. Knowing them, they were probably going just to intimidate."

"Are you serious?" Kay asked.

"Yeah, I'm surprised you didn't hear about it."

Kay shook here head. "Are you going to drink your tea?"

"No," Doug said, fetching it from the table and putting it into Kay's waiting hands. Then, pacing the floor, he said, "You know, getting in there, into the mill, might just be the thing to do, like going right to the source, but I just can't see how to do it."

Kay dumped a cupful of detergent into the dishwasher, straightened up, and turned toward Doug, still holding the box. "That plant is huge. I don't see how you'd find out anything even if you had the freedom to try."

"Well, before Frank retired, he was in there all the time peddling cleaning stuff. He said there's pipes running everywhere, all exposed, a lot of them overhead, and they're marked really well. The labels show content, direction of the flow, you can follow them just like a map. But like you said, you'd never get the chance. I know they got their own security up there, and no doubt cameras and the like. Besides, my days of that kind of thing are over. There are plenty of legitimate ways to see this thing through, they may take longer, but who cares."

"That reminds me, didn't DEP send you some discharge pipe plans with that other stuff?" Kay asked.

"Yeah, but they're piecemeal, and copies of copies with small type you can't read. I couldn't make any sense of them."

"Well if you want my opinion you ought to get some help from the council. I know it's always been your way to go it alone, but I think in this case you should get some help."

Doug was annoyed. "I have. I told you I've talked with Frank and some of the others. I just came from the library, there's nothing there and there's only one person who can run the interlibrary computer and she wasn't there. I could drive to the state library in Augusta but I don't think it would be worth it. I need stuff that is specific."

Kay was insistent. "I don't mean information. I think you should get the council directly involved."

Doug figured Kay's suggestion was at least partially selfish. She knew he might be setting himself up for disappointment like had happened so many times in Dracut and if that happened she would have to live with his episodes of moodiness. He also suspected she sensed a degree of danger in what he was doing, particularly because he was doing it alone. Maybe he shouldn't tell her everything.

"You know I prefer to work alone," he said. "Don't worry, it won't be like before and there really isn't anything to worry about. But regardless, I can't get any help with this anyway. You know how the council is. They just want to grandstand. Other than Frank and a few others they aren't interested in something small and specific, which is what this amounts to right now. They like things like the clear cutting ban, high profile stuff, with a lot of punch, which gets a lot of attention. It's like you said, they ignore their backyard in favor of saving the world."

Kay nodded. "I know you'll do what's best, dear. I'm going to take a short walk around the block. I'll bring in Sam when I get back."

As soon as Kay and Sam were out of the driveway Doug went to the telephone directory and looked up the number for Roland Gendron, the council's secretary, and dialed it. He answered on the first ring.

"Hi, Roland, this is Doug, Doug Andrews."

"Oh, hi, Doug. How are you?"

"Fine. And you?"

"Fit as a fiddle. What's up?"

"Well, I was wondering what you might have for material on paper mills? I know you said once that you get a lot of material as secretary."

"That's an understatement. Not a day goes by that I'm not receiving something and some days it's two or three pieces. When I allowed the council to use my mailing address way back when it wasn't bad, but now I'm thinking of asking that we rent a post office box."

"Which would only cost us, what is it, ten dollars a year," Doug said.

"Something like that. Now, you said paper mills, right? Yeah, I got a lot on them, that's a hot topic all over these days…actually…yeah, I do still have it, I got a good sized file on North American from when we were involved in that consent agreement with them a while back. You remember that don't you?"

"Yeah, I guess."

"Did you want everything I got or were you looking for something in particular?"

Doug was explicit. "Waste water discharge to rivers."

"Sounds interesting, and yeah, I can probably scare up an arm load of stuff for you if you want it. I keep most everything recent, and like I said that's a hot topic right now."

"Sure, that would be good. I'd really appreciate it."

"If you don't mind me asking, are you taking a class, or are you on to something?"

"I got a hunch about the mill in Waterford."

"Ho, ho, National, huh, I bet it's something juicy."

"What do you mean?" Doug asked.

"Well, ever since National changed hands things have been going to hell. Word is that the Japanese owners are running it into the ground, you know, cutting corners, no capital improvements, that kind of thing."

"Really. Are you aware of anything specific?"

"No, it's just telltale stuff, one of those things that seems to be simmering. You think maybe they got discharge problems, huh?"

The independent streak in Doug took over. "I don't know for sure, I just thought I'd brush up on things just in case, it's all new to me."

"Yeah, I know you said once that land use was your baby. Well anyway, I'll have the stuff ready if you want to pick it up and you don't have to bother to return it, either. I won't be around at all during the day tomorrow, but I should be home by four, four-thirty or so, you can stop by then if you want. You remember where I live, right?"

"Yeah, I can find it. Well that's great then, I really appreciate it, Roland."

"No problem, we'll see you tomorrow."

Doug's interest in National was on the rise, and despite the fact he knew he was probably getting overly involved, he was anxious to do more. That evening he was quieter than usual as he mulled over what else he could do. Going to the mill was out of the question and snooping around White Woods probably wasn't a good idea either. That left the river. He'd just have to try and access the river again, preferably at another location. While he didn't know what exactly he was looking for, there had to be something to strengthen his case.

Still dwelling on the developments of the day and an evening of pondering, Doug spent a restless night, getting up earlier than usual, which pleased Sam.

At quarter of nine, with Kay looking after the shop, Doug set out to find access to the river at a different spot. He drove north along the state highway to the outskirts of town, where he zeroed the trip odometer, which might be the only fast way of relocating whatever road he might find.

As he sped along he was thankful for the snow cover that acted to eliminate a dozen possibilities in the first few miles, even if one or two of them might go to the river. Woods roads were a plentiful thing in these parts, but most of them, Doug knew, didn't go far. Occasionally they would end up somewhere, like a forty-acre hay field or an overgrown clearing that had once been a gravel pit. But mostly they got thick with bushes a ways in, or rutted bad enough to claim an exhaust system, which usually meant backing out for lack of a place to turn.

He struck out on the first two roads he tried. They started out promising, dotted on both sides with houses and trailers, but no more than a mile in, they ended as driveways.

The third one he tried, with the odometer reading 4.7, turned out to be what he was looking for. It hadn't started out much wider or smoother than the other two, but it kept going, far enough he figured, to be getting near the river. As the odometer rolled over to 7 the woods flattened out and opened up on both sides of the road. Not too far ahead he could see a metal mobile home longer than any he'd seen before, so long in fact, that he figured it must be two units placed end to end, but with the fancy pitched metal roof that ran the length of it, drooping over the sides like a hat that was to big, you couldn't tell.

Without hesitation, Doug rounded the final curve and pulled in front of the trailer, surprised to find that the entire yard, the size of a regulation hockey rink, had been cleared of snow. Ahead of him an odd collection of outbuildings dotted the landscape along with mounds of snow in the shape of the firewood that was buried there.

Two small kids, dressed like Eskimos were out of the house before Doug was out of his car.

"Good morning," he said.

The littlest stuck his thumb in his mouth while the older one yelled something Doug couldn't quite make out while pointing his mitten-clad hand toward the larger of the outbuildings. A tall man in greasy coveralls, with a cap to match, stood just outside the door, holding a long shiny wrench.

"Can I help ya?" he asked in a raised voice, obviously not intending to walk over.

Doug approached him, eyeing the late-model snowmobiles parked behind the building.

"Hi, My name is Doug Andrews. I hope I'm not bothering you," he said, stopping short of hand-shaking distance.

"Don't know yet," the man said.

"Excuse me?"

"I said I don't know yet if you're bothering me, 'cause I don't know what ya want?"

Doug stopped himself from smiling, or worse, laughing. Instead, he pointed in what he assumed was the direction of the river. "I've been trying to find access to the river and I thought maybe you could help me."

"Get to the river?"

"Yeah, there's a project I'm working on, kind of a research project, and I need to get to the river. As you probably know, it's tough getting access around here."

"Yep, well, I've kind of been expecting ya."

"I…I don't understand," Doug said.

The man turned slowly around, threw the wrench into the building where it must have found a soft landing because Doug didn't hear it hit, and walked toward him, plunging his dirty hands deep into his front pockets.

"Cause the river is all screwed up is why. It fucking stinks, and it ain't no good for fishing."

Doug's heart was pounding. "What do you mean?"

"I mean what I said, it's fucked up like it ain't never been before."

"What's wrong with it?" Doug asked.

A toothless smile swept across his thin face. "If I knew that I'd be the one driving the fancy car, now wouldn't I?" he said, chuckling at his own humor as the younger of the two kids tugged vigorously at his pant leg without him showing the slightest bit of notice.

"Yeah," Doug said. "Do you suppose we could go take a look?"

He shooed the kid away like a dog. "Sure thing mister, you want to go down on my sleds. I got me two of the finest machines known to man there. I bet they're faster than that car of yours."

He was nodding now, apparently waiting for Doug to say something.

"Yeah, they do look good. How far is the river?"

"Just a ways beyond," he said, motioning in the same direction Doug had pointed.

Doug said, "Well if it's okay with you, I'd just as soon walk."

"Okay with me, it's not bad going. I got it plowed almost all the way."

They walked briskly along in silence, through the cleared yard, past the clothesline where a load of white laundry was flapping in the wind, and along the plowed path. A couple hundred yards from the house, they reached the edge of the river.

"Looks okay from here," Doug said. The man didn't answer, instead, he ventured onto the river, toward several small places that were clear of snow that looked to be ice-fishing spots. Doug stayed on shore, scanning the riverbanks.

When the man got to the first clearing, he turned around. "Well, you got to get close to smell it," he said, motioning Doug toward him like he was being coaxed into doing something he didn't dare do. By the time Doug reached the clearing the man was on his knees chopping frantically at the hard surface with a small hatchet as slivers of ice, and occasionally a chunk or two, flew in every direction.

"This was open day before yesterday," he said. "Now it's all frozen ice."

"Oh," Doug said.

Without missing a swing, the man continually jumped from place to place on his feet like a kangaroo, seemingly oblivious to where Doug was standing. The longer it took him to break through the harder he seemed to beat the ice. Finally, with a dull thud, the hatchet head broke through into the water with the handle coming to rest on the solid surface. Water and chunks of ice splashed from the hole as the man leaped to his feet, throwing the hatchet behind him, where it disappeared into the snow. The man leaned over the hole, poking his head toward it like he was trying to get the aroma of cooking food from a ground level hibachi.

"There," he said straightening up, "take a whiff of that shit."

Doug leaned over and drew in lightly to minimize the effect of whatever it was, despite the fact he didn't anticipate much.

He was right. There was an odor, like sulphur, but it wasn't particularly strong. Doug got down on his hands and knees and drew in deeply. He regretted it. Up close, the smell was obnoxious.

"So what do you make of that?" the man said. "Pretty bad ain't it."

Doug got up. "I don't know."

"Well, it stinks don't it? If you ask me it smells like rotten eggs."

"Yes, no question about that. How long did you say you've lived here?"

"I don't remember saying."

Doug was silent.

"It'll be eight years come spring and I know what you're thinking, and no, this river never stunk like that before. It ain't bad today, it's been worse."

"Oh, I almost forgot," Doug said, reaching into his jacket pocket and pulling out a small container. "I 'd like to take a test if you don't mind?"

"It ain't my river, mister. I've always said that, nobody ought to be able to own a river."

Doug smiled, pulled a piece of pH paper from the container, and submerged half of it into the cold river water. Pulling it out, he observed it for a short time, making note the paper didn't change color.

He was putting it away when the man spoke. "If you don't mind me asking, what did it say?"

"It really depends," Doug said, not wanting to share the result. Actually, he didn't trust the result. The pH paper he was using was from a package he had purchased almost five years earlier to test the water in their house. He had found it rummaging through a box of odds and ends in the shop while looking for something else and figured it was worth a try.

The man grumbled something Doug couldn't understand and started for shore.

Doug stooped down again, lowered his head toward the hole and drew in heavily, making sure he got a strong enough dose of the stink so he wouldn't soon forget it. Back on his feet, he walked the few steps back to shore, and again scanned the river.

"So it's never been like this before then?" Doug asked the man who was leaning against an aging white pine.

"I told you it ain't. Neither is it pretty to look at."

"I see you snowmobile on it. How far do you go?" Doug asked.

"I don't run my machines up and down," he said, his arms flailing about as he tried to illustrate what he meant. "That wouldn't be too swift. This may be dead water, but irregardless, doing that could get ya into a heap of trouble, especially with that spell of rain we had."

"When you say dead water, you mean…"

Irritated by Doug's ignorance, the man sighed. "Slow running. Most all of the year except springtime of 'course."

Doug nodded. "So where do you go?"

He pointed across the river. "Mostly to Jackson's Pond and I got a trail between here and Ray's place up above. I can make it to just shy of Waterford but the trial ain't so good so it's slow going which is why I stay down this way for the most part."

Doug pointed down river. "What about this way?"

"Same thing. There's a decent trail that will take ya clear to Rock-well."

"What about the dam?" Doug asked.

"The dam ain't not bother, the trail veers around it. 'Course like everything else this year, it's fucked up."

"Oh," Doug said, hoping the man would comment further.

"Yeah," he said, taking the bait. "It's running real high behind it, and there's nothing to speak of below it. I never seen nothing like that before either."

With his suspicions confirmed, Doug quickly changed the subject. "How far do you go upriver?"

"Well I ain't never clocked it, mister, so I don't rightly know, but it's a couple miles to Ray's, maybe more I guess. I regularly go above his place a piece."

"Does Ray live on the river?" Doug asked.

"I thought I said he did."

"Do you think he'd mind if I went up and talked to him?"

"I wouldn't know, but I'd give it a try. Just make sure you make yourself known, he don't take too kindly to strangers you know. Just last fall during leaf season he thumped the shit out of some guy that was trying to get a snapshot of the river."

"Really."

"Yeah, that's right. I guess the fella had taken a liking to the way the colored leaves were reflecting in the water and all. I guess he'd all but snapped the shot when Ray latched on to him good."

Doug raised his eyebrows. "Maybe I ought to call him first."

The man snickered. "Ray won't run you out, so long as you show yourself."

Doug nodded. "So how would I get there?"

"In your car."

Doug held back a developing smile. "Okay."

The man continued. "Just go back out to the state road and take the next road up and follow it out."

"I thought you said it was a couple miles."

"I did. And it is. On the river. The river veers around like a moving snake."

"Oh."

They walked back toward the trailer, stopping halfway across the plowed clearing near Doug's car. As soon as they came into sight, the two little kids bailed out of the house and ran briskly to them. What do they do, Doug thought to himself, sit in the window watching? The littler of the two took up a position behind the man while the older one just kind of stared at Doug with blue eyes that were as round as quarters.

"I was wondering if it would be all right with you if I came back again, that is, if I need to. Maybe to take some tests."

The man nodded. "I thought you just did."

"Excuse me," Doug said, tilting his head.

"I said I thought you just took a test."

Doug nodded. "I did. I meant that I might need to take a water sample."

The man shrugged. "Like I said, mister, nobody owns the river. Never have, never will. It wouldn't be right. Besides, if you got a fix for it, the river I mean, I figure that would be a good thing."

The younger of the two kids suddenly spoke. "Are you a policeman?" he asked Doug, taking his thumb from his mouth just long enough to shriek the words that Doug barely understood.

Doug smiled down at him. "No, not me."

The kid giggled and stamped his feet in rapid succession.

"Cute kids you got," Doug said, looking up at the man.

"They ain't mine. Now you two get," he said, shooing them away. Giggling, they ran to the trailer as fast as they had come.

The man figured Doug's puzzled look deserved an explanation. "They ain't used to people coming by, most people don't venture down here, not with the signs and all, so they ain't used to folks. But you come back if you need to, it's no skin off my nose."

Doug thanked the man and left, watching for the signs he mentioned on the way out but never seeing them. He followed the man's directions to Ray's residence, which turned out to be a fairly decent farmhouse that sat on a knoll overlooking the river. It didn't look like the home of somebody who would have beaten up a sightseer. Doug knocked firmly on the outer wooden door. When it opened a minute later, a burst of warm, sweet smelling air preceded the suspender-clad man, who filled the opening. Doug introduced himself and stated his interest in the river.

"Well it's good to see somebody is interested," bellowed the man as he stepped backward, relinquishing the doorway.

"What do you mean?" Doug asked.

"Come on in," the man said brusquely, leading the way to the kitchen while he mumbled something Doug couldn't understand. He motioned for Doug to sit down at the big round kitchen table, pushing back the condiments and pill bottles that lined the backside with his two big hands.

"My wife's resting, she's been baking bread and sweet rolls all afternoon, otherwise I'd have her open up the front room for us."

Doug, who was still standing, shook his head. "No need for that, this is fine," he said, motioning toward the kitchen table and chairs.

"Well, sit down then."

"Thank you."

"So you've come about the river. Who did you say you were?"

"My name is Doug Andrews."

"And who do you represent, Doug Andrews?"

"Nobody really, I've just got concerns about the river, the health of it you might say."

The man squinted, obviously leery. "So if you're not a government man, who are you then?"

"Like I said…well, I'm on the Natural Environmental Council, but I'm not here on their behalf. I have reason to believe that the mill, the paper mill, is discharging untreated waste water into the river."

The man stared coldly back. "So what are you going to do about it?"

"Well, first I need to know what's wrong."

"That's the easy part. Go poke a hole in it and take a whiff, it's something like it was back in the 40's."

"Oh."

"Sure, we've been here 57 years last October, Helen and me that is, and that river ain't never sparkled mind you, but it's been okay since they started treating, but for the last month or so it's been like it used to be. That's not something you forget, it stays with a person."

Doug contained his bubbling excitement. "Really."

"Oh yeah, we used to call the mill Nasty National for what they did to this river, but things changed, a mite slow mind you, but that's the government way, you know."

"Nasty National, that's what they called the paper mill?"

"Oh sure, around these parts anyway, not so much up in Waterford where the mill was their bread and butter. Folks up there just said the smell is money. Course, you had to be down river anyway and most of the town isn't, we got the worst of it, no doubt about that. They used to dump mostly at night, and 'course during warm weather we'd turn in with a window or two open, but we'd get wakened by this suffocating stink and have to close the windows up."

"So it was really that bad?"

"Oh, sure it was. Helen, that's my wife, she's taking a nap, she used to liken it to a root beer float. 'Course it was worse in Rockwell below Saint Louis, which is a bigger operation. They say it was so strong down there that it took the paint right off the sides of houses within two blocks of the river and it turned the places painted white a yellow color."

"Really."

The old man was obviously happy to have someone to talk to. "Oh yeah, it's one of the things that got better over time instead of worse. When you think about the old days you mostly look back with fond memories, but that was an exception."

"So up until last month you said it was okay."

"Sure it was, not swimming water okay, surely not drinking water okay, but I would have bathed in it quick if I had to. That's the thing about it, it came back from what it was. You see, young man, a river is like a living thing, you hurt it and it will heal, it may take time, but it will. It's got a natural cleansing flow to it. That's one thing those folks that are always raving about the environment don't understand. They're right to want to put a stop to some things. But they're dead wrong when they say it can't be undone, the damage and the like, 'cause it can. Nature's like that, like us kind of, give us time to mend ourselves and we're good as new."

"Yeah."

"Now you take Helen's sister, she's smoked all her life, two, two and a half, maybe three packs a day. The doctor told her to quit, but she said there was no reason, the damage was done. But it just ain't true. If she quit today she'd be that much better off."

From the fading light outside the window Doug knew he needed to be going. It was time to bring the conversation around to the present.

"So it's pretty bad right now then?"

"For her it is, because she won't quit."

"No, I...I mean the river."

"Oh, well, yeah, it is. 'Course you can't tell a whole lot with it froze over, but it looks and smells the part. I don't get around as much as I used to, especially in winter. You might want to talk with Paul, the fella that lives apiece down the river, he'd know better than I would."

"Does he live in a mobile home right near the river? Has a couple of little kids."

"Yeah, that would be him."

"I just came from there."

"Oh. What's he'd have to say?"

"Pretty much what you said, he sent me here."

"Oh, well then."

"I guess I really ought to be going."

"Before you do, tell me, what are you fixing on doing about the river?"

"Like I said when I got here, I'm not in a position to do anything myself. I got involved…lets just say it came to my attention that the river might be polluted so I'm checking it out. Today is the first time I've been able to get close to it. That reminds me, have you reported it to anyone."

"Reported what?"

Doug fought back a smile. "Reported the river being polluted?"

"Not yet."

"If you don't mind me asking, why?"

"Because they'd make me put my name to it, and then they'd come down here poking around with the newspaper and TV people in tow, and they'd be asking a bunch of questions I had no mind to answer. And before long there would be more people here than you could shake a stick at—asking questions, probing the river. You just don't know where something like that would lead these days. Besides, you don't know whose feathers you might be ruffling."

"I see."

The man looked away. "Besides, a man ought to have something first-hand before he meddles in it."

Doug's heart sank. "What do you mean?"

"Just that I only know what Paul told me, what he showed me, over his place."

"Oh, I guess I thought you had..." Doug paused and motioned toward the river. "That you had been to the river yourself...I mean, here."

The man turned his head back toward Doug, but not his eyes. "Like I said, I don't get around so good anymore. It was different years ago. It's not that I don't try, mind you, but I got two bum knees, not one, but two. If I got down there I'd probably never get back. It used to be that I knew that river in any season like the back of my hand. That's probably what Paul remembers, which would account for him sending you."

"Well, I guess it doesn't matter, here or down there, it's the same thing. You said you were down there, right?"

"Yeah, half a dozen times of late. Helen takes pity on his little ones. She's always sending me down with treats. Helen baked all morning, so I suspect I'll be paying them a visit tomorrow."

"Well, I have to be going, but I really appreciate your help," Doug said, pushing back in his chair.

The man did the same and stood up, prompting Doug to follow suit.

"I hope I was a help to ya," the man said, his face expressionless.

Doug knew that the truth of that statement was more important to the man than it was to him. So he put on his best smile. "Yes. You've been a big help. Really."

But already the man's debilitated mind was elsewhere. "Like I said, if Helen wasn't taking a nap she would have opened the front room. But she's been baking since lunch and she laid down just before you come."

"Sure, no problem. You've helped me a great deal."

Doug eyed the door he had entered through, wondering if he should lead the way out, when the man ushered him toward it and down the dark hallway. Not another word was spoken till Doug was on the stoop.

"I was wondering if it would be okay with you if I come back should the need arise?" Doug asked, wondering why he had waited so long to pose such an important question.

The man's reply was spoken warmly. "You come back and visit us anytime," he said.

"Thank you, thanks for everything," Doug said, letting the door slip from his hand as he turned away and walked to his car.

Initially he had the feeling the visit with Ray had been wasted, but the more he thought about it he realized it really didn't matter. Did it? After all, Ray had been to the river at Paul's house, and what Ray had said about the past stood. Ray had probably figured that if he told Doug right up front he hadn't been to the river himself he might not want to talk to him, or maybe it was hard to admit he couldn't get there any more, at least not in winter. Yeah, Doug concluded, that was it. Ray must have been finding it difficult to admit his newly developed inability to do what had probably been a lifetime trek.

When Doug arrived at Roland's house just before five-thirty, Roland wasn't there, but a short fat woman who said she was the baby-sitter let him in without hesitation, directing him to a foot-high pile of material held by a black bungee cord that was sitting on the otherwise empty kitchen table. Doug thanked the woman, put the material in the back seat, and drove home, going over and over in his mind what the river dwellers had said.

Kay didn't ask about his afternoon and he didn't offer anything. It was best to keep quiet until he had a chance to sort things out, particularly because she'd probably prod him again to get the council involved. He spent the early part of the evening pouring over the material Roland had assembled, marking information that he thought might be helpful with purple sticky notes that he pulled from a pad on his armchair. At quarter of nine, slightly better than halfway through the stack, he decided to quit. Fastening the bungee cord around the done pile, he pushed it behind his chair, placing the to do pile on top.

"That's enough for one night," he said, sitting back down in his chair, tossing the pad of sticky notes on the table.

Kay looked up from the book she was reading. "There's a movie at nine that looks pretty good, if you want to give it a try."

Doug took off his glasses and rubbed his eyes. "I think I'll pass. I'm beat," he announced, standing up. "I'm going to turn in, if you don't mind."

"Please do, dear. I'm just going to finish this chapter," she said, flipping a dozen or so pages ahead. "I won't be far behind."

Doug nodded and started for the bedroom.

The next morning Doug rose at dawn and crept downstairs, being careful not to wake Kay. He settled himself in the den with a cup of instant coffee, intending to finish off the stack of material. It was just before nine-thirty, long after Kay had risen, and Sam was snoozing in his pen, when he came across a packet of data grids showing toxic chemical discharges directly to water for pulp and paper mills in the Northeast. The small italics type in the right bottom corner of every page indicated the information had been complied by several environmental watchdog organizations, which were familiar to Doug by name. Despite the fact that EPA data was listed as the source, Doug was leery. He knew such information was often presented out of context or skewed in some other way that was complimentary to the writer. Regardless, it gave him an idea.

From the telephone directory's yellow pages, he copied down the numbers of several water testing companies. Even though it was a holiday, Doug figured there was a good chance they'd be open, so he went to the kitchen, taking the data grid and some other papers with him for reference.

The first company he called sounded eager, but they quickly made it clear that their forte was fixing water, not testing it. Unimpressed with the second one, whose recorded message directed him to leave a message or call another number with an unfamiliar prefix, he dialed the third number on his list.

"Good morning, Central Maine Laboratories. How may I help you?" The voice was young and cheerful.

"Ah, yeah, I was interested in your water testing services."

"Sure, residential or commercial?"

Doug wasn't sure why he said residential, but he did. Before he could decide what to do, she was asking for his name and address, promising to send him a water test kit by first class mail.

The water testing kit arrived the following Monday, a rectangular shaped box with two cloudy plastic 250 cc bottles lying in a bed of green foam and a flyer that listed a variety of tests, recommended collection methods, and an order form. None of the stated tests included Biochemical Oxygen Demand, or BOD, which Doug had read was crucial for flagging untreated wastewater from pulp and paper mills. Neither were any of the chemicals listed on the data grids mentioned, so he dialed the lab's toll free number. An older but equally pleasant woman answered.

"I was wondering about what tests you conduct besides those listed on the fact sheet you enclosed with the kit you sent me."

There was no hesitation on the other end of the line. "One moment, sir, I'll connect you."

Ten seconds later a male voice came on the line. "This is Scott, may I help you?"

"Yes, I was wondering about what tests, water tests, you perform besides those listed on the sheet you sent me?"

"Sure. What did you have in mind?"

"Do you do BOD?"

"Sure, we do BOD."

"So I should use the residential test kit you sent me then?"

"Ah, no, not really. You need to have a liter bottle, a sterile liter bottle, we could send you one, along with some chain of custody forms."

"Okay, good. I have some others tests I was wondering about."

"Sure?"

"What about acetone?"

"Yes, we can do that."

"What about chloroform?"

"What was that?"

Afraid that he had pronounced it wrong, Doug spelled it out.

"I'm not sure on that one," the man replied.

"What about ammonia?"

"Yes."

"Methanol?"

"Yes."

What about zinc compounds?"

"Ah, yeah, zinc, we test for zinc."

"Good, so you can test for these based on me submitting a liter-sized sample?"

"Yes."

"What about Dioxin?"

"Dioxin?"

There was a brief silence on the other end of the line.

"No, I'm being told no, we don't test for that."

Doug was quick to move on. "That's all right. The BOD is the important one."

"Sure. If you'll give me your name and address, we'll send you a sterile liter bottle and a chain of custody sheet."

Doug gave the information and hung up, satisfied that if he could get a water sample tested it would clinch his suspicions.

▼

COMING TOGETHER

Above two thousand feet, where warm air from the southwest gushed northward, it was raining, but in the mountain valley, where cold air was trapped as though caged, it fell as freezing rain. The precipitation had started mid-afternoon as snow, quickly changing to sleet, chasing nearly everybody from the mountain. Most opted to get an early start for home, not knowing it was clear sailing through the foothills and coastal plain where warm spring-like air had preceded the precipitation.

With a forecast for rain, plain or otherwise, Joe went to work early and canceled the crew. Just after dark he left the pump house to a layer of ice a quarter inch thick that coated every exposed surface. Walking flat-footed like a novice on stilts, he carefully made his way across the parking lot to his truck, its cab encased by an uneven layer of ice speckled with air pockets. Pulling the door open, the ice cracked and broke like shattering glass and fell to the ground where pieces the size of toast and the shape of Texas cascaded down the parking lot's slight incline like runaway sleds with nowhere to go. Scraping was out of the question, so he started the motor, cranked the defroster to high, and returned to the pump house. He could hear talking on the radio at the control desk, so he started that way, knowing the resort's two sand trucks would be out. As he approached he could make out their simple words.

"How much ya got on, Eddy?"

"Bout half a load."

"What ya got left?"

"Just the North Slope circle, Lester."

"Okay, see ya when you get in."

Joe turned off the radio so he wouldn't forget to do so on the outside chance it would be silent until he left. Reaching into his jacket pocket, he pulled out a cigar and was halfway through it when he decided the truck's windows must be clear. As he carefully crossed the parking lot, a sharp crack echoed from the distance as a weak limb succumbed to the weight of the ice and snapped, tumbling through a thicket of branches as it plummeted to the ground, coming to rest with a dull thud.

With all but the tops of his windows clear, Joe started down the access road, pumping his brakes lightly, hoping to find trouble before it found him. He knew the freezing rain that was falling steadily could glaze a surface, even a sanded and salted one, in short order. Dodging the white pine and hemlock branches that sagged into his path, Joe turned onto White Woods Road and slowed to a crawl. It wasn't sanded.

Just around the first bend a car was stopped, beyond it Joe could see a second car, three quarters of it in the ditch. He joined the man and woman who were standing by the car discussing what to do. When they turned to him, he offered the services of his truck to pull the car out "just as soon as a sand truck comes through." But it was well after eight and Joe was pretty sure that Cannon's Road Commissioner wasn't even working. He returned to the dry warmth of his cab, turning up the heat for himself and the windows, and dialed the resort's maintenance building. One, two, three rings. Even if they were there, they might not answer. Four, five rings. He let it continue. On the eleventh ring Lester answered.

"Maintenance" he barked.

"Lester, this is Joe."

"Yeah, Joe."

"Listen, I'm down on Whites Woods Road, about a quarter-mile from the access road, it's a sheet of ice down here and there's a car off the road. I'd like to pull it out, but I can't do anything without sand, you can hardly stand up down here."

"Yeah, okay. Quarter mile you say?"

"Yeah," Joe said as he watched the other motorist say goodbye to the woman, get into his car, and creep away.

"Okay then, I'll get Eddy, we'll load up, it's a damn lucky thing you caught us, we were just getting ready to call it a night. It's pretty much changed over to rain up here and the salt is cutting it good at this temperature. Yeah, okay, Joe, a quarter mile you say, we'll be there in about ten minutes, sit-tight."

Joe hit the end button and hung up the handset. He had difficulty keeping his footing on the slick surface as he returned to the woman and announced a sand truck was coming. Joe was having trouble making small talk with the snobbish-acting woman, so he was relieved when a shabby vehicle that had served most of its years as an ambulance creep up the road and stopped, blocking the opposite travel lane. The middle-aged driver, with long bushy sideburns, leaned across the cab and rolled down the window.

"Need some help?" he asked, his eyes moving vertically on the well-dressed woman who had turned away as he approached.

"No, I think we're all set. I've got a sand truck coming down from White Woods so I can pull her out. It shouldn't take more than a little tug, as long as I got traction. Thanks anyway though."

It suddenly occurred to Joe that he hadn't offered the woman the opportunity to sit in his truck, where it was warm and dry.

"Excuse me," Joe said to the man as he turned to the woman. "Ma'am, would you like to sit in my truck while we wait?"

"Yes, that would be nice, thank you?"

Joe escorted her to the passenger's side and opened the door, expecting she'd need help climbing in, given the truck's sixteen-inch clearance. But she hoisted herself up easily. Joe gently shut the door and returned to the old ambulance, leaning slightly backward to read what it said on the door.

"So what brings you out on a night like this, all the way from Waterford?" Joe asked.

The man smiled broadly and motioned vaguely back in the direction he had come. "I've been down at the Clifford woman's house. She was sure her sump pump wasn't running and with all the rain coming I guess she got nervous."

"Was it, working I mean?"

"'Course it was working. Her hearing aid was turned down is all it was."

Joe laughed. "No, really."

"Sure. That's nothing. This past fall she had me come shut off the water in the shed like I do every year cause there's no heat out there. This is no shit. The next day, the next day mind you, she called up my answering service complaining there wasn't any water in the shed. It was a Saturday and I was coaching my boy's flag football team, so all I got was the page which of course didn't tell me much of anything, so I drove all the way out there."

"Are you serious?"

"Oh yeah. It's pathetic, but you feel sorry for her if you know what I mean."

"Yeah, I do," Joe said, putting on a serious face.

"I don't do much down this way anymore. But I got a few old customers I keep working for, mostly olds folks like Mrs. Clifford who are alone and don't trust nobody else. I mean they would I suppose if they had to, but they don't want to, and I figure they shouldn't have to, they got enough worries, enough things to contend with if you know what I mean. So I keep servicing them even though I got a subbing contract at the mill three years ago. Actually, I enjoy getting out and meeting folks. I didn't take the mill job because the money was any better. I took it because it was steady work, a regular paycheck every two weeks. It's tough raising a family when you can't depend on a decent paycheck. You got to have steady money to make ends meet."

"Yeah. I know what you mean. I work at the resort in snowmaking and it's tough for the guys when they don't get their hours. As a matter of fact, that's where I was just coming from. I had to cancel the crew for tonight because of this weather."

"Oh, so I guess you're the boss up there then?"

"Yeah, snowmaking."

"Did you get your troubles smoothed out?" the man asked.

"It looks that way," Joe said, even though he didn't have a clue what the man was talking about.

"Well I feel for you. That's a hell of a thing to be up against. It's been three years since they privatized some of the operations at the mill and things still aren't healed up completely. Now me, I'm union all the way, and I would be even if I wasn't a Master, but when you people called about the pump house job, I wasn't about to turn it down. I knew you'd pay up fast, and who the hell knew what it might lead to with all the building you're doing. 'Course it might have been different if I had had to cross paths with your regulars, which I didn't. It's different at the mill. Everybody knew trouble was coming for the longest time. You had three guys up there doing one man's job, so the way I figure it the mill has the right. Regardless, they still considered you a scab and all, but after things settled down there was no danger or nothing, they accepted it and just went about their business. But anyway, I think sometimes the guys get pigheaded and get in the way of a business changing with the times, doing what they need to do to stay competitive, if you know what I mean. There aren't any easy answers, most of the time it's six of one and half a dozen of another."

Joe still didn't have any idea what the man was talking about so he decided to cut to the chase.

"You said you did a job at our pump house?"

"Yeah, that's right."

"What did you do?"

"Oh, just a service check. Like I said, I'd have turned it down except for the feeling I had that it might lead to something more."

"When did you do it?"

"Oh, I don't know, I'd have to have Barbara, the gal that does my books, check the invoices. But it was a couple or three days before I heard about the fire you had which would put it toward the beginning of December, right?"

If there was ever a time to be aloof this is it, Joe thought to himself, content in the fact he was thinking quickly for once.

"Oh, okay. That check was at the pond, right?"

The man looked confused. "No, I checked the river. I gave it a once-over, not that they needed it or nothing. Those Siemens you got are the best in the business."

Joe nodded, doing his best not to act surprised. The talkative man started in again.

"Well I suppose I better be going, Misty, that's my wife, God bless her, she likes it when I get home before the little ones get tucked in. We got twin girls, two of the cutest six-year-olds you ever saw, even if I do say so myself. They're ours and then we got a couple teenage boys, which are hers, 'course, they're just like kin to me, the boys that is, it don't matter to anybody but the judge that they aren't blood if you know what I mean. You sure you're all set, 'cause I'll stay if need be. I got a hopper full of chains and J hooks just waiting to be stretched."

Joe smiled. "Really, I think we're all set. I got one of the trucks from the resort coming down, one of the sand trucks."

"That must be the beauty of being the boss. Well then, it's been nice talking to you. If you ever need anything just holler, I'm in the book."

"Okay, I will, and thanks."

"Sure thing."

The rickety truck pulled slowly away, its left taillight dimmer than the right. When it disappeared around the bend, Joe walked slowly back to his truck, not in any hurry to join the condescending woman who occupied the passenger's seat.

He was almost to the truck, feeling the warm air Lester had mentioned on his face when he heard the distinctive beeping of a back-up alarm in the distance. When it didn't stop, Joe knew Lester and Eddy must be backing down, which sometimes was the only way to safely proceed in such conditions. With the spreader spewing sand from the rear of the truck, it created a sanded road as it proceeded. The truck rounded the corner, its alternating amber strobe lights mounted on each side of the tailgate reflecting off the glass like surface ahead of it. Squeezing between Joe's truck and the gully, Lester backed the truck up until the spreader cleared the ditched car's back bumper. Then, reversing direction, he crept steadily forward, covering the road surface with a thick wet blanket of brown sand. Fifty feet later the spreader stopped and Lester let one long blast on the air horn go as the big truck lurched forward, quickly disappearing.

Joe hitched up the rusted chain that he retrieved from behind the seat of his truck and easily pulled the stranded car back onto the road. The woman offered him a folded twenty-dollar bill, which he shooed away.

"I'm glad I could help, really, there is no need. Now you should take it real easy the rest of the way out. The state road should be okay, but between here and there it might be slick."

"I wish that sand truck had kept going," she said snidely.

Joe was quick to explain. "This is a public road Ma'am, and they were from White Woods. They were doing us a favor coming down at all."

The woman frowned. "Well, thank you."

Joe watched her climb into her car, adjust the seat, fling back her hair, and ease the vehicle into drive, inching away ever so slowly. Just as he had watched the plumber go, Joe waited till she was out of sight before he returned to his truck and started for home.

Staying in the middle of the crowned road, he allowed his mind to think about what the plumber had said for the first time. It could only mean one thing, couldn't it? That Warren expected—no, Warren knew—that the Jordan Pond pump house was going to burn, and he was making sure that the Salem River pump house was ready to take up the slack. A cold dark feeling engulfed Joe, accentuated by the darkness and the dreary weather. It was one more thing, one more bit of information, that foretold of something. But what? He crept along, the speedometer barely able to register his speed, as his mind wandered. The picture of Warren Taylor, with the ski shaped bookends in the background, that he had been so pleased to get, still sat in his file cabinet, and the snowshoes that ski patrol had turned in, no doubt the property of Henry Pike, still sat beside it. But those things were useless, weren't they? So what was he going to do about the mess they were in? It wasn't that he couldn't tough it out, because he could. He had done that a few times before.

Like when he was thirteen, still an uninitiated farm hand, a sizable sum of money turned up missing from a cash crop sale he and two others had delivered to a no credit buyer at the produce market in Bangor. For a week a furor raged amongst the trio about who was guilty, sucking in other workers who were quick to take the side of the popular kid that Joe suspected. When Joe overheard the kid bragging one day about stealing the money, he confronted him, giving him one hour to turn himself in. When he didn't, Joe did. The kid was fired, prosecuted, convicted, and forced to make restitution. While Joe fell into the good graces of his uninsured boss, he was banished by the others workers. Despite the hammering they gave him, he stuck it out. It was his first experience as a whistle blower, but not his last.

Each time Joe was put to the morals test, he passed, which gradually solidified his reputation as a person who did right, regardless of who or what was at stake. But the trouble that beset him now was altogether different. It was insidious. As much as he tried to grasp it, he couldn't. It was too big, to unwieldy.

He took a left onto the highway, sped up, and tapped his brakes lightly. No ice. Either a heavy dose of salt had cleared it or the warmer air had finally displaced the pockets of valley cold. In any event, it was clear sailing. He slowed as he approached The Johnson Road but didn't turn. He still had thinking to do. He wasn't sure why, but he did his best pondering on dark, deserted roads at about thirty miles an hour in the solitude of his pick-up. As his thoughts deepened, he quickly forgot about the road conditions.

If it was just him, he knew what he'd do. Nothing. Not only was that his way, but the situation didn't yield a clear response. Again he mulled over everything that had happened, searching for something that might guide him. But there was nothing. As he passed the Welcome to Waterford sign his mind was made up. He'd have to talk to Warren again. Surely he would have an answer or excuse for everything Joe could say, but he had to do something. It was raining again, hard, and he suddenly had the urge to get home.

*   *   *   *

Joe stopped at the store for coffee, disappointed that Ethel wasn't there. He figured she had heeded his advice and hired somebody to look after the store for a portion of the day. After all, why not? At seventy-four the length of her day needed to be shorter. Her mind was still sharp as a tack, but her arthritis pained her and her legs no longer allowed her to stand from opening to closing, at least not without letting her know how they felt.

But the young high school girl behind the counter, absorbed with trying to do the job at hand, had nothing for the customers but feeble smiles and heartless words. Regardless, Joe didn't care. He pictured Ethel upstairs in her modest apartment resting, and the thought of that somehow soothed him.

When Joe got to the counter with his coffee and handed the girl a dollar bill she studied the cash register as if it were a mathematical problem to be solved, pushed the keys like they were going to break, and jumped when the cash drawer slid open. Joe pocketed his change, flashed her a smile, and left without a word.

His coffee was half gone when he turned off White Woods Road onto the roughness of Reservoir Road, his truck easily absorbing all but the worst of the bumps. He didn't remember passing Jordan Pond and was only jerked back to the present by the strange unoccupied car that was parked near the dam in his path, a full hundred feet before where anybody who knew better would have stopped.

"What the hell," he said out loud. A BMW on the mountain was as common as skis, but it had no place here. He pulled to within a foot of the car that looked to have been recently washed, and shoved the truck into park, his eyes never leaving the horizon in search of the vehicle's driver. He figured it must have been the sound of his truck that summoned the middle-aged man from river's edge a half a minute later. He appeared from above the banking, holding a small cardboard box in his hands, peering at Joe like it was *he* that didn't belong. Leaving the truck running, Joe exited quickly and walked briskly toward the bearded, well-dressed man who didn't move despite Joe's confident stride. Still thirty feet out, Joe spoke.

"Hello," he said, raising his voice with an authoritative tone that came naturally to him.

The man continued to look at him, but didn't immediately speak, apparently preferring to let Joe close the distance between them.

"Hi there," he finally said, as Joe stopped his approach at ten feet.

Joe's accent was inquisitive, his face blank. "Can I help you?"

"Ah, I was just...just taking some water samples, I..." Doug said, his meek voice trailing off in obvious defeat of his purpose.

Joe was confused. He'd expected somebody and something different. Sightseers, that was what he had expected.

"Oh," he said.

Doug advanced across the crusted snow toward Joe, closing the distance faster than Joe would have liked. "Yeah, water samples, I was just taking some water samples."

Doug could see that Joe was no passerby. Clad in dark blue Dickie's with sharp creases, he was obviously a worker of some sort, probably somebody from the mill or maybe somebody from the mountain. Except for his scrolled first name, Doug couldn't read the blue embroidered script writing on the white patch above his right pocket. He thought the last word was services but he wasn't sure and he didn't want to move closer or make it look like he was staring at it. Since the odds of being caught at the dam had not ended in his favor, he knew he needed to say more before the situation escalated. Stepping from the snow onto the plowed road he spoke again.

"My name is Doug Andrews," he said in a more assertive voice, extending his hand toward Joe, who was now within clasping distance of it. "I was just taking some water samples for analysis." Doug knew that too little or too much information at this crucial point of contact could have devastating consequences. He carefully watched Joe's face for a sign he was too far in either direction, but nothing that could be taken as a cue came forth.

Joe squeezed the stranger's hand tightly as his mind sorted through the multitude of explanations that justified the man's stated purpose.

"Joe Littlefield," he said, still lacking the words he was searching for as they stared at each other for longer than was customary.

Doug decided to change tactics again, hoping humility would carry the moment.

"I suppose I shouldn't be here?" he said.

Joe was relieved. "Well, this is private property you know, from here all the way out to the paved road. What did you say you were doing down here again?"

"Taking some water samples," Doug said for the third time.

"What for? Are you with DEP or something?"

Doug was quick to dispel even the slightest perception of impersonation, which under such circumstances might get him in trouble. "No, nothing like that."

"So what then?" Joe asked, sensing he had the upper hand for the first time. Silently he suspected that Doug might somehow be connected to the flock of problems that had besieged the resort in recent months. But even if he had, a laid-back approach was best for drawing out the truth.

Doug sighed. "I've been doing some research, nothing that started here, but I think...I thought, that taking some water samples from here, behind the dam," he said, motioning toward it, "would be helpful. I'm truly sorry if I shouldn't be here, but I just needed access. As I'm sure you know, there aren't a lot of places you can get it from around here."

"Yeah," Joe said, feeling a rush of superiority. "I don't have a problem with that I guess, as long as you got permission."

He could see Doug tense up at the word permission, which meant he probably didn't have consent to be there.

Doug knew the moment called for frankness. "I don't have permission, like I said, my only interest is in the river, I'll leave right now if you want. You can have this if you want," he said, thrusting the box forward as if by doing so it proved he wasn't suspicious.

Joe waved the box away.

"Do you want to see some ID?" Doug asked, intent on satisfying Joe he was legitimate.

Joe nodded. Why hadn't he thought of that?

Doug carefully placed the box he was holding onto the ground and pulled a large attractive-looking alligator skin wallet from his back pocket and plucked his driver's license from the perfect row of cards that lined its right flap. Joe studied it, finding some relief in the fact that Doug was from Cannon. Silently, he read the name, address, and date of birth several times, trying to memorize them, when it occurred to him it would look better if he wrote the information down.

"I've got to get something to write with," he said, motioning toward his truck. With a pen from the dashboard and a dirty payroll envelope that he fished from under the seat, Joe wrote down the information. When he finished he eyed his two-way radio on the passenger's seat, wondering if he should call Marty and tell him to call security. He felt he should, especially considering all the trouble they had had this season, but something about Doug stopped him. Instead he turned off the truck, leaving the keys in the ignition, threw the pen back onto the dashboard, stuffed the folded envelope into his back pocket, and returned the license to Doug. For ten minutes more they talked, narrowing their focus with questions and answers, until they arrived at the heart of the matter.

"So let me get this straight," Joe said, pointing toward the river, "you think the water here is polluted?"

"Yes," Doug said, purposely choosing not to qualify his words.

Joe stepped closer to the cardboard box that was on the ground and peered into it, but beyond its flaps, which were three quarters closed, there was nothing but blackness.

Doug immediately picked up the box and thrust it forward like an offering of truth, but Joe waved it away for the second time.

"Polluted how?" he asked, squinting his eyes.

Returning the box to the ground, Doug said, "By the paper mill in Waterford. I think there is a pretty good chance they're not treating their wastewater. If I'm right, it's a serious thing."

Joe thought for a moment. "So...so you think the mill's dirty water is here," he said, pointing toward the river again, "because...you realize this is our snowmaking source, right now, anyway. I mean we usually pump from the pond."

"Yes, that's part of it, that's how the mill is getting away with it, you see, this dam is closed, you're using all the water they're discharging. It's not going downstream."

For a few seconds, Joe locked eyes with Doug. Then he looked away, toward the river, then at mountain, his mind processing Doug's puzzling words. When he finally spoke, he still hadn't collected his thoughts. "If that's so, how...how long has it been going on, I mean...?" His voice trailed off.

"I don't know," Doug said confidently, "quite a while, over a month anyway."

"So what you're saying is, that all the water we've pumped from here has been polluted."

Doug nodded. "I know it sounds...bizarre, but I've been working on this for a while now. By the way, how much have you pumped from here?"

"From here," Joe said, tilting his head, "we've been pumping from here since the pond pump house burned in early December. Three, maybe four hundred million gallons, maybe more. I don't know. I'd have to do the math to know for sure."

"Really," Doug said, "that much, huh?"

"Yeah," Joe said.

Doug looked surprised. "I didn't realize how much was involved. I mean, I guess I should have, if the dam is closed it has to be going somewhere, but three or four hundred million, gee, that's a lot." Doug took a quarter turn and looked at the mountain for a few seconds. "So would you say half of what's up there came from the river?" he asked, turning back to Joe.

Joe frowned. "Who knows, with natural stuff, runoff, nobody could know that. But what's the significance of it? I mean, the snow has been okay, it looks the same, quality hasn't been a problem, nobody has gotten sick or anything like that."

Doug nodded sympathetically. "Up there," he said, tossing his head toward the mountain, "I don't know what this all means, probably nobody does. But in the river this stuff does tremendous damage."

Joe shook his head and smiled. "I just don't know. I mean it's crazy. If the water is polluted and the mill knows it then they closed the dam, because...if the dam wasn't closed what would happen?"

"There's a government testing station down river and another mill that would undoubtedly detect it. But regardless, the river flows right through Rockwell and it's mostly open downtown because of the temperature of everything going into it, it doesn't freeze over, and you can access the river just about anywhere down there, so people would see it, certainly smell it."

The picture was suddenly coming clearer for Joe. "So then," he said, "if this whole thing is as you say, it only works if the mill knew we would pump it."

Purposely, Doug didn't say anything, he just nodded his head, hoping Joe would continue. When he didn't, Doug spoke. "If you don't mind me asking, why were you pumping from here? You said the pond was where you usually pump from."

"Because the pond's pump house burned down in December." Immediately, Joe realized the gravity of what he had said and again his mind was in chaos. The only safe thing to do was to change the subject.

"So you're going to take a water sample from here and have it tested?"

Doug pointed at the box. "I've already taken it, but I'll pour it out if you want."

Joe ignored the offer. "So what will the test be for? What will it tell you?"

"The primary test, I mean the one I think would be best, is what they call BOD, Biochemical Oxygen Demand. It measures the level of oxygen in the water. That's one of the primary things a mill does to a river when they discharge without treatment, they deplete the oxygen level to a point where fish or really anything can't survive, basically the river dies. With this sample we can also test for other things that National is likely to be discharging."

Joe hadn't heard much of what Doug said. He was thinking. His mind replaying the events of the past season. Doug was still talking.

"...I didn't really think too much of it until I talked with the guy who remembers what the river was like before treatment. He says it's just the same now, just like it was years ago."

"How's that?" Joe asked.

"In a nutshell, it's brown and smells bad."

There wasn't any particular reason that Joe could put his finger on that suddenly made him believe Doug was for real. It was just a feeling, a sense, that Doug was being straightforward. It wasn't his fluent speech, his nice clothes, or his styled hair neatly parted just left of center, and it wasn't the nice car he drove, at least he didn't think it was those things. It was more than that.

With the sun dipping behind the snow-capped peaks of White Woods and a new moon visible in the darkening blue sky, they stood there in the sparseness of the plowed way, occasionally shifting their weight from leg to leg, rehashing the important points and telling more and more, their belief in each other increasing with time, until they had spilled their guts. Perhaps it was the abnormality of them meeting, or the certainty they would, or maybe it was something else, but as daylight faded on the western horizon and the cold invaded their still bodies, Joe and Doug came to trust each other.

But Joe knew he was late for work and his radio wasn't on. Resisting the temptation to look at his watch, which he felt would be rude, he decided to end the conversation.

Motioning toward the river pump house, he said, "Well, I've got to turn on the pumps, and then I've got to get to work."

Doug took the cue. "Sure, I understand. Well, I'd appreciate it if you'd keep this under your hat, everything, until the results are available."

"Sure, no problem, it's the only way."

Joe moved his truck to allow Doug room to back out and went about the routine task of turning on the pumps. But increasingly, he felt like a traitor. In ten years at White Woods he had always stood behind Warren and stood up for White Woods, sometimes blindly perhaps, but always with sincerity. Now in the span of an hour he had crossed the line to the other side. Hadn't he? An unsettling feeling engulfed him. The more he thought about it, the worse he felt.

He spent the night immersed in the issue, allowing his mind full rein to grope for justification. He could still come clean, he reasoned, by going to security or to Warren and turning in Doug, letting them deal with it. After all, maybe he was being unfair to Warren. He had ideas about what had transpired at White Woods this past season, none of which he liked, but they fell short of being anything tangible. Surely he had smoke, but no fire. Weren't his concerns rooted in the fact the mountain, the resort, wasn't being well served by whatever it was that Warren was up to? Wasn't he protecting the mountain? Weren't people more important? Wasn't Warren and all he had built White Woods into worth a few mistakes, maybe a transgression or two?

They were questions that Joe didn't have answers for, but he knew what he had to do. Talk with Ethel. Depending on how the conversation went, he'd still have a chance to go to Warren on the way to work the next day without it looking like he didn't report Doug the first convenient chance he had.

CHAPTER 16

▼

POETIC JUSTICE

Only Joe, Andrew, and Jason, who were taking a break in the summit ski patrol shack, heard the explosion. Everybody else was either in the pump house or on gun runs, where the noise level was too great to hear the boom that reverberated through the valley like commercial fireworks, shaking the ground.

Andrew, who was sitting closest to the door, sprang to his feet, unaided by his hands. "What the hell was that?" he said loudly, pulling open the door and clearing the shack's two steps in a single leap. Joe was right behind him. From the steps of the building they scanned the star-specked blackness. Nothing. "I'm gonna check the backside," Andrew yelled to nobody in particular as he bolted away.

Joe figured a transformer had exploded, but he wasn't one to jump to conclusions, to panic, to order an emergency shutdown, at least not yet. Whatever it was, he had to wait for it to show itself. Jason, who had finished lacing up his boots inside the shack, came out.

"What was it?" he asked tentatively.

Joe shrugged. "Don't know yet," he said, hoping to quiet him so he was free to think.

A minute later Joe took several steps toward Universe and stopped, standing as still as a statue, his right ear trained on the hissing guns in the distance, trying to detect the increased level of air or water that would escape from the guns if the flow of either had slowed or stopped.

Unable to decipher a difference, he decided to radio Marty, but just as he was about to key his microphone, Mike's voice, teeming with excitement, came over the radio. "510, pump house," he said, not waiting for Marty to answer, "we're losing water pressure on Infinity."

There was a short delay before Marty answered. "Yeah, well, we got the same damn problem all over," he said calmly. "I ain't getting nothing from the river, the pressure is on a free fall, hang on."

With his finger an inch from his radio's transmit button, Joe contemplated what he should do, quickly deciding to gamble with freezing up the top third of the mountain on the chance the dropping water pressure was a power blink—a momentarily loss of electricity. Knowing that Marty would be busy, he radioed 510.

"I'm at the summit shack with 507 and 512, can you see if the power is out anywhere?"

A bewildered voice answered. "Negative, we can't see much of anything from where we are. You want us to move to higher ground or shut down or what?"

"Standby. 501, 509."

"509. We're just above the lodge on North Slope, Joe, the lights are on there, everything looks okay from here."

"10-4," Joe acknowledged just as Andrew returned from the backside with nothing to report. Joe nodded and keyed his microphone.

"501, pump house."

"Pump house," Marty replied, his voice as steady as ever.

"Is the hill pressure still dropping?" Joe asked, trying to mimic Marty's calm diction.

"Like a rock," Marty snapped.

Joe turned to Andrew who was eagerly awaiting instructions. "Damn," he said, "it looks like we've lost the pumps. You and Jason shut down Exception as quick as you can, I'm going to head for the pump house." Joe figured Andrew must have had questions, but fortunately he didn't choose to ask them. Joe instructed 509 and 510 to shut down their runs as he trotted along the path to Abbot Peak, where he took care of getting himself down on the lift. When he got to the pump house Marty had just finished opening the back drain valves. He followed him to the control desk. As they entered Al dangled the keys to the pick-up and raised his eyebrows. "I waited for you."

"Let's go."

They were quiet as they jogged to the truck and jumped in, slamming their doors in unison. As Al barreled down the access road, driving faster than Joe would have dared, he called Marty, instructing him to have Johnny meet them at the pump house "just in case." The truck rounded the corner from the access road onto White Woods Road too fast and fish tailed, spewing sand and rocks and kicking up a cloud of dust that hung in the air long after they had passed.

"Take it easy, will ya," Joe scolded.

"Sorry, there's a shit load of loose sand there," Al said, unfazed by Joe's tone of voice.

Al's approach to Reservoir Road was slower and he took the turn onto it easily, but he quickly sped up again on the unpaved surface, the truck careening wildly from side to side as he dodged the potholes and puddles that lay in the truck's path.

As soon as they passed Jordan Pond, Joe fixed his eyes straight ahead to where he figured the twin lights that flanked the door of the Salem River pump house would be. For fifteen seconds he searched the darkness beyond the truck's headlights, while his mind continued to process the event. What had he forgotten to do? The shadow of the trees on his right disappeared and they were in the clearing, but there were no lights ahead. Nothing.

"I don't see the lights, must be a power outage," Joe said.

Suddenly, Al jerked the wheel to the right and slowed. "Sorry," he said, "that wasn't my fault, there was a piece of…shit, what the hell…"

Al stomped on the brakes and cut to the left, barely missing two chunks of ragged cinder block that lay a foot apart. Al slowed to a crawl, his eyes fixed on the road ahead as he tired to dodge several more pieces of cinder block. "Somebody has been screwing around down here," he said, crowding the steering wheel to get a better look at what lay ahead. Without giving the pieces of cinder block any thought, Joe peered into the darkness off to his left through the truck's rear window, trying to catch a glimpse of the power line he figured was the culprit. He hadn't been looking away for more than a few seconds when Al swore.

"Fuck."

Joe looked straight ahead. Horrified at the scene that lay before him, his eyes flickered in disbelief as his heart pounded. The pump house was gone. Al turned the truck's wheels hard to the left, putting the headlights directly on the remains, and slid the truck into park.

Silently, they leaped from the cab, first Joe, and then Al, leaving their doors open. But then they stopped, as if some invisible force was holding them back. For a full minute they stood there, speechless, surveying the illuminated pile of rubble and the jagged pieces of wood and concrete that littered the snow-covered ground around it. Cautiously, Joe took several steps forward, but again, he stopped.

"What do you suppose?" he said slowly, his eyes still fixed straight ahead.

"I don't know," Al said, "I just don't know. But I sure as hell wouldn't get too close. There is no fucking way that thing blew like that on its own. It couldn't have…it just couldn't have. For all we know it's rigged or something."

Joe's head bobbed up and down as he backed away.

"I can't believe it," Al said, tearing his eyes away from the debris for the first time to look at Joe. "I suppose we better get on the horn and have Marty call the fire department. What do you think?"

Still mystified by the rubble that lay before him, Joe managed to respond coherently. "Yeah you better, and that reminds me, there should be some lives wires over there," he said, motioning toward the darkness, "have him notify MMP."

Al pulled his radio out of its chest holder and called the pump house while walking toward the truck. Joe followed, realizing they were going to have to call the sheriff. He was about to tell Al to do so when he saw a set of bouncing headlights bearing down on them. A few seconds later, Johnny braked hard, bringing the Suburban to a stop inches from the truck's rear bumper, and jumped out, oblivious to the destroyed pump house.

"Sorry, Chief," he said, tucking his light blue uniform shirt into his dark blue trousers and arranging his belt. "I was taking a crap when Marty called, wouldn't you know it. What's going on?" For the first time Johnny looked up and out.

"What the hell," he said, walking past Joe toward the rubble.

"Don't get too close, Johnny," Joe instructed. "Does your phone have an outside line?"

Johnny turned around, his face a sea of bewilderment. "What did you say?" he asked.

"Does your phone have an outside line that I can use?"

"Yeah…yeah, sure it does, it's just like any cell phone."

"Can I use it to call the pump house?"

"Yeah, sure."

Johnny walked briskly back to the Suburban, retrieved the phone from its holder between the seats, and tossed it to Joe.

"It's just like any other, punch in your number and push send," Johnny said.

By the time Joe finished talking to Marty, which included instructions for him to report the explosion to the Sheriff's Department and notify Warren, the first firefighters were arriving in their personal vehicles. They came in faster than they should have, jumped from their cars, threw open their trunks, and grabbed their turn out gear, which they donned in a matter of minutes. With a powerful searchlight in his hands, the largest of the three carefully scanned the remains of the pump house, gradually increasing the area he was inspecting, talking on his radio as he did it.

"Who the hell called the fire department?" Johnny asked no one in particular.

Joe said, "We just figured they better check things out."

Johnny sighed. "They'll just screw things up. Evidence, everything. This could be a crime scene, no, this is a crime scene, which I've got to protect. We've already lost any hope of finding tire tracks," he said, motioning up and down the road. "So I've got to preserve any suspicious foot prints, give me a hand over near the building, will ya, Chief, before there isn't anything left."

Joe was a bit apprehensive about getting too close, but he knew Johnny was right on both counts. One, there might be foot prints in the snow that belonged to whoever had done this, and two, if there were any they wouldn't be there in ten minutes, not judging from the line of vehicles with red dash-mounted flashing lights that was making its way toward them on Reservoir Road.

Joe and Johnny scoured the ground around the three accessible sides of the pump house without finding any prints of value. By then the area was crawling with outfitted firefighters. Johnny talked to the officer in charge, explaining to him the importance of not disturbing possible evidence. But it was hopeless. Three firefighters, standing on top of the jagged remains of the walls, were flipping small pieces of rubble with long sticks and jabbing slabs of concrete they couldn't turn over. Several others waited patiently, hoses ready, to spray the debris, while the rest of them milled about the perimeter, shining flashlights, pointing, and talking.

So much for the potential of more explosives in the remains, Joe thought to himself as the firefighters perched on the walls probed deeper into the building's footprint. Joe walked back to his truck, which was blocked in. Not surprisingly, Johnny followed, muttering something Joe couldn't understand.

"What?" Joe asked.

Johnny shook his head in disgust. "They're nothing but a bunch of idiots. They're so damn unprofessional it's pathetic."

Joe groaned. "Don't worry about that, Johnny. There's nothing we can do about it. Maybe we shouldn't have called them, but it's too late now."

Unknowingly, Joe had given Johnny more of a chance to spout off.

"That isn't it, the fact they were called I mean. We should have been able to do that without them prancing around everywhere and jabbing the shit out of everything. But fuck it, it isn't my fault. You were here, you saw it…God damn it."

They stood quietly in the cold for a few minutes, staring at the scene of the explosion, which was now bathed in fire department lights.

"Still hard to believe isn't it?" Joe said, his eyes never leaving the debris.

"Yeah, sure is," Johnny agreed. "What do you make of it?"

Joe shrugged his shoulders. "I don't know, I just don't know."

Suddenly there was pandemonium amongst the firefighters. Heads turned, hands motioned, and voices were raised, but Joe couldn't make out their words over the steady roar of the throttled fire trucks.

"Now what?" Johnny said.

"I don't know," Joe replied, raising his voice as he hurried toward the pump house remains, "but I'd say they found something in the foundation. I just hope it isn't more explosives."

"You and me both," Johnny said, hustling to catch up.

When they reached the debris field, the firefighter with the white hat and coat, the one Johnny had pleaded with earlier, was herding everybody away with raised arms and a barrage of commands. Joe ignored his requests, intending to take a look at what the fuss was about, knowing that Johnny, who was at his side, was his ticket to do so, but he changed his mind, stopping beside the officer in charge, who, according to the inscription on his hat, was a captain.

"What's going on?" Joe asked just as Al joined them.

The captain looked at Joe's nametag, then at Johnny's uniform shirt. "You're from White Woods, right?"

Joe nodded. "That's right."

The captain tossed his head toward the pump house. "There's a body in there," he said calmly.

Joe was speechless.

"No shit," Johnny said, his eyes widening.

"Excuse me," the captain said, turning away, his radio up to his ear. He acknowledged something Joe couldn't hear. Dropping the radio to his side, he turned back to Joe, who had regained his composure. "Are you sure?" he asked.

The captain shrugged. "There's an arm and there's a shoulder. I assume the rest is there."

"It must be whoever did this," Joe said, pleased that he was thinking clearly again, but thinking twice about his observation. There was more talk on the captain's radio, and a couple firefighters were at his side, asking questions. Joe and Johnny stepped back and waited. When the captain was through, Johnny spoke up. "So I assume you've called the police?" he asked.

"I've called the Fire Marshal's Office," the Captain answered gruffly. "They got jurisdiction."

Johnny ignored his ignorance. "Good," he said. "Now this is a crime scene, so we've got to get everybody out."

Again the Captain had the upper hand. He pointed to the area behind Johnny, where a group of firefighters had started circling the pump house with bright yellow plastic tape from a big roll they had acquired from the bowels of their rescue truck. Johnny nodded approvingly, not getting the opportunity to say anything more.

"Don't attach it to the truck," the Captain yelled toward the tape crew as he started in that direction.

Joe, Johnny, and Al exchanged knowing looks and returned to their vehicles in silence. When they reached their vehicles Joe turned to Johnny. "I've got to use your phone again, if that's okay."

"Sure," Johnny said.

Joe dialed the pump house. "Did you get a hold of Warren yet?" he asked Marty.

"Sure did, he's all set, he wants you to call him, though."

"Okay, thanks, and the Sheriff's Department, are they coming?"

"They said they'd assign a deputy, but you know how that is, there's probably only one on and he's somewhere in the pucker brush."

Joe instructed Marty to call them both again to inform them about the discovery of the body and to emphasize to Warren his intentions of calling him the minute he got to the pump house. Fingering the end button, he handed the phone to Johnny.

"So you called the cops anyway?" Johnny asked.

Joe nodded. "CYA."

Al spoke up. "So do you think it's the same guy that did it?"

"Who else," Joe replied, sharing the conclusion he had reached.

"I suppose. It's just so fucking unbelievable."

Johnny joined in. "Christ, can you imagine this happening on top of all the other shit that's been going on. This place is going to hell."

"You got that right," Al added. "In a hand basket."

Joe shrugged. "How do you figure it?" he asked, preferring to keep their talk focused.

"Easy," Al said, pointing toward what was left of the pump house, "that somebody over there wanted to put us out of business once and for all."

"And they've succeeded. Right?" Johnny said, looking at Joe.

Joe nodded. "I guess. At least for the time being."

Al said, "I was just talking with one of the fire guys that lives up my way. He used to work highway construction where they blasted a lot of rock. He was saying this was some explosion, considering the damage and how far the stuff flew."

Johnny was eager for more. "How much do you figure they used, dynamite I mean?"

Al squinted. "Who said anything about dynamite?"

Johnny's face went blank. "I just assumed that…" he said a moment later, wetting his lips.

Al laughed. "Had ya there for a minute, didn't I?"

"Yeah," Johnny said.

Al pointed to a cluster of bushes fifty feet up the riverbank that were nothing more than a black silhouette from where they stood. "You can't see without the light, but the tops of them bushes are all snapped off. The guy said nothing less than a hundred pounds would do that."

Johnny looked skeptical. "A hundred pounds."

Al shrugged. "That's what he said. He ought to know."

Nobody spoke for several minutes as they watched the firefighters finish erecting the yellow barrier. Joe kept looking back at the pump house foundation, reminding himself there was a body in there, trying to imagine what it looked like.

Finally, Joe turned to Johnny. "You're going to stay, right?"

"Oh yeah, I guess I better."

"Looks like we're all staying for the time being," Al said, motioning toward the vehicles that blocked their departure route. Then, pointing to the open snow covered area that paralleled the road he said, "Do you suppose we got the clearance to get through there, I'd like to get out of here."

Joe looked at the height of the truck's undercarriage and nodded his approval. "With four wheel drive, yeah, we can make it. They got those fire trucks by us, didn't they?"

As expected, the truck passed easily along their intended route and they headed for the pump house. Joe went directly to his office to call Warren, leaving Al to what would undoubtedly be a barrage of questions from Marty and everybody else.

*   *   *   *

When Joe called about the pump house being destroyed and the body that was found buried in the rubble, Warren briefly considered going to inspect the damage, but thought better of it. After all, what purpose would it serve except to satisfy his curiosity, which at this stage in his life was limited. Still feeling tipsy from his evening round of martinis, the last of which he had had during the eleven o'clock news, he crept down to the living room, slumped into his chair and picked up the telephone handset all in one motion. Victor answered sleepily on the third ring.

"Hi, Victor, this is Warren, listen, sorry to bother you, but we got an ungodly fucking problem." He paused to let his words sink in before he continued. "The pump house at the river has been destroyed."

"Destroyed?"

"Yeah, destroyed."

"How?"

"I haven't gone down. It blew up I guess. I'm surprised the mill didn't call you."

"They probably won't, unless the dam is affected…is it?"

It was a thought that hadn't occurred to Warren. "I don't know. Joe didn't say anything about the dam, only that the pump house was gone."

"So what happened?"

"I'll be dammed if I know."

"But you said it was blown up."

Warren sighed and cleared his throat, eyeing the almost full bottle of vodka on top of the liquor cabinet across the room. "Yeah, and it was. But that's not all of it."

"What do you mean?"

"They found a body in the remains."

"A human body?" Victor asked.

Warren sighed. "No Victor, the body of some fucking rodent."

There was a long pause before Victor spoke. "So who is it?"

"They don't know yet. Conventional wisdom would say it's the prick that did it, blew up the place I mean."

"Oh." There was a long silence. Then, finally, Victor said, "Well this does us in for sure, right? I mean what are we going to do? What can we do?"

"Be damned if I know. Just hope the pumps aren't wrecked, I guess. Maybe we can, oh, I don't know, there's no sense in speculating, we might as well take a ride down, don't you think?"

"Yeah, I suppose."

Warren picked up on the reluctance in Victor's voice. "What's the matter, don't you want to go?"

"Not really. I don't see any point in going."

They talked for a few minutes longer, with Victor promising to call Warren first thing in the morning. When he hung up, Warren fetched the Dewar's and a shot glass from across the room, snapped on the television, and slumped back into his chair, where he sat for over an hour, sipping warm vodka. A John Wayne movie was on, one he hadn't seen before, but he wasn't paying it any attention.

He was worried, which for him, was unusual. The explosion at the river pump house, he reasoned, had to be connected to the pumping of the dirty water. While he doubted Victor had the balls to double cross him, he couldn't see how destroying their capacity to pump from the river could possibly be part of a scheme that would benefit him. Besides, he knew Victor fairly well, and there wasn't an iota of evidence that pointed in that direction. So who then? And why? Warren kept turning it over in his mind to no avail. He had just decided to go to bed when the telephone rang. He snatched it on the first ring. It was Victor.

"I've thought about it," he said, "we'd better go. Besides, I can't sleep."

"You and me both. Get dressed and I'll pick you up."

Warren pushed the connector button and dialed again.

"Pump House," Marty bellowed.

"Marty, this is Warren. Is Joe there?"

"Sure thing."

Warren could hear voices in the background as the telephone was passed to Joe.

"Yes," Joe said.

"Listen, I'm coming after all. Meet me down there in say, an hour."

"Will do," Joe said.

Warren hung up the handset and got ready to go, thinking about how it probably wasn't the best idea for him and Victor to been seen together. But he was beyond caring about such trivial matters. Besides, Warren reasoned, by the time they got there they would probably have the place to themselves. But he was wrong. Two dozen cars and trucks, half of them police vehicles, clogged the parking area, forcing Warren to leave his car in the road.

"My boys are already here," Victor said quietly as they inched their way along the packed snow surface in their leather-soled shoes "There must be a dam problem or a good possibility of one, otherwise they probably wouldn't have come at this hour."

Warren didn't answer.

As they cleared the vehicles, the lighted remains of the flattened pump house came into view and they stopped, silently studying it. A full minute passed before Joe and another man in his fifties, wearing a blue hard hat and blue coveralls met them.

"How bad is it?" Warren asked Joe directly, foregoing his usual greeting.

Joe shook his head. "Not good, the pumps are shot, and even if they weren't, the intakes are screwed up, but that isn't the worst of it." He turned toward the other man. "This is the engineer from the paper mill, the police requested he come."

The engineer tipped back the brim of his hard hat. "I'm sorry, I didn't know you were coming, sir," he said, addressing Victor. "We're debating whether to conduct an emergency inspection consistent with an extraordinary event."

Victor nodded, waiting for more, but Warren spoke up. "What do you mean an extraordinary event?" he asked.

"Well, the force of the explosion, coupled with its proximity to the dam, would appear to indicate that we handle this like an earthquake. We've called for a geologist and…"

Warren interrupted. "You called for a gynecologist?"

The man looked at Victor and quickly back at Warren, his face remaining expressionless. "No, sir, a geologist. We work closely together in these types of situations," he said, turning his attention back to Victor. "I've also called for one of our structural engineers, again, I wasn't aware you were intending to come, sir."

Victor nodded approvingly. "So how's it look?"

"We're doing a preliminary inspection now, sir."

Warren changed the subject. "Anything new on the explosion?" he asked, looking at Joe.

Joe looked at the pump house remains and back. "No. They removed the body and they're collecting evidence, but they don't know anything yet, or at least they're not saying."

"Did they ID the body?"

"They haven't said."

"Did you ask?"

"Yeah, somebody did. But they won't say, if they know. They have to notify next of kin."

Warren turned his attention back to the engineer and motioned toward the dam. "Given what it did to the pump house, what's your opinion of the dam?"

The engineer's answer was immediate. "Gravity dams are characteristically safe, even on poor foundations. But we may have some subsurface problems, the force of the explosion may have undermined the foundation, or even the structural integrity of the dam itself."

"Put that in English," Warren snapped.

The engineer tipped back his hard hat. "Well, sir, like I said, this is preliminary, but we've probably got a weaker dam than we had. I can't really say more than that till we do a full inspection, but it doesn't help that she's holding a lot of water right now. That's really the whole problem. For some reason the dam is closed, the reservoir is very full. As I recall this reservoir elevation may be at an all-time high."

"Really?" Victor said, playing dumb.

"That's right. We can check the operational history of the dam, but I'm almost certain it's never reached this level, which only complicates figuring out what may happen. But at best we're jumping to conclusions."

Warren resisted the temptation to look at Victor. "So the threat is the water then, the build up?"

"Yes, sir. No question about that. Water is heavier that most people realize." He paused. "Let's see, this dam is about ten meters high, maybe a little more, which means the water at the bottom has a pressure of say, roughly, 10,000 kilograms on a square meter."

Warren smiled. "Could you put that in U.S. please?"

"Yes, sir. About a ton on each square foot."

Warren thought for a moment, and then said, "So what about releasing some of the water."

"That's probably our most serious problem, the outlet gates appear to be sprung. They're not responding to manual operation. Whether it was the force of the explosion, a settlement of the structure, ice build-up, or maybe a combination of things, we don't know. Right now we don't have any power and the auxiliary isn't working."

"What about the spillway?" Warren asked.

"Same thing, maybe worse," the engineer replied. "The gate apparently hasn't been exercised for a while."

"What do mean exercised?" Warren asked.

"Operated, sir, under actual conditions."

"In other words they haven't been maintained."

The engineer looked at Victor, obviously not interested in answering a question that strayed from straightforward technical matters.

Victor rubbed his hand across his face and spoke. "The spillway here rarely gets used. Usually only in the spring. But as I recall, last spring we had a slow melt, so they probably didn't get used even then.

Another thing is Jordan, since it was built it's taken a lot of runoff from the watershed which has reduced the need for holding capacity here."

"So what you're saying is, we can't open any of the gates?" Warren said.

The engineer looked at Victor again, looking for his blessing to answer the question. Although Warren couldn't see Victor's face the engineer must have got his approval because his words suddenly became explicit.

"You're correct, the spillway gate has not been properly maintained. This is certainly not an opportune time to be finding out about it, but that's what it looks like now. We'll know more soon. But regardless, the power and control systems aren't working either."

Warren smiled. "Jesus Christ. Does anything work?"

Again the engineer looked at Victor, wet his lips, and answered. "I know what you're saying, sir, I know what you mean. If every possibility, every probability if you will, was addressed here, we would have power and control systems that were redundant and…well, I don't believe I'm at liberty say anymore."

"So what next then?" Warren asked.

The engineer raised his eyebrows. "The fastest and least expensive way to reestablish the safety of the dam is to lower the reservoir level, which means we've got to open the gates. Until we do, the dam is at risk. It's that simple."

"So it could break from the weight of the water then?"

"Possibly. But the biggest threat is over-topping."

"What do you mean, over-topping?"

"Just what it says, eventually the water will go over the top. Which for a concrete dam isn't fatal in itself. It can probably withstand that for a limited time without damage. The question is the foundation, whether it can sustain the impact of the free falling water, and that's anybody's guess since it's never happened here to my knowledge."

Warren was surprised. "I wouldn't have thought water going over the top was that bad."

"If my memory serves me correctly, it's the number one cause of dam failure," the engineer said.

"Sounds ominous," Warren said.

"Really, sir, I think we're getting ahead of ourselves. In fact, I know we are. First we need to do the full inspection, and then we'll probably have the answers you need. We'll do our best, anyway."

But Warren wasn't through. "Do you know anything about the explosion?"

"Again, this is only preliminary, but based on the apparent positioning of the charges it appears to me that whoever did this was after the pump house, nothing more, and in that way they knew what they were doing. But if I'm right, and like I said, we're still talking about an if here, they used more explosives than they should have, more than they needed to, and that's why the dam was affected. It's only a theory at this point, but it might just hold water, no pun intended."

"So in some respects it's like the dam was bombed?"

Again the engineer looked at Victor before he answered. "I guess I know what you mean, but in this particular instance there isn't much to base an informed decision on. The consequences of hostile action against dams has been comparatively low, mostly, if not entirely, from war. My opinion, and the geologist may dispute me when he arrives, is that an earthquake is probably better suited for a case study here, because the dam was not the target. I don't mean to sound like a broken record, but we just don't know at this point in time, we really need to do the full inspection. Now if you gentlemen will excuse me, I've got things to do," the engineer said, quickly mustering a smile he shared with all of them before he marched away.

Warren motioned toward the ravaged pump house. "So what did you say about the pumps, Joe?"

Joe shook his head slowly. "They're shot to hell, I imagine. Maybe they can be rebuilt, but they're going to have to be pulled either way."

Warren took a few steps forward to get a better look and turned around.

"Well," he said, addressing Victor, "I don't know about you, but I've seen enough here, you ready?"

"Yeah."

They were halfway back to the car when Joe trotted after them.

"What do you want me to do…about operating I mean?"

With the excitement of everything else, Warren hadn't given any thought to what Joe was now asking. "Call it a night," he finally managed to say.

Joe nodded. "What about…"

Warren interrupted. "We'll think of something. I'll get back to you."

Neither Warren nor Victor spoke until they were back on White Woods Road.

"Sounds like we're fucked," Warren said.

"Maybe not, it depends on the dam. If it's sound, we got a few days, maybe a week, the capacity is there. What about temporary pumps?"

"To make some snow with, yeah. To bring down the reservoir, I doubt it. The only reason this thing worked was because of the volume we can do. Temporary pumps will probably only do a thousand, maybe two thousand gallons a minute at best."

"There must be something we can do," Victor said.

"Well, I don't know what the hell it would be, it's inevitable, even if you shut down now there's enough of your dirty water in the reservoir and in the trough to trigger every damn testing station from here to Portland. That reminds me, I've been meaning to ask you, why aren't there any testing stations below your mill?"

"There is, one, just like there is below every mill in the state."

"Well how the hell could there be, it would have triggered by now, right?"

"It's not working," Victor said softly.

"What do you mean, not working?" Warren said, raising his voice.

Victor shrugged. "Just what I said, it's not working."

"Why isn't it working?"

"It's not funded."

"Christ, Victor, would you try constructing some whole sentences. What do you mean, it's not funded?"

"The testing stations are owned and operated by the United States Geological Survey, they've got funding problems like everybody else. They were forced to discontinue operation of five stations so they chose the ones below the five smallest mills, which included us."

"So we haven't got anything to worry about then."

"Not exactly. It's on an inactive status."

"Inactive status. What does that mean?"

"It's unfunded."

"So what you're saying is that if they find the money they'll turn the frigin thing on."

"No, it won't get funded, not until the new fiscal year at the earliest, which doesn't start till October. I mean, they may free up some money somewhere else, they could, but at this point it's the least of my worries."

"You should have told me about this going in. What else haven't you told me?"

Victor bowed his head. "Nothing."

Warren squeezed the steering wheel with both hands. "Well, this is great."

There was a long silence before Victor spoke.

"The testing station isn't a big deal anyway."

Warren shot back his answer. "No, it isn't, not until they turn the fucking thing on."

"On the outside chance it gets activated," Victor said, "which isn't going to happen, its data would be contrary to everything we give them. All the testing, the stuff that counts, is done by us, it's under our control. We collect our own samples, whenever and wherever we choose. We could take samples in the executive washroom if we wanted to, or from the spring water bubbler. We submit the results to

DEP, that's the only oversight they have, what we give them. They have nothing, zip, zilch."

"Really, I didn't realize that."

"Oh sure, DEP lost their field workers. When people were laid off, they were the first to go. They'll tell you themselves they're lucky to be able to respond to complaints and incidents."

"Well anyway, do you want to get something to eat?" Warren asked.

"Yeah, I guess."

In an increasingly unquiet corner of the Mill Diner, they ate breakfast. Victor mostly picked at his food as they hashed over their dilemma that seemed to loom larger with each passing hour.

"Well, I guess we've beaten it to death," Warren said, gliding a folded piece of toast across his plate to pick up the small puddles of juicy egg yoke that remained.

"I suppose, but we really ought to have a plan, don't you think?"

Warren popped the last of the toast into his mouth and pushed his unused-looking plate away. Then, with a sarcastic grin, he said, "Funeral planning, you mean."

Victor's face remained expressionless, his eyes empty. "You ready? I've got to be getting back," he said, dabbing a paper napkin on his forehead to soak up the beads of sweat that had suddenly collected there.

"Yeah, but Jesus, Victor, you didn't eat anything."

Victor was on his feet. "I'm not hungry."

"You better eat while you can. I hear prison food isn't too good."

They paid their separate checks and went to the car in silence. Warren shot out of the parking lot, streamed through the downtown on green traffic signals, and started up the hill toward Victor's house. Three minutes later, as he made a right turn onto Victor's street, Warren spoke.

"So you all set?"

Victor threw up his hands. "I guess there really isn't anything more we can do at the moment. Call me if anything comes up on your end, and I'll do the same."

"Right."

Warren dropped off Victor and went to the office, where he sat at his desk downing shots of vodka in the darkened room that was lit only by the light that streamed in the windows. As the eighty proof Dewar's hit his system he leaned back in the softness of his chair and swung his legs onto the desk top, pushing back a heap of papers to do it.

He didn't know how long he had been asleep when he was jolted awake by a loud bang. Disoriented, he jumped to his feet as the shot glass tumbled across the carpet and rolled under the conference table. Getting a hold of his senses, he scanned the windows and walked to the closest one, arriving just as the distinctive beeping of a back-up alarm filled the room. A few feet back from the window he watched the trash truck finish backing and speed off. Then it was quiet again. Unable to find the shot glass, he took three swigs from the bottle and called the pump house. On the tenth ring Joe answered.

"Where the hell were you?" Warren asked.

Joe was taken aback. "I...I was just leaving, everybody's left."

"Oh, yeah," Warren said with a slight slur. "Everything okay?"

"Well I guess, everything considered. The biggest problem is people talking and I don't know how much longer we're going to keep a lid on things, the guys are anxious and I don't blame them."

"If anybody gives you any shit just tell them to take the door."

Like he always did, Joe ignored Warren's hostile words. "I told them they'd probably only be out for a few days."

Warren grunted.

"Is that right?" Joe asked.

There was a prolonged silence. Finally, Warren said, "Call Somersworth. See what they got for pumps."

Joe was confused. "For what?"

"Whatever," Warren snapped back.

"I guess I don't understand," Joe said, feeling a surge of boldness. "Do you mean replacements for the river or temporary ones?"

"I don't give a damn, a pump is a pump. Call Somersworth and see what they can do, and if it doesn't sound good call that one in Portland. Go to Boston if you have to."

"Okay."

"And let me know what you find out," Warren ordered, hanging up without waiting for a reply.

Warren puttered around the lodge till Dwight arrived. Behind closed doors they discussed the situation at length. Mid-morning, Warren called Victor.

"Any word yet on the dam?" he asked.

Victor sounded distraught. "Yeah, the engineers just got back, we better get together, we really must get together."

"Okay, I'll meet you halfway, at that little convenience store, you know the one I mean."

"Yeah, the one with the antique shops on both sides. I'll see you there in 20 minutes."

Seventeen minutes later, sitting in Warren's running car in the back of the store's small parking lot, Victor delivered the bad news.

"It's just what they thought," he said, "the explosion really screwed things up, somehow shifted things, there's no way to get the gates open."

"Not that we want them open," Warren shot back.

Victor sighed. "But that's the problem. I'm up to my elbows in questions about why it was closed in the first place."

"Why is that a problem? Everybody knows about Jordan, and that we were pumping from the river. Your guys even knew it was closed."

"They're just workers, doing what they were told. Since the explosion things are different, different people are involved, people that know better." He paused. "In terms of dam management, your needs come last."

"What the hell is that supposed to mean?"

"The Salem is a multipurpose dam, but its first priority is flood control, then power generation, then as a snowmaking source, which means…"

"You never told me I was last."

Victor frowned and continued. "Which means that the reservoir is supposed to be low enough at all times to contain flood waters. We've got it almost to flood stage and there isn't any flood, which raises eyebrows, lots of them. There's a danger it will fail, particularly if it was weakened badly enough by the explosion and there is a good chance it was. At the very least we could have some serious damage, which means leakage. There's just a lot of pressure there, especially with the ice build up."

"Well, we don't want it open anyway. It's a fucking blessing in disguise the gates won't open."

Victor's eyelids flashed. "But that's the point, I can't tell them not to try to open them or order them not to do it if they find a way to, it puts me in a hell of a jam. I mean, think about it, what the heck am I supposed to do?"

"You mean you'd open the gates?"

"I'd have to, to do otherwise it would be like…like asking for the safety valve to be closed on a boiler going full tilt."

"So then, where does that leave us, big guy?"

"We've got to find a way to pump."

"We can't pump without pumps."

"So what do you want to do?" Victor asked, his impatience wearing thin.

"Have a drink," Warren said, as he jumped from the car and disappeared into the store, coming back two minutes later with a bag-less six-pack of Budweiser.

"We'll have to settle for beer," he said. "They don't have anything stronger."

Victor was silent, obviously furious about the introduction of beer.

"What's the matter with you?" Warren asked as he wrestled a can free from the plastic holder, cracked it open, and took a long drink.

"Nothing. I was just thinking, we're dammed if we do and dammed it we don't. When they find a way to raise the gates, which they will, I can't stop them, but even if I did, it's going to fail sooner or later."

Warren sighed. "I just don't see why the fucking dam has suddenly taken center stage," he said. "This didn't have anything to do with the dam. I didn't buy into the dam and its host of problems."

Victor was definite. "Yeah you did, when you signed on to disposing of the dirty water."

"Yeah, okay maybe I did, but I didn't know I did. I didn't know my fucking future depended on it, now did I?"

"No, because it wasn't supposed to. We've had an unanticipated turn of events. I didn't expect this either, it's blind-sided me just like you."

"So what's the bottom line then?" Warren asked.

Victor shook his head. "Before I was CEO, when I was heading up operations, I was in charge of the dams, so I know a little about them. The Salem is an old dam and..."

"What do you mean, an old dam, you told me it was like new."

"It is, as dams go, but...well, they're like anything else, I mean we haven't had a fraction of the capital we need for the mill. Figure it out, why would the dams get anything."

Warren took a sip of beer. "I don't think I like what I'm hearing."

"With old dams, there has to be regular inspections, regular maintenance, periodic testing of the equipment, alternate power sources, that kind of thing. That hasn't happened, you heard the engineer."

"Wonderful. I agree to pump your dirty water and now it sounds like my fate is dependent upon the reliability of your fucking dam which is nothing but a piece of shit because you didn't take care of it." Warren paused. "Have a beer, Victor."

"No thanks."

"Oh, for Christ sakes, have a beer."

"Okay then, one."

Warren took two long swallows that almost drained his can. "You're right, big guy. One of two things is going to happen. Either the fucking dam lets go, or one of your wonder boys figures out some scheme to open the gates, which you know damn well you'll have to allow. Either way, that fucking water is headed downstream sometime soon, say, in the next five days, max."

"There's no chance for making repairs to your pump house?"

"Don't be ridiculous, you've seen the damage. Even if we had spare pumps, which we don't, that's a poured concrete foundation they sit on, then the intake system is no doubt destroyed. No, that thing is history till spring, and we both know it."

"So what about temporary pumps?"

"I've got Joe working on it. But like I said earlier, it's not the answer for you."

"But you'd be doing it anyway, right?"

"What do you mean?"

"I mean that regardless of the mill, you'd still be trying to restore your pumping capability, wouldn't you?"

"Yes."

"Well then. Why don't I see what I can get for pumps at the mill."

Warren shrugged. "If you want."

"The more the better, right?"

"Right," Warren said, crumpling the empty can in his hand and tossing it onto the floor behind Victor. Then, without hesitation, he latched onto another one, cracked it open, and took a swallow.

"It also shows that we're, the mill I mean, is doing everything we can," Victor said. "Even if we don't lower it, at least we tried, a lot can be said for that, right now anyway. We've got some big pumps at the mill, the type you pull behind a vehicle. I don't know how many gallons a minute they'll do, or anything like that, but they got four, maybe five inch intakes." Victor shifted in his seat. "Do you think you'll be able to rent pumps?"

"This time of year, with no construction going on, sure, we can rent some."

Suddenly, Victor seemed upbeat. "I can have a crew from the mill set them up and deal with the intake issues and that stuff. Can we run them around the clock?"

"Yeah, right."

"Why not. You can dump the water like you did before. My boys could deal with maintenance during the day."

Warren frowned. "You talk about attracting attention. Christ, Victor, you start unloading a thousand gallons of water a minute trial side, what are people going to think."

"I didn't realize those discharges were so close."

"Even if they couldn't see it, they'd hear it."

"Well then, we still got, what, fourteen, fifteen good hours."

"Something like that."

"That reminds me, what about the pump house at Jordan, hasn't it been rebuilt?" Victor asked.

"Of course it hasn't."

"What's that supposed to mean?"

Warren took a swallow of beer. "If I rebuilt it, I'd have to use it."

"I guess I don't understand."

Warren sighed. "Jordan being unavailable was the justification for pumping from the river. Because I had no way of knowing how long we'd need to pump from the river, I couldn't rebuild it."

Victor thought for a moment. "But Jordan burned...I mean..."

Warren looked at Victor and lifted his eyebrows.

"You burned it down?" Victor asked.

"No, I didn't do it. I had it done."

Victor shook his head. "I just figured that old man you were having trouble with did it."

"You and everybody else, including the insurance company. And I still had loss of service insurance on it from when we didn't have the river pump house, so the payoff was decent."

Victor changed the subject. "That reminds me, what about the investigation into what caused the explosion."

"The fire marshal was down there this morning poking around again. I haven't heard anything new."

"In all our concern about you know what, I forgot to ask if it was that old man again."

"No doubt."

"No doubt what?"

"That he's the stiff they're trying to identify in Augusta," Warren said, finishing his second beer. "Anyway, send over your pumps, and have your guy get in touch with Joe about hooking them up, he'll have to deal with that."

Victor grasped the door handle and pulled. "Okay, I'll do it, stay in touch."

"Sure will," Warren said, dangling the three remaining beers from his index finger. "You want these?"

Victor looked at the beers then at Warren. Slowly he shook his head, pushed open the door, and climbed out. "See you later," he said, slamming the door.

Warren returned to the office and passed the remainder of the morning flirting with Doris. If she hadn't had a twice-postponed lunch date with a coworker and a parent-teacher conference to attend at three o'clock, he'd have probably coaxed her into going up to Ridge House where he could unwind. Instead he pushed the private button on his telephone and puttered around his office behind a closed door for almost an hour after she left, unable to focus on anything for more than a few minutes.

It was close to one when he fished the bottle of Dewar's out of his desk drawer, filled his coffee cup and sat back, resting his feet on the corner of the bookcase. The muffled sound of car and truck engines—some going, some coming—peppered with doors slamming and occasionally an animated voice, drifted into the room from below. But they were distant sounds. He settled deeper into the softness of his chair and closed his eyes.

When he woke up an hour later the room was darker. Dropping his feet to the floor with a thud, he stood up, stretched, and walked to the window, peering at the sky that was a blanket of thick gray clouds. If it rains, he thought, it will up the ante. Returning to his desk, he downed a glass of vodka, filled his flask, which he stowed in his raincoat pocket, and started for the dam, slipping out a side door that exited twenty feet from his car.

The balmy wind that was tossing the bare branches of the young maple trees that stood between the lodge and the Reception Center was ample confirmation that rain was inevitable. At any other time during his ownership of White Woods, he'd have been tracking down Joe to find out the latest forecast, hoping to hear the rain would limit itself to the valleys, sparing the mountain, or that the storm was expected to suck in colder air, giving way to a change-over. But those were thoughts of the past.

Pretending not to see Dwight, who had suddenly appeared across the pedestrian plaza waving madly for him to stop, he backed out quickly and sped away. Just as he reached the dam it started to spit rain, big drops that splattered on the windshield. Fetching his rain coat from the passenger's seat he got out and put it on, buttoning it from top to bottom and pulling the collar snugly against his neck, holding it in place.

He picked his way through the packed snow and hoisted himself onto the concrete deck of the dam where he hung from the chain link fence, surveying the down-river side. Everything looked normal until his eyes settled on a spot at the base of the dam, where several arches of water poured forth, like there were two men down there, out of his sight, below the overhang, pissing. But this, he knew, was water, dirty paper mill water from behind the dam, which had seeped through its aging foundation.

There wasn't much of it, at least not from what he could see at fifty feet, and it was falling harmlessly into the snow and ice and mud, no doubt being absorbed. It would be days, maybe a week or two, at that rate he reasoned, before it would start to pool and flow and find its way a hundred feet down river and mix with the discharge from Jordan. Regardless, Warren knew it would only worsen, and there were probably other leaks, ones you couldn't see.

Returning to his office, Warren telephoned Victor, getting through to him immediately. "The dam is leaking," he told him bluntly, foregoing their usual practice of not talking on the telephone, which Victor followed.

"I know, I know," he said tensely. "My guys just left there."

"Well I didn't see them. Anyway, it's leaking near the bottom."

"Yeah. Yeah, anything is possible with structural damage, the water will find even the slightest crack and follow it."

Warren reached for the near empty Dewar's bottle.

"Well, I'd say it's crunch time," Victor added.

"Whatever," Warren said, pouring what remained in the bottle into his coffee cup.

"We still have a chance to come clean, you know," Victor said.

Warren swallowed the vodka he had been sloshing through his teeth. "What the hell is that supposed to mean?" he asked.

"Nothing, I guess."

"No, no, you brought it up, what do you mean by that kind of happy horse shit remark?"

Victor ignored the insult. "We could...I don't know, maybe say what happened and gloss it over somehow, I don't know. I just don't know anymore."

Warren laughed. "Christ, Victor, don't even consider it, it concerns me you're talking like that. I thought I had to be worried about the dam cracking, it sounds like it's you that might crack."

Victor didn't say anything.

"Anyway, we'll just watch it, the dam I mean."

Victor sighed. "You don't understand." He paused. "Like I told you, the engineers just came back from there. I can't play this game, or whatever it is we're doing, any longer. Dams are regulated, period. If I stave off the engineers any longer, it's just a matter of time until they do something on their own. As bad a things are now, at least we have control."

Warren grunted.

"And that's not all of it. It's only a matter of time before the Bangor paper gets wind of this thing. I'm surprised they haven't yet. You haven't heard from them, have you?"

"No. Not that I know of anyway, but I'm been keeping myself unavailable. But yeah, you're right, they'll be on this like flies on shit when they find out."

"What about that weekly paper you got in town, they must have heard something by now."

Warren thought for a moment. "Well, it's probably because they aren't working. They put that paper out Wednesday morning and they pretty much close up till the following Monday."

"Lucky us," Victor said.

"Lucky shit," Warren snapped back. "It's one of the fringes we get for doing business in this quaint little hamlet. Nobody is watching. Remember."

They hashed over the situation for another half hour, resolving nothing. If there was a solution, it escaped them. Warren hung up the telephone and took the last swallow of Vodka from his glass. Then he chucked the empty Dewar's bottle into the desk drawer and pulled his flask from his raincoat pocket, using it to fill his glass. With his feet planted on top of his cluttered desk he leaned back, cradling the glass in his lap, trying not to think about the dam. At quarter of five he called home, leaving a message for his wife that he would be late. He didn't have any plans, but he was in no mood to go home.

When the flask was empty he stuffed it back in his pocket and emerged from his office to an empty third floor. As he passed Doris' desk he picked up the wad of message slips that were tucked under her blotter and thumbed through them. He was almost through the pile when he saw the one from the *Bangor Herald*. "Shit," he said out loud. True to Doris' ways, it didn't have a time on it or a reference. Warren snatched it from the pile, crumpled it up, and threw it in the wastebasket. He managed to slip out of the building with only a few hellos, making a beeline for Stars where he lingered for two hours, drinking vodka and munching pretzels.

*   *   *   *

The pumps Victor sent arrived early Thursday morning and the ones Joe rented from Somersworth were delivered just before noon. With the help of a crew from the mill and three laborers Mickey sent, Joe and Al were able to get them set up and working by dusk. Except for the limited supply of water the pumps produced and the frequent trips to refuel them, they operated normally Thursday and Friday night, making enough snow to freshen Planet and a couple of the trails at North Slope.

Saturday morning, when Warren made what must have been his tenth visit to the dam, the water level hadn't dropped, at least not so it was discernible. Returning to the privacy of his office, he called Victor at home.

"What about more pumps?" he asked.

"We haven't got anymore, not portable ones. What about renting more?"

"Somersworth doesn't have anymore. I guess they overhaul most of theirs in the winter, so they're in pieces. We called Portland but they sent everything they had to some big water project in Boston."

"What about the fire department?"

Warren laughed. "The fire department."

"Yeah, the fire department."

"Well, I suppose they'd jump at the chance to play with their equipment, and this thing is legit, at least on the surface…but, no…their trucks can probably only push a thousand gallons a minute at best and we'd need them to be right there, they'd be tied up there, it would create a lot of attention."

Victor sighed.

"Besides," Warren added, "surer that shit they'd call EMA. They're like peas in a pod you know. Then where would we be?"

"I suppose you're right. We should consider ourselves lucky they haven't gotten involved."

"Anyway, the fire department probably wouldn't do us any good. If we haven't dropped it, we probably can't."

"What do you mean?"

"There isn't much going into the river except our discharge. We've cut the Johnson dam flow to near nothing, so there isn't any dilution going on, which in itself may be a problem. But regardless, if we can't bring it down with what little we're discharging and what's getting into it between here and there, we're not going to."

"But you're still operating, right?" Warren asked.

"Yeah."

"So?"

"That's out of the question," Victor said, sounding sure of himself. "We can't possibly discontinue operations again. There's just no way. Regardless, it probably wouldn't make any difference anyway."

"But it might."

"It doesn't matter, we can't shutdown."

"Why not?"

"Because we can't, I'm not going to go into it."

"So even if it might make a difference you won't do it."

"That's right."

Warren sighed. "What's happening with the dam itself? Are your people making any progress?"

"Not really, they're out of solutions and asking for help is something I'm trying to stall them on, like you said, word could get back to EMA. Even though it's just a little dam in the middle of nowhere that isn't likely to do more than uproot a bunch of trees, claim a few docks, and probably flood a few basements, they'd blow it all out of proportion?"

Warren laughed. "Yeah, of course they would. They activate themselves at the drop of a hat. They'll do it for anything, so long as there isn't a good ball game on or something. And if they did activate, surer than shit, the place would be crawling with them."

"That's for sure."

They talked for a while longer, not because Warren wanted to, but because he needed to. Besides drinking, it was the only thing that took his mind off their predicament. That was why when he hung up he pulled the nip bottle of vodka from his jacket pocket that he had stashed earlier from a six-bottle set somebody had given him for Christmas. Twisting off the cap, he settled back in his chair and took a long swallow, emptying nearly half the bottle. He hadn't been sitting there long, maybe ten or fifteen minutes, when Victor's indifference to curtailing operations started to gnaw at him. Who the hell did he think he was? He was tempted to call him back and give him a ration of shit, but thought better of it. Victor wasn't the type of person you did that to because he just took it. There just wasn't any satisfaction in badgering him.

Instead, he found himself toying with the idea of jettisoning Victor, an act that was still within the realms of possibility. All he needed to do, he reasoned, was blow the whistle, claiming he had switched to pumping from the river following the destruction of the Jordan Pond pump house. Everything else would be a pack of lies that would pit he and Victor against each other, but despite a meticulous perusal of the facts, he couldn't recall a single thing he had said or done that would lend credence to what Victor would claim.

But for whatever reason, he shied away from that course. Instead, he unleashed on everybody else, including Joe. Joe knew that Warren's out-of-character actions were the product of something significant, and he suspected that the course of events that had started months earlier were to blame. In fact, Joe was convinced of it. As much as it bothered him, there was only one thing Joe could do. Help Doug expose the whole mess. But increasingly, he became concerned it would blow up in his face, and he would be left looking like a part of it, which of course he unknowingly had been for the past two months.

He knew with each passing day the chance of something, if not everything, being brought to light increased. Sure, they were making snow with the portable pumps, but the intakes were jury rigged to the main, so only slightly better than half the five hundred gallons per minute that each of them was capable of pumping was reaching the mountain.

As word spread about White Woods' reduced capacity to make snow, people would inevitably ask why, which would lead to other questions. Joe also knew that unlike the other happenings on the mountain, the discovery of a body in the river pump house remains made that event newsworthy in itself. While Doug would undoubtedly vouch for him if the need arose, he didn't think it would be enough. It was one of those dark thoughts he couldn't dispel, the kind that gnawed at him in a subliminal sort of way that made him uneasy, and therefore, hard to be around.

∗   ∗   ∗   ∗

Doug expected to get his water test results in the mail, so he was surprised when Kay summoned him to the telephone just before dinner on Monday saying it was the laboratory.

"This is Brian Gordon, the senior chemist at Central Maine Laboratories in Bangor."

"Yes," Doug said, expecting to hear that his collection method was flawed, despite the fact he had followed the instructions carefully.

"I was calling about the water testing you requested. I had a few questions?"

"Yes."

"What was the source of the water?"

It's none of your business, was the thought that popped into Doug's head. "Ah, well...I," he said, stumbling over his words, "I'd rather not divulge that."

There was a prolonged silence before Brian spoke. "Okay. I understand. Let me tell you why I ask. The dissolved oxygen in your sample is almost zero, which..."

Doug interrupted, eager to know more. "Is that bad?"

"The bad depends on where it came from."

Doug knew that Brian had skillfully converted his question into a second request for the sample's source. Doug didn't like the idea of sharing information he hadn't intended to without the opportunity to think about it, but he didn't figure he had much of a choice.

"It's river water," he blurted out, immediately regretting his manner of delivery.

"Then it's bad, very bad," Brian said calmly. "If your sample came from a river, it's a very sick river indeed."

Doug's mind was whirling. "Really," he managed to say.

"Oh yes. It likely wouldn't support fish or other aquatic species. Apparently you don't feel comfortable sharing with us what river the sample was taken from, which might shed some light on its condition."

Doug was finally thinking clearly. He was the customer. He ought to be asking the questions. "Would untreated waste water from a paper mill do it, make the river that way I mean?"

"Oh, sure it would."

"Well then," Doug said, "you've given me what I need. When will the results be available?"

"That's the other purpose of my call. In light of what we've detected, depending on what use you have for the results, you might want a duplicate sample to ensure that a measurably different outcome is not generated. But that's up to you."

"You mean obtain another sample?"

"Precisely. We've done a duplicate on the sample you submitted, but a second sample is often suggested. Obviously, it would cost another $25. I'll send you another bottle and custody sheet this afternoon, if you want."

Doug thought about the delay in collecting and testing another sample. "Is that really necessary?" he asked.

"Like I said earlier, it depends on the purpose of your testing, which logically leads to what is required by whoever you're submitting the results to, if anybody. I mean, if you're satisfied, fine. But others may not be. There are a lot of variables here."

"I see. Well, why don't we leave the door open to another sample then."

"That's fine. We'll wait to hear from you then."

"Yes."

"Good bye, Mr. Andrews."

Doug lowered the handset slowly to its cradle, planted his palms on the edge of the kitchen counter, and lowered his head, standing as still as a statue as he processed what Brian had told him. He didn't see the point in a second sample. Surely it would generate the same result. But maybe he should have them test for some of the chemicals he had identified in the materials Roland had given him. That would definitely strengthen his case. But he already had corroboration. Didn't he?

"Honey, are you all right?" Kay asked.

Jolted back to reality, Doug spun around and smiled. "Yeah, I'm fine. I was just thinking, is all."

Kay nodded and continued on her way to the linen closet with an armload of perfectly folded towels. "You can start the soup if you want, honey, and light the oven, I'm running a little late," she called back, raising her voice as she turned the corner into the hall.

Doug turned on the oven, setting the temperature selector at 400, and wrestled a medium sized pot out of the drawer below the oven, which he placed on the counter. Kay was still down the hall stowing towels in the linen closet. Doug knew it would be only a matter of minutes before she'd pass back through the kitchen, giving him the opportunity to divulge to her the developments of the past ten minutes, which he was anxious to do.

But instead he found himself contemplating his next move. Given that the lab seemed very professional, he figured that the analysis was safe, which meant that everything else was under his control. He was ready to blow the whistle. The only question that remained was how to expose it. Selfish feelings of glory and visions of a council seat were starting to envelop him, when he remembered that he and Joe had made a gentlemen's agreement that they would share new information. Briefly, he considered tracking down Joe at the mountain, but thought better of it.

Instead, he went to the telephone and dialed the pump house at White Woods. On the sixth ring a gruff sounding person answered, talking loudly into the mouthpiece to compensate for a steady humming noise in the background.

"I'm trying to reach Joe Littlefield," Doug said, unsure if he needed to speak loudly but nonetheless doing it.

"Yeah, he's here someplace, let me see if I can round him up for ya," Pete said. The telephone didn't go on hold, so Doug waited for what must have been close to three minutes listening to the steady hum that was occasionally peppered with the sound of men talking and doors slamming. Pete had summonsed Marty from the bathroom and Marty radioed Joe, who was at the base of Exception. Thinking it was Warren, Joe hurried to the pump house and took the call in his office.

"Joe Littlefield," he said, immediately realizing the control desk extension was still off the hook. "Excuse me, hold on a minute," he said, not letting Doug speak a single word. With the telephone handset squeezed tightly between his head and shoulder he keyed the mike on his radio. "501, pump house, hang up the phone, would you please."

No reply came over the radio, but the click and subsequent silence on the telephone line was ample acknowledgment. "Yes," Joe said.

"Joe, this is Doug Andrews, we met down at the river a…"

Joe interrupted. "Oh yeah, hi, Doug."

"I hope it was all right to call you at work, I didn't know of any other way to contact you."

"Yeah, it's okay," Joe said, wondering if it was such a good idea. He remembered he and Doug had discussed talking again, but they never really got specific about how it would be arranged.

Doug got right to the point. "I have some information I think you'll be interested in. Is there sometime we can meet?"

"Ah…yeah. You mean right off?"

Doug was explicit. "Yes. As soon as you possibly can."

"Yeah, no problem, let me see, things are just getting going here, so how about an hour from now, at six o'clock?"

"Fine with me. Where?"

"Oh, I don't know," Joe said, "how about the dam?" He wasn't sure why he said it, maybe it was because he knew Doug was familiar with it or because it was private, but he immediately had reservations. But Doug had already agreed. It was too late to change it without making it look worse.

As Joe hung up the telephone, a wall of uneasiness spread through him. Despite all he knew and his bitterness at what he figured was happening at White Woods, he didn't like the idea of meeting an outsider at what could be considered his workplace, on company time, in a vehicle that belonged to the resort. A second meeting with Doug would also cement his allegiance to Doug's cause, which meant he was now truly opposing Warren.

Regardless, he shelved his concerns and went back to work, slipping away unnoticed at quarter of six. Doug wasn't at the dam when he arrived there five minutes later, which was what he had hoped. He

turned the truck around, parking a hundred yards shy of the noisy gasoline powered pumps that dotted the riverbank. Helping himself to a
cigar from his jacket pocket, he settled back, pulling his right leg onto
the bench seat. He was four deep satisfying drags into the cigar when
Doug's gray BMW sedan meandered down the road, stopping ten feet
from the truck's front bumper.

They exited their vehicles simultaneously, shook hands tersely, and
talked. After five minutes, Joe knew Doug's excitement was rubbing off
on him, but for some reason he was powerless to stop it. He found
himself being swayed by the confidence spewed forth with every word
Doug spoke. Either he's trying to suck me in, or he's sure about this,
Joe concluded, his mind racing forward. Given what Doug was saying,
what was he going to expect from him? Was this the end of the line?

"So that's pretty much the extent of it, what do you think?" Doug
asked.

"Well, it sounds like you're convinced."

A confident look settled on Doug's face. "There isn't a shred of
doubt in my mind," he said nodding.

"So what now?" Joe asked.

"Well, that's why I looked you up, we've got to decide the best was
to expose this thing, and we've got to do it right away. Like I told you
on the phone, there isn't a minute to waste."

Joe helplessly tried to keep the sinking feeling, which had suddenly
encompassed him, from showing on his face. But he lost the struggle,
remaining speechless.

"You're still with me on this, aren't you?" Doug finally asked.

Joe cupped his hands in front of him and briskly rubbed them
together at waist level. Then, making eye contact with Doug, he nodded slowly, still searching for the right words.

"Well then," Doug said, trying not to let his concern about Joe's
eagerness show. "I think we should just call DEP in the morning and
give them everything we got."

"What about the test results, do you have them?" Joe asked, seizing on the literal even though it was of little interest to him.

"No, they weren't ready. But they're convinced of their findings."

Joe nodded.

Misinterpreting Joe's question for genuine interest, Doug elaborated. "They have DEP and EPA certifications and they have an extensive quality assurance policy," Doug said. "Besides, they got the state contract, so you know they know what they're talking about. Which means DEP will take notice. I'm not worried about that piece of it, if that's what's bothering you."

Joe still didn't say anything.

"They seem to be a topnotch lab in every way. Take my word for it, there isn't anything to worry about on their end."

"I wasn't really doubting the lab, I was just wondering why they wouldn't release the results."

A flash of understanding spread across Doug's face. "Oh, well, it's because they didn't know where the samples came from, I...I purposely didn't tell them. But all that is squared away now. They're all set with everything."

His head bowed, Joe didn't say anything as he shuffled his feet, crushing little pieces of ice that were within standing radius.

Doug decided to verbalize what Joe couldn't. "So what do you do now?" he asked. "I mean, for you it's...it's different, you got..." His voice trailed off.

His words were Joe's exact thoughts. Up until now everything had been possibilities. But this changed that. But for some reason, Doug's mention of the matter that was dear to his heart suddenly enabled him to rise to the occasion. He lifted his head, looked Doug squarely in the eyes, and took a deep breath. "These are the kind of things that separate the men from the boys," he said confidently. "It's no problem, it's just a matter or when and where, as far as I'm concerned. You can make that call. What is, is."

Doug nodded slowly, silently admiring Joe's candor. Nonetheless, years of activism had taught him things weren't that simple. "I don't mean to pry into your business, Joe, but in my opinion you need to be shoulder to shoulder with me when we do this thing, you need to make a clean break, that will not only protect you short term but it should serve to protect your future, if you know what I mean."

Joe eyes narrowed. "I guess I don't understand."

"I just mean that, well, you're either in or out, if you know what I mean. You're either going to defy your boss and turn him in, or go back to work and let the cookie crumble as it may. If you choose the latter, Joe, I'll understand, and I bet everybody else will too. You just aren't culpable in this mess. You have my support whatever you decide."

Joe thought for a moment. "You're right, this thing has been a long time coming, over two months. I'm ready to do what needs to be done. Don't get me wrong, it isn't easy. I wish none of this stuff had ever happened, but it did. No, I won't sleep at night if I don't do what's right, no matter how much it hurts."

Doug tilted his head back slightly. "I understand. Then why don't we do this. Tomorrow morning, first thing, we'll call DEP, both of us. We'll tell them what we got, that way there isn't any question. We can make the call from my house if you want."

"Yeah, that's fine with me."

"Okay then, you want to set a time, maybe nine?"

"Okay."

"You know were I live, right?"

Joe nodded.

Doug smiled. "Okay then, thanks."

They shook hands again and left. As he drove back to the pump house, at a speed that was distinctively slower than his usual pace, Joe felt scared, but mostly he had a sickening feeling. He'd have liked to drive right past the access road and keep going, but he knew that if there was ever a time in his life he needed to hold the course, it was now.

When he got back to the pump house he tried to immerse himself in work, but couldn't. After just forty-five minutes on the mountain he was back in his office, smoking a cigar, feeling like he was out on a limb that was about to be cut off. Sure, the plan was for him to be at Doug's side when he made the call to DEP. But would that be enough to set him apart from everything? Probably not. Just before eight o'clock, with a knot in his stomach, he dialed Brenda's number. She answered on the fourth ring, slightly out of breath.

"Brenda, this is Joe."

"Oh, hi, Joe. I just came in the door. I was trying to answer it before the machine did. How are you?"

"I'm okay. Have you got time to talk?"

"Yeah, sure, hold on just a minute, let me get the other bag from the hall."

A minute later she was back.

"There," she said, still winded, "what's up?"

Joe cleared his throat. "I was wondering if you know what is going on over here?"

"No, not really, not beyond what we already talked about."

"Well, I'd like to tell you, no, I need to tell you, and not only that, I think you'll have a scoop."

There was excitement in Brenda's voice. "Yeah, sure. Do I need pen and paper?"

"Yeah, lots of the latter."

"Sounds intriguing, hold on."

"No, wait a minute," Joe blurted out.

"Yes."

"What I'm going to tell you has to be anonymous, at least for the time being. Is that okay?"

Some of the excitement that had been in her voice seconds before was gone. "Well sure it is," she said without hesitation, "we do that all the time."

Despite her response, Joe still felt like he was a heel to hide his identity, but figured there was nothing to gain from discussing it.

"Okay then," he said.

"Just let me grab a pen and paper," she said.

Again she was back in a minute.

"Listen," she said, "if this is going to take a while why don't I call you back. I can put in for reimbursement."

It was something that hadn't occurred to Joe. Without realizing it, he had direct dialed Brenda, forgetting to use his calling card or charging it to his home telephone. His immediate thought was that there was now a record he had called Brenda on this date and time from the pump house. But surprisingly he didn't care. Neither did he care at this point who paid for the call.

He had already thought through how he was going to handle the disclosure. He would start at the very beginning and tell her everything, even what she already knew, being as straightforward as he could possibly be, holding back nothing. So that is what he did.

Twenty minutes later, he was finished, and he felt better than he expected. Brenda started asking questions, which he answered to the best of his ability. But the more she asked, the less he knew, until finally she announced her plan.

"Okay, I think I've got enough for now. I'm going to head for the office, well, maybe I'll call ahead, but whatever, I'm going to get right on this. Can I call you later if need be?"

"Oh sure."

"You'll be there, right?"

"Yes."

"Okay then. It's almost eight now and we go to press at eleven, so I don't know what, if anything, we'll get published for tomorrow unless they hold the press, which they might do, but regardless, I'm sure the editor will want to do something, otherwise we won't break it."

She's rambling, Joe thought. But why wouldn't she be. He had just given her a scoop of national, maybe international interest.

"I'll be here if you need me," Joe said. "I'm sure we'll be talking again soon. And I'm sorry about this being anonymous. I hope you understand." He didn't think she did, understand that is. But it didn't really matter because that was the way it had to be, at least for now. He had broached the subject of anonymity again only to remind her of it.

"I do," she said, "and I'll honor it. I really appreciate this, Joe, really."

Joe hung up the handset slowly and straightened in his chair to a melody of squeaks. He was about to head back to the mountain when he realized that he'd gone ahead and called Brenda without consulting with Doug. "Damn, why did I do that?" he said out loud. Briefly, he considered not calling Doug, but quickly realized that wasn't fair. So he dialed Doug's number and held his breath while he told him. If Doug cared, which Joe didn't think he did, you'd have never known it.

"They were probably already on to it anyway," Doug said. "And tomorrow it's not going to matter one way or the other. Is it?"

"I guess not," Joe said, silently trying to convince himself Doug's last two words weren't a challenge of some sort.

"Actually, it's for the best. The sooner they unleash on it the better. Did you mention the test results?"

"No," Joe replied. "I didn't want to bring you into it and I know we don't have them in writing yet."

"Yeah, that's fine. Well, I'll see you at nine tomorrow."

"I'll be there," Joe said.

Surprisingly, Joe felt a little better about things. He went to the control desk and helped himself to a cup of coffee, ignoring Marty, who was slumped down in his chair watching a fishing program on television. With only enough water to run thirty or forty guns at a time there was only one crew on the mountain, so there wasn't much for

Marty to do. Joe stood there silently, sipping his coffee until the commercial break.

"Everything going okay?" he asked as Marty thumbed back the volume.

"Haven't heard that it isn't," Marty said. Then, for no apparent reason, he spun around in his chair and faced Joe. "So is this going to be it for the season?" he asked.

It was a conversation Joe didn't want to have. Anything he said would be a lie.

Marty spoke again. "Because if it is, we might as well call it quits right now. Those fucking diesels down there ain't worth shit and you know it. We could haul more water up the mountain in a bucket brigade."

Joe managed a smile. "I know, but it's only temporary," he said, pleased he had been able to craft a reply that kept him from lying.

Marty frowned and turned away.

Joe finished his coffee in silence and went back to his office. He knew he ought to go to Exception, where the crew was working, to check snow quality. But he just couldn't bring himself to do it. He'd be faking it, and they, like Marty, would probably have questions he'd have to fabricate answers for. So he left for home early, figuring he'd need a good night's sleep for what tomorrow held, whatever that might be.

CHAPTER 17

▼

GETTING CAUGHT

Leaving himself plenty of time before his nine o'clock meeting with Doug, Joe drove to Heath's Variety in town to get a look at the *Bangor Herald*. He hadn't been in the store in years, so he wasn't known there, which would give him the opportunity to buy the paper and read the story, if there was one, before talking about it with anyone. He'd rather have gotten a copy from a vending box, which assured privacy, but there weren't any in town and going to the mountain, where there were half a dozen, was out of the question. With two quarters in his sweaty palm, he walked into the store, picked a copy of the paper from the stack without looking at it, folded it in half, deposited the coins in the clerk's outreached hand, and walked out without speaking a single word.

He drove to the rear of the store's parking lot, where the lone vehicle was a beverage delivery truck, and stopped. Leaving the newspaper lying on the seat he unfolded it and scanned the upper section of the front page. Nothing. Flipping it over, his eyes immediately locked on the headline. *One dead following White Woods explosion.* But it was the sub-headline that gave him a rush of excitement that was slow to subside. *White Woods brimming with suspicion, page 12-A.* Disregarding the front page story, he flipped the paper over and began reading the article, which was prominently displayed with the same headline in a text box at the end of the explosion story.

> *White Woods Ski Resort, located in the tiny Western Maine town of Cannon, has been a hotbed of suspicious activity since early December. According to a source close to the resort, who requested anonymity, White Woods has been plagued with a series of strange events, one of which disabled a veteran snowmaker in December of last year, and, most recently, the explosion of a pump house and the discovery of a body in the remains (see related story, page 1-A).*
>
> *Based on several tips received over the course of the past two months and information culled from a variety of sources, the Herald has learned that White Woods experienced at least three instances of "deliberate tampering" with snowmaking guns which was followed by a fire at the resort's pond pump house which totally destroyed that structure, forcing White Woods to pump from its backup system on the Salem River.*
>
> *The Herald has also confirmed the arrest of 72-year-old Henry Pike of Cannon on trespassing charges in late December of last year, which according to Herald sources, was "undoubtedly connected" to some or all of the suspicious activity. Finally, and perhaps most significant, are unsubstantiated claims that White Woods may have knowingly or unknowingly been pumping millions of gallons of polluted water from the Salem River that was used to make snow, which was, according to the anonymous source, "part and parcel" to everything else.*

The story did not identify the source of the pollution but it did mention several industries located on the river upstream from White Woods, including National Pulp and Paper. The story went on to say the *Herald* had assigned an investigative reporter to the story and they expected to have considerable coverage in Wednesday's edition. As Joe reread the story, he started to feel weak at the thought of it. Certainly he had known this would be the outcome of his conversation with Brenda, but to see it in print, knowing there were seventy thousand some odd copies of it out there, was scary.

He flipped the paper back and read the other article, which detailed the river pump house explosion and the discovery of the "still unidentified body" found in the remains. Cannon's fire chief was quoted several times in the story, which went on to say the deceased was not a resort employee, the explosion was of suspicious nature, and the Fire Marshall's Office was investigating. It also said that attempts to reach the owner of White Woods were not successful up until press time. Joe pushed away the paper and looked at his watch. It was only eight twenty-five. With a half hour to kill before his meeting with Doug, he headed out Route 62, intending to turn around at the town line. But his thoughts about the newspaper article and all it meant consumed his mind and before he realized it he was in Clifton. He turned around in a deserted gas station and drove faster than he liked back to Cannon, arriving in town with only minutes to spare.

Doug greeted Joe with a big smile and a freshly brewed pot of French Vanilla coffee. They sat at the shiny kitchen table and talked until about nine-thirty, mostly rehashing their conversation of the evening before, when Doug got up, announcing it was time to call DEP. He must have had the number ready, because he simply went to the telephone on the kitchen counter and pecked away rapidly at the number pad.

With his hands cupping the smoothness of his heavy warm mug, Joe listened as Doug described in perfect chronological order everything that had happened, including a few things Joe wasn't aware of. After what must have been about five minutes of almost nonstop talking by Doug, followed by a short question and answer period, Doug placed his hand over the mouthpiece, dipped it down, and turned to Joe.

"This is too easy," he said, grinning, "something is going on."

"Are you on hold?" Joe asked softly.

Doug nodded. "Yeah."

"What's happening?"

Doug raised his eyebrows and shrugged his narrow shoulders in obvious confusion.

"I don't know, it just seems strange the way they're acting."

Doug stayed on hold for a few more minutes, and then talked for another five minutes or so, mostly responding to questions that had the same answers as those asked earlier in the conversation. When Doug hung up there was a satisfied look on his face as he walked back to the table and sat down.

"I think we're all set," he said. "Judging from their reaction they know exactly what I was talking about."

"What do you mean?"

"I don't know, I couldn't put my finger on it, but they just seemed to be in tune with what I was telling them, almost like they knew, yeah…like they knew what I was talking about."

Joe shrugged his shoulders. "But how?"

Doug tightened his lips. "I don't know. But I've dealt with loads of these people before and made plenty of calls like this one," Doug said, has arms moving like a conductor. "This was too…too easy, for lack of a better way of putting it. In my opinion, somebody, maybe something, has already spilled the beans."

Joe's face hardened as confusion consumed him. What's going on? It would be just like Warren, or whoever, to twist and turn things. But they couldn't blame him. Could they? "That figures," he finally managed to mumble.

"Excuse me?"

"Oh nothing," Joe said, trying to regain his composure, "it's just everything."

Doug smiled. "Let me warm you up," he said picking up the coffee pot from the table warmer. But Joe waved it away politely.

"So now what?" Joe asked, not really expecting the type of reply that would decide the issue.

Doug's answer was on the tip of his tongue. "We wait. Either they do what needs to be done or we go the next step. Trust me on this, I've been through it a few times before. You've got to give them the opportunity to do their job, and fortunately in this case there isn't any reason to believe they won't. It also comes down to letting them save face, allowing them to believe they were the ones who raised the red flag. Government is like that, you've got to let them think they are in control, even if they aren't. But I'd say we're golden on this one, all we have to do it sit back and relax. But if things don't start happening by, say, noon, we'll play the rest of our cards."

Joe finished his coffee and got up. "Well, I best be going," he said.

Doug didn't try to stop him. "I'll keep abreast of things from here. What are you, I mean, are you going to go to work this afternoon?"

"I don't know, maybe I should, it might not look right if I don't, but on the other hand, what's the point, I don't know, maybe it won't be up to me, maybe going to work won't be an option. I'll just play it by ear."

Doug moved closer, narrowing the distance between them to three feet. "Listen, Joe, don't underestimate what's going on here. If you need to talk I'm available. I've been around this kind of thing before. Don't get me wrong, in the end it will have shown itself for what it really is. But there may be a day or two, maybe, God forbid, a week or two, when people will be confused, things may be said, flashed on the news, reported in the newspaper, that will bother you. I haven't known you long, but if there is one thing my dad gave me, it was his ability to judge a man at his core. You did the right thing, for the right reason, and the record will reflect that in the end."

Joe hadn't missed a word of what Doug had said, but the closeness of the moment was more than he could handle. He backed away. "I'm all set, really, I...don't...don't worry," he said, stammering over his words like an accused schoolboy. "I'd better be going."

When Joe left Doug's house that morning, he didn't know which direction to turn. Despite the fact he knew he'd done the right thing, he couldn't help but feel confused. He went home, hoping the telephone would ring. Each time it did, he let his mother answer it, and was disappointed when he'd hear her talking to one of her friends about things he couldn't help but feel weren't important.

Just before four, he surrendered to his vow of staying put, and went to the store, trying to act normal as he fetched himself a coffee. But when he got to the counter Ethel quickly jolted him back to reality.

"What the devil is going on?" she asked, her hands planted firmly on the edge of the worn wooden counter.

Joe didn't mean to act dumb, but nonetheless it was how he came across, answering her question with a question. "What do you mean?"

Ethel held her ground. "You know darn well what I mean."

Joe sat his coffee cup down on the counter and leaned on the mount of his palms, slowly nodding his head. "Let's just say it's the beginning of the end," he announced confidently. Then, without waiting for a reply, he continued. "Everything that's been happening?" he said, phrasing it as a question he answered, "has come to a head."

Ethel eyes narrowed. "For better or worse?"

Joe's mind raced as he fashioned an answer that seemed tailor-made for her.

"For the store, I guess maybe it's for the worse, the mountain may not survive this, actually, it probably won't."

The gravity of Joe's words hardened her face. "What about you?"

Joe took a big swallow of coffee. "Oh, I don't know. I mean…there's really nothing left."

Her face flushed with worry, Ethel hadn't had time to speak when the door slammed in rapid succession as a parade of acne-faced high school kids that had emerged from a late-model van filed in and fanned out, filling the store with high pitched voices. Joe and Ethel exchanged a knowing glance, and silently watched them as they canvassed each isle in search of nothing in particular but paying homage to the almost barren Hostess rack and the soda cooler. Joe impatiently shifted his weight from one foot to the other just as one of them approached the counter. Despite the rings that hung from both ears and the crotch of his dirty, frayed belt-less blue jeans that dipped close to his knees, the boy was soft spoken and polite. "Excuse me," he asked, "have you got a slush machine?"

The corners of Ethel's face curled into a sweet smile, the kind Joe used to get from his grandmother. "No, young man, I'm sorry, I don't."

"Thanks," he said turning away, rejoining a couple of his buddies halfway down the utility aisle where Joe heard him declare the results of his inquiry.

Not three minutes had passed since the troupe had entered, when a calm acting man with graying temples, wearing a navy blue Lawrence Academy pullover came into the store and strolled along the top of each aisle, telling the kids they were leaving in precisely two minutes. When he was done, he turned toward Ethel and smiled faintly. "I guess we picked the wrong day to come here, that place is a mad house," he said, motioning vaguely toward the mountain.

Joe looked at Ethel. When she didn't say anything, he did. "What do you mean?"

"Didn't you hear, they shut down at two o'clock, no notice or anything, they just stopped people from getting on the lifts. It was the strangest thing I ever encountered in thirty years of skiing. I mean usually there's a reason, like wind or something, and they offer you a half-day ticket, but this was nothing like that. We pretty much got booted out. No explanation, no nothing. One minute we were skiing and the next we weren't."

The man's departure announcement had driven a flock of kids to the counter, who formed a winding line between Joe and the man.

"Really," Joe said.

"Yeah, it's like a zoo, people complaining, asking questions, but nobody knows anything, not even the employees. It was crazy, we just loaded up and left."

A kid with a clean-shaven head, holding two twenty-ounce bottles of Mountain Dew and a box of Nissen frosted donuts spoke up. "Yeah, we're going to sue them for the two hours they gypped us," he said, setting off a chorus of approval from his buddies.

The man stepped forward and said something Joe couldn't understand, as a few other kids chimed in with their opinions. Joe smiled, stepped back and waited. He'd have left any other day, but he knew Ethel wanted to know more and he felt obligated to share his knowledge with her. As the last kid disappeared through the door, Joe edged back to the counter and forced a smile.

"So what have you heard?" he asked.

"All I know is there's some commotion up there," she said, easing shut the cash drawer. "They got the road blocked, and they're only letting people out, even the condo owners, can you imagine, only letting people out. The television news was up there too, they stopped in here on their way out looking for me to say something."

"Did you?" Joe asked.

"I talked with the reporter a bit but I wasn't about to talk into the camera. It's the damnedest thing though. I just can't believe it's happening. Here of all places."

"Yeah, that guy made it sound pretty bleak, I mean I guess they just shut down."

If Ethel suspected Joe knew more than he was letting on, she must have decided to let him off easy. She shook her head. "Yeah, it's a bad thing all right. We'll just have to see how it shakes itself out."

Joe nodded. Suddenly he remembered how helpful Ethel had been providing him with information and she had steered him to Buck and to the lawyer. But mostly she had given him the strength to go on. He didn't feel like talking, but figured it was the decent thing to do. "You know, something like this builds for a long time, somehow you know where it's leading, but there just isn't any way of getting there without letting it run its course, so you do, let it run its course that is, but when it happens, no matter how bad it might be, it's a relief." Joe paused and looked out the window, his eyes following a loaded logging truck as it zipped past the store. He continued. "I guess it's like a volcano that's simmering, you know it's going to erupt. Even if you're one of the villagers that live in its shadow, the day it blows isn't the worst day, if you know what I mean. I never liked cliché's, but it's like that, something like that. I know what happened today isn't good, but there's some degree of comfort in the fact it happened, things can't get any worse now, they can only get better."

Ethel was silent for a little while. When she spoke her words were soothing. "You're a good thinker, Joe, I always knew that. It will all come out in the wash, and whatever happens, you'll end up on your feet."

A shabbily dressed man entered the store followed by a young couple clad in ski clothes. Joe retreated toward the door. "Well, I've got to be going, I'll see you later, Ethel, maybe tomorrow."

Ethel raised her raspy voice to compensate for the distance he was creating. "Hang in there, Joe, let me know if I can do anything."

Joe raised his arm, fingers spread, and backed out the door. As he climbed into his truck he weighed his two choices. Go home or go to the mountain. Those were the only things in his life. The former didn't interest him and the latter was out of the question, at least in his book. Instead he drove around town a few times, keeping an eye out for anything that might be happening that was connected with what he was convinced was White Woods' demise. He didn't find anything.

There was the usual number of cars parked and moving on Main St., the dark church, the closed library, the elementary school lighted from end to end but seemingly empty. He passed slowly by Doug's house, peering in the curtained windows. He wanted to stop, but somehow couldn't muster the nerve. They were probably having dinner or about to, he thought. Besides, he was too self-conscious to stop. He despised people dropping in on him, so he figured everybody did, even though he knew that didn't make a whole lot of sense given his quirks.

After cruising the downtown for fifteen minutes he remembered what Ethel had said about the television news being at White Woods, so he decided to go home and watch the six o'clock broadcast.

When he got there his mother offered him supper, but he declined, mentioning he wanted to watch the news. It was five forty-five. Joe scooped up the remote from beside his mother's chair, stretched out on the couch, snapped on the television, punched in channel six, and muted it. His mother sat quietly doing her crossword while he rambled on about the day's events. When the grandfather clock in the foyer struck six, he propped himself up on one arm and ran the volume up loud enough so his mother would know better than to try to compete with it. As the music faded, the smooth talking anchor belted out the headline.

"White Woods Ski Resort, located in the Western Maine town of Cannon, was abruptly shut down earlier today by an army of officials led by state and federal environmental regulators. We go live now to Mary Mason, who's standing by at White Woods. Mary."

Joe slowly shook his head in disbelief as the reporter, standing in front of the blocked access road, filled the screen.

"That's right, Dan, it happened at about two o'clock this afternoon," the young woman said, snuggling the microphone close to her mouth with her right hand. "Details are still sketchy at this hour, but we have learned that some type of environmental exposure, to use the words of officials, has occurred here at the state's largest ski resort. However, officials are stressing that people who have been here today or at anytime in the past should not be concerned at this time and they are assuring residents of the area that the situation is under control and there is no reason to be alarmed. We've also been informed that the exposure is not an airborne incident. Again, those are their words." She paused for effect, using her free hand to pull back the strands of long brown hair that kept blowing across her face. "However, the sudden unexplained closure that happened at about two o'clock this afternoon apparently took everybody by surprise, including the more than one hundred employees who were working at the time."

The coverage switched from the reporter to footage taken that afternoon of the mass exodus, and included interviews with skiers, workers, and nearby residents. The remainder of the report focused on possible sources of the contamination, including a telephone interview with the general manager of a New Hampshire ski resort who tried in vain to shed light on what it might be.

Despite the fact they had spent close to ten minutes covering the story, Joe was convinced they didn't have a clue about what had happened, at least not yet. He flipped to the other two local news channels, but one of them was doing world news and the other was already on the weather. He got himself a beer from the refrigerator and returned to the living room, where he and his mother talked for an hour or so, until he knew she had had enough.

Joe was tired, but clearly too wound up to sleep. He longed to know more, to be a part of what was happening. He knew he needed to talk more about it. But going to White Woods and hobnobbing with whoever might be milling around the entrance was out of the question. At least for him. So he had another beer and went to bed, hoping his lack of rest and the alcohol would allow him to sleep. It did.

Except for a flood of media calls, which he ignored, the day after the closure was surprisingly quiet for Joe. He had anticipated more happening, although he hadn't really thought about what he expected.

DEP and Doug each called back to back on the second day. Joe made arrangements to meet with Doug at three o'clock that afternoon and made an appointment with DEP for nine o'clock the next day. He didn't really want to meet with Doug. After all, what was the purpose of it? But it turned out to be the right thing to do.

"You deserve a lot of credit for what you did," Doug said as they settled down at his kitchen table with cups of coffee lightened with real cream, and toasted bagels dripping in butter.

"Yeah, thanks."

"No, I mean it, Joe, not too many people would have done what you did. As an innocent bystander, you had the most to lose, most people would have turned the other cheek."

"I really don't feel I did anything."

"Of course you did."

Joe sipped his coffee. "I suppose, but there are things I should have done differently."

"Hindsight is always 20-20," Doug snapped back.

Joe nodded.

Doug's serious expression gave way to a smile. "Look, what they did was wrong and unnecessary to boot. You got caught in the middle of that. If you don't mind me saying so, you expect too much of yourself."

"It's just that...I know it isn't worth playing Monday morning quarterback, but I just wonder why I didn't put things together sooner, I mean, it was all there, right?"

"I know where you're coming from, but you've got to realize this was bizarre as hell, who...excuse me, honey," Doug said making eye contact with Kay who had entered the kitchen with an armload of papers just in time to hear him swear. There was an awkward silence before Doug turned back to Joe and continued.

"Like I was saying, this whole thing, it was bizarre, whoever would have suspected it. Not as much on the mill end, but certainly on your end. Furthermore, I don't know if you get the *Bangor Herald*, but DEP was quoted as saying it was by far the largest and most blatant case in their history. And the EPA didn't show up for nothing."

Joe nodded. "I suppose. It's not so much what happened, but that it happened at all, I mean, why? We, White Woods, had it all. A solid record of growth, a good reputation, expansion potential. We didn't have any of the problems other resorts have. We weren't on Forest Service land, we had plenty of water. I may be wrong, but given our size and our skier visits and Warren owning everything, we would have been okay even without Carter." Joe hadn't explained things the way he would have liked. He didn't think he was making sense.

"On your end it was greed all right," Doug said. "But at the mill it was different. The paper did a nice job of prying into the mill's motivations. It turns out it was more than them adverting a temporary shutdown. It appears they were trying to avoid a permanent one. Nowacki, which is the parent company of the mill, is in the process of serious downsizing and National was on the short list. They were scared stiff that if their bottom line didn't look just right, they would get the booby prize. Hard to believe, but true."

"You mean the mill arranged the whole thing to protect itself?"

Doug nodded. "Exactly, you need to read the article."

Doug went to the recycling bin by the kitchen door and rummaged through a messy stack of newspapers, giving up a minute later.

"I'll try and find it and get it to you," he said, walking back to the table and sitting down. "If we didn't get so many papers it might help, but you know how it is, it was probably that very one we used for the dog. Anyway, the mill was sure that corporate contraction was knocking, so they did the only thing the home office and Wall Street would take notice of, they protected their bottom line."

Joe scratched the back of his head. "Really."

"Yeah, most of it was right in the paper, they had it labeled analysis, but that doesn't mean anything."

"Wow."

"From what I've heard and read, National was a troubled mill, operating with ancient machinery. Their environmental and safety record was dismal and they had a strong unrelenting union. And most importantly, they had a bottom line that teetered all too often into red. Now you tell me? What would you do?"

"I'd like to think I wouldn't have done what they did."

Doug motioned toward Joe's almost empty cup. "Do you want a refill?"

"Sure, thanks."

"So you think that Nowacki is to blame?" Joe asked.

"No more than White Woods. It wouldn't have worked without both of them. But I expect White Woods to suffer the most. I've been through enough of these, shall we call them proceedings, to know that the punishment won't necessarily be or look right. I compare it to electricity taking the path of least resistance. The consequences will likely follow a course that does the least economic damage to the area. Like everything else, it all goes back to money."

"I guess I don't follow."

"What I'm saying is that White Woods is a seasonal business that mostly pays minimum wage, the mill on the other hand has full-time jobs, that pay well and have benefits. Don't you think they'll find a way to protect the mill?"

"But the mill was at greater fault in my opinion. I know you say it couldn't have worked without both of them, but it was the mill's dirty water. They did more wrong than Warren."

"Sure they did, at least in terms of violations. You've got operating a mill without treatment capability, violation of the terms of their license, violation of water quality standards, falsifying records, and who knows what else. But violations or the lack of them won't be deciding the fate of those two businesses."

"Well, at the very least, they both ought to be held equally liable."

"In a perfect world, yeah, but I'm telling you, a bunch of political hacks will decide this behind closed doors, not the regulators. Don't expect that things will play out in the same way the music is written. It isn't, at least based on my experience, likely to happen."

"Yeah, I suppose."

Joe tried to remain relaxed even though Doug's detailed assessment of the situation had rattled his normally composed attitude. He knew it was only Doug's opinion, but it did seem to make sense, regardless of how disgusting it was. Joe ran his sweaty palm through his thinning hair, mopping up the sweat that had collected on his head. Perspiration had a way of flowing from him when he was confronted with the harsh reality of injustice.

Doug was smiling. "Listen, I didn't mean to politicize the discussion," he said, following his rule that no conversation should remain serious for more than a few minutes. "Like you said the other day, what is, is, and you and I did what had to be done, end of story. Besides, they were cooked anyway."

Joe was puzzled. "What do you mean?"

"Oh, I didn't tell you that, did I. I've been talking to so many people, council people, everybody, that I forgot. I called DEP after the lid came off and got it out of them that they did know when I called Tuesday morning. Turns out they had had a few other calls."

Joe stayed for another ten minutes. He didn't really want to leave, but Kay kept passing through and asking Doug questions, like they had something planned.

Doug walked Joe three-quarters of the way to his truck, stopping on the walkway. "Take care," Doug said.

Joe waved, climbed into the cab, and backed out of the driveway. For the first time in many days, Joe felt better. But he knew he was just on the up side of his roller coaster of emotions.

He took a cigar from the box on the seat and had it unwrapped, cut, and lit before the truck rattled over the railroad tracks on the way out of town. It was a good time to take a ride. Not only did he need to think, but spending time at home when his mother was there was becoming increasingly difficult.

As smoke filled the cab, he cracked the passenger's side window and allowed his thoughts to turn to his meeting with DEP the next day. He expected they would have a battery of questions for him, maybe questions he wasn't prepared for, and since he was never good caught off guard, he might look bad, or worse, he might look guilty. He was also unhappy with the fact the meeting was in the morning, because he wouldn't be at his best. But as always, he'd do his best.

∗   ∗   ∗   ∗

The next day Joe got up early and left the house just past eight o'clock, intent on not being rushed for the meeting. Ethel was busy behind the counter when he walked into the store, so he fetched himself a cup of coffee. He'd just finished snapping on the lid when Ethel hollered from the front of the store. "Where are ya, Joe?"

"I'm coming," he said, letting his boots land loudly on the wooden floor in case she'd missed his answer. When he got to the counter Ethel was waving a copy of the *Bangor Herald* around like a curbside street vendor. "They finally identified the body," she said. "It was Henry all right, just like we thought."

Joe took a deep breath. "Well I guess that's the end of it then. Now we'll never know. Does it say anything new?"

Ethel laid the newspaper down on the counter facing Joe. "No. Just that it was him."

Joe quickly scanned the article. Then, after a swallow of coffee, he said, "It's really unfortunate we'll never know for sure what he did and why. I mean, I guess it's obvious, he just couldn't take Carter being developed, but it would have been nice to hear a confession or see him get convicted or something."

"Yeah, it would have been better for the sake of closure. But like you said, it seems obvious he got himself all fired up over Carter and there just wasn't any going back."

Joe thought for a moment. "Which means, I guess, that everything we've been through was triggered by one thing—the expansion onto Carter Peak. It's really too bad, don't you think?"

Ethel didn't get a chance to answer. A young man, neatly dressed in a brown uniform, poked his head in the door. "The back door is locked," he announced.

Ethel waved at him and scurried out from behind the counter. "I'll just be a minute, Joe."

"I've got to go anyway," he said. "I'll see you later."

"Okay then," she said, disappearing into the dimly lit stock room.

Joe drove around town for a little while, arriving at the abandoned lumber company office on the outskirts of town—the ad hoc headquarters for the White Woods' investigation—at ten minutes of nine. He was met at the door by two causally-dressed men in their forties who spoke in short sentences. They were polite but serious. The exit interview, as they called it, lasted close to four hours. They wanted to know everything he knew, which, judging from what he did know, wasn't much. It wouldn't have taken half the time it did if they hadn't insisted on going over the same ground two and three times, rephrasing the same questions differently like they were trying to confuse him. But if they were, they didn't. When they asked him if he had anything he wanted to add or had any questions, he couldn't think of anything, and was concerned when they acted surprised, almost like he was supposed to say something.

Except for the constant flow of media calls, which Joe continued to ignore, the days following the interview were uneventful. Actually they were downright boring for Joe, who was used to working seven days a week. He spent his time at home, watching television or puttering around the house. Judging from their strained relationship, he knew he was pestering his mother, whose coveted routine had been turned upside down by his sudden presence.

He had given up trying to break himself of sleeping till noon everyday. With nothing to do, nowhere to go, there was no reason. Besides, it gave the house to his mother in the morning, and to him in the late evening, after she had gone to bed. The only thing that kept his sagging morale propped up was the constant action that still swirled unabated at White Woods. Every day there was some sort of new development, although nobody really knew what was happening. The government didn't have much to say. On most days they simply repeated that there continued to be no reason for people to be concerned, and encouraged them to call the toll-free number that had been established if they had questions.

A few local people had been into the sealed resort for one reason or another, mostly vendors and contractors who were doing work for the government, but they were mum about what they did or saw. Condo owners were being allowed in to retrieve personal belongings from their units, but their visits were guided and short.

The newspapers continued a feeding frenzy that bordered on being a witch-hunt on the days that nothing newsworthy surfaced for them to print. Joe got into the habit of going to the store every day and getting a copy of the *Bangor Herald* and a coffee. Then he would drive to the rest area on the highway and read the paper. It was a full week before the story left the front page. Halfway through the second week the horde of reporters that had been covering the story slowly dwindled, but Brenda stayed assigned, probably, Joe reasoned, because it had been her story in the beginning, something Joe was pleased about.

On Tuesday evening the telephone rang while Joe and his mother were watching a movie. He muted the television and grabbed the caller ID. It was Brenda.

"I suppose I better talk to her," he said to his mother. Depositing the remote on the arm of her chair, he raced off to the extension in the kitchen so he wouldn't bother her.

When he pulled the handset from the wall, Brenda was just finishing her message, none of which he had heard.

"Oh, you *are* home."

"Yeah."

"How are you?"

"Okay. I see you've been busy."

"Oh yeah, very. It's been crazy, ten, twelve-hour days, it's good experience though, and a lot of the stuff is going on the wire. We've even done some exclusive stuff for other publications, so the money is great and the exposure I've gotten is priceless. I really can't complain."

"That's good then. I just wonder what's going to happen."

"I really don't know any more than you've been reading. They just aren't saying. So you're doing okay, I mean under the circumstances."

Joe knew an immediate and upbeat answer would quell her concerns. "Oh yeah, sure, I'm fine, a little bored maybe, but I'm doing okay, really."

"Well that's good, I've been thinking a lot about you. I mean I know how it must be for you."

"Yeah. Thanks."

"But that isn't the only reason I called."

"No?"

"I don't want it to seem like I'm using our friendship, but I was wondering if you would consider an interview." Brenda was talking fast now. "If you don't want to, I understand completely, I just thought I'd ask. I don't want it to come between us."

But Joe wasn't surprised she had asked, only that she had taken so long to do so. As the chief of snowmaking at the demised resort, the media had been clamoring to talk with him, but he hadn't said a thing publicly. Not a single word. He hadn't seen any reason to.

"I guess you know I don't want to," he finally said, leaving the door to her request open.

"I know, and I understand. I fully respect your decision not to, but we thought you might agree to a profile kind of thing, you know, more about you than anything else."

"Who is we?" Joe asked.

"My editor."

"Oh."

"Yeah, something that would focus on you. You could control the content, I mean, anything you didn't like we wouldn't have to run. You'd get to see everything beforehand and reject what you don't like."

"Regardless, I guess I don't see the reason for it."

"How do you mean that?" Brenda asked.

"What purpose will it serve?"

"Well, I won't use my usual lines, I'll be honest with you. There are two reasons I asked, both of which really are part and parcel of our friendship. First, I think it would be best for your story to be told, best for you I mean, best for your future. And second, it would help me, not that you haven't already done that with the scoop."

Joe didn't immediately answer. "It would help you then?" he finally asked.

"Oh sure it would, it would be an exclusive."

"That's always what it comes to, isn't it. That's what started this whole thing in the first place, if you know what I mean. People trying to be first. Egos in search of money. More is better. That kind of thing."

An awkward silence lingered. Finally, Brenda managed a few words. "I understand. I...I really didn't want to ask...but, I'm sorry, Joe, I shouldn't have."

Joe glossed over his previous words. "I don't mean you, it's not you, it's the system. If you don't try to be a part of that system, you'll fail. I know that. I know how it works. You have to go along to get along. That's all you're doing. It isn't your fault. You'd have been wrong if you didn't ask."

"Does that mean you'll do it?"

"I suppose, for you, I mean, if it will help you, I'll do it."

"Well, that would be great," Brenda said, managing to contain her excitement.

"So when, where?" Joe asked.

"Ah, you name it."

"Are you going to be over this way anytime soon?"

"I can be, I'm on unrestricted travel."

"Why don't we meet at that restaurant, what's it called, Friends, it's about halfway between here and Bangor. Why don't I meet you there at three tomorrow."

"That sounds great, I'll look forward to it."

"Good, I'll see you then."

"All right, thanks, Joe...and...I just hope this was the right thing."

"Don't worry about it. See you tomorrow."

As he hung up the telephone, Joe couldn't help but feel depressed. It wasn't that he blamed Brenda, because he didn't. She was nothing but a rat in a rat race. He'd do the story for her, find out what edition it was going to be in, and make sure he didn't see it. So that was what he did. But the very day it ran, Jack Place, the Chief of Snowmaking Services at Shapleigh, called him.

"I saw the piece in the paper about you," he said to Joe after introducing himself with more fanfare than necessary. "I was wondering what your plans were."

Joe's heart was pounding, his mind racing. Whose plans? Mine? "Well, nothing...nothing right now, why?" he asked, immediately wishing he hadn't cut to the chase so quickly.

"Because we'd like to talk with about the possibility of you joining us."

"Really."

Join them as what, Joe thought to himself, groping for a way to phrase such a crucial question. But Jack was talking again. "We're making some changes down here, restructuring things if you will, and we think you might fit in nicely in a number two spot we've created, as the manager of snowmaking operations who would oversee everything." He paused. "It isn't a done deal yet, by any means, but talking with you is a part of our decision making. It really comes down to whether or not it would be a good fit, for you and for us."

Joe couldn't believe his ears. The telephone rings and your whole life changes.

Groping for the right words, he said, "Certainly, I mean, yeah...I'd be very interested in that."

"Good, we'd like you to come down sometime soon."

"Anytime."

"Well then, why don't we schedule something for the first part of next week, say Monday?"

"Fine with me, what time?"

"What's good for you?" Jack asked.

"Afternoons are best, but I can be there anytime you say, just name it."

"Why don't we say two. You know where we're located, right?"

"Oh sure," Joe answered, immediately realizing he had been too quick to answer. Jack probably hadn't meant the resort itself. "I know where the resort is," he quickly added.

"Okay then, we'll meet in the conference room at the corporate offices which are located at the top of the access road on the right. It's the only building on the right, it's across from the parking areas, and before you get to the base area, it's well marked. So we'll see you on Monday at two then."

As he hung up the telephone, Joe felt good, really good. This was the best news he had had in months. His mother was out on her usual afternoon errand run, so he didn't have anybody to share it with. Instead he paced the floor, going from one room to another, looking out the windows at nothing in particular, thinking about the possibilities. He wanted to be happy about it, but he was afraid it wouldn't work out. Things had been so difficult lately, he had lost so much. While he was grateful for the offer, he couldn't help but feel it was a carrot being dangled in front of him, which might be taken away. He knew at this point in time he didn't have the capacity to count on something so important and not get it.

A car door slammed and the garage door started up. It was his mother. He helped her carry in the bags of groceries she was struggling with. He was anxious to tell her his news, but waited until she had put away the food and was settled comfortably in her big upholstered chair in the living room. They discussed it pretty much non-stop until they went to bed. Joe had a need, which he knew his mother recognized, to hang his hat on something during these troubled days. There hadn't been anything before. Now there was.

Joe spent Saturday doing chores around the house and taking his mother for a long ride, her favorite pastime. When he got up Sunday morning at eleven he was unsure how to spend the day. But when he pulled the Sunday paper, the only one they had delivered, from the box, a good part of his day was spoken for. Splashed across the front page, and continued on three inside pages, was an in depth profile on the resort called *White Woods—rags, riches, nothing*. It chronicled the history of the resort, reviewed the past season, and reported at length on its future and what that meant to skiers, condo owners, residents of Cannon, and the skiing industry in Maine and New England.

Despite the fact Joe spent three hours reading every article, several of them twice, his thirst for information was still not satisfied. He carefully cut out all the articles and added them to his growing collection, which he kept loose in an old scrapbook.

That night, after watching a movie with his mother, he lay in bed, propped up on his elbow, and went through the entire stack of clippings. When he laid the scrapbook on the hardwood floor at quarter of twelve and put out his light, he felt pretty good.

The meeting at Shapleigh went well, or at least Joe thought it had. He wasn't sure if the gracious treatment he received was simply Shapleigh's way of doing business or an attempt to woo him, but either way, it left him feeling even better.

On Tuesday, with the spread in the Sunday paper still fresh in his mind and wanting to share his job offer at Shapleigh, he decided to go see Doug. It was rare for Joe to seek out people. It was more like him to wait until they crossed paths, but this was different. The prospect of getting the job at Shapleigh had boosted Joe's confidence like nothing else could.

More importantly, he felt Shapleigh's job offer spelled vindication. Despite people's dismissal of his concerns as nonsense, Joe felt some of the responsibility for what had happened at White Woods belonged to him. He had convinced himself that he hadn't figured things out as soon as he ought to have, and when he did, he didn't act soon enough. No words, even those shared by his mother day after day, were sufficient to lay his claim of failure to bed. The only true exoneration for him was the job offer at Shapleigh.

He found Doug in the shop with Kay, in the process of rearranging an entire corner.

"If this isn't a good time, I can come back another day," he said.

But neither Doug nor Kay would hear of it. "We're ready for a break anyway," Kay said, wiping her hands on a checkered cloth that had been draped over her shoulder. Doug ushered Joe to the kitchen table, put the water kettle on for tea, and sat down. Joe purposely didn't bring up Shapleigh until Kay served the tea and a plate of assorted cookies, and excused herself, disappearing into the den.

When he announced the job offer, Doug seemed genuinely pleased. "Really," he said, "that's great, Joe."

"Yeah, it's the number two position. I suppose it'll be hard playing second fiddle at first, but I'm sure I'll get used to it over time. Besides, they've expanded their snowmaking a lot lately, so it's a bigger job than this one, and," he said smirking, "they'll no doubt benefit big time from White Woods, especially if it's closed for good."

Doug was tempted to say that permanent closure was about as sure a thing as the sun rising in the morning, but he knew better than to let the conversation drift back in that direction.

"That sounds great. I'm glad things worked out for you, you deserve it, and Shapleigh is lucky to get you."

"Yeah, they kind of created the position for me."

"Really, that's impressive."

"Yeah. What about you?" Joe asked. "What are you going to do now?"

Doug laughed. "Well, as you know, I didn't go into this thing for any reason. It just kind of happened. But the position of executive director for the council's New England chapter is up for grabs. I probably wouldn't have had a chance a year ago, probably wouldn't have even considered applying, but considering how high profile this case has been and my role in it, well, let's just say there are those who are trying to draft me. It's wholly undeserved as far as I'm concerned, but they got the crazy notion this thing wouldn't have been exposed if it wasn't for me, and if it hadn't been exposed, Maine wouldn't be getting its first chlorine free mill with closed loop technology, which is a big deal, at least in environmental circles."

"You did it, you deserve the job."

"Not really."

"Well, I think you do," Joe said.

"Regardless, it's not as easy as it might sound. We still got a faction of radicals in the council, but I think the tide is starting to turn."

Joe nodded, wishing he knew what to say, but nothing came to mind, so he took a couple of sips of tea.

"Well, it sounds like we're both headed for better things," Doug said.

"Yeah, I guess," Joe said. "So have you been following things in the newspaper?"

"Oh yes, very closely. We really enjoyed Sunday's coverage."

Joe nodded. "Yeah, that was good, real complete."

Faintly, Joe heard the doorbell in the shop ringing. He looked at Doug, expecting him to go, but tending to business, at least at this moment, must have been Kay's job, because within seconds she scurried through the kitchen and disappeared into the shop just as the telephone rang. Doug excused himself and answered it. It was Roland, who, as council secretary, had become the intermediary in Doug's elevation to executive director. With a guest at his kitchen table, Doug cut the call as short as he could and returned to Joe's side, trying to put Roland's questions out of his mind.

"Sorry about that," Doug said. Joe shook his head. "Don't worry about it. I've got to be going anyway," he said. Popping a cookie in his mouth, he washed it down with a swallow of cold tea and got up stretching, looking at the dishes, silently wondering if he should clear them.

Doug read his mind. "Oh, just leave those there," he said, motioning toward them, "really."

They walked outside and paused on the wide, neatly shoveled path. Joe tilted his head back slightly, allowing the sun to drench his face.

"Great day," he said.

"Sure is."

Joe straightened up, looked Doug in the eye, and extended his big hand. "Thanks, Doug, thanks for everything."

They shook hands.

"Thank you, and take care of yourself," Doug said.

Joe started down the flagstone path. "I will."

"And good luck at Shapleigh, Joe. Maybe Kay and I will get a chance to come over for some cross-country skiing. If we do, we'll look you up."

Joe raised his voice to a yell. "Please do, that sounds good, take care."

But as he pulled himself into the cab of his truck he couldn't help but think he didn't even have the job yet. Maybe Doug's pronouncement that he did was the product of not listening, or maybe it was just that Doug was confident he would be successful. Either way, it didn't matter two days later when Jack called.

"We're convinced you're our man," Jack told him, "but we got a few things to iron out here before we can bring you on board. First, the restructuring is a budgetary thing. Unlike White Woods, Shapleigh is a public company, so it's different than what you're probably used to, we got a board of directors, and believe it or not, some people here aren't convinced we need to further prioritize snowmaking. To me they got their heads up their ass, but anyway, that's that. The other thing is, we've ruffled the feathers of a few of the foremen with talk of bringing you in. They don't have a leg to stand on of course, but our GM doesn't have any backbone, so we have to tread lightly, if you know what I mean. But none of this involves you. We just need some time is all."

Joe didn't like what he was hearing. His hopes of getting the job at Shapleigh dwindled.

The next day he went to the store late morning, as he had become accustomed to doing. As soon as he walked in, Ethel hollered to him, holding up a copy of the newspaper. He could see the headline. *White Woods, National reach accord with DEP.*

Joe grabbed a copy from the stack on the counter without saying anything and started reading. A smaller headline read *White Woods Ski*

Resort and National Pulp and Paper have entered into a conditional con-sent agreement with the Maine Department of Environmental Protection in the aftermath of the state's largest case of industrial pollution. Below it were two stories, one about National and the other about White Woods. Joe read the story on the right first, the one about White Woods.

> *Beleaguered White Woods Ski Resort, Maine's largest alpine destina-tion, has reportedly reached agreement with the Maine Department of Environmental Protection to settle what has been widely touted as the state's largest case of industrial pollution. Warren Ainsworth, White Woods' owner, and state officials, have hammered out a consent agree-ment that appears to have served the interest of both parties.*
>
> *If the consent agreement is approved, Ainsworth would be immune from criminal prosecution for his part in pumping as much as half a billion gallons of dirty water onto his mountain where he used it to make snow. The water, untreated effluent from National Pulp and Paper located upriver from White Woods, has yet to prove itself danger-ous outside of the river basin.*
>
> *According to the terms of the consent agreement, Ainsworth's wholly owned skiing empire, estimated to be valued at 250 million dollars, would be dismantled and sold. Ultimately, his five thousand acres, which spans five mountains peaks, about half of which is undeveloped, would be donated to the state, where it would become part of a pending Green Zone that borders its western edge.*
>
> *The proceeds of buildings, equipment, and other assets that are sold, would be used to establish an elaborate network of unobtrusive ground-water testing stations and the operational costs associated with ten years of monitoring. Remaining funds would be used to restore the resort to its natural state.*

Joe didn't bother to finish reading the article, which was continued on an inside page. Instead he turned to the story about the mill, scan-ning ahead to the focus of the story.

> *Under the terms of the consent agreement, which still requires a host of approvals, National's Chief Executive Officer, Victor Doucette, will*

plead guilty to several criminal and civil charges including intentional discharge of untreated mill waste water and a multitude of reporting violations. Doucette could serve as much as two years in prison. National's parent, Nowacki, a Japanese company with considerable holdings in this country, was absolved of direct knowledge of what Doucette was doing.

However, the agreement requires Nowacki to supply capital for the mill to upgrade its wastewater treatment process to state of the art levels, and to switch to a totally chlorine free process within eighteen months and install closed loop technology. Despite the apparent leniency extended to Nowacki, environmentalists are hailing the switch to chlorine free papermaking and the closed loop system as a victory.

Like the other story, this one was also continued. Joe looked up at Ethel, who had been silent while he was reading, and shook his head. "Unbelievable," he said.

"Sure is, sounds like the whole deal was orchestrated."

"I can't believe Warren isn't going to jail, I mean, he had to have known everything."

Ethel was talking but Joe wasn't listening to her every word. He suddenly remembered what Doug had said when they last met at his house. That the way it played out wouldn't necessarily make any sense, and it sure didn't. Joe also found it interesting the mill was spared, even strengthened with new capital, but White Woods was going to be annihilated. It was just what Doug had predicted.

"What do you think?" Ethel asked, raising her voice.

"I'm sorry, I didn't hear you."

"I said you can't trust the government, they're sly. You know as well as I do that Warren no doubt had the money, the connections, whatever, to get himself a sweet deal while the other poor soul didn't. Of course, Warren may not be going to the slammer, but he's lost everything."

"True," Joe said.

"I get a kick out of his defense though, he was just pumping from the river like he had a permit for, can you imagine?"

Joe stared at her with a blank look. "What's that?" he asked.

"Oh, you haven't read inside, oh yeah, Warren says that when the pump house burned down he was forced to pump from the river, period, that's why he was."

"No way," Joe said, thumbing through the pages to find the continued section of the article. He found it just as several noisy customers entered the store. Joe knew them by sight. Ethel greeted them by name. Joe read most of the two continued articles and scanned several related stories. By the time he finished the customers were gone, allowing Ethel to turn her attention back to Joe.

"What I don't understand," she said, "is that Dwight supposedly sang like a bird for the investigators. You'd think that would have cooked Warren's goose, but it don't seem to have."

"Yeah, I heard the same thing, that he spilled his guts, but I find it hard to believe. I mean he was always such a yes man, I just can't see it. But even if he did, talk that is, it would have been just like Warren to keep him out of the loop, a least to some extent."

There were more customers in the store now and Ethel got busy answering questions and checking people out. Joe wasn't in the mood for waiting and he didn't feel like reading the rest of the newspaper. He needed to talk. But he knew that any resumption of their conversation would be short lived with the noon hour so close.

Even though it was out of character for him to drop in on somebody, he started for Doug's house, hoping to get his take on the agreements. Since the shop was open, Joe felt that using the barn door was the right thing to do, but he immediately regretted it. The shiny gold bell attached to the upper inside corner clanged loudly as he pulled the door open. Embarrassed, he quickly passed through and guided the door to a closed position, a maneuver that succeeded in calming the bell. There was no obvious path to the back of the shop, where Joe could see the counter, so he just started in that direction, walking cautiously through the dozens of pieces of antique furniture, most of which were topped with unique figurines and colorful glassware. He reached the back of the store just as Kay appeared from the house.

"Hi, Joe," she said smiling.

"Hi, I was wondering if Doug was around."

"No, he isn't, he went to Waterford on business, he should be back this afternoon."

"Is it something to do with the job?" Joe asked.

Kay hesitated. Then, with a smile she couldn't conceal, she said, "I'd rather he told you, but yes, he did get it."

"Oh wow, that's great, he deserves it."

Kay nodded, still smiling. "I'm sure he'll want to tell you all about it."

"I'll look forward to that," Joe said. Then, after a short silence, he waved his right arm across the contents of the store and said, "I didn't realize you had so much stuff in here."

"It's the same old story. We've been taking in more than we've sold."

Joe nodded, even though he wasn't sure what she meant. "Well I've got to be going, tell Doug I stopped by. I just wanted to touch bases with him about things. I'll catch up with him later. Thanks."

Joe turned and started for the door.

"I'll tell Doug you stopped by, Joe," Kay called after him. "It's nice to see you."

In the narrowness between a wooden dining room table and a perfectly restored sea captain's chest with the picture of a sailing ship etched on the top, Joe turned his head back but kept moving. "You too," he said, waving.

As he backed out of the driveway, he thought about why he didn't like to drop in on people. It was rarely fruitful, and more often than not inopportune. He passed by Doc's, thinking how if he was like most of his crew, he'd stop for a beer and a little company. But he knew while he would no doubt find talk there, it wasn't likely to be of the type to satisfy him.

Instead he drove home, cut the latest articles from the newspaper, added them to his growing collection, snapped on the television, and channel hopped for almost an hour. At three-thirty the telephone rang. It was Doug.

"Kay said you dropped by this afternoon."

"Yeah, I was curious what you thought about the agreement, you know, between White Woods and DEP."

"I heard about it, I guess you might say I couldn't really help but hear about it. But I haven't read the paper yet, every stop I made today led to another. It sounds like what we expected though."

"You mean what you predicted. Especially the part about the mill being spared. I find it interesting that they crafted it so the mill gets improved."

"Yes, that's most often how they play it, people don't realize it, but it gets political like that."

They discussed the agreement for a few minutes, and Doug told him about getting the job with the council, but the conversation was stiff. It just didn't flow freely like the other times they had talked. Maybe it was talking on the telephone that made things awkward, or maybe it was because things were settled now, and whether they knew it or not, they didn't have anything more in common. In any event, Joe was anxious to end the call.

"Well anyway, that was all I wanted, thanks for calling back." He could hear Kay's voice in the background.

"Sure, well, maybe we can get together sometime and talk about it some more."

"That would be great, thanks again, bye."

"Good bye," Doug said.

Gently, Joe returned the handset to the cradle, thinking about how them getting together would likely never be arranged. Confronted with the prospect of separation, people often said things like that, but such meetings rarely took place. He was still pondering the question when the telephone rang. It was Jack at Shapleigh. The job was his. They wanted him to start the following Monday and suggested he come over the next day. He jumped at the chance, while still protecting his preferred schedule. He planned to get there about mid-afternoon and stay into the evening, later if they wanted him to.

The next day, he got up at ten. When he planted himself in front of the bathroom mirror to shave, he found himself looking at a face he hadn't seen in a long while.

Accepting his mother's invitation of fried eggs, bacon, and toast, he left the house at twelve-thirty, with plenty of time to spare, pleased that his mother would get a decent stretch of privacy which was sure to be like medicine to their tattered relationship.

The late winter sun, which was growing stronger every day now, had warmed the cab of his truck nicely. He pushed up the sleeves of his heavy cotton shirt and lit the cigar he had carefully prepared prior to leaving the house.

He wasn't sure why, but instead of sailing by White Woods Road as he had planned, he turned onto it. He hadn't been back to the mountain since the day all hell had broken loose. With no set time to arrive at Shapleigh, maybe today was a good chance to check things out.

As he approached the access road with the unlit cigar in his hand and a knot in his stomach, it immediately occurred to him he had been right not to return. A solid line of concrete barriers lined the road from end to end, with only a small designated opening on the far right that was marked with a half dozen bright orange pylons. The barrier, assembled with free standing slabs of cement eight feet long and three feet high that were often used at highway construction sites, must have been trucked from a hundred miles or more he thought, remembering the time Art had tried to get them for the Olympic ski trials but had thought better of it when he found out what the price for round trip transportation would be.

Joe inched his pick-up truck closer, his eyes locking on the official-looking car sitting just above the opening. It was a dark colored Ford Crown Victoria, with black-wall tires and a couple of small antennas on the back. A small blue light, in the shape of a bubble, sat on its roof just above the driver's seat.

Should he go straight toward the opening, turn around, or proceed along the continuation of White Woods Road? Should he make out he was a person from away who was really surprised by what confronted him, or just another curious local looking at the unimaginable? A man with sunglasses, wearing a bright red crew neck sweater, got out of the passenger's side of the car, looking directly at him. Joe snapped on his right directional signal and accelerated. The man who had exited the vehicle got back inside. Once he was safely out of sight, Joe slowed down and kept driving.

He knew he could get an almost full view of the top two thirds of the mountain from a vantage point three miles down, a place where the road opened into a large field on both sides. Still reeling from the sight of White Woods being gated, he was again surprised to find two orange wooden barriers, placed in a V shape, across a woods trail about a mile down on the left. While he had never traveled that particular path, he knew it to be a hiking trial that connected to the resort's three-mile novice trail from the summit. He was tempted to stop and read the notices that were stapled unevenly to the barriers, but he didn't.

Instead, his thoughts raced ahead. Maybe I shouldn't be here. Maybe they'll think I'm up to something. Then again, maybe they don't even know who I am.

As the road entered the open field area he pulled his pick-up truck off to the right and stopped. Slowly, he turned his head to the left. There before him was his beloved mountain, looking every bit as good as it did in its most attractive advertising literature. He studied it for a long while, running his eyes slowly up and down the trails as he silently uttered their names. Exception, Planet, Starburst, Leader of the Pack, Orbit, Thin Air, Pipeline, Universe, Infinity. From peak to peak his eyes traveled, straining to see something. But there was nothing out of the ordinary. Nothing that caught his attention anyway.

When he figured he had fully etched a picture of it in his mind he checked his rearview mirror, made a tight U turn on the sand-less snow covered road, and drove away, not bothering to take advantage of the partial glimpses of the mountain that came and went as he sped along. He had seen enough.

His thoughts settled on Shapleigh. He knew they were in a strong position to operate past June 19, the previous record. Their goal? Ski beyond the official start of summer, which this year, happened to be 2:17 p.m., Sunday, June 21. He knew, because he had checked. The more snow Shapleigh made now, the better their chance of doing it. As he turned off White Woods Road onto the smoothness of the state highway he reached down and turned on the weather radio.

The End

0-595-26460-3

Made in the USA
Lexington, KY
25 February 2013